WAKING THE SNOW LEOPARD

Forrest E. Morgan

This is a work of fiction. The characters, names, incidents, dialogue, and plot are products of the author's imagination or are used fictitiously. Any resemblance to actual persons, companies, or events is purely coincidental.

Edited by Susan Canterbury

Cover design and original artwork by Kara L. Morgan

ISBN-13: 9780997681703
ISBN-10: 0997681705
Library of Congress Control Number: 2016909149
Wexford Point Publishing
Wexford, Pennsylvania

In loving memory of Seth Joseph Edgar Morgan
May 21, 1979 – May 28, 1983

CHAPTER ONE

Southwest England—December 31, 2000

N one of them said a word. Moving in silent precision, twelve figures robed in rough brown wool formed a circle inside the crumbling walls of a ruined abbey. Hoods covered their heads and concealed all but the lower portions of their faces, but each knew the others and knew his own place among them. The day was cold. The ruin lay open to a leaden sky, and beyond the clearing where it stood, barren trees trembled in the wind.

When the circle was formed, one of the figures brought out an ancient codex—a large, yellowed manuscript bound in brittle leather—and placed it on the broken remains of a stone altar. Just then the wind rose in anger and he paused, steadying the old book's fragile pages. The others figures stood silent, stone straight, impervious to the chill and the passage of time. After the gust subsided the man with the codex addressed his associates in a firm but solemn voice.

"Fellow Keepers of the Covenant, we are approaching a critical juncture in God's plan. The third millennium is upon us, and recent events have revealed to all who preserve the Word in its fullness, and who know the prophecies within, that the time of decision is close at hand." Then, as if foreordained, the wind abated, and the waning breeze carried the faint sound of church bells tolling the noon hour in a nearby village. "At this historic moment, let us read from the sacred text…"

At a respectful distance outside the abbey, other figures waited by the cars. These men and women were dressed in business suits and topcoats, yet they winced against the wind's bite. Some clustered together while others stood alone, whispering into microphones hidden in their lapels. They watched each other warily. They also watched the narrow dirt road that passed the ancient ruin and scanned the wooded moor around them.

When the hooded figure finished reading from the codex, he carefully closed the book. The other robed figures remained quiet for several moments, their countenance as heavy as the ashen sky above them. Finally, one of them spoke in English seasoned with a thick Latin accent.

"What can we do to prepare ourselves? There must be measures we can take to—"

"Are we certain this is the time?" another man said. "What if we're wrong and—"

"Of course this is the time. This has to be the chosen millennium. We've all seen the signs. There was even a partial eclipse on Christmas Day. The face of darkness—"

"The question is," a third voice broke in, "from where will the danger come? The old empires are gone, and no modern enemy strong enough to threaten us knows we exist."

"What about the Paulines?" said a tall man, his deep, accented voice revealing his African heritage. "Rome knows we are still here."

"Rome?" barked another man sarcastically. "What can Rome do? There are no more papal states, no papal armies. Will Rome launch another inquisition?" he went on with a sneer. "The Pope is a toothless lion relegated to riding around in a plastic bubble, making empty pronouncements and dispensing useless blessings."

"The persecution needn't come from Rome," the Latino said. "Pauline sects have multiplied a hundredfold since the Reformation. And intolerance isn't limited to Pauline Christianity. Others have tried to exterminate us too. The attack could come from anywhere."

That triggered a flood of protests, some angry, others fearful.

"Brothers, Brothers," said a shorter man with an Asian accent. "This is no time for fear or discord. We are blessed to be living in this historic time." The Asian's voice was confident. The other men fell silent, eager to be reassured. "The answer to our problem is obvious. The prophecy is clear. God has placed our fate in the hands of the Arbiter. He must wake and make a choice. If the Arbiter chooses goodness and light then we are saved. So all we need to do is wake the Arbiter and guide him to—"

"No!" yelled a man from across the circle. "We must not tamper with the prophecy. The scripture says the Arbiter will wake and be tested. We must let the prophecy be fulfilled without our interference."

Once again the circle erupted in a clamor of protests, this time more heated than before.

"Brother Ezekiel!" the Asian man shouted angrily above the din. This outburst was unlike him, and the other men stopped arguing at once. For a moment he reveled in the silence, savoring the power he commanded. Then he continued softly. "Brother, I share your desire to carry out God's will faithfully, but my translation of the *Apocalypse of Joseph* says that the Arbiter will *be* awakened."

"The Brythonic codex is older," Ezekiel snapped. "It's the oldest transcription we have."

"But it isn't the original. Only by seeing what Joseph of Arimathea actually wrote will we know what to do, and the Arbiter has the original Aramaic scroll. That is why we must wake him."

"But can't you see the danger?" Ezekiel said. "Keepers of the Covenant have made this mistake time and again. Every time we've meddled in God's plan, sooner or later, disaster has followed. Think of the calamities we've caused: the Crusades, the sack of Jerusalem, that ugly Templar affair."

"We didn't cause all of those things. The Pope launched the Crusades and ordered the Templars burned, and besides—"

"Of course we caused them! We may not have ordered them directly, but we put events in motion and shaped them just the same. For centuries we've whispered into the ears of men of power, guiding their decisions to suite our own ends. Kings and generals have done as we have counseled, and even you must see how that has turned out."

"Come now, Ezekiel," the Asian said, his tone patronizing. "Hearing your words, one would think we are malicious or even evil. We are neither. We are the children of God, the anointed keepers of his sacred covenant, the only followers of the one true faith. We may sometimes influence the way events unfold, but we only do that because we have to. It's for our own survival. And if we occasionally guide some head of state to a policy that serves our interests then where is the harm? After all, are we not doing God's will? Are we not working to fulfill his ultimate plan on Earth?"

"God's plan is it? You think God is incapable of having his will without our help? And how many times have our kindred manipulated events solely to line their own pockets? Is that God's will?" Ezekiel's voice rose in messianic fervor. "Well, my brothers, if history has taught us anything, it's that God condemns our meddling!

Think of the plagues, the world wars..." He paused for dramatic effect then hissed, "Think of the Holocaust!"

꘎

A gray stillness had settled on the clearing by the time the robed men emerged from the abbey ruins. On seeing them, the men and women in suits stopped talking and started moving toward their cars. "God be praised," one of them said. "Now we can get out of this exposed place."

Then they heard the distant rumble of an approaching vehicle. All of them turned to see an old lorry come into sight and lumber down the road toward the ruins.

"How did that truck get past the checkpoint?" one man said as they looked on in momentary confusion.

The robed men continued walking toward the cars, but some of them slowed apprehensively. Several of the people in suits looked at them then back to the approaching truck, gauging the distances.

Deciding at once, they broke into a run toward the abbey, trying to screen the robed men from the oncoming truck, but it was too late. The truck swerved off the road next to the ruins and squealed to a stop. The back doors flew open, and several figures in military-style sweaters and black ski masks leaped to the ground and opened fire on the robed men with automatic weapons. Almost simultaneously, the suited men and women produced submachine guns and pistols from beneath their coats and returned a hail of fire toward the truck. In the confusion, the robed men ran for the cover of the abbey walls. One of them fell, tried to get up, and then collapsed face down.

The people in suits continued firing as they ran toward the truck. The masked men turned to face this unexpected threat, eyes wide in disbelief. Two of them fired their guns at the approaching guardians with no effect. The others tried to run. They all went down in seconds. Other masked men appeared in the truck's open doors, only to tumble out over the tailgate and onto the bodies of their comrades.

Reaching the truck, the guardians quickly encircled their objective, pouring fire into the vehicle from all directions, pausing only to change clips, until they were certain the threat was eliminated.

When at last the shooting stopped, an eerie silence blanketed the scene, punctuated by the hiss of steam escaping from the truck radiator. A blue-gray haze hung in the dead air, a fog that carried the acrid smell of burned powder and blood. For a moment, no one moved. Time seemed suspended.

Then came the faint heehawing of distant sirens.

The clearing burst into movement again, this time even more chaotic than before: men and women yelling in a half dozen different languages; men stripping off robes while running to the cars; suited guardians flinging doors open and pitching their masters into back seats; tires spinning on winter grass and throwing up clouds of dust as cars veered onto the road, some nearly colliding with each other.

Amidst it all, one of the robed men, his hood thrown back to reveal a bearded face and head of curly gray hair, ran to the fallen brother and knelt down.

A man in a suit approached the bearded man and said in a tone that was deferential but anxious, "Brother Joshua, we have to get out of here." Two other guardians took up tactical positions behind them, scanning the road and tree line, guns at the ready.

"Get the codex safely into the car," Joshua said without looking at the man. Then he gently rolled the wounded man over and cradled him in his arms. The man's eyes were wide with pain and fear. Joshua was about to ask him how badly he was hurt, but he saw the gaping wound in the man's chest. He saw the bright, foamy blood and knew. He looked at the man's face. Their eyes met and the man struggled to speak. Joshua blinked to clear tears from his eyes then put his ear near the man's lips.

"Why?" A gurgled whisper was all he could manage, blood welling in his mouth.

Joshua turned to face the man again, hesitating, wanting to find a way to avoid the answer, but there was no point. "Because it's begun," he finally said.

Joshua watched as the words sank in and the pain in the man's eyes turned to horror. Then the eyes glazed into a stare. Joshua laid the lifeless body down.

"Go with God, Brother Ezekiel. Go with God."

CHAPTER TWO

Maryland—Spring 2001

The man stood, hands clasped behind his back, gazing into the plumes of water that danced above the fountain in front of McPherson Library. He wore a rumpled topcoat, and though he faced away, Owen Powell knew that beneath that coat would be a midgrade business suit—not cheap looking, but not expensive—something inconspicuous, something a man could afford on a government salary. Powell knew how the man would be dressed because he knew who it was. He could not see the face, but he knew that silhouette and it made his stomach churn.

It had been almost five years since he had last seen the man, and he had sworn that if he ever saw him again, he would kill him. He wouldn't, though, not here in the warm spring sun, not in the middle of the university campus.

All around them young men and women were hurrying from one class to the next. Others moved at a more relaxed pace, done with another week of studies and chatting about their plans for the weekend. Powell and the man standing before him, the man deliberately showing him his back, seemed an island out of phase with this tide of young humanity, like phantoms from another dimension only marginally existing in the present reality. No one seemed to notice, but Powell sensed it intensely, and it made him furious.

He had once thought he could fit in with the crowd around him. At a glance, one would think he did. Striding across campus in faded jeans, knit sweater, and a gray tweed sport coat worn soft at the elbows, he could almost pass for a graduate student heading to a lecture or to help some professor grade undergraduate test papers. But he wasn't a student and he never quite managed to feel like a member of the faculty.

He had come here four years ago, a freshly minted Ph.D. in political science determined to settle into a quiet, comfortable life as a scholar. But he soon learned he would never be one of them. He never managed to bond or even identify with his fellow professors, most of whom had gone straight from their parent's suburban homes to college, from there to grad school, and from there to faculty positions to teach about a world they had never experienced firsthand.

Nor did many of his colleagues accept him as one of their own. These textbook academics loved to flaunt their mastery of abstract theories in airy discussions over drinks in quaint little bars, but they reddened and shrank away whenever Powell pointed out how often the messy world contradicted their neat, logical explanations. It was not long before they stopped inviting him to their gatherings. He didn't care.

Powell felt much more comfortable talking with his students, lounging in noisy coffee houses with dirty floors and young waitresses flirting for tips. He would sit there for hours, draining pots of coffee and explaining the world in ways that tempered the theoretical principles he taught in the classroom with rich, contextual examples.

Sadly, during the last year or two, he had begun to lose interest even in these sessions. He didn't want to admit it. For months he had pushed it to the back of his mind or blamed it on the weather or told himself it was but a passing shadow on his mood. On a day like this one—the first mild day of the year, the first whisper of the summer ahead after an unusually hard Maryland winter—he could almost believe it. Maybe it really had been the weather, he had told himself only five minutes earlier.

Then he rounded the corner at McPherson Library, glanced at the fountain, and saw Jack Fowler. In a single heart-chilling instant, he knew he had been wrong—he would never fit in at the university. And that made him despise the man all the more.

Powell stepped up to the fountain a few feet from Fowler, folded his arms across his chest, and gazed at the water. He could see why Fowler had chosen this place. The white noise of the fountain would make it impossible for anyone to eavesdrop on their conversation. The buildings on each side and the spray of water in front of them screened their faces from anyone with a telescopic lens, trying to read their lips. Tradecraft.

Powell waited, outwardly placid as he contemplated coldcocking the man beside him.

"Hello Owen," Fowler said, not turning his way.

"What do you want, Jack?" Powell, too, stared straight ahead.

"Now, is that any way to greet an old friend?"

"Our friendship ended when you abandoned me in northern Iraq."

Fowler sighed, but still did not look Powell's way. "We've been over that. The operation went bust. The Peshmerga sold us out to Iraqi counterintelligence. They were rolling up the network and—"

"You managed to get your own people out."

"Yeah, well, like I told you before, Agency personnel have priority over private contractors. I offered to put you on the regular payroll before we sent you in. Staying private was your decision. Besides, you managed to find your way over the mountains and across the Turkish frontier without my help. A hundred miles of cat and mouse with the Special Republican Guard—damned impressive, I'd say. I guess I trained you pretty well." He gave Powell a sidelong glance and grinned then turned back to the fountain.

"What do you want, Jack?" Powell enunciated each word slowly, his jaw tight.

Fowler sighed again. "We need your help. An American diplomat was killed in England, and the whole thing's turned into one big clusterfuck. It looked like some kind of terrorist attack, but it happened out in the middle of nowhere and there are a whole lot of pieces that don't fit. We don't even know why our man was out there."

"Why come to me? Aren't the Brits investigating? Why don't you work with MI5 or Special Branch?"

"They're on it, but they've frozen us out. We don't know why. For some reason, MI6 is involved."

"Again, why come to me? I'm out of that business. Besides, I've got no expertise in criminal investigation. Why aren't you working through the FBI?"

"Our relationship with the Brits has gotten complicated, lately. We thought you might be able to help because you have contacts there. You went to grad school with the upper crust, people who now have important jobs in the bureaucracy, some in intelligence."

"That's bullshit. No one who went to school with me would be in a key position this soon. Your contacts are better than mine, and you know it. Why are you here, really?"

Fowler shifted awkwardly then turned to face Powell. "I'm here because the man who was killed, Michael Dunross, was a friend of your father's. They were in Tokyo together when your dad worked at the embassy. We think Dunross's death might have something to do with your father's."

Owen Powell gave Fowler a hard stare. "That was almost twenty years ago. My father died in a fire. How could that have anything to do with a recent terrorist attack in England?"

"I can't say more here. Let me give you a full briefing then you can decide what you want to do." He handed Powell a business card. "I've got a temporary office on Broad Street. Come by at four."

Before Powell could say anything else, Fowler turned and walked away.

⇥ ⇤

Arriving at the School of Public Policy, Powell quietly slipped into the back of the main lecture hall and sat down in the last row of seats. On the stage below, Dr. Elaine Chen walked gracefully across the floor, speaking in a strong, confident voice lilted with that peculiar singsong British accent unique to the affluent Chinese native to Hong Kong. She was just wrapping up her lecture.

"Yes, humankind is clearly making progress. Every year more and more people everywhere are becoming educated. Education leads to prosperity, and prosperity empowers individuals and inspires them to seek political reform. Democracy is spreading around the world and, just as Immanuel Kant predicted more than two hundred years ago, democracies don't fight one another because their citizens are loathe to paying the costs of war in blood and treasure..."

As Dr. Chen spoke, Powell watched the hundred or so students in the hall. All of them seemed captivated by the young professor. Owen had heard that she was something of an icon among the female students. She was brilliant and beautiful, and other faculty members envied her ability to inspire such a devoted following. Now, seeing these awestruck young women in the lecture hall, he decided the rumors were not exaggerated.

The male students were equally transfixed, but Powell wondered how many of them were really listening to the lecture. He couldn't blame them if they were distracted. Elaine Chen exuded a sensuality that was both primitive and refined. Repressing a smile, Powell watched the young men follow her every turn on the stage as her knit dress clung to her willowy form.

"...And so, as we move into the twenty-first century," she was saying, "the trends are clear. International cooperation is increasing, and tensions between states are becoming less every decade. The latter half of the twentieth century saw a veritable explosion of intergovernmental and nongovernmental organizations. Combined with other transnational interest groups and empowered by the information revolution, these organizations are making it increasingly difficult for states to inflict violence on other world actors and even on people within their own borders.

"In closing, let me give you something to think about over the weekend. It is not unreasonable to expect that, even before the end of your lifetimes, war will have become a thing of the past. As archaic an institution in the future as slavery and dueling are today, war will have become unthinkable. It will be obsolete.

"Ladies and gentlemen, that concludes today's lecture. I am open to questions."

Several hands shot up. She called on a young woman.

"Professor Chen, I think I can speak for all of us when I say how impressed and encouraged I am by all you've told us today."

Powell rolled his eyes.

"But there's something I don't understand," she continued. "Given all the evidence you've presented, how can anyone dispute the trends? I mean, don't the supposed 'realists' paint a much gloomier picture of international relations? How can they deny all these facts?"

A momentary rustling passed through the lecture hall as students nodded and whispered, echoing the woman's sentiment.

"Well," Professor Chen said, looking in Powell's direction. "Why don't we ask one?"

Uh oh... Surely, she's not going to...

"It just so happens that, today, we have in our presence a distinguished advocate of the realist theory of international relations."

Oh God, she is...

"Doctor Powell, please stand up for us." Powell pulled himself out of the seat and shifted awkwardly as Elaine Chen continued. "Students, allow me to introduce Dr. Owen Powell from the School of Government and Politics across campus. Doctor Powell, can you answer Charlene's question and give us a thumbnail sketch of how realists view the world?"

"Well," Powell began, his face flushed. "I'm at a bit of a disadvantage, being asked to defend realism following an hour-long lecture on liberal idealism. Let me just say that, after more than three thousand years of recorded history in which human beings have killed one another in increasingly brutal wars, I think it's a bit premature to declare war obsolete."

"But isn't that the problem with realism?" another student said. "It's stuck in the past. It isn't progressive. Can't you see that economic interdependence is growing? Can't you see that transnational corporations are already constraining state behavior?"

A murmur of agreement rose from the students. Professor Chen smiled.

"Economic interdependence flourished in Europe at the beginning of the twentieth century," Powell said, "but that didn't stop states from starting the First World War."

"But education and prosperity are spreading, and people are learning that war is unprofitable," Charlene said, her voice becoming more strident. "There are more efficient ways to settle conflicts than fighting. War just doesn't pay!"

"War pays for those who aren't satisfied with the status quo, those who are desperate," Powell said, struggling to keep his voice level.

"Troglodyte," muttered one of the students loud enough for Powell to hear.

"And though you may think that states are constrained from violence, states retain a monopoly on the legitimate use of force. As long as they have the means, states will use force to protect their interests. Prosperity may be spreading in some parts of the world, but there will always be winners and losers in the economic market. Meanwhile, in the arena that really counts, the marketplace of world power, force will always be the final arbiter!"

Powell realized he had raised his voice despite himself, and many of the students had turned around in their seats, muttering, and were staring at him angrily.

"Students, settle down please," Professor Chen said.

The hall became quiet.

Powell decided it was time to disengage from the debate. "On the other hand," he added calmly, "the trends Dr. Chen cites are undeniable. We can only hope her predictions are right. After all, there's always hope."

This olive branch rang cliché even to Powell's ear, and it didn't satisfy many of the students, but most of them were already looking for an excuse to break away and start their weekend. Several got up and headed for the door, and that was enough to trigger an exodus.

As the students filed out of the lecture hall, Elaine Chen called out, "Remember your readings for Monday," and began packing up her papers. Powell sat back down and waited.

As the last students left the hall, the elegant professor gathered up her bag and started walking up the aisle. Powell stood up and met her halfway.

"You are an evil woman," he said sternly.

"Why, whatever do you mean, Dr. Powell?" her eyes wide with innocence.

"You know what I mean, siccing your cubs on me that way."

"My cubs?" an edge coming to her voice, "So what are you saying, that I'm some kind of bear or something?"

"More like a lioness, I'd say."

They glared at each other for a moment then the facade fell and both of them laughed.

"All right, I was a bad girl. So, are we still on for tonight, or are you going to punish me? Are you going to send me to bed without dinner, Dr. Powell?"

Elaine smiled coyly and Owen hesitated, but he decided to ignore the innuendo.

"Actually, that's why I came by, to confirm for tonight and tell you something came up that will make me later than expected. How about we meet at the restaurant at seven?"

"That will work for me. Chinese, right?"

"No," Powell said, pretending to be stern again. "We had Chinese last week."

"But we can have civilized person's food two weeks in a row, can't we?"

"Chinese last week. Japanese this week."

"Okay, okay! Raw fish and green tea!" Elaine tried to make a sour face, but couldn't suppress a smile. She turned to leave then said over her shoulder, "By the way, you fare pretty well in the lioness's den, Dr. Powell."

CHAPTER THREE

"So exactly what kind of work does Tidewater Consulting do?" Powell said.

The young woman sitting at the reception desk cracked her gum and stared blankly for a moment. "Consulting," she said, a wrinkle forming on her brow.

"Consulting on what?"

She frowned a few seconds longer then flashed a gotcha smile. "You mean you don't know? You've got an appointment here. You don't know what they do?"

"I'm not a client," Powell said, returning the smile with unassuming candor. "I work at the university. I've just been asked to stop by and review some... data."

Her smile broadened. "Consulting to consultants, eh?"

Powell grinned and winked.

She blushed, but the smile stayed on her lips and her eyes brightened. "Tell ya the truth, I'm not really sure what they do. I'm only a temp, but Mr. Fowler said if it works out, he'll hire me on full time."

Yeah, I'll bet he did, Powell thought. He wondered how she would feel the morning she came in and found the office empty with no forwarding address. Knowing Fowler, he would leave at the end of a pay period, before cutting her a check.

"Tracy, you can bring Dr. Powell back now," Fowler's voice said through the intercom on the woman's desk.

"Yes, Mr. Fowler," she said, her eyes still on Powell. She buzzed him through the door and appraised him with fresh interest. "Doctor, eh?" She led him down a short hallway, her tight skirt accentuating the wiggle of her hips. They were nice hips, and she wanted Powell to notice. He did.

"This is as far as I go," she said when they reached a second door, "Some kind of security thing." She pressed a button by the door. A couple of seconds later it opened. Jack Fowler welcomed Powell into the inner office and led him to a small conference room. A ceiling-mounted projector shined a midnight-blue slide on a wall screen at the end of the table. The title of the briefing, *The Dunross Affair,* was emblazoned on the slide in amber. The image was labeled "TOP SECRET" in white-boxed, red block letters at the top and bottom, followed by a series of code words indicating intelligence sources and access restrictions.

"Are you sure you want to show me this?" Powell said as they took their seats. "I was debriefed after—"

"You're still cleared," Fowler said briskly.

Without further preamble, he clicked a hand-held pointer, and a picture of a distinguished looking man in his mid sixties appeared on the screen. "Michael Dunross was a career diplomat with postings in Japan, Southeast Asia, and Western Europe," Fowler began. "At the time of his death, he was serving as the charge d' economic affairs at the U.S. Embassy in London. He was married—his wife, Clarissa Hemsley Dunross, lived with him—and they had three grown children living back in the States.

"On New Year's Eve, 2001, at approximately 10:30 P.M. local time, Clarissa Dunross called the embassy and then Scotland Yard to report that her husband had not returned from a meeting he had left for early that morning. She didn't know where the meeting was supposed to be held or with whom, and the embassy had no record of it. As far as they knew, he was home for the holiday."

"Was Dunross CIA?" Powell said.

"No, he was not one of us." Fowler's tone was matter of fact. "He was a legitimate diplomat, a State Department professional."

Fowler clicked up the next slide, a picture of Dunross's body lying on the ground in some weeds. "Two days later, his body was discovered in a vacant lot in an industrial neighborhood north of London. Cause of death: a single gunshot wound to the back. His wallet was missing. The police found his car about two blocks away—blood in the trunk, none on the seats."

"I thought you said he was killed in a terrorist attack," Powell said. "This sounds more like robbery."

"Someone set it up to look that way, but the pieces don't fit. The wound was caused by a high-caliber weapon. The bullet exited his chest, so we don't know what it was, but there were no powder burns on his back. He was shot from a distance."

"That doesn't rule out robbery," Powell said. "The assailant could have shot him from a few feet away. He probably did it in a parking lot or garage, someplace close to Dunross's car. I'd be more concerned about this mysterious meeting no one seems to know about. Sounds like your charge d' affaires was on someone else's payroll."

"That's what we are concerned about. Let me give you the other side of the mystery, the side the Brits were not willing to share. This story begins in Somerset County, in southwestern England.

"At shortly after noon on December 31st, 2000, the police station in the town of Yeovil received a flood of calls from alarmed residents who reported hearing heavy gunfire in a rural area near the village of Glastonbury. When the police arrived on the scene, this is what they found."

Fowler clicked through a series of pictures showing an old panel truck, bodies and automatic weapons strewn around it, several corpses piled beneath the tailgate. A sidelong shot of the truck showed its windows shot out, its tires flattened, and bullet holes perforating every exposed surface. The door was open, and the driver was hanging out upside down, rivulets of blood striping his neck and face, a pool in the dirt below. All of the bodies were wearing black, military-style sweaters, and all but the driver had on ski masks.

"Looks like the terrorists got the worst of it," Powell said. "SAS ambush, right?"

"Wrong. A reliable source says the SAS had nothing to do with this."

"Then who did?"

"That's part of the mystery," Fowler said, leaning back in his chair. "The Brits quickly identified the dead as former IRA terrorists—they had been inactive since the Ulster ceasefire—and traced their movements back to Belfast. They've gathered quite a lot of information about them: how they and their weapons got into England, where they gathered for the raid, where they rented the truck they used, and what have you. But our source insists they know nothing about the group of people the terrorists attacked—the Brits call them 'Group X'—and how these mysterious people managed to vanish after wiping out thirteen veteran IRA killers."

"You can't be serious," Powell said. "Certainly, they must know something. How could a group of people large enough to win a firefight with thirteen heavily armed men disappear into thin air? Someone must have seen them come or go. They must have taken some casualties. What did the police find when they checked local hospitals?"

"Zilch," Fowler said. "Not a single emergency case with any-thing resembling a gunshot wound. And the police were unable to find any reliable witnesses. When they first canvassed residents in and around Glastonbury, several reported seeing expensive cars speeding away from the vicinity of the attack shortly after noon that day. But when MI5 tried to follow up a few days later, they all adamantly claimed they had been mistaken.

"But I'll tell you what they do have: all together, they gathered up more than three thousand spent shells fired by Group X. They all came from small-caliber, high-rate-of-fire, automatic weap-ons—mostly MACs, UZIs, and Walthers—but there were a variety of other types too."

Powell turned back to the picture of the bullet-riddled truck with the bloody bodies strewn around it. "Looks like whoever these people were, they were trying to make a statement."

"Yeah, but what were they saying, and to whom?"

Then Fowler clicked up a slide showing a map of the crime scene, complete with circles and arrows. He got up and walked to the screen. Pointing to the left side of the map, he said, "The shells were scattered over an area beginning here and running to and around the truck. In this area there were also tire tracks from a dozen cars and, based on the footprints, the Brits believe Group X consisted of at least thirty-five people, all wearing dress shoes."

"So what are you telling me," Powell said, "that a team of terror-ists raided some kind of Mafia gathering?"

"I'm not suggesting anything, yet. I'm just showing you what we got from MI5. Actually, some of the footprints were from women's shoes, something we wouldn't expect to see at a Mafia meeting."

"But you're sure none of these thirty-five people was wounded in the attack."

"Like I said, the Brits found no evidence that Group X took any casualties at all. They did find a pool of blood separate from the IRA men, but not associated with Group X. There's a ruin of a fourth-century church over here," he said, pointing to the map. "There's not much left of it, just some waist-high remnants of the walls, actually. The blood pool was located in front of the church ruin amid the footprints of a different group of people, this one all men. The Brits call these guys 'Group Y'.

"Based on the footprints, they calculate that Group-Y consisted of a dozen men, all wearing expensive shoes—Gucci, San Loren, that sort of thing." Fowler pointed to the map again. "Their footprints are alone inside the church where they stood in a circle. From there, they seem to have come out and then run back to the church, probably fleeing the IRA attack, before heading for the car park."

"So the Group X people were bodyguards for Group Y," Powell said.

"Our conclusions exactly. Scotland Yard Special Branch had a DNA analysis done on blood from the pool in front of the church. It turned out be—"

"Let me guess," Powell said. "It was Michael Dunross's blood."

Fowler smiled and put his index finger on the tip of his nose. Then he returned to his seat, crossed his legs, and leaned back, his eyes fixed on Powell's.

Powell leaned back, too. "So we've got an American diplomat secretly involved with a wealthy group of people in some religious cult," he began, "and then—"

"What makes you think it was a religious cult?" Fowler interrupted, still smiling in anticipation of where Powell was going.

"Obvious isn't it? Secret meeting on the last day of the last year in the millennium, standing in a circle in the ruins of an ancient church? And not just any church—a lot of people believe Glastonbury Abbey was Britain's first Christian church. There's a legend that Joseph of Arimathea, the man who gave up his tomb for Christ, founded it in the middle of the first century."

"You're talking about that tourist trap over in the village," Fowler said.

"No, that was built later. Most historians now believe the ruin in the woods predates the one in town. Even that one isn't the original building, but it does reside on the original foundation. So I'd say Group Y was holding a ritual to celebrate the dawn of the new millennium."

"So why meet at noon, in broad daylight where they're liable to be spotted? Why not do it at midnight?" Fowler said.

"Because noon in England's Greenwich time zone is midnight on the international dateline half a world away. That's where the calendar rolls over first, where time and the new millennium begins, figuratively speaking."

Fowler stared at Powell a moment then lunged forward and slapped his hand on the conference table. "That's why we need you on this case! You know, it took the Brits several days to figure out the religious-cult, millennium-celebration angle, and they only managed it then because one of their constables was an amateur scholar in medieval literature."

"Yeah, well, the bigger mystery is how a group of people standing in the open can mow down a team of terrorists and get away with only one casualty."

"No, the bigger mystery," Fowler said, "is how the IRA squad could have brought down even one target."

"I don't follow."

Fowler paused, holding Powell's gaze, and said, "The magazines in all the IRA weapons were loaded with blank cartridges."

Powell stared at him, dumbfounded.

After a moment, Fowler said, "Most of the Brits think someone set up the IRA guys to be killed. Their families and friends in Belfast are convinced it was the SAS, but as I already told you, they've denied any involvement."

"So how did anyone get a group of IRA thugs to stage an attack using guns loaded with blanks?"

"According to the squad's sole survivor, a guy who missed the raid because he got locked up for drunk and disorderly the night before they left Belfast, it was a pretty elaborate scam. It seems that in the fall of 2000, his brother and one other member of their IRA cell was approached by an unknown Irishman who claimed to be outraged that a cult group was planning to defile a sacred Christian site in southwestern England. The man said he represented a group of wealthy Catholics who wanted to stop this desecration in a way that would discourage it from happening again. He offered to pay their cell a hundred thousand pounds to attack the group at the site using blank ammunition. They were to hose down the cultists with mock gunfire then tell them that, should they ever try to conduct occult rituals at Christian sites again, the next attack would be real.

"As this guy tells it, when his brother brought the proposition to the IRA cell, they thought the whole idea was daft. But the mystery benefactor seemed serious and obviously had a great deal of money. In later meetings he presented a detailed plan that convinced them he and his colleagues were serious and competent. After a long debate, the cell decided to carry out the scheme. The Ulster ceasefire had left several of them restless for action and, of course, there was the money.

"Unfortunately for their families, they never saw a cent of it beyond the cell's expenses for the raid. The rest was to be paid when the job was done. When news of the massacre hit the press, the guy who missed taking part rang up the Irishman's contact number, but got no answer. He had disappeared."

Powell rubbed his temples. This was getting more and more complicated. "Any leads on the mystery Irishman?" he said.

"No, but the IRA contact mentioned that, immediately before one of their meetings, several cell members overheard the guy talking to someone on his cell phone in a foreign language. They weren't certain, but thought it was an Asian language, perhaps Chinese or Japanese."

"That would explain MI6's interest," Powell said.

"Maybe"

"But why are they trying to avoid American involvement?"

"We don't know, but they've slammed the door in our faces. We can't get squat from MI6, Special Branch, or even MI5, officially. If it weren't for our..." He paused, searching for the right word. "... our contact in MI5, we wouldn't have this much."

Powell knew he meant the CIA had a spy in MI5, something the American intelligence agencies were officially barred from doing when it came to the United Kingdom, a country with which the United States enjoyed a "special relationship." He thought for a moment. "I'm guessing the whole IRA attack was a diversion so someone could assassinate Dunross."

"Why would you think that?"

"Because it's the only explanation that makes sense. Someone wanted Dunross dead, but he and all the other members of Group Y were heavily guarded. None of the IRA guys had live ammo; there had to be another shooter, probably a sniper working from a distance. The IRA raid was a smokescreen to cover the gunshot from the sniper."

Powell sighed, looked up at the ceiling, and pondered for a few seconds. Then he leaned forward, put his forearms on the table, and turned his icy stare on Fowler. "Alright, Jack," he said, "this has been an amusing tale, but what has it got to do with my father?"

Fowler gave him a wan smile and clicked the next slide. It was a picture of a younger Michael Dunross standing at the rail of a balcony on a high rise overlooking downtown Tokyo. He had his hand on the shoulder of another man, one about twenty years older than him, and their faces were close in what appeared to be intimate conversation. Fowler clicked again, and a picture appeared of the same two men sitting at a table in a sidewalk café. Powell couldn't tell where it was, but the setting looked European. The men leaned close across the table and, once again, seemed deep in discussion. A third picture showed them in hiking garb, walking across what looked like a meadow in the Scottish highlands. Again, the same intense expressions, and they walked side by side instead of in file as most hikers do. The pictures were grainy, obviously shot from a distance with a telephoto lens, but the faces were unmistakable: one was Michael Dunross, the other Owen's father, Rhys Powell.

"So what are you saying?" Powell demanded, his anger rising. "Are you suggesting Dunross and my father were lovers or something?"

"Oh, for god sakes, no," Fowler said immediately. For once, he looked genuinely surprised and more than a little uncomfortable. "Both of them were investigated for security clearances repeatedly in their careers, and we know they were straight. But they obviously had a special relationship of some kind."

"They were friends," Powell said, his voice sounding more strained than he would have liked. "They both worked at the embassy in Tokyo. What's so unusual about a couple of coworkers becoming personal friends?"

"Nothing at all. But you've got to admit it is unusual for friends to meet in a variety of far-flung places around the world and to keep those meetings secret. We pulled up their travel records and compared them. There were trips to the same destinations, or to ones nearby, on matching dates several times a year from the late seventies until your father's death in 1982. They weren't noticed right away because Dunross worked for State and your dad worked for Defense."

"So why did you photograph their meetings?" Powell snapped. "Why'd you have them under surveillance?" Fowler didn't answer.

"Look, why don't you just put it on the table," Powell said. "What are you trying to say?"

Fowler folded his arms across his chest and sighed in resignation. "We think your father was involved in this cult group, whatever it is, with Dunross. We think that he, like Dunross, may have been murdered for some reason related to that group. We don't know the reasons for either murder, but given their positions and the wide access they had to classified information, we are concerned that they may have compromised national security."

"That's absolute bullshit!" Powell yelled. "My father was not in any cult. He was loyal to his country and wouldn't have even considered betraying it. And he wasn't murdered. He died in a house fire after falling and hitting his head."

"Owen," Fowler said, his voice level, "you're father's death was very suspicious. The cause of the fire was never determined, and the nature of his head injury was not consistent with what one would expect to see from a fall. The case was never resolved to American satisfaction, but the Tokyo police insisted on closing it quickly."

"Well he wasn't a traitor!"

"Prove it! Go to England and pick up the trail on the Dunross murder. Help us with this, Owen and clear your father's name in the process."

Powell considered it for what seemed like a full minute. The Dunross thing was a fascinating puzzle, and he couldn't stand the thought of his father's name being dragged through the mud. But something smelled about Fowler and his story. He had caught the first whiff when Fowler had him come to a cover location in town. Langley was within easy driving distance of the university. If the CIA wanted his help, why didn't Fowler have him go there for the briefing? Maybe, Powell thought, it was because Fowler hadn't even given the Agency the full story. Maybe it had something to do with the agent he was running in MI5, in clear violation of national intelligence policy. Whatever it was, he knew Fowler wasn't being straight with him. This man had burned him once before—he wasn't going to let him do it to him again.

"I think I'll pass," Powell finally said. He rose from his chair.

"What?" Fowler blurted, "But what about your father?"

"My father was a war hero who served his country all his life. He's been dead for eighteen years. There's nothing you could dredge up now that would damage his reputation." Powell turned and started for the door.

"But what about Dunross? We need to find out what that was about. We need you, Owen."

Powell stopped abruptly and turned to Fowler, "Yeah, right. I'm a college professor now, Jack. My students need me. I can't just drop everything and fly to England." He started to leave again. Then, as an afterthought, he said, "I'll tell you what: the semester ends in a few weeks. If you haven't sorted this out by then, call me. But before I get involved you'll need to brief me at Langley—you and your boss."

CHAPTER FOUR

I t was ten after seven by the time Powell got to the restaurant. Inside the air was warm and alive with cheerful voices and the mixed aromas of tempura and miso. The sushi bar was full and the hostess told him there would be a twenty-minute wait for a table. He was about to give her his name, but he caught sight of Elaine sitting in a private room behind a partially closed *shoji* screen, so he headed on over. Elaine saw him coming and flashed a warm smile. Then the screen slid back to reveal a bearded man sitting across the table from her. When Powell reached the booth, the man got up and stepped to Elaine's side of the table.

"Owen, this is Randall Preston. He works up on the third floor at Public Policy," Elaine said.

Preston was lanky and tall, several inches taller than Owen's six-foot-two stature. Powell put out his hand, and the man responded with a limp handshake.

"Do you go by Randall or Randy?" Powell said.

"It's Randall... to my friends, anyway," he said, looking away.

The men sat down and a middle-aged Asian woman wearing a brightly colored polyester kimono brought them tea and took their order. After she left, Elaine tried to get the men talking.

"Owen, Randall's a philosopher by discipline. He heads up our Ethics in Policy program."

"Ethics in policy, eh?" Powell said. "We can certainly use more of—"

"I got a call on the book today," Preston said to Elaine.

"Oh, good," she said. Turning back to Owen, "He's just finishing a manuscript and hopes to find a publisher by summer."

"Got one," Preston said. "Davis University Press wants it bad."

"Why, that's wonderful, Randall!" Elaine said.

Preston beamed. For the next fifteen minutes he told Elaine every detail of his phone conversation with the Davis editor. Elaine smiled enthusiastically throughout the monologue, providing an occasional "Oh, that's good" or "You must be very proud." All the while, she kept stealing glances at Owen who sat back in his seat watching Preston talk. Finally, after what seemed an eternity to Powell, the waitress appeared with a tray of sushi and the conversation turned to food as the three of them selected their first pieces and mixed their sauces.

Once they had begun eating, Preston said, "So Powell, Elaine tells me you've got quite a past—raised in Japan, undergrad at Oxford, Army Ranger, CIA… To hear her tell it, you're some kind of cross between Indiana Jones and James Bond… Or was it Tom Jones and Maxwell Smart?" He grinned at Elaine.

"Nothing so exciting," Powell said, "or entertaining," he added, also looking at Elaine.

She blushed.

"Actually," Preston said, "I rather think we could do well enough without the Rangers or the CIA. They've both caused more than enough trouble in the developing world." Owen didn't respond, so he continued. "So what did you do in the Company, eavesdrop on foreign political leaders so you could blackmail them over their tawdry little affairs?"

"Well, to begin, no one in the CIA calls it 'the Company'. That's the stuff of novels and B-movies. And I wasn't actually in the CIA; I just did some work with them when I was with Army Intelligence in Korea." *And once afterwards,* he thought, but he couldn't tell anyone about that.

"So why'd you get out of the Army? Couldn't get promoted?" Preston smiled, but his eyes were taunting.

"I left with the drawdown following the Gulf War, took the separation bonus and went to grad school at Yale."

"Ah, yes, you became a professor. So what have you published, Professor?"

"Not much," Powell said, pushing back a flush of anger, "A couple of papers in minor journals, certainly nothing as impressive as a book on ethics."

Elaine shifted nervously.

"Well, I think military people would do well to stay out of academia, and vice versa, for that matter," Preston said.

"Oh?" Powell said. "I think Sir William Butler had the right angle on that issue."

"How so?"

"He said that the nation that insists on drawing a broad line between the fighting man and the thinking man is liable to find its fighting done by fools and its thinking by cowards." Powell was smiling now. "By the way, Randall, have you done any military service?"

This time Preston blushed and Elaine smiled discretely as she stared into her teacup.

Owen Powell almost regretted having told Elaine about his colorful past. He hadn't told her the whole story, of course. He had left out the darker parts.

He had grown up in Japan, the son of Rhys Powell, a Defense Intelligence Agency officer working out of the American Embassy in Tokyo. His mother, an English schoolteacher his father had met on a brief assignment to London, had been killed in an accident when Owen was a toddler. Growing up the son of a single parent who worked long hours, Owen spent much of his childhood in the care of a Japanese nanny and housekeeper who taught him to speak Japanese as well as he could speak English.

Owen enjoyed a degree of freedom most American children could never imagine. Fluent in the local language and frequently unsupervised, he ventured ever farther from home, exploring his neighborhood and the surrounding area. By the time he was in high school he had gathered an eclectic circle of friends, an odd assortment of Japanese kids and the children of diplomats from several countries as well as a handful of sons and daughters of U.S. State Department and military personnel.

Owen and his band of young bohemians were known in every district of Tokyo. They rode the subways all hours of the night. They knew every pachinko parlor in town and all the dance clubs in Shinjuku that served alcohol without asking for ID. Their exploits became something of a legend among the other American kids in Japan.

Owen's father took a laissez-faire attitude when it came to the boy's wanderings, but he paid careful attention to his progress in two key areas: education and combative sports. He enrolled Owen in a local judo club when he was still in elementary school, and encouraged him to take up karate-do in junior high. Rhys conferred with Owen's instructors regularly and never missed attending any test or tournament in which he was participating.

Like the State Department kids, Owen attended the American school downtown, saving him the trauma of being a cultural outsider in the intense Japanese education system. Even so, when he was eight years old, he took up learning to read and write Japanese on his own initiative and became literate enough by high school to undergo the grueling general examination for admission to the Japanese university system. He also learned to speak passable Korean over the course of a summer he spent on the peninsula after high school graduation.

All in all, Owen had had a happy childhood, if an unusual one. His relationship with his father had been reserved, but living alone in an exotic land without a mother in the house, they had been close in their own way. Owen loved his father and felt loved by him. And Owen loved living in Japan. There, free to roam and enjoy the countless diversions available in the world's largest city, he was in his element. He was content.

But all of that changed the summer his father died. He was in Korea when it happened. He had just lost someone there that he cared about deeply when he returned to Tokyo and discovered he had been orphaned. Suddenly, with no living relatives available to lean on—at least, none who cared enough to take him in—he was uprooted from his world and sent away to college in England.

There, disoriented and consumed with grief, Owen entered the dark phase of his life. He avoided the university social scene and became a loner, speaking to those around him only when he could not avoid it. He lost all interest in combative sports, focusing instead on Jikkishinkage-Ryu Aikijujutsu, an obscure Japanese martial art that he studied under the tutelage of one Takagawa Masao, an eccentric graduate student he had met at school. Jikkishinkage-Ryu was Takagawa's family system, having been passed from one generation to the next since 1600. Owen was the first person outside the Takagawa family permitted to learn its secret techniques, and Masao became Owen's only friend. The two of them spent countless hours practicing jujutsu. Otherwise, Owen threw himself into his studies, graduating a year and a half early.

But Owen's mood had darkened further by the time he left Oxford. His grief was evolving, and its expression had progressed from brooding to anger—anger at himself for not being home when his father was killed and anger at the world for letting such an injustice occur. As a result, though he had several lucrative offers to join import/export concerns doing business in Asia, he shocked everyone who knew him by walking into the American Embassy in London and joining the U.S. Army. His father had been an Army officer during the Second World War, and Owen told himself that he wanted to follow in his footsteps, but mostly he wanted to throw his life to fate.

Army life opened many avenues to a man with little regard for his personal safety. Immediately after finishing Officer Candidate School and receiving his commission at Fort Benning, Georgia, he went on to Airborne School there then stayed on for Ranger School. During the 63 punishing days of Ranger training, Owen and his fellow candidates endured everything from jungle treks to alpine assents while averaging less than three hours sleep a night. The strain broke many of the soldiers in Owen's class, but he thrived on it. Driven close to the limits of his physical ability, he temporarily forgot the burdens he always carried, not only his endless, gnawing guilt for being away when his father died, but also the memory of a deeper failure that summer.

Upon graduation, he sought immediate assignment to a ranger battalion where he would have the best chance of seeing combat, should the United States intervene in some brushfire war. But to his frustration, the Army saw a valuable resource in his language abilities and sent him to yet another school, the Human Intelligence Operations Course at Fort Huachuca, Arizona.

Once again, Owen excelled, and when he was done with intelligence officer training he finally got what he longed for—a dangerous field assignment. The Army sent him to South Korea where he worked with a multiagency team of intelligence operatives and special operators from that country and the United States tasked with combating North Korea's incessant efforts to infiltrate commandos into the South. The work was invigorating. When he wasn't interrogating captured soldiers or assessing intelligence leads on enemy movements, he was leading special fire squads sent to intercept and capture, or, when given no alternative, liquidate North Korean infiltration teams.

He extended his tour in Korea several times, but as the years passed, he became increasingly independent and began taking ever-greater risks. To his commanding officer's mounting frustration, he started conducting his own one-man, night reconnaissance missions in the mountainous region around the eastern end of the Demilitarized Zone, generating a great deal of speculation among his colleagues as to what he might be doing on these forays.

Whatever the case, he had already received several reprimands for his rogue behavior, and his commander was on the brink of filing criminal charges against him when Iraq invaded Kuwait in 1990. Seeing an opportunity to get involved in a shooting war, Powell immediately requested a transfer to the 5th Special Operations Group, supporting U.S. Central Command in Saudi Arabia. His commander was more than happy to oblige and, in the process, rid his unit of this irksome, if talented, officer.

The Gulf War gave Owen Powell exactly what his demons craved—a chance to spit directly in death's face. On a moonless night shortly before coalition air forces began bombarding Iraqi positions, Powell and eleven other special operators boarded a black Pave Low helicopter that spirited them into southern Iraq. In the weeks that followed, the team operated behind enemy lines directing air strikes and providing bomb damage assessments by satellite link while reporting movements of Iraq's Republican Guard divisions. They became more aggressive when the ground war began, blowing up bridges, attacking communications nodes, and cutting the fiber-optic cables that linked Iraqi field units to their headquarters.

After the ceasefire, when U.S. forces drew back into liberated Kuwait, Powell stayed behind with a handful of other special operators to organize Shi'a dissidents in southern Iraq and encourage them to rise up against their Baathist oppressors. They relayed guarantees of American support—air power would keep the Iraqi army off the freedom fighters while they seized the cities.

But the men in Washington failed to keep their promises, and when the Iraqis did rise up against their overlords, the backlash was awful. From their covert encampment on a hillside overlooking a village outside Basrah, Powell and his team watched in horror as the Republican Guard swept into the town and exterminated everyone they suspected of being rebels, including their families, their neighbors, even their livestock. Dispirited and hunted now by both the Baathists and the bitter, vengeful Shi'ites, the American special operators gave up on their doomed mission and signaled for a covert extraction. On the next moonless night they boarded the black chopper and left Iraq in forlorn defeat.

When it was all over, Powell had won himself a Silver Star, something for which he cared absolutely nothing. What really mattered was that he had become a different man, a wiser man, or so he thought then. He had lost all faith in political authority. He was also less driven. More importantly, he had finally come to terms with himself. He had finally exhausted his reckless self-disregard and with it, his interest in the Army. The only thing that could put a gun back in his hands, he told his Army comrades, was a chance to get the psychotic son of a bitch who had all those people murdered in southern Iraq, a chance to get Saddam himself.

Then, several years later, the day after Powell defended his doctoral dissertation; Jack Fowler showed up on his doorstep at Yale and said he could give him that chance.

God, Owen thought, *how could I have been so stupid?*

Owen, Preston, and Elaine finished the last bites of dinner without speaking. Then, after dabbing the corners of her mouth with her napkin, Elaine tried once more to find a topic the men could discuss with a degree of civility.

"Owen, Randall practices martial arts. Perhaps the two of you could get together sometime."

"Yeah, Powell, I hear you run a little studio in town."

"It's a dojo," Powell said.

"So what do you teach? I haven't seen you around any of the local tournaments."

"I teach martial arts, not combative sports."

"Yeah? What's the difference?"

"My students study Japanese and Okinawan *bugei*—jujutsu and karate-jutsu, mainly. We don't play games."

"Ah, now I see," Preston said, leaning back and crossing his arms. "You're one of those ultra traditionalists—meditation, forms, that kind of stuff. Well, no offense, but I just don't buy all that crap. If there's one thing I've learned, it's that all the best fighters compete. You hone your skills and test them in the ring."

Elaine looked into Owen's pale, ice-blue eyes and started getting uneasy about what she saw there. But Preston continued, oblivious to the danger.

"In the thirty years that I've been training, all the instructors I've known who told their students not to compete were just afraid—"

"Thirty years?" Elaine said. "That's an awfully long time for a young man like you to have studied anything as demanding as martial arts." She gazed at Preston and smiled. It worked.

"Well, I started when I was four years old. I made black belt before I was six. Now I'm a certified master and..."

You're certified all right, Powell thought.

Preston turned in his seat to face Elaine and described how he had been a child prodigy in the martial arts, earning one belt after another and dominating the tournament circuit from his teen years onward. Powell settled back and watched, marveling at how easily Elaine manipulated the man. Every time Preston seemed about to wind down, she smiled and batted her large, almond-shaped eyes and he remembered a whole new chapter of his life story, one he just had to tell her.

After a few minutes, Powell grew bored. He quietly slid back the *shoji* screen and motioned for the polyester kimono to bring over a bottle of sake. He wondered how long it would take Elaine to tire of this game. He didn't have to wait much longer.

"So now I've got more trophies than I have room to store," Preston was saying. "Anyway—"

"Excuse me, Randall," Elaine said. "I hate to interrupt, but could you let me out. I really need to freshen up."

"Oh, certainly." He and Powell stood up. Elaine slipped out of the booth and headed for the ladies' room. Both men watched her graceful gate, showcased by the formfitting knit dress. "Exquisite!" Preston said.

It was the one thing on which he and Powell agreed.

"So," Preston said as he and Powell sat back down. "What's the deal with you two?"

"Excuse me?"

"You know, what's your relationship? Everyone knows you see each other a lot. Are you dating or what?"

"Not that it's any of your business, but Elaine and I are very close..." Powell hesitated, the word sticking in his mouth. "... friends."

"So she's not your woman?" Preston said, his face lighting up.

"Elaine Chen is no one's 'woman' but her own," Powell said, an edge coming to his voice.

"So I'm still in the game."

"I guess that's for Elaine to decide."

The waitress appeared with a tray holding a small, porcelain bottle of warm sake and three cups just as Elaine returned to the table.

"No, boys, don't get up. It's been a long week and I'm tired. I think I'll go soak in a hot bubble bath." Powell saw Preston's pupils dilate and knew he was visualizing. Glancing at the bottle of sake, Elaine added, "And I think I'll have some wine from a civilized country." Then, watching Owen's expression, she winked and said, "I mean France, silly."

CHAPTER FIVE

After Elaine was gone, Powell poured the sake and they drank in silence for a minute. Then Preston looked up from his cup and said, "So Powell, just what do you do in your little martial arts studio—"

"Dojo"

"Whatever. I mean, how do you attract students, since you're afraid to compete? "

"I don't have to worry about attracting students," Powell said, the edge returning to his voice. "There are still a few people in the world that recognize quality when they see it. I teach the real thing and people come."

"And what is that?" Preston said, smirking.

"I start by teaching them how to fight, how to defend themselves on the street. Once they're advanced enough, I begin guiding them in the Way; I use *bugei* to lead them to *budo*."

"Gobbledygook," Preston sneered. "Now that Elaine is gone, let me tell you what I really think. You're not only a coward; you're a charlatan, too. All this talk about *budo* and some mystical Way, it's all just a smokescreen to hide the fact that you don't really know anything of value. You're pretending to be some warrior guru, but you're afraid to test yourself in tournaments and afraid to let your students compete because if they do, they'll discover how little you've taught them."

Preston was becoming increasingly animated now, waving his arms to emphasize his argument. Powell, meanwhile, had gone very still, his pale blue eyes locked on Preston's.

"You say you don't compete because you don't play games," Preston continued, getting up and stepping around the table as if to leave, "but competition is the only way to develop the lightening speed and razor-sharp reflexes that only true masters have."

To illustrate his point, he suddenly snapped a back fist at Powell's face. But before Preston could register what had happened, Powell deftly caught it and, in one smooth motion, turned the tall man's wrist and jerked his arm forward. Rising from his seat, Powell swept his other arm across Preston's, putting him in an arm bar. He cranked Preston's wrist upward, violently levering his shoulder downward and smashing Preston's face into the table, scattering cups and dishes.

Crying out in pain, Preston yelled, "What the hell do you think you're doing? Let me go, goddammit!"

"Randall, you just made a serious mistake. I've put up with your boorish behavior all evening, and I couldn't do anything about it before now."

"Let me go you bastard!" he screamed, his eyes wide in panic as he tried to turn his face to see his captor. "When I get loose, I'm going to kick your ass!"

"No you're not," Powell said calmly. "You see, you're just a ka-rate man... No, make that a karate player. You've only learned how to defend against someone kicking and punching at you in a ring with a referee to stop the game before anyone gets hurt. But you've just taken a swipe at a different kind of animal, and there's no referee here to save you. You're in my power now. I've got you, and there's nothing you can do about it. I can break your arm at the wrist, elbow, or shoulder anytime I want to."

As he said this, Powell torqued the lock sharply at each joint, eliciting yelps from his helpless prisoner. Then he leaned forward and slipped his free arm around Preston's neck, setting up to apply *hadake jime*, a deadly choke. Putting his lips close to the bearded man's ear, he whispered, "In fact, I can kill you any time I choose, and there's nothing you can do to stop me."

With that Powell flexed the arm around Preston's neck, pinching off the blood to his brain. Preston's eyes bulged for a moment then rolled up into his head as he lost consciousness.

Powell let go of Preston's neck and let his head bump facedown on the table. He stepped back and waited a few seconds to see if he would need to resuscitate him. Preston's body jerked a couple of times then he groaned. Reassured that the tall man was coming to, Powell opened the *shoji* screen and found himself facing the wide-eyed stares of the polyester kimono and several other members of the restaurant staff.

"Please call my friend a cab," Powell said. "I'm afraid he's had a bit too much to drink." He started to leave then added, "Oh, and he'll get the check."

※

It was after nine when Powell parked in the gravel carport and fumbled open the kitchen door of his dark house. Stepping inside, he shoved the ill-fitted door closed and froze, his senses tingling. He turned, peered into the darkness, listened intently. Nothing. He sniffed the air, but caught only a faint, stale whiff of bacon from breakfast. Still, he knew someone else was in the house. He could feel it.

Stepping silently, he moved across the moonlit kitchen and into the blackness of the hall. Coming to the living room doorway he paused, stretching his awareness into the soundless gloom. No one was there, so he carefully worked his way toward the back bedroom of the rundown, single-story bungalow, staying in the shadows and avoiding the pools of moonlight that flooded through the windows of each room.

Reaching the master bedroom, he eased open the door and saw that the room was dimly illuminated by a light coming from beneath the door of the adjoining bathroom. Relieved, he hesitated just long enough to confirm that no one was hiding in the bedroom then stepped to the bathroom and pushed open the door.

"Where have you been?" Elaine moaned. "My skin is wrinkling like a prune."

She lay in Owen's tub beneath a rolling white landscape of suds. Her face was serene; its delicate features framed by raven curls pinned up on her head and snowy bubbles below her chin. The room was steamy and filled with the sweet aroma of bath oil.

"I was dealing with that pompous ass you left me with," Owen said. "By the way, where's the Audi? I didn't see it and thought you'd gone home."

"It's parked around the corner. I slipped in and left the house dark so that nosey neighbor of yours wouldn't see me.

"Fooled me too."

"No I didn't." She shifted, parting the suds for a moment. "But I did forget to get the wine before climbing into the tub. Be a darling and get it, will you? But first, hand me that towel."

Owen grabbed the clean towel Elaine had left folded on the counter and held it out, but only close enough for her to reach if she stood up, exposing herself. She scowled momentarily then smiled and nodded for him to put it down on the side of the tub. "Get the wine, Owen." Her voice was teasing but firm.

Owen chuckled. He put the towel within her reach and went out the door.

When he returned, Elaine was wearing a bathrobe and standing in the bedroom in front of a full-length mirror that hung on the back of the closet door, brushing her hair. Owen crossed the room and placed the open bottle and two glasses on the bedside table.

Turning to Elaine, he noticed how the silver-blue, silken robe clung to every curve of her body. He stood there a moment, mesmerized by the way her lustrous, black hair glistened each time the brush pulled it straight then bounced back into large, soft curls around her shoulders as it sprang free of the bristles. Then his thoughts returned to earlier in the evening. "Why on earth did you have that blowhard join us for dinner?"

Elaine giggled. "He is insufferable, isn't he? But I thought it was about time you got to meet some of the people I work with. Besides, you need a little competition now and then." She dropped the brush into a makeup bag that hung on the doorknob and turned to face him. "Keeps you on your game, don't you think?"

"Competition like him I can do without. He's an imbecile."

"He's a respected scholar!"

Owen didn't like the reproach he heard in her voice. "You know he just wants to get into your panties, don't you?"

"That would be impossible," Elaine said.

"How's that?"

"I'm not wearing any."

With that, she pulled open the robe and let it slip off her shoulders, pooling on the floor around her feet.

CHAPTER SIX

A white limousine carefully negotiated the narrow street that wound through an exclusive neighborhood built on the steep mountainside. The gleaming, 25-foot behemoth would have drawn attention almost anywhere else, but it was a common sight on Oahu where hundreds of cars like it plied the streets of Waikiki, shuttling affluent Japanese tourists between the airport, their hotels, and the many attractions on the island. Anyone who saw the car in this particular neighborhood might have guessed it was taking a wealthy resident to or from the airport. They would have been wrong.

Drawing to the end of a quiet lane, the limousine barely had to hesitate when it reached the entrance of a walled estate. The motor-driven gate rolled back immediately, and the car slipped past the alabaster pillars and between the stone-faced men who stood on either side of the driveway. As the gate closed behind it, the car followed the drive up a steep rise around the main house and stopped in a large carport in back. The doors sprang open and half a dozen guardians, mostly Caucasian, spilled out.

A comparable number of Asian men converged on the car from around the house. The two groups eyed each other cautiously, but without rancor. After a moment, a tall blond man in a gray silk suit emerged from the car and an elderly Asian stepped out of the house to greet him.

"Welcome to Hawaii, Brother Zechariah. God's wisdom upon you," said the Asian, smiling. He bowed briefly then extended his hand.

"And upon you, Brother Saul," Zechariah grasped the Asian's hand warmly and they shook, each man clasping his left hand over the other's right. "You've chosen a beautiful place to meet."

Saul led him into the mansion and through several lavishly furnished rooms before stepping out and across a breezeway to a large, covered lanai on the other side. There, the men beheld a panoramic view of southern Oahu with the downtown Honolulu skyline to the west, Diamond Head to the east, and Waikiki directly below them to the south. Bounding it all was the sea, stretching out in brilliant bands of emerald and azure.

Saul ordered a servant to bring them tea as they seated themselves in rattan chairs. Two guardians—one Asian, the other Caucasian—stood quietly in the breezeway, maintaining a respectful distance, but staying close enough to defend their masters if needed. The others remained vigilant in the house and on the grounds below.

Once they were alone Saul said, "My beloved brother, let me begin by congratulating you on your recent ascension. The House of Benjamin will prosper in your illumination, and the Great Circle will benefit from your wise counsel."

"Thank you, my friend. I think you know how much this means to me. Representing the Sons of Benjamin in the Great Circle of Illuminati has been my lifelong dream."

"I am intrigued by the ascension name you've chosen," Saul said. "Zechariah, *the Lord remembers*."

"That's ironic," Zechariah said, smiling. "I've always been curious about yours. Why would an illuminatus want to be called Saul, the name of the traitor?"

Saul hesitated a moment. "My name alludes to the great king of Judah, not Saul of Tarsus." He laughed quietly, but his eyes were hard. "Anyway, no matter what name you choose, I know you will bring your acolytes spiritual insight and prosperity."

"Thank you, Brother. Such praise from an enlightened man of your stature flatters me." Zechariah hesitated, his face darkening. "But when I think of the awful event that brought me to power... Not only was Brother Ezekiel a great illuminatus, he was my mentor." Zechariah's eyes seemed to lose focus for a moment. "I almost can't believe he's gone," he said to himself. Then, looking back at Saul, "I'm not exaggerating when I tell you his murder shook our house to the core."

"Yes," Saul said, rubbing his chin. "I share your grief. These are dark times." Then he leaned forward, looking into the blond man's eyes. "That is why it is so important that we act now to put our plan into effect," his voice low. "If we move with conviction, we can head off any more violence and bring the Tribulation to an end consistent with God's prophecy."

"Well, about that..." Zechariah hesitated, looking down. "I'm not sure acting so soon after my ascension would be wise." He shifted nervously.

Saul remained quiet and kept his eyes on the other man's face. *Yes*, he thought, *I saw this coming. You are a weak man, ambitious and opportunistic, but weak.*

⊷⊷ ⊶⊶

Saul and James Wingate, who now called himself Brother Zechariah, had been secretly meeting for several years. They had kept their association secret because, had others in the Covenant known of the relationship, it would have been ruinous for both of them. Both men were *pneumatics*, spiritually enlightened Gnostic Christians of the highest order. Wingate had served on the House of Benjamin's Council of Twelve, the body that administered the house's routine affairs and advised its illuminatus. Saul was the Illuminatus of Asher, the leader of one of the most powerful houses in the Covenant's Great Circle. Had it become known that a councilor of Benjamin was conspiring with the House of Asher, it would have been scandalous for Saul and might have cost Wingate his life. Yet, both men were willing to take such risks—at least, both of them had been up until now.

Each man had seen a personal advantage in these covert liaisons. Saul wanted the House of Benjamin as a political ally in the Great Circle, something its former illuminatus, Brother Ezekiel had brusquely denied him at every opportunity. Wingate wanted power. He wanted to succeed Ezekiel as the Illuminatus of Benjamin. But though he was the leader's protégé, he was not well regarded in that house's Council of Twelve. Unless he could convince his brethren that his ascension would bring greater wealth and power to their house than would accrue under the policies of another candidate, he stood no chance of being anointed illuminatus.

That was where Saul came in. Almost three years prior, Saul had contacted him through an intermediary offering to provide some Asian business connections that might prove lucrative for the House of Benjamin. After exchanging several cautious communiqués, Saul and Wingate met in an alpine villa in Switzerland to discuss the particulars.

From that meeting onward, each man had courted the other. Wingate complained expansively about Ezekiel's shortsighted stubbornness and repeatedly assured Saul that, should he become the Illuminatus of Benjamin, he would steer the house on a course more agreeable with Saul's interests. Saul, in turn, showered praise on the younger man for his insight and wisdom. More importantly, he directed a steady stream of business deals Wingate's way, contracts that fed the House of Benjamin's coffers and improved the young pneumatic's reputation in the Council of Twelve.

Yet, even with Saul's help, Wingate probably would not have become the Illuminatus of Benjamin had Ezekiel not been so tragically murdered. The revenue Wingate brought to the great house's treasury had raised his standing, but the other councilors still doubted his maturity, and several of them whispered that they sensed what might be a dark shadow in his spirit.

But the whispering stopped when Ezekiel was killed. The council was overwhelmed with grief—Ezekiel had been their blessed illuminatus. He had led them with insight and wisdom. Now he was gone. Yes, he was gone, but his protégé was still with them.

For months, Wingate basked in Ezekiel's glory and the council's grief. When it finally came time to select the next illuminatus, the debate raged for hours, but eventually, Wingate's growing circle of followers prevailed and he was anointed Brother Zechariah, the ninety-seventh Illuminatus of Benjamin.

Yes, Saul thought, *you've come a long way, my young friend. When you needed me, you were quick to pledge your support, but now... Now you show yourself for the weakling you are. Well, that's all right. That is why I chose you. That is why you fit into my plan.*

Saul continued watching the young man's face. After a few moments, Zechariah looked up and Saul locked his eyes in a steely glare. "I think we need some privacy to discuss this more fully," he said.

Without taking his eyes off Zechariah's, he waved away the guardians in the breezeway. The Asian turned to leave, but paused when he saw his counterpart had not moved. Zechariah hesitated a moment, looking perplexed, then nodded in resignation. The guardians turned and went into the house, sliding the glass door shut behind them.

"You know our agreement," Saul began, keeping his voice level. "Once you were anointed an illuminatus, you would bring the House of Benjamin into the Eastern Alliance and commit your support to me."

"Yes, I know. But everything is different now. Ezekiel's been murdered. Everyone's on edge. If I change the house's policies now, it'll look suspicious." Zechariah's voice sounded strained.

"Why are you worried about what people might think? You did not have anything to do with Ezekiel's death." Saul noticed the younger man's hands were trembling. Ezekiel reminded him of a rabbit, hiding in a thicket, hoping the fox would pass by without discovering him there.

"No, of course not," the young man said. "But Ezekiel was such a strong leader, so outspoken. Every pneumatic on the Council of Twelve knew how set he was against interfering in the fulfillment of prophesy. My God, every—"

"Do not profane the Lord's name in my presence!"

"—Every Son of Benjamin knew how committed he was, and they all shared his views. I can't just change directions with no warning or explanation. What do you expect me to do?"

One of the guardians standing by the glass door turned and looked out.

"Keep your voice down!" Saul glared at the door and the guardian turned away. He turned back to Zechariah. "You made a commitment and you will keep it."

"Yeah, but, but..." Zechariah looked out toward the sea and struggled to get his breathing under control. After a few moments, he turned to face the Asian again. "I know we talked about what the Great Circle might achieve if Ezekiel would just be more cooperative. And yes, I said that if I ever led the House of Benjamin, I would support your ideas and lean more toward the Eastern

Illuminati," he said, his voice becoming steady. "But we didn't talk about dates, and I didn't sign any pact. Now is not the time to change Benjamin's policies. I am an illuminatus, the spiritually enlightened head of the House of Benjamin." He was sounding more confident now, and he liked the sound. "I will decide when... no, *if* the House of Benjamin will join any secret alliances. Now is not a good time. Perhaps I'll consider it in a year or two."

Zechariah sat back in his chair looking pleased with himself.

Well, my young rabbit, Saul thought. *In one hand I have honey, in the other I have thorns. Which shall I give you first? I think it will be thorns.*

"Beloved Brother," Saul said, his voice like granite, "You are an illuminatus because I made you one. It is time you understood that you serve at my pleasure."

"What do you mean, you made me an illuminatus!" Zechariah said. "That is absolute nonsense. I ascended when Brother Ezekiel died..." Zechariah's eyes opened wide in shock. "You don't mean that you... You would go so far as to have a fellow illuminatus assassinated... an enlightened, spiritually anointed man of God?"

Saul maintained his icy glare and smiled.

"That's abominable! You can't just kill an Illuminatus of Benjamin. I won't stand for it. I'll impeach you before the Great Circle."

"And what will you say, that I told you that I killed your mentor?" Saul hissed, his voice cutting like a razor. "Why would they believe you? What motive would I have had for killing a brother? It seems to me that the only person with something to gain from Ezekiel's death was you."

Zechariah's eyes opened wide in shock. "They wouldn't censure me... They couldn't, there's no evidence."

"No, the Great Circle would not censure you. But every Benjamite knows of your ambition. How would you fare with your own Council of Twelve?" Saul smiled. "How would you handle

Ezekiel's former guardians? Don't I recognize some familiar faces in your escort detail? Weren't some of those men Ezekiel's? Just how long do you think you will live if this gets out?"

Saul settled back in his chair and took exquisite pleasure in watching the color drain from Zechariah's face. The blond man seemed to deflate before his very eyes, his shoulders sagging, his head drooping forward in submission. After a few moments, Saul continued.

"So this is what we will do. First, do not say anything notably pro-Eastern in meetings with your Council of Twelve, and you need not make any overt changes in policy just yet. Soon, I will call Joshua to convene the Great Circle. Just follow my lead and support my initiatives there."

"What are you going to do?"

"We—you and I—are going to change the balance of world power," Saul said, suddenly leaning toward the younger man, a tremor of excitement in his voice. "I'll present the newly awakened Arbiter for confirmation, and this one will not be a lapdog for the Houses of David and Levi like his predecessors. He will be in my pocket. With your support and the Arbiter's favor, the Eastern Alliance will control more votes than the illuminati from the West. And then… then…"

Saul paused, his eyes ablaze. He saw Zechariah staring at him. With considerable effort, he reigned in his excitement and sat back in his chair. "Well, that is not important now. Just be ready to respond when Joshua calls the Circle to convene."

Zechariah didn't respond. He sat staring at Saul a moment longer then returned his gaze to the sea, his eyes looking tired. Saul noticed that the younger man suddenly seemed old. It pleased him.

Now it is time for a little honey, he thought.

"Oh, don't be so morose," Saul said. "There will be plenty in this for you, too. Your house can profit nicely from our… association."

Zechariah looked at the Asian. "What are you talking about?"

"The House of Benjamin is heavily invested in a certain American aerospace company, right? You also hold a good deal of stock in a Japanese firm that makes missile guidance systems. Well, Beijing wants to develop a new generation of cruise missiles, but they lack some of the essential technologies. They would pay well to get them. I will see that those contracts come your way."

"That's an empty promise. The United States and Japan both restrict sales of critical technology to China."

"Do not play coy, Brother," Saul said. "Benjamin has operatives in key positions in the U.S. Department of Commerce, and I have people in Japan's Ministry of Economy, Trade and Industry. You know as well as I that we can turn the right screws to get export licenses pushed through for our contracts."

Zechariah looked out at the sea and pondered the situation for several minutes. Saul waited patiently, knowing his prey was fully ensnared. Finally, Zechariah nodded abjectly then pulled himself out of the chair. He started to leave then paused.

"So when will you awaken the Arbiter?" he asked.

"Those wheels are already in motion, my young friend. All you have to do is await the Great Circle summons from Joshua."

Zechariah turned his back and walked away.

"Go with God, Brother," Saul called after him.

Zechariah did not respond.

CHAPTER SEVEN

Elaine stood at the counter in Owen's kitchen slicing fruit for their breakfast. She paused now and then, taking care not to cut her fingers, as she divided her attention between wielding the paring knife and watching Owen through the window. He was in the backyard going through his morning *kata*, the complex patterns of movement that comprise the core of traditional karate training. Morning *kata* was a daily ritual for Owen. Rain or shine, summer or winter, he always got up early enough to put in at least thirty minutes of rigorous training before breakfast.

Elaine always loved the morning. Morning was her quiet time, time for her to reminisce about the past and contemplate her plan for the future. Morning always seemed to draw her thoughts back to her earliest memories of Hong Kong, where her grandmother, Su-wen, would get her up at dawn and take her down to the harbor to fish.

Su-wen had grown up among the *Shui Min Yan*, the people who lived on the vast sea of sampans lashed together forming a floating village in Aberdeen harbor near Hong Kong. Like so many

Shui Min Yan children, she was nearly grown before she ever put her foot on dry land. Unlike her playmates, however, she eventually escaped that life of toil and poverty when her daughter married a wealthy shipping magnate she had met while dancing in one of the many gentleman's clubs that crowded Hong Kong's pleasure district. Suddenly, Su-wen found herself separated from the hard but simple life she knew so well and living in splendor in a hillside mansion overlooking the city. Yet, as much as she appreciated her son-in-law's generosity, she never felt comfortable in her daughter's luxurious home. So every morning she rose at dawn and left the exclusive hillside neighborhood, walked through the city, and went down to the docks where she would sit and fish. Not long after Elaine was born, Su-wen began taking her along, strapped to her back until she was old enough to walk on her own.

These were Elaine's happiest memories, sitting and fishing with her grandmother. There, sometimes sitting on the dock, sometimes drifting in a dingy, both of them holding lines in their bare hands, Grandma taught little Lainie the mysteries of life. Time and again, she recited the history of her family and all the legends passed to her in her own youth. She taught her to feel the rhythms of the Tao, how to read tealeaves, and how to orient herself in any setting to achieve the proper *feng shui*. This was a carefree time, a time before they sent her abroad for school, before she had to learn logic and rationality and so many other things foreign to her nature.

Watching Owen in the early morning hours always brought her back to this happy time in her life. This morning Owen was clad only in sweatpants and sneakers, and steam flowed from his nostrils and rose from his sweat-glistened back as he drilled in the brisk dawn air. Elaine watched him with wonder and pride. His body was lean and powerful, with well-articulated shoulders and a broad chest above a narrow waist, all borne on stout, agile legs.

"Do you know how to catch a man?" Elaine remembered Su-wen asking her so many times.

"No Grandma," she would always say, though she had heard the story nearly every day for years.

"Well, catching a man is just like catching a fish," Su-wen would begin. "You have to show him the bait, but never let him see the hook beneath it. Sooner or later he'll nibble, but you must be patient. Never try to set the hook too soon or you'll lose him. Only after he's tasted enough to know you are the sweetest morsel in the sea do you jerk the line and bury your hook deep in his jaw."

"Do I pull him in then?" Lainie would always ask excitedly, already knowing the answer.

"No child, you must still be patient, especially if he is a good catch. Remember, you are fishing with very light tackle. If you try to land him too soon, he'll run and break the line. No, you must play him until he tires. Gently pull on the line until he runs then give him lots of slack. When he turns back, pull him closer to the boat until he runs again. If you set the hook deeply and play him long enough, sooner or later he'll be so exhausted he'll beg you to pull him into the boat." At this point, Elaine and Su-wen would always throw back their heads and laugh. "Just remember, Lainie, the bigger the fish, the longer you have to play him."

Well Owen, Elaine thought, *you are a very big fish indeed.*

Elaine was humming softly when Owen came into the kitchen. She stood at the counter with her back to him, and he almost laughed when he saw her faded running shorts and his ragged, old Oxford sweatshirt with the sleeves pushed up to her elbows. Instead, he crept up behind her and snaked his arms around her waist.

"Good morning," he said and kissed her neck below the ear.

"Good morning," she cooed, squirming slightly, but pressing against his kiss.

He held her tight for a moment then moved one hand up and slipped his fingers into a gaping hole under the sleeve of the sweatshirt.

"Stop it!" she giggled, not really meaning it. She turned suddenly and slipped out of his reach. "Sit down and eat."

Owen sighed then sat down at the table and eyed the bowl of fruit disapprovingly. "Where's my bacon and eggs?" he said as Elaine poured his coffee.

"I told you, I don't feed you that poison. You can eat whatever you want when I'm not here, but when I fix you a meal, it will be something good for you." She scooted into the only other chair at the tiny dinette. "You know, as often as we do this, I'm going to have to remember to leave some clothes over here. I've got an aerobics class across town, and I'll have to rush home and change for it."

"You wouldn't have that problem if you'd just move in."

Elaine's face suddenly darkened.

Damn, he thought. He hadn't meant to spoil the playful mood they shared that morning, but as soon as the words left his lips, he knew he had.

"You know how I feel about that," she said. "I'm a professional woman with a reputation to protect. I don't want students and colleagues whispering behind my back, saying 'there goes Dr. Powell's bed wench.'"

"Good God, Elaine, this is the twenty-first century. Nobody says 'bed wench' anymore. And nobody cares who anybody's dating or sleeping with as long as it's not a student. Do you know what a pain in the ass it is to tell buffoons like Randall Preston that you and I are just buddies?"

"Please don't curse, Owen. You know it makes me uncomfortable."

"Well?" he persisted. "Do you know what it's like listening to Preston gloat that he's 'still in the game,' just because I had to tell him you're not my woman?"

"Is that what this is about?" Elaine said, suddenly raising her voice. "Is this about claiming your prize in some juvenile contest with Randall?"

"No!" Owen said, shoving the bowl away in exasperation. "That's not it at all." He took a deep breath and let it out slowly. Then he turned his chair to face Elaine more directly. "Look, I only meant that I care about you and I'm not ashamed to let other people know it. For the life of me, I can't understand why you don't feel the same way about this. What's the big deal? So we're dating. So we're intimately involved. Who gives a flying f—" he caught himself before the word came out.

Elaine's almond eyes flashed fire for a few more seconds then the muscles in her jaw relaxed and she softened. "Owen, we've been through this before. You know how hard it is for a woman to achieve a professional reputation, and you know how easy it would be to flush all that down the loo if rumors started going around that I'm sleeping with a colleague. Besides..." She hesitated a moment, poking her fork at the remaining pieces of fruit in her bowl. "I don't believe in living with a man before marriage."

"Then let's get married." The words slipped out almost before he realized what he'd said.

Elaine looked up in surprise and met Owen's startled eyes.

They had been seeing each other for nearly two years and had been on intimate terms for most of that time. They had never really discussed a future together—certainly, neither of them had said anything about marriage. The thought had crossed Owen's mind, and he had considered trying to bring it up with Elaine in some casual way if he could find the right mood and moment. Clearly, this wasn't it.

Neither of them spoke for a few seconds. Then Elaine sighed. "I can't marry you Owen."

"Why not?" He felt the marrow draining from his bones.

"How can I say this?" She hesitated. "You don't know who you are."

Owen was dumbfounded. Then he felt a heat rising in his face as if steam were forcing out the last traces of bone marrow. "What the hell does that mean?" he yelled.

"Well..." she struggled for words. "Look at your life. Your father raised you overseas. You had everything going for you. You were a prodigy, immersed in the local language and culture, brilliant enough in high school to get a free ride at Oxford. Then, out of the blue, you joined the Army, of all things. Even there, you excelled. But just when it looked like you had a promising career ahead, you reversed course again. You quit the Army to go to grad school."

"Well what's wrong with that? So what if I decided I'd rather teach college than command a battalion in some dirty, Godforsaken armpit of the world? After all, if I hadn't changed the direction of my life, I wouldn't have met you."

"That's fine, Owen. I'm glad you came here. But that's just it." She leaned forward, holding Owen's eyes with her own. "You're not glad you came here. Look at yourself. You're a terrific teacher. You're talented enough to be one of the top scholars in your field, but in the four years you've been on the faculty, you've hardly published a thing. Instead, you spend all your time practicing and teaching martial arts."

"Elaine," Owen said in exasperation. "You've got to understand, that's an important part of my life. If you can't understand that then you'll never really know me."

"Of course, I understand, Owen. I know you better than you realize, better, I think, than you know yourself. Martial arts are an important part of your life. That's fine, but it can't be your whole life. You've made it a refuge, a hiding place to escape facing the fact that you're not satisfied here. But the worst part is you don't know what you want to do. You don't know where life will take you next. And if you don't know that, how can either of us know whether your life will include me after you change course again? Owen, I have a career that's very important to me. I'm rooted here. I can't marry you if I don't know whether I can be in your future."

"Elaine…" now Owen struggled for words. "Marriage is about commitment and trust. If we were married, I wouldn't just change careers without working it out with you. You've got to trust me."

"Yes, marriage is about commitment and trust," she said, her voice turning brittle. "But how can I trust you to include me in your life if you don't know where that life will take you?"

"Don't you love me?"

Owen winced as soon as the words left his mouth. He knew the question wasn't fair. In all the time he had been with Elaine, he had never used the word "love". Not that it had ever seemed to matter to her—she had never said anything about it, never told him she loved him, or asked him how he felt about her. Just the same, over time he had come to sense a deep, intimate bond between them. He had assumed she must love him, but now that the question was out in the open, he suddenly wondered if he had been fooling himself. He desperately wished he could pull those words back.

Elaine looked at him long and hard. The air in the kitchen grew heavier with each passing second that neither of them spoke. Owen's pulse accelerated.

Finally, she moved to break the tension. Gently placing her hand over his on the table, she looked into his eyes and said, "Owen, let's not talk about love right now. We've got plenty of time. Neither of us is seeing anyone else. Life flows like water. Right now our lives are flowing together. Why don't we just let this stream take its natural course and see where it leads us?"

Owen recognized the Taoist fabric beneath her words. Ordinarily, he loved the way Elaine's quirky Chineseness always seemed to bubbled up and overcome her stodgy, British rationality at times he least expected it. But this time the words cut him like a knife.

Then she abruptly changed tone. "Oh, I'm going to be late for my class." She gave his hand a quick squeeze then sprang up from the chair and put her dishes in the sink. "I'll be home all weekend grading quizzes and preparing for Monday's class. Call me if you think of it."

As Elaine headed for the door, Owen rose from his chair, mouth open. He wanted to say something, but couldn't find any words. She grabbed a paper sack that held her clothes from the evening before and pulled open the ill-fitted door to the carport. Stepping out, she turned and met Owen's eyes for just a moment. "Call me, okay?" she said softly. She mouthed a kissed in his direction and pulled the door closed behind her.

Owen stood there several seconds, waves of conflicting emotion washing over him. Then he picked up his fruit bowl and pitched it at the sink. It shattered, spraying shards of porcelain across the counter.

CHAPTER EIGHT

Hot water streamed over Owen's head and shoulders. It felt good. He closed his eyes, regulated his breathing, and focused on the tingling sensation of the water hammering his skin. He willed it to wash away the tension that lingered in his body reminding him of the humiliation Elaine had dealt him.

He had always used breathing to center spirit. From the time he learned to walk, perhaps even earlier, the adults in his world had urged him to control his emotions, to maintain his *wa*, his peace. Some of his earliest memories were of his nanny, Keiko, sitting him down when he was upset and telling him to stop sobbing and breath. Later, when he was in elementary school, she made him sit on his heels in *seiza*, the traditional Japanese kneeling posture, for up to 20 minutes a day, focusing on the rhythmic intake and outflow of his breath and learning how to clear his mind, how to stop his inner dialog. By the time he had begun junior high school, Keiko had him sitting in Lotus posture for an hour a day in deep meditation. He resented the discipline when he was young, but by the time he was a high school student, he recognized its value in the heightened intuition and powers of concentration it had gained him.

So why couldn't he calm himself now?

The phone rang.

"Shit!" Owen cranked the water off and threw back the vinyl curtain. His head crowned in lather, he grabbed a towel and ambled across the bathroom and into the bedroom where the phone jangled again on the nightstand by the bed.

"Hello," he said, trying to wedge the phone between his slick, wet cheek and shoulder to free his hands so he could wrap the towel around him.

"Are you out of your mind?" a woman's voice yelled in his ear. It was Elaine.

"What the hell are you talking about?" he yelled back, immediately angry.

"You know what I'm talking about. Randall! He just called and told me what you did to him." She was screaming in his ear.

Owen had never known her to be so angry. It shocked him and, at the same time, made him furious that she would get so mad on Preston's behalf. "So, he had to go whining to you about what happened to him, eh? What's the matter? The great master can't fight his own battles without hiding behind a woman's skirt?"

"Oh, grow up, Owen! Stop being such an immature little boy. You can't go around tearing into every man who gives me a second look, and I'm certainly not going to stand for you beating up my colleagues. Don't you get it? I have to work with that man!"

Owen stopped struggling with the towel and grabbed the handset. "That man is an absolute buffoon! He's an idiot! Worst of all, he's a lout! He insulted me, my students, and my dojo!"

"Your dojo! Your dojo! It's always your dojo!" Elaine sounded madder than ever, now. "When are you going to realize there are things in this universe more important than your dojo? There's a whole world out there, forces of good struggling against forces of evil, people dying by the thousands every day. And all you can think about is playing little power games in your dojo, holding up your silly artificial pecking order of who outranks who, propping up your self-deluded façade, pretending that all that crap is important."

Now Owen was as angry as she was. "You've got a lot of nerve mocking what I do, and you've got a hell of a nerve screaming at me for putting Randall-Asshole-Preston in his place! It was you who pitted the two of us against each other. 'You need a little competition,' you said. 'Keeps you on your game," you said. Well, damn it woman, I was on my game last night, and I put Preston on his ass. That ought to teach him a lesson for nosing around my woman, and it ought to teach you a lesson for being such a tease!"

"How dare you!" Elaine hissed. Her voice was cold as steel now, and that startled Owen even more than her earlier yelling. "How dare you refer to me in that manner. I am not your woman, and if you are so insecure that you have to assault any man who shows an interest in me..." She hesitated as if weighing whether to say what was on her tongue. "Well... then maybe it's time we stopped seeing each other."

"That's fine with me!" Owen shouted just as he heard Elaine hang up. "For all I can tell, we haven't really been dating anyway," he yelled into the dead line. He slammed the phone down and clumsily gathered the towel off the floor before heading back toward the shower. "Damn crazy, fickle bitch!"

He stomped through the puddles he'd left on the bathroom floor and tossed the towel on the counter then cranked the hot water tap on full and shoved his hand into the shower. Relieved that it was at least warm, he put one foot in the tub when the phone rang again.

"Son of a bitch!" he yelled as he wheeled and charged back into the bedroom. "What do you want now?" he shouted into the phone.

"Uh, I'm not sure, now that you put it that way," came the startled reply. "Is this Owen?" It was Richard Falstaff, Owen's department chairman and boss.

"Oh, Richard," Owen said, suddenly embarrassed. "Jeez, I'm sorry. I thought it was someone else."

"Well I'm sure glad to hear that," Richard said, still sounding a bit rattled. "I don't know what you're so mad about, but I've got some news that I bet will cheer you up." He hesitated a moment for effect. "Pack your bags, buddy, you're going to Japan!"

"What?"

"You're going to Japan, Owen. You got the grant!"

"Richard, I don't know what you're talking about. Back up and give it to me from the beginning."

"The grant, Owen, the grant. I went into the office this morning to catch up on some paperwork. You know how it always seems to come crashing down in waves near the end of the semester. And it never fails, just when I plan a weekend antiquing trip with Monica, Friday afternoon I get—"

"Richard, the grant?"

"Oh, yeah, sorry. Like I was saying, I went into the office this morning and found a letter from Tokyo on the fax machine. The Ministry of Economy, Trade, and Industry has approved the research proposal you submitted for the study of Japan's governmental coordination of private industry. They're really hot on the project. Not only do they want to fund the research, but they're going to—"

"Whoa, whoa, Richard, slow down. I still don't know what you're talking about. I didn't submit any research proposal to METI or anyone else in Japan. You've got the wrong guy."

"No, there's no mistake. The fax included a copy of your proposal—you know, the one you sent out about two months ago—and this Inoue Tsugumichi, the guy who wrote the METI letter, was very pointed in specifying that the funding is strictly contingent on you carrying out the research personally. Looks like you really impressed them."

"Richard, I'm telling you, I didn't send any proposal."

"Owen, it's got your signature on it. Maybe you just forgot. Maybe it was something you threw together on a whim then pushed to the back of your mind because you never really expected to get a response."

"No, I'm sure I would have remembered something like this. You've definitely got the wrong guy. Someone else in the university must have put this thing together, and somehow, it got my name on it."

"Well, however it happened, the Japanese want you and no one else. In fact, they want you there Monday."

"Monday?" Owen said, yelling again despite himself. "That's less than two days away—one, considering I'd be crossing the date line. I'd have to catch a plane—"

"Tonight," Richard said. "I've got you booked on a five o'clock out of BWI, connecting with a redeye out of L.A. I tried to call you earlier to discuss the arrangements, but you must have been at your dojo."

"But Richard, I can't just drop everything and leave the country on an hour's notice. The semester's not over. We've got final exams in a couple of weeks. Who's going to look after things at my—"

"I know you're busy, but you're going to have to drop everything and do this. When I couldn't reach you this morning, I called the dean to tell her about the METI offer, and she's all excited. You see, what I've been trying to tell you is the Japanese aren't just agreeing to fund your research; they're also offering the university a sizable grant for us to use at our discretion. But it's all contingent on you being in Tokyo on Monday.

"Besides, there's nothing we can't handle without you. Your exams are already written, and you have a teaching assistant. Have him administer them. I'll cover your last few lectures and oversee grading the exams. I'll keep an eye on your house and cover for you at the office."

"But Richard," Owen said in exasperation, "I don't want to rush halfway around the world on what will ultimately turn out to be a wild goose chase."

"Owen, let me tell you how it is," Richard's voice was firm now. "The tenure board meets in September, and your contract is coming up for renewal again this fall. You haven't published squat in more than two years. This is a research university, and you know the old saying: 'publish or perish.' Well, my boy, I managed to carry you through your last contract review, but to be perfectly honest, your chances of being retained on the faculty for the fall semester are pretty grim if you don't produce some publishable research before this board meets. Now, I know you've got a lot going on, but this is life-and-death for your career. You need to show up in Tokyo and follow through on this project whether you proposed it or not."

Owen sighed in frustration. "Okay, Richard," he said. "Here's what I'll do: I'll go to Tokyo and untangle this mix up. If I can't figure out who really wrote the proposal, or if I can't persuade the Japanese to fund the grant when that person turns up—and believe me, he or she will turn up sooner or later—then, with that person's permission, I'll do the project myself. But I'm telling you, Richard, there's something fishy about this whole thing. If it falls through, I'm on the first plane home, tenure board be damned."

"Fair enough, Owen." Richard said, his voice betraying the immense relief he felt at getting Owen to do this. "Pack your things and call your teaching assistant. I'll pick you up in an hour—and don't forget your passport."

Owen hung up the phone and headed back into the bathroom. "What else can possibly go wrong today?" He put his hand in the shower. The water was ice cold.

CHAPTER NINE

Owen peered into the fog and tried to get his bearings. He didn't know where he was or how long he had been standing there, but the mist was cold on his face and the dampness had soaked his outer layer of clothes and begun to reach his skin. He shivered. He looked around, trying to spot some landmark, some identifiable feature on the surrounding terrain.

Then he heard it.

The sound was very faint at first, but he knew immediately what it was, and it stirred in him a deep and all too familiar sense of dread. He stood absolutely still and held his breath so he could hear it better, so he could determine where it was coming from, so he could get a bearing on what direction to walk to see what he dreaded seeing and try once more to stop what he had never before succeeded in stopping.

The sound was louder now, and there was no doubt about what it was. It was a woman sobbing. It was a pitiful sound. She wasn't screaming in pain or terror or crying for help. She wasn't even weeping in that open, shameless, self-indulgent way that people weep when they want someone to acknowledge and comfort them. She was just sobbing, quietly and pathetically, sobbing in a way that said she knew there was no help for her, that no one who cared would hear her, sobbing in a way that said she had been hurt beyond healing and that she knew she was going to be hurt some more. The woman was sobbing the way a woman sobs when she is physically and emotionally broken, when life is anguish, when death is release. The woman's sobs were quiet and pathetic and pitiful, and each one of them was an icy blade cutting into Owen's soul.

The sobs were louder now, but Owen still couldn't tell from where they were coming. They seemed to echo in the fog, coming from all directions at once. He began to walk, not knowing which way to go, but knowing he would end up in that place, the place to which he had to go, but didn't want to be. The sound grew louder but somehow less distinct. It seemed to change, becoming more resonant, taking on the tone and timbre of a voice coming from a cave, or a well… or a tomb.

Owen walked faster, though there was no distinguishable difference in the terrain, no landmarks to indicate his progress or gauge his speed. He walked on and on, straining his eyes to see through the mist, fighting to remain calm, to keep his rising panic in check. Then the fog parted before him and he saw what he knew he would see.

He found himself looking into a shabby room—tattered walls of unpainted masonry with rotted studs peeking through jagged holes, a rough plank floor below, a single, naked light bulb hanging on a cord from a rusty electrical fixture above. What he could see of the room was empty save for a large, heavy wooden table standing in the center beneath the harsh light.

And on that table he saw her.

A young woman was naked and tied there, her wrists bound together above her head, her legs spread and hanging over the end of the table from the knees down, her ankles lashed to the table legs. She had been beautiful once, a Viking princess with a strong, defiant jaw and flowing blond hair. But now her hair was grimy and matted and she looked half starved. The bruises on her body and face—bouquets of bright, purple blossoms scattered among fields of older blotches of yellow and brown—spoke of numerous beatings. She lay there sobbing pitifully and hopelessly, unable to move, unable to cover her nakedness, unable to escape the harsh, glaring light and the anguish she knew was coming.

He heard the men before he saw them—rough, male voices speaking a familiar language, but carrying on a conversation that Owen couldn't quite make out. The voices were coarse and gritty from the smoke of countless cigarettes, and the words were slurred. The men spoke loudly, each throwing out a cacophony of words as if to drown out the others, but there was no tone of contention, no sense of discord. These men were cheerful. They were drunk and cheerful.

Owen groaned and felt his gut tighten when he saw the men come into the room. There were four of them, Asians clad in un-kempt military uniforms, their shirts open, their hair disheveled, their pockmarked faces sweating. They continued their bawdy conversation as they walked around the table, leering and laughing and saying words that Owen could not make out but under-stood all too well.

The woman did not acknowledge their presence. She just con-tinued sobbing, her half opened eyes fixed on the cruel light above. One of the men reached out and kneaded her breast roughly, and she cried out just a little. They laughed. These cheerful men laughed.

This was more than Owen could stand. He started running, desperate to reach the room so he could stop this unthinkable thing, but he couldn't seem to get any closer.

Then the men stop circling. The tallest of them now stood at the foot of the table, between the woman's knees.

Owen cried out in panic and ran as hard as he could, throwing all his strength into the effort, willing himself to succeed, but he felt as if his body were under water, pushing against a formless but unyielding force.

Then, to his horror, as the three smaller men looked on, laughing and goading their comrade to do what was unthinkable to Owen, but what came so casually to them, the tall man, grinning around crooked, yellow teeth, slowly began unbuckling his belt.

"No!" Owen cried out. And as he yelled a hissing noise filled his ears and got louder and louder until it became a roar, drowning out the sound of everything else…

Owen jerked his eyes open and found himself belted into the seat of an airliner crossing the Pacific Ocean, the sound of air and engines filling his senses. He tried to swallow, but his mouth was all sand and cotton. His forehead was clammy.

"Are you all right, Sir?"

He looked up into the concerned face of a young woman in a flight attendant's uniform. "I'm okay," he said in a raspy voice. She continued looking at him, her expression unchanged. He wondered if she thought he might cause a disturbance here, so high above the ocean and far from the safety of land. "I'm fine," he said again.

"Can I get you anything?"

"Ice water… and a cup of coffee, please."

A look of relief came over her face, as she seemed to decide this passenger wasn't going to cause trouble after all. She turned and headed for the galley.

Owen looked out the window. Far below, a solid deck of clouds was ablaze with the orange glow of a sunrise that had finally caught up with the plane.

Owen was shaken. The dream from which he had awakened was a recurrent nightmare that had haunted him for years. He knew what it was about. He knew it had arisen from the shame he felt about his failure in Korea that summer so long ago. But he hadn't had the dream in more than a year, not since... not since he had been with Elaine.

His thoughts turned to Elaine. She didn't know about the Japan assignment. He had not called her before he left. Now he wished he could talk to her about this riddle, share his puzzlement over the mysterious research proposal and METI's peculiar demand that he come immediately. Maybe she could make some sense of it. Maybe they could reason it out together. But he could not think of Elaine without becoming angry again.

Damn her, he thought.

How could she even think of siding with Preston over him? Yeah, okay, she wanted to keep their relationship quiet, but they were about as close as any lovers could be. At least, he thought they were. There had been times when he could almost read her mind. God knows, she often read his, he mused, a momentary smile coming to his face.

But then there were times when he felt like he didn't even know her. What was it with her and Preston? What was he to her?

He looked out the window again. It was morning, Monday morning.

After the flight attendant brought his drinks, Owen picked up the fax copy of the research proposal that had lain in his lap as he slept and read through it again. It all seemed to be in order. In fact, it was quite good: a precisely worded research question followed by a thorough exposition of what data would be collected and how it would be analyzed, all carefully laid out in rigorous detail.

A section entitled "Qualifications of the Researcher" described Owen's background, emphasizing his language skills and familiarity with Japanese culture, ruling out the possibility that his name had accidentally been attached to someone else's project. No, this proposal was deliberately written with Owen in mind and just the way he would have done it. The cover letter had his signature on it, in his own handwriting. It was all in perfect order…

The only problem was, he didn't write it.

CHAPTER TEN

I noue Tsugumichi was sitting behind a spacious desk leafing through a stack of official looking papers when the secretary, Ms. Naguma, showed Owen into his office. The desk was an ultramodern, stainless steel and glass affair, all angles and curves beneath an immense clear top, and Owen noticed how the satin-silver contours perfectly set off the man's salt-and-pepper hair and Italian-cut suit. The deputy assistant minister looked up as Owen walked in and immediately rose to his feet and smiled.

"Dr. Powell, how do you do? I am so glad to finally meet you," he said in precise English with only the barest trace of an accent. "I hope you had a pleasant trip." He came out from behind the desk and extended his hand. As they shook, both men bowed cordially. Then they exchanged business cards and Owen observed that Inoue moved with the kind of poise that seems to come naturally to men of breeding.

"I trust there were no problems at the airport. I know Narita can be very confusing." As he spoke, he guided Owen to the far side of the office where a sofa and two contemporary-styled chairs were arranged around a low table beside an immense plate glass window. "Naguma-san, *ocha kudasai*," Inoue said, asking the secretary to bring them tea. She bowed and left silently.

Owen could see that Inoue was a man of considerable standing in Japanese society. In the obligatory small talk that followed, Inoue mentioned that his father and grandfather had both been government men like himself. Civil service is an honored profession in Japan, one to which access is reserved almost exclusively to those who have graduated from the finest schools. Not only was Inoue a high-ranking bureaucrat, but his family tradition of government service indicated that he undoubtedly had a samurai heritage.

Owen glanced around the office as he chatted with his host, and everything he saw confirmed this appraisal. The room was spacious and elegant—high ceiling, tea-green walls and expensive plush carpet—obviously the product of a professional designer. The tasteful décor with its expensive furniture and greenery were chosen with a discerning eye and precisely placed to convey an ambiance of grace, dignity, and power. Inoue was obviously a key player in the power structure here at the Ministry of Economy, Trade and Industry.

Making no more sound than a cat moving across a grassy meadow, Ms. Naguma came into the office holding a tray with an elegant teapot and two small, porcelain cups. Inoue continued talking about life in Tokyo and seemed to take no notice of her as she set the tray down on the low table and poured a cup of the steaming, pale-green brew for each of them.

Owen, on the other hand, could not help but notice her. Not that she was remarkable in any way—a middle-aged woman, neither pretty nor plain, smartly dressed in a well-tailored suit the same tea-green hue as the office walls. Her hair was pulled back and wound in a tight bun giving her, if not a severe countenance, then a quintessentially professional one. Her skin was pale as the white china into which she poured the tea, and that, combined with the color of her suit and her silent, subservient manner, projected an impression that she might have been a part of the tea service—that the pot, two cups, and woman were a matching set one might order from a catalog or purchase in one of the upscale department stores downtown.

Indeed, it was this very absence of presence that first caught Owen's attention. Like the master prop handlers that move unseen across the theater stage during a Kabuki play, Ms. Naguma seemed to have perfected the art of social transparency, that peculiar ability to hide in plain sight.

Although Owen was exhausted from the long flight, he was now fully alert, his nerves tingling, his senses tuned. As Inoue droned on, oblivious to the secretary's presence, Owen covertly watched her and wondered whether her peculiar invisibility was accidental—the simple product of a lifetime of behavioral conditioning in a highly regimented society—or a deliberate affectation. He suspected it was the latter.

Then he realized what had so prickled his senses. It was not what he could discern from this woman that was so intriguing; it was what he *could not* discern from her. As Ms. Naguma poured the tea, moving in her silent, flawless grace, Owen could see no evidence of conscious thought. Looking into her catlike eyes—black, bottomless pools, fixed and unblinking beneath heavy epicanthic folds—Owen realized she was in *mushin*, the thoughtless state that master warriors enter during combat.

This Owen found intriguing, and though he knew both Inoue and the secretary might consider it a breach of etiquette, he was seized by an urge to break the illusion the woman had so masterfully created. He wanted to disrupt, if only for a moment, this sly enchantress's subtle spell of invisibility, just to see how she might react. So, when the secretary extended to Owen his cup of tea—an act she did with utmost grace and flourished with a subtle bow—Owen reached out with both hands and deliberately placed one hand on the back of hers as he took the cup with the other.

"*Domo arigato*, Naguma-san," he said softly as he returned the bow.

In Japanese society, such deliberate physical contact from a stranger is acutely embarrassing. Momentarily startled, Ms. Naguma's eyes met Owen's for just an instant, and he saw in those deep, black pools the briefest flash of irritation followed by... What was it? He couldn't be certain, and as quickly as the connection had come, it passed.

The secretary looked down and bowed. "*Do itashimashite*," she whispered politely.

This exchange broke Inoue's patter for a moment, but he didn't seem offended. He looked briefly at the secretary, noticing her for the first time, and leaned forward for his tea as she extended the cup. He took it without replying then returned his attention to Owen, continuing his monologue from where he had left off, mid-sentence. Having finished serving the tea, Ms. Naguma resumed her invisibility and left the room on the same silent cat paws that had brought her in.

After several minutes of small talk, Inoue began asking Owen about his teaching job at the university and his previous research. Owen could sense his host was finally coming around to the point of the interview. They chatted on, comparing the academic cultures in Japan and the United States then Inoue offered, "I must say, Dr. Powell, that we at METI are elated that an American scholar with your degree of cultural sensitivity would be interested in doing research on how we coordinate commercial activities in Japan. I know many Americans think our system is not a valid example of free enterprise."

Trying to be polite, Owen wrinkled his brow and shook his head slightly.

"Oh yes, Powell-san, I know it's true. I read American newspapers and magazines: 'Japan uses trade barriers to protect its industry,' they say, or 'the Japanese government prohibits domestic competition.' Such accusations disturb us deeply. We are very sensitive about what Americans think. We want your leaders to understand that, despite their misgivings, Japan's economic system is capitalism; it's just a different kind of capitalism, one that benefits from governmental coordination.

"A report from a project like yours could be very influential. I am confident that if one examines our system objectively, it will become evident that the way we conduct business is no less a form of free enterprise than that in Western European nations or even the U.S. But you must be aware that few Americans could possibly understand Japan's political and business cultures well enough to assess our complex system objectively. We believe you are one of those few, and we are delighted that you are interested in conducting a study here."

Seizing the opportunity to direct the conversation toward the mystery Owen most wanted to solve, he responded, "Well, about that, Inoue-san, I have some questions about the research proposal you approved."

"Yes, the proposal. It was very effective—the level of detail you put in it was very helpful when it came to selling your project to the directors—a very nice piece of work that helped me convince them the project was worthwhile."

"Well, thank you," Owen said, feeling awkward. "It's just that… well, I didn't write it."

"I don't understand."

"The first I heard of this project was on Saturday when you faxed your approval to my department chairman. I didn't write the proposal."

Inoue's patrician face went blank, and he stared directly at Owen in a way the Japanese only do when a sudden shock causes them to momentarily forget their social propriety.

"But you signed it," he said after a moment.

"It's not my project. Someone else signed my name to it. I think we need to find out who really wrote this proposal so that person can carry out the research."

Inoue looked perplexed. Then he began sucking air through his teeth as he leaned forward to set his teacup on the table, his eyes darting side to side, avoiding contact with Owen's. Owen recognized the mannerism, a defensive behavior the Japanese unconsciously employ when they sense a confrontation may be imminent, one that could cause someone embarrassment. Following Inoue's lead, he placed his own cup on the table.

After a couple of tense moments, Inoue spoke in a voice that seemed to have lost much of the confidence he had displayed earlier. "But we don't want someone else to do the research. I persuaded the directors to fund the project and the chief executives of the corporations involved to participate in it based on your unique ability to carry out this analysis in a culturally sensitive fashion." When Owen didn't respond, he added, "Certainly you must be mistaken about this."

"No, Inoue-san, I'm not."

More air sucking. More eye darting. Seconds passed.

Finally, Inoue said, "Powell-san, you must understand the position this puts me in. I worked very hard to build a consensus among some important people to make this project possible. We spent a considerable amount of money to bring you here. In fact, the reason we gave you such short notice for travel was because we wanted you to meet the presidents and chief executive officers of the Asano and Mijikawa Corporations tonight, before they fly to Europe tomorrow. All the arrangements have been made." His voice trailed off until it was almost a pleading whisper. "Powell-san, I have not only invested my personal reputation in this effort, I have placed the ministry's standing in the corporate community at risk."

Now Owen was embarrassed. Inoue's open admission of a potential loss of face before his countrymen, both inside and outside of METI, was, in fact, an unconditional surrender of face before Owen. Now Owen looked from side to side, unable to meet Inoue's vulnerable eyes. Seconds passed in painful silence. Then Owen could stand it no longer.

"Inoue-san, let me propose this solution. I'll meet the Asano and Mijikawa men tonight, and tomorrow I'll begin the preliminary research—you know, gather up files here in the building, copy relevant documents, and begin organizing the data. Meanwhile, we should both try to find out who really wrote the proposal you approved and—"

Inoue drew in a quick breath as if to object, but Owen reassured him.

"Don't worry, I'll stay on the project. But my professional ethics require me to find the person who really proposed this research and see if he or she still wants to go through with it. If they don't, I'll finish the job. If they do, then by all rights, it's their project, but I'll stay on in name so your colleagues inside and outside the ministry don't become alarmed, and I'll review the final report to ensure the findings appreciate Japan's unique cultural environment. But Inoue-san, I want you to understand, I have responsibilities back in Maryland, so if this mystery scholar does take over the project, I'll be spending most of my time back there. Do we have a deal?"

"Dr. Powell, you are a natural diplomat," Inoue said, his buoyant confidence returned. "Yes, we have a deal."

At the conclusion of the meeting, Inoue escorted Owen out of the office and bade him farewell at the elevator. After the doors closed, he stood staring at the elevator for a moment, smiling. Then a short, balding man with small eyes and a recessive chin stepped out from around the corner. He was wiry and nervous, and he walked with a slight stoop.

"How did it go?" the man whispered eagerly. "Is he everything they say he is?"

"He is that and more, Teguchi-san."

Inoue turned and looked at the Director of Trade Coordination, Teguchi Kenji, and could see why everyone in the ministry called him "the Ferret" behind his back. He turned away and walked back toward his office. Teguchi scampered along beside him.

"So what was he like? Was he suspicious? Is he going to stay? Do we have him in our control?" Teguchi breathlessly whispered a fountain of questions as they walked into Inoue's outer office.

"Yes, he was suspicious, of course. He knows he's been brought here under false pretenses, but I don't think he suspects we're behind it."

They stopped in the waiting lounge of Inoue's outer office and continued talking, raising their voices slightly above a whisper now that they were safely away from the ears of passersby in the corridor.

"And I have him under control, at least for now. He's a remarkable man, so American, yet so like a Japanese. That is how I controlled him—I shamed him into staying on this bogus project just to protect my face. Imagine, Teguchi-san, a *gaijin* putting his neck in a yoke to save face for a Japanese stranger. And it's all the more amazing when you consider who he really is. But, of course, he has no idea about that."

"Remarkable!" Teguchi said, staring off in thought. Then his ferret face turned back to Inoue. "But his eyes... Tell me about his eyes. Do they really look like what everyone says?"

"They are the palest blue you could imagine. He has eyes like that snow leopard in the Ueno Zoo."

"Remarkable!" Teguchi said again.

All the while, not five feet away, Ms. Naguma sat at her desk, invisible.

CHAPTER ELEVEN

Click, click, click, click—Elaine watched the shiny ball bearings swing back and forth, the one on the right striking the next in line, transferring its kinetic energy down the row to the ball on the far left, it leaping out then swinging back, returning the energy to the right—Newton's first law of motion verified once more. She couldn't care less.

She didn't really see the balls any more than she saw the pile of term papers on her desk where they had lain for two days, waiting for her to grade. Over the past week she had become increasingly distracted. She had managed to go through the motions of her daily routine—she had come to work every morning, gone to faculty meetings, given lectures, and even put up a cheerful front with colleagues and students—but it had gotten harder with each passing day.

She started the balls swinging again. Click, click, click…

She continued staring at the kinetic energy machine, but in her mind's eye, she saw only the phone. *Ring… ring…* she concentrated.

In the educated, rational part of her brain, she knew such exercises are silly. She could not make a phone ring simply by force of will. But deep down in her psyche, she could hear her grand-mother's voice telling her not to be so literal, or her spirit would remain bound in the illusion of physical reality.

"*Stop thinking, Lainie!*" the voice kept saying. "*Let your spirit float. Free it of your rational mind and it will expand and merge with the universal consciousness. Then it will reach out and touch his spirit, and he will call.*"

Click, click, click...

Ring... Ring! She struggled vainly.

Then, for the hundredth time that week, her mind wandered back to the fight with Owen. Had she been too hard on him? She didn't think so. What he did was insufferably childish—beating up one of her coworkers out of jealousy. What was he thinking? How could he expect her to work if he caused a scandal and got everyone on campus whispering behind her back? And to think, he tried to blame it all on Randall's behavior.

Now he was only making things worse by not calling her. She knew what he was doing—trying to punish her with his silence. He thought that if he waited long enough, she'd call him and start sniveling about how much she missed him. Men were so childish, and stubborn, and, and... foolish! It would snow in Hong Kong before she'd call him!

Her face flushed with anger.

On the other hand, she knew she had upset him that morning. He was angry and feeling rejected because she didn't get all gooey and stroke his male ego when he asked her if she loved him. So, what did he expect? He asked in the middle of an argument. Did he think she wouldn't know he was just using that angle to get her to move in with him?

She reached out to start the balls swinging again then stopped. She sat back in her chair and sighed. No, she thought, that wasn't true. He wasn't trying to be manipulative. He was just feeling inse-cure. He asked her a painfully honest question, and it frightened her. She froze. He let down his defenses and opened his heart. And what did she do in return? She brushed him aside.

She flushed again, this time in frustration and embarrassment. She leaned forward and started the balls once more. Click, click, click...

If only he'd call, she would find a way to end this spat. She'd be patient and tender and give him lots of ground to apologize. Little by little, they could edge into a compromise and agree to meet that evening to work things out. Then, when she had him alone, she could communicate in the language he understood best. Her body would speak to his and make him forget they had ever fought. If only he'd call!

Suddenly, she could sit still no longer. She picked up the phone and dialed. Several rings later, she heard her voicemail recording start, and she poked in the additional five-digit PIN to access her inbox.

Four new messages!

She took in a short, quick breath and held it. At least one of them might be from Owen. She called up the first one, a message from her department chairman reminding her to turn in her quarterly expense report. She scrolled to the next. It was Randall responding to a message she had left asking him to help her install a new modem on her home computer. He said he would do it in return for dinner and... She deleted it before it ended. The third was a wrong number, and the fourth was Randall again.

Frustrated, she was about to punch in the code to clear the mailbox, but caught herself. What if Owen called just as she was clearing it? What if he'd already called but, for whatever reason, the message didn't cue the New Mail register in her inbox? She decided to simply leave the messages where they were, just as she had all week, just in case.

She had a sudden urge to dial Owen's number—her fingers stopped, poised over the keypad—then she slammed the phone back in the cradle.

"No snow in Hong Kong today," she said aloud.

※ ※

Owen stood beneath a canvas awning in the breezeway of a closed tobacco shop in Shinjuku Kabukijo, juggling the two Styrofoam cups that held his dinner: *soba* and *ocha*, noodles and green tea. He didn't need to subsist on dinner out of Styrofoam cups. He had politely turned down an invitation to a night out with a group of Mijikawa Corporation executives and opted, instead, for an evening of personal nostalgia.

It was the first evening he'd had on his own since arriving in Tokyo five days earlier. He had begun his research in the METI files on Tuesday and, by Thursday afternoon, had gathered and reviewed enough preliminary data to want to ask some dicey questions about METI's relationship with the Mijikawa board of directors. He wasn't ready to broach those issues, however, until he had reviewed the corresponding files at Mijikawa's corporate headquarters, so he had spent late Thursday afternoon and all of Friday there, in the industrial sector of Yokahama, thirty minutes away by commuter train.

Whenever he had an opportunity, whether at METI or Mijikawa, he asked the people with whom he dealt what they knew about the mysterious research proposal. Each time he got the same response: puzzlement at first followed by sincere assurances that they had no idea who might have written the document or why that person would have signed Owen's name to it.

On Wednesday morning he managed to catch Inoue in the corridor after a meeting and asked him what progress he had made in clearing up the mystery. Reverting to his routine of air-sucking evasiveness, Inoue said he was late for another meeting, but promised to speak with Owen later that day. When Owen went to his office that afternoon, Ms. Naguma—she was very visible this time, and as immovable as the Great Buddha of Kamakura—told him the deputy assistant minister was out of the office for the rest of the day.

Meanwhile, every evening his hosts—first, a rotating crew of mid- and senior-level METI officials then an ever-eager group of Mijikawa company men—had taken him to dinner and bouts of *hashigo* that extended far into the night. As the week drew on, the constant partying became monotonous. They had been in the same bars so many times that the hostesses were starting to call Owen by name. By Friday, he'd had all the revelry and male bonding he could stand.

So tonight he was on his own. He had spent the evening roaming the streets of Shinjuku Kabukijo, a somewhat seedier part of town where locals and tourists come to find the kinds of entertainment that missionaries rail against and tour groups from stateside churches avoid. Here a man could drink, gamble, and get a massage, with or without extra services. On the other hand, some of the best restaurants and shops were in Shinjuku. The district was a strange patchwork of upscale businesses and lowbrow diversions, a place where anything was obtainable, if you had enough money.

Owen didn't have much money, but he didn't care. He hadn't come here to satisfy any licentious desires. He had come because it was one of his old haunts as a boy. Tonight he walked the streets he had roamed almost twenty years earlier, reliving his memories, basking in the warm glow of nostalgia as he wandered in and out of the bars and clubs he had haunted as a kid. In a strange, indescribable way, he felt like he was home. He almost expected to hear one of his friends yell his name. He almost believed that if he turned down the side street to his right, walked two blocks down to the subway station, and caught the train out to his old neighborhood, that he could tiptoe into his old house and find his father sitting in his reading chair beside the dim lamp, his glasses perched on the end of his nose. He almost believed it, but not quite.

Deftly maneuvering the disposable wooden chopsticks, Owen managed to get the last noodle out of the cup. He downed his tea then tossed the trash into a barrel in front of the shop. It was time to head back to the hotel. This had been good, but the old memories were just that—memories. Those times were gone.

He rounded the corner past the *soba* stand and headed up the side street toward the subway station. This night was like so many of those twenty years ago. An early evening rain had tapered off, only to be replaced by a steamy mist that was not quite fog, but made the back streets very dark just the same. The businesses on this street consisted mainly of shops that closed at 6:00 P.M., so the block was deserted with the only illumination coming from distant streetlights reflecting on the store windows and wet streets. Owen worked his way along, focusing his attention on avoiding puddles on the uneven sidewalk.

Then he felt a tingle race up his spine and realized it had been there for several moments, hovering just beneath his awareness. He turned and looked behind him. There, silhouetted in the light from the main street a block and a half back, he saw the broad forms of two big men walking shoulder to shoulder and closing on him fast. Instinctively, he swung back around to look ahead and saw exactly what he expected. Two more men, brutes stamped from the same mold, were just stepping out of the alley about twenty yards ahead. They took up positions blocking the sidewalk.

How could he have been so stupid? Here he was, waxing nostalgic and forgetting the first lesson he learned here as a kid: never let down your guard!

He quickly gauged the distances and considered his options. He could run for it—they didn't have him completely surrounded. The other side of the street looked clear, and he figured he was quicker and more agile than these gorillas, but he didn't know whether there were more of them waiting in a nearby car. Besides, running was not his style.

But fighting was not an appealing option either. Owen was well trained and tough, but he could tell by the way these guys walked that they were not paper dragons like Randall Preston. They were professional thugs—big, strong, street fighters with lots of experience and savvy. And being Japanese, they would have had some amount of training as well. He might be able to fight his way out, but it would be no walk in the park.

He didn't have much time to decide—he was approaching the men blocking his way, and the guys behind him were closing fast. When he got within fifteen feet of the human barricade in front of him, he coiled his muscles and prepared to launch into a charging attack. Then the men stopped and one of them spoke.

"Dokuto Pawu," he said in a loud, gravelly voice. It was not a question.

Owen stopped. He turned sideways so he could focus his attention equally on the men behind him and in front. He noticed that the men behind him had stopped as well, keeping their distance about ten feet away, leading Owen to wonder if they were as reluctant to tangle with him as he was with them.

"Who are you, and how do you know my name?" Owen demanded in curt, dismissive Japanese. He had learned long ago to never show fear in the face of a challenge, and if your enemies waiver, you should show your teeth.

With that, the man who had spoken cautiously sank into *hanta-chi*, a traditional samurai posture in which a warrior kneels on his left knee and extends his right hand, his sword hand, palm upward beside his right knee as a gesture of temporary truce. The intended message is: *I will not draw my sword while we talk.*

None of these men had swords, but Owen recognized the routine and immediately understood who they were. In modern times the yakuza had adopted this custom. These guys were yakuza foot soldiers, and someone had apparently sent them to speak to him.

"Dokuto Pawu, bigu man wantu talku," the man said.

"Speak Japanese," Owen said. "My dog speaks better English than you!"

He watched the men closely to see if the insult had found its mark, but shadows concealed their faces and none of them visibly flinched.

"You will come with us, Pawu-san," the man said in Japanese. "A very important man wishes to speak with you. We will drive you there."

"My mother always told me to stay out of cars with strangers and mangy animals," Owen replied in Japanese.

"There is no need for fear or hostility. We mean you no harm or insult. Our orders are simply to chauffeur you discretely across town to the important man's residence and ensure you arrive there safely."

"Who is this important man?"

"We are not at liberty to say."

"Then I'm not going anywhere with you."

"You will come with us, Pawu-san, one way or another."

Once again, Owen considered his options. Running was out of the question, now that all the thugs were within ten feet of him. On the other hand, his chances in a fight were substantially reduced as well. The men had maintained enough distance so that Owen could not achieve surprise in a sudden attack, but each of them stayed close enough to come to the others' aid if Owen sprang at them. The way they positioned themselves suggested that these guys had been trained to fight as a team.

And now Owen had something else to consider. These yakuza knew who he was and had been sent specifically to get him. Someone wanted to speak to him, so they said, and he sensed they were telling the truth. What was this about? He suspected it had something to do with the mystery proposal and the reason he had been brought to Japan, whatever that was. Maybe this was a chance to find out what was going on. Maybe it wasn't. Either way, he'd never know unless he spoke to Mr. Big... or whoever he was.

"Okay," Owen said. "Take me to the head gorilla."

CHAPTER TWELVE

The yakuza men escorted Owen to an alley where a late-model, black Subaru was parked. They got in and drove across town using a circuitous route of back streets and alleys. After twenty minutes, they pulled up in front of a high rise in an exclusive neighborhood in Asakusa. Owen could see several well-dressed men milling in the lobby—sentries, he thought, recognizing the look of them. They had apparently been watching for the car, because on seeing it drive up, one of them stepped partway outside the double glass doors and brusquely motioned for them to pull around the corner. The driver complied then drove down the side street and turned into an alley behind the apartment building.

At the end of the alley, they came to a heavy steel garage door, the kind typically used at loading docks, with two more men in suits standing beside it. They stopped briefly while the driver identified himself to one of the suits, and the door creaked upward revealing a heavy-gauge steel accordion gate behind it. When that barrier rolled aside, the black Subaru eased into the garage and parked, nose-in, against the far wall next to a forest-green Rolls Royce. Everyone got out.

As soon as their feet hit the pavement, they found themselves surrounded by a half dozen more guards. These guys were toting submachine guns, and Owen was puzzled to see that they didn't seem to share any kinship with the yakuza men who had brought him there. They didn't level their guns at them, but they didn't welcome them back to hearth and home, either. They just held their distance and glared. His chaperones responded to this frosty reception with deliberate caution, moving slowly and keeping their hands in the open.

"We have brought Dr. Pawu," the driver said to the guy who seemed to be the headman in the garage. "We need to take him up."

"You can take him up, but you'll have to go by yourself. Your partners must wait for you in the car. And you must go unarmed."

The men from the car looked at each other, worried and momentarily uncertain whether to split up. But the driver nodded, and the headman and one of the other garage guards led him and Owen to an elevator. They searched the driver thoroughly, removing a 9mm Glock from a shoulder holster beneath his ill-fitted suit jacket and knives from sheaths strapped to the small of his back and his right leg above the ankle. They didn't search Owen.

The headman then picked up a phone beside the elevator door and, after a few seconds, said some words that Owen couldn't hear. He hung up and inserted a key into the elevator button panel; the door opened, and Owen and the driver stepped inside. The man leaned in and pushed the top button, the one for the fortieth floor, then leaned out and let the door close.

When the elevator opened, Owen and the driver stepped out into what appeared to be a lavish drawing room. It was richly carpeted and furnished with several Victorian chairs and a sofa. Tiffany lamps stood on cherry side tables, and oil paintings adorned the walls depicting various scenes around Tokyo at what Owen guessed to be about the turn of the twentieth century.

The overall effect was one of repose and relaxation, which stood in sharp contrast to the tension Owen felt between the yakuza driver and the four men who were gathered around the elevator when Owen and the driver stepped out. Silent and stone faced, their eyes immediately locked on the driver then moved to Owen and back to the driver again.

"I have delivered Dr. Pawu," the driver said, his voice loud in an obvious effort to sound unafraid. "This discharges Otaki-san's obligation to Nomura-san. All debts of honor have been repaid."

"Nomura-sama will decide whether your *oyabun* has fulfilled his *giri* in this matter," one of the men said.

Nomura-sama? Owen thought. Did he hear that man say "*sama*"... *Lord Normura?*

"Then let me speak to Nomura," the driver barked.

The men flinched in barely suppressed rage on hearing this man say Nomura's name in such a demanding tone and without adding even an honorific "san". Owen readied himself for the explosive violence he knew was close. The men here obviously loathed the man who had brought him up, and the sheen of sweat on the driver's forehead indicated that he knew it.

"Nomura-sama does not waste his time on men like you," the other man growled. "You forget your station. Your lack of manners exposes you as the gutter dog you are. If you want to live long enough to rejoin the rest of your pack, you will get out now."

"But Otaki-san said—"

"Get out!"

No one moved or even blinked for at least five seconds. Then the yakuza driver, his eyes trained on the men around him, slowly backed into the open elevator. He pressed the button and the door closed.

The four men turned their attention to Owen.

After a few seconds, the man who had confronted the driver, re-laxed and bowed. "How do you do, Dr. Pawu," he said in Japanese. "Welcome to the Nomura household. I am Abe Shintaro, captain of Nomura-sama's personal guard. You may go up now. Nomura-sama has been expecting you."

Not waiting for Owen to answer, Abe led him to another eleva-tor and poked a code number into a keypad on the wall beside it. When the door opened, he gestured for Owen to step in then bowed as the door closed. There were only two buttons on the panel: one up, one down. Owen pressed the up button and felt the elevator rise several more floors. When the door opened, a short bald man dressed in a white coat and black bow tie and trousers stood at attention waiting for him.

"Good evening Dr. Pawu," he said, smiling and bowing low. "Please come this way."

The man led him down a powder-blue hallway, tiled in white stone. Chinese ink and watercolor drawings hung on the walls. Recessed lighting provided soft, indirect illumination. The hallway opened into a garden atrium with a perfectly formed Japanese ma-ple tree in the center. A skylight, some twenty-five feet above, would have provided light during the day, but foot lamps shined up at the tree now. Owen followed the houseman around the garden, across the atrium, and through a doorway on the other side. There, Owen found himself in a large study. At the far end of the room stood an immense ebony-wood desk, its front decorated with ornate carvings. Owen guessed it to be Chinese in origin. Closer to the door, a sofa and two armchairs were arranged as a sitting area.

"You may wait here. Nomura-sama will be with you shortly." The houseman bowed and left.

Owen regretted that it was so dreary out. One entire wall of the study was glass, and he guessed the view would have been mag-nificent on a clear night. But turning around, he discovered some-thing equally fascinating on the opposite wall. There, hung rack after rack of antique weapons—swords, spears, halberds, bows and arrows—every imaginable implement of war from Japan's medieval era. A mannequin stood in the far corner dressed in samurai armor.

This Nomura guy must be one tough thug if he's got his people calling him "Lord Nomura." But he certainly lives like a lord, Owen thought, looking around again.

Then he noticed a small rack standing alone on the far wall next to the armored mannequin. It held a solitary sword, resting blade-up in its *saya*, its wooden scabbard. He walked over and examined the sword as closely as he could without touching it. It was obviously quite old. The weapon's graceful curve and the design of the *tsuba* and *menuki*, the hand guard and hilt ornament, suggested that it was forged sometime in the late sixteenth or early seventeenth century.

"That *katana* has been in my family since 1592," said a voice behind Owen in perfect English.

Owen turned to see a small man standing in the doorway with wispy white hair and translucent skin stretched over a skeletal face. He wore an elegant brown kimono—one costing several thousand dollars, Owen guessed—and his body was reed thin. At first glance, Owen thought he must be a hundred years old, but when he looked closer, he noticed the man stood perfectly erect without postural signs of age. On seeing Owen's bemused look, he grinned and walked to him in an easy, nimble gait. He bowed slightly and put out a gnarly hand.

"How do you do, Dr. Powell. I am Nomura Eizo." The voice was a rasp, but the words were strong and confident.

Owen shook Nomura's hand and was startled by how strongly it gripped his.

"Would you like to examine the blade?"

"What? Oh yeah, the sword," Owen said. "Yes, I would like that very much."

Nomura turned to the rack, bowed, and reverently lifted the weapon out, holding it horizontal in both his outstretched hands. Turning back to Owen, he positioned the hilt to his left with the blade's cutting edge turned toward his own body, a traditional courtesy meant to reassure a guest that he would not draw on him. Then he gracefully turned the sword, hilt over blade, crossing his forearms, so that the hilt was now on Owen's left, and extended the sword to Owen while bowing. Owen, in turn, bowed and took the sword in both his outstretched hands, turned the blade toward his own body, and straightened. He slowly moved his left hand to the hilt, positioning it carefully in the reverse draw position, then looked to Nomura. The old man nodded his consent, and Owen slowly drew the sword about a third of the way out of the scabbard.

It was magnificent—an exquisite handmade blade showing the wavy lamination lines of a thousand folds on the forge. It was as shiny and unblemished and razor sharp as the day the master sword maker delivered it to its first owner.

"*Kore katana ga shibumi desu, yo!*" Owen whispered in awe. "This sword is extraordinarily elegant!"

"*Domo arigato gozaimashita,*" Nomura said, bowing deeply, thanking Owen in the most formal phrasing possible.

Owen slowly re-sheathed the sword, and the men reversed the earlier ritual as they transferred it from Owen's hands to Nomura's. Then the old man put it back in the rack and both men took one step back. This time, they both formally bowed to it.

As they turned to face each other once more, Owen wondered about the old man's truthfulness. The yakuza have a centuries-old history in Japan. Tradition has it that they began as the *machi-yakko*, a society of lowborn men devoted to protecting defenseless villagers from the rapacious abuses of local samurai overlords. In time, however, they evolved into an elaborate network of organized crime syndicates that controlled all the vice—mainly gambling and prostitution—within their respective territories. They operated along clan lines. Membership tended to center on certain families, passed from one generation to the next down to the present day.

With all that in mind, Owen found Nomura's claim that this sword had been in his family for centuries highly suspect. In feudal times, ownership of a *katana*, especially one as fine as this, was the exclusive privilege of the samurai class. No lowborn yakuza family, no matter how rich or powerful it was in its own domain, would have owned such a weapon during the Edo period, which stretched from the seventeenth to the mid-nineteenth centuries.

Your family must have bought this after 1872, Owen thought. *There were some fine swords on the black market when the samurai class was legally abolished and banned from carrying them. Or, more likely, you stole it.*

"It is gratifying to meet someone who still observes the formal ritual for handling a revered sword," Nomura said. "Such refinement has become increasingly rare in this modern age, even among Japanese. It is sad state of affairs."

Owen did not respond. He hadn't come to chitchat with a gangster, no matter how elegant and refined.

Seeming to sense Owen's thoughts, Nomura said, "I must apologize for the way I had you brought here. I only recently heard you had come to Japan. I felt it very important that I speak with you, but it would have been dangerous for both of us to be seen together or for any of my men to be seen approaching you."

"What possible interest could you have in me? Why would you care whether I came to Japan, or whether anyone saw us together?" Owen's questions were curt and direct.

"I believe you are in great danger, Dr. Powell. I believe you have been brought here under false pretenses by some very dangerous people for motives beyond your understanding."

"Well, you'll get no argument from me about being brought here on false pretenses. But what is all this nonsense about dangerous people with nefarious motives?"

"I regret that I cannot be more specific."

"Well you'll have to do better than that. Look, I only agreed to see you because I thought you might clear up the mystery about why I was brought to Japan. Otherwise, I could have left your men—"

"Otaki's men—"

"Yeah, okay, Otaki's men—I could have left them in a pile on the sidewalk in Shinjuku. So stop speaking in riddles and give it to me straight. What is all this crap about?"

Owen was glad Abe and his men were out of earshot. The way he was speaking to Nomura was unconscionably rude, particularly as he was in the man's house. Having seen how the guards bridled at the yakuza driver's lack of respect, he knew they would have responded violently had they witnessed Owen's ill-mannered behavior.

Owen, in fact, felt very uncomfortable acting this way, but he was determined to maintain the social high ground. He was a college professor, a respected professional, while his host was a thug—a wealthy, cultured thug, perhaps—but a thug nonetheless. Besides, he had been brought there under duress, so he held the moral high ground as well as the social advantage, and he was determined not to let Nomura forget it.

But strangely, Nomura seemed insensitive to Owen's barbs. He stood at ease throughout the abrasive questioning, showing not the slightest sign of irritation. Owen could sense no tension in his body, and his face looked, if anything, serene.

He spoke softly. "All of this 'crap', as you so quaintly put it, is very complicated. Neither of us has time for me to explain it to you and, quite frankly, the more you know, the more danger you will be in. Please trust me on this, Powell-san. It is extremely important that you return to the United States as soon as possible. Get out of harm's way while you can."

"What danger? What harm?" Owen was almost shouting now.

"I cannot tell you," Nomura responded even more softly.

"Well I'm not going to just pack up my tent and leave. I can't back out of the commitments I've made without some explanation."

"I urge you to reconsider," Nomura persisted.

"Why?" Owen said in exasperation. "Why do you urge me to reconsider? What is in this for you? What possible reason would you have to give a rat's ass about me being in danger?"

"Because I owe it to your father to look after your wellbeing while you are in Japan."

Good God! That statement hit Owen like an oncoming train, leaving him breathless for several seconds. "Are you saying you knew my father?" he finally gasped.

"Yes."

"Yes? Yes what? How could you have known him? He died almost twenty years ago."

"I know. He was my dearest friend. I carry his *on*."

"No… No, I don't believe it. I can't believe it. How could you and he have been friends? How could a man like…" Owen hesitated a moment wondering whether he should say it, but his emotions were washing him over the brink of propriety. "…a man like *you* carry *on* for a man like my father?"

On is a Japanese concept for a debt of honor. If Nomura carried *on* for Owen's father then Rhys Powell had done him some extraordinary favor or service, something for which Nomura would have been hard pressed to repay in his lifetime.

"Once again, Powell-san, I cannot tell you more."

"Well I don't believe you! You couldn't have been one of my father's friends. It's impossible. I would have seen you… I would have met you sometime."

"We have never been introduced, Owen-san, but you have seen me. Think about it. Think hard. You saw me with your father the night before you left for Korea... the last night you saw your father alive."

CHAPTER THIRTEEN

Tokyo—June 1982

It was ten after twelve when Owen rounded the corner and ran up the narrow lane into his neighborhood. When he finally reached his house, the lights were still on—not a good sign. His father was an early riser and usually turned in shortly after dark on these long June days. Tonight he was up and apparently waiting for Owen.

On impulse Owen decided to steal around back and go in the kitchen door. He didn't know what that would accomplish—he'd have to face his old man one way or another—but something told him that if he just slipped in quietly and got ready for bed, whatever beef his dad had with him might wait until morning. He cut across the patch of grass that tried hard to be a front yard and started tiptoeing past the side of the house.

Then he stopped and listened. Through the open windows and flimsy plank-and-plywood walls, Owen heard angry voices. They weren't yelling, but they clearly weren't discussing the virtues of gardening, either. He held his breath so he could hear them better. He recognized his father's voice, and it sounded like he was arguing with one other man. He concentrated harder. He thought they were speaking English, but he couldn't make out enough of the words to figure out what the row was about.

It didn't make sense. Rhys Powell was a gentle man. Owen could not remember the last time he had heard him speak to anyone in anger. But "the Mace," as everyone called him at the Embassy, had led Filipino guerillas on Japanese-occupied Mindanao in the Second World War, and no one who knew him ever took his soft-spoken words lightly. For that matter, few people ever trifled with the elder Powell, whether they knew him or not. So who would be challenging him now in the living room of his own home at midnight?

Owen heard the front screen door slam. He edged to the corner of the house and peeked around it. He saw a late middle-aged Japanese man start down the narrow street. The man stopped and looked in Owen's direction. Owen quickly pulled back into the shadow between the houses. He was sure he was hidden in the inky blackness, but the man looked right at him for several seconds before turning and going down the street.

Relieved that the quarrel was over, Owen slipped in the kitchen door, but was unable to put off talking to his father as he had hoped. Rhys was waiting for him. As it turned out, what he had to say had nothing to do with the late hours Owen was keeping.

━╫ ╫━

Rhys Powell was an oak tree. Having wrestled at Yale and boxed in the Army, he had a penchant for physical culture and remained vigorous and powerfully built well into his sixties.

He was a late-life father. He'd met Owen's mother, a slender, auburn-haired schoolteacher named Olivia Parker, while on liaison duty at MI6 headquarters in London, and though there was nearly twenty years difference in their ages, they had felt an immediate rapport and soon fell deeply in love. They were married in three months, and Owen was born nine months after that.

Rhys never regretted marrying Olivia, though he frequently felt pangs of guilt during their short marriage. He never said a word about it, but he was certain that he would die before her, leaving her widowed and alone. He never imagined she would beat him to the grave, the victim of an inexplicable one-car accident on a rural road in County Kent on the eve of their second wedding anniversary.

Now, some sixteen years later, Rhys was a single father and aging warrior with a sad, deeply lined face and a granite jaw. His high widow's peak of short-cropped hair matched his eyes—steel gray, the color of ten-penny nails and just as piercing. Tonight those eyes bore into his son, who squirmed on the living room sofa, struggling to hide his anxiety. When Owen found out what was on his father's mind, his anxiety turned to indignation.

"Son," Rhys began, "you've been practicing the martial arts for several years now, and I'm pleased with how well you've done." He hesitated, waiting for Owen to respond, but the boy just sat, waiting for the other shoe to fall, so he continued. "Now I think it's time you finally started learning how to fight."

Owen was stunned and for a moment didn't know what to say. When he did manage to find his voice, it was tinged with equal parts of shock, hurt, and disbelief. "Dad, what are you talking about? I just won the biggest military karate tournament in the Far East! And didn't I win two of my last three judo tournaments?"

"Yes you did, Owen. I am very proud of how well you've done in combative sports. But you need to understand that those events were not fights, they were games. Your judo and karate-do training have been valuable. You've learned techniques that will help you become a good fighter. But the tactics they taught you in those schools are tactics for winning games, not real fights. Had you faced that guy you beat tonight in a real fight, he would have killed you. Believe me, son, fighting is different. You'll see."

Rhys went on to explain that he had arranged for Owen to spend the summer studying under an old man who ran a camp up in the Taebaek Mountains of Korea, a man who learned karate-jutsu and jujutsu from the Japanese when they occupied that country and much of eastern China before the Second World War.

"This man took what he learned from his oppressors, combined it with other skills, and eventually turned it against them on the battlefield. He killed a lot of men..." Rhys's voice trailed off as if he regretted revealing that detail. After a moment, he added, "He's been secretly teaching his art to a small, handpicked group of people ever since."

Owen wanted to ask how his father knew about this man and his camp, but he knew better. His dad was an intelligence officer, and Owen had learned long ago that some questions were better left unasked. But Rhys did tell him more about the old man's camp, and Owen's indignation started to fade. In one respect, he was disappointed—he had been planning a graduation trip to Hawaii that summer with his friends—but, on the other hand, he couldn't deny he was intrigued with what his father told him about the camp and what they taught there. Beyond that, he saw how much this seemed to mean to Rhys, and not disappointing his dad was more important to him than a few days of fun on the beach in Waikiki.

"Okay, Dad, he finally said. If it's that important, I'll go to Korea."

Owen stood on a high ridge, deep in the mountains of Korea, wondering if he had made the right decision. It had been a long day.

He had gotten up before dawn to catch a MAC flight from Yokota Air Base, Japan, to Osan Air Base, South Korea. There he was met by a sullen Korean teenager who drove him into the mountains and, when the road ran out, led him on a six-hour hike into what seemed like the middle of nowhere.

Now, as the sun slid between the southwestern peaks, Owen looked down from the ridge into a vale where there lay a village of sorts, though it was not a village, exactly. It didn't have roads or vehicles or shops or livestock, or any other signs of commercial activity. Rather, it was a motley assortment of structures in varying degrees of permanence and dilapidation. Some were long, wooden, barracks-like buildings with tin roofs, solid doors, and glass windows. Others were mere shacks. On the outskirts of the settlement lay a scattering of wood-frame structures with tented, canvas roofs that Owen recognized as military-style hooches—probably Korean War surplus. Many lacked doors or windows or both, and some leaned precariously, their rotted frames and tattered fabric just waiting for a stiff wind to knock them down.

At the center of this hodgepodge, a large pentagonal pavilion stood out in stark contrast to the ramshackle buildings around it. It was a sturdy structure built of heavy, freshly painted white timbers and roofed in bright red clay tiles. Looking down from the ridge above, Owen could not see beneath its Chinese-style, pagoda roof, but the structure was open on all sides and streams of people were filing in while others were coming out. In fact, the entire settlement seemed alive with activity.

Owen surveyed the strange cantonment in wonder. Then a small orchard near an open area beyond the settlement caught his eye. There half a dozen large, dirty canvas bags were stuffed tight and hanging on chains from tree limbs—he immediately recognized them as heavy punching bags—and a row of sturdy posts lined the field like an unfinished picket fence. Even in the waning light, Owen could see rice-straw pads lashed to the posts and flattened grass midfield, grass he imagined had been trampled by hundreds of bare, calloused feet.

This was the place. He had arrived at camp.

Owen was just about to ask his guide if he was going to take him down and introduce him to the head instructor when the kid walked away, heading back the way they had come. When Owen called to him, he looked back over his shoulder and flashed a grin that was more a jeer than a smile and said, "Good luck, Pawu. Hope you make friends real good."

Owen started down the winding path leading into the vale. He hadn't gone far when he noticed people coming out of the pavilion, pointing his direction and yelling. Then a tall figure appeared. The others fell in behind him and they started marching Owen's direction. Just as Owen reached the outer line of shacks, the crowd drew up and halted about thirty feet away, blocking his path. The tall figure was a Korean man in his late twenties with broad shoulders and a heavy brow. He stood at the head of the mob, feet astride the path, hands on his hips, glaring at Owen.

Owen stopped, not knowing what to do. No one spoke for a moment then Owen offered, "Uh, I'm... I'm Owen Powell. I was told to come—"

"You go back!" the big man barked, gesturing toward the ridge.

"Is this Yi Chung-hae's training camp?" Owen said. "I was invited to come here and—"

"You go back!"

"No!" Owen yelled, angry now. He slipped the straps of his duffle bag off his shoulders and dropped it behind him. "You get Yi Sabumnim and tell him I'm here."

The Korean shook his head then strode forward until his nose was in Owen's face. He thrust out his chest, bumping Owen's. Resisting the urge to shrink back, Owen pushed forward defiantly. Then the Korean brought up both his palms and slammed Owen's shoulders, shoving him back. Such naked aggression startled

Owen, but he recovered quickly, dropping into a fighting stance with a loud *kiai* and an angry glare.

Seeing this, the man gave the crowd behind him a sardonic smile then raised his hands to his face in mock fear. The mob broke into laughter. The man laughed with them for a moment then suddenly wheeled around and whipped a roundhouse kick into the side of Owen's thigh, buckling his leg.

A wave of white-hot pain washed up into Owen's hip—*Oh God, he's broken my leg!*—then the Korean's fist hit the point of his chin, unhinging both his jaws.

Owen's next sensation was his back hitting the ground. He lay there dazed for a moment, not seeing anything, but hearing the mob laughing and taunting. He forced the cobwebs from his head and struggled up on his elbows just in time to see the crowd part for a short frail-looking Korean man with wisps of white hair on his scalp and chin. The hecklers fell silent.

The old man walked up to Owen's assailant, who bowed deferentially, and they spoke for a minute in Korean. The white haired man said little, and his face betrayed no emotion. Finally, he turned to Owen.

"You Pawu?" he said, his voice as flat as if he were asking the time.

"Yeah." Owen considered complaining about the way he had been treated, but thought the situation spoke for itself.

"You want to learn to fight?"

"That's why I came."

"Then fight."

"But I'm hurt. I think my leg may be broken."

A wave of chuckles rippled through the crowd gathered around them. The tall Korean rolled his eyes, but the old man remained expressionless.

"You not injured," the old man said. "You want to fight then fight. You want to lay on the ground and whine then go home."

Owen blushed crimson. He bent his hurt leg at the knee then straightened it gingerly. The old man was right—it wasn't broken. He worked his jaw from side to side, confirming it too was intact, then climbed to his feet to face the big Korean again. Steeling himself for the fight, he put his hands up and assumed a classic T-stance.

Owen watched the big man as if he were a snake about to strike, but the Korean didn't bother to take a stance or even raise his hands. He regarded Owen with undisguised disdain as the boy began bouncing in stance then weaving as if he were looking for an opening in a competitive match.

Seizing the initiative, Owen shot out a back-fist/side-kick combination and followed it with a quick roundhouse kick. The Korean leaned back slightly to evade the back fist and casually slapped the kicks down. But he was not at all casual when he followed Owen's second kick with a roundhouse kick of his own, burying his instep in Owen's gut.

The air whooshed out of the boy's lungs, and he stumbled back, trying to get out of the man's reach. No luck. The Korean's hand found Owen's shoulder and clinched a handful of his sweatshirt. With a powerful crosscutting motion, the man pulled him in with one hand and drove a hook punch into his gut with the other.

Owen had never been hit so hard in his life, but rage and adrenaline numbed him to the pain, at least for the moment. He wrenched free of the Korean's grip and lunged forward with a front kick, aiming for the man's abdomen. It never found its mark.

The big man turned sideways, blending with Owen's attack, and hooked his arm under the kicking leg. Before Owen realized what had happened, the Korean round kicked the inside of Owen's standing leg. Owen's feet sailed up, and his back slammed the ground again. Holding onto the captured leg, the big Korean stepped in and drove the blade of his foot into Owen's groin.

This time, not even rage was enough to block the pain. With an angry wail, Owen curled into a ball and rolled over on his side, facing away from his assailant.

No one said anything for a moment. Even the mob was silent, and the only sound Owen could hear was his own strangled groaning. Then came the old man's flat, deadpan voice. "You not live long in a fight if you lie down and turn your back."

What? Is this guy serious? Owen could not believe what he was hearing. Did the old man really expect him to keep fighting after being knocked down and kicked in the groin? Surely, no man could. And surely, no adversary would continue attacking a man made so helpless.

"If you want to live, get up."

Owen thought he could ignore the old man, but after a moment, he went on.

"If you lie on the ground, the enemy will kill you. If you turn your back, the enemy will kill you. No enemy will have mercy on you. No one will feel sorry for you because you are hurt. This is your first and most important lesson, Owen Pawu. As long as you have life, you can fight. To give up is to die." He paused again then added, "If you don't get up, this will be your only lesson at this camp."

With a supreme effort, Owen uncoiled from his fetal pose and pushed himself up to his hands and knees. He retched twice, but he finally struggled to his feet, his knees wobbling.

He turned to face the big Korean and was shocked to discover the man had gone. Bewildered, he scanned the crowd, but the man was nowhere to be seen. The old man remained, though, staring at him as expressionless as ever.

"Alright, Owen Pawu, you can stay."

CHAPTER FOURTEEN

Owen's first weeks at camp were tortuous. Worse, they were one humiliation after another. The big Korean that had given him the beating was Pak Je-man, Yi's senior student and the camp's assistant instructor. Pak went out of his way to make Owen's life miserable. He put him in the most dilapidated, tumbledown hooch in the settlement. He bullied him constantly and never missed an opportunity to berate him in front of the other students.

During those dark days, Owen had very few friends. One was a burly, red-faced Australian named Patrick Nagleson whom Owen met while standing in line for breakfast his first morning at camp. The man's intimidating size and Fu Manchu moustache reminded Owen of pictures of mercenaries he had seen in pulp magazines, but his eyes were warm. As he and Owen inched their way towards the pentagonal pavilion, the open-air structure that served as the camp's dining hall and community center, Nagleson told Owen how the camp operated.

"It's kind of a co-op, Lad," he said. "Everyone here pitches in when there's work to be done, and we all share the fruits of our labors. Old man Yi has a strong bond with the people who live in these mountains and in the village a couple miles north of here. They look out for him, you might say. They're his eyes and ears. No bugger gets within miles of this place without the locals dobbing the old man. So, in return, he teaches them *Tangsu* and—"

"*Tangsu?*" Owen said.

"Yeah, *Tangsu*. That means 'Tang hand', as in the Tang Dynasty in China, just like the word 'karate' means 'China hand' in Japanese. At least, it used to before they changed the written character from 'China' to a homonym meaning 'empty' so they could call the modern stuff 'empty hand' and turn it into a bloody game."

Nagleson paused a moment suggesting he would not continue until Owen agreed with this claim, so Owen nodded.

"Anyway, Yi holds *Tangsu* classes every morning and afternoon for the local kids and only charges them token dues—a few cups of rice, an occasional chicken, or whatever they can spare, sometimes nothing at all. We take part in the day sessions and help him teach. In return, he holds special classes for us in the evening.

"During the day, it's straight Tangsudo—you know, Mate, standard forms, sport sparring, the kind of thing you would find at any decent school in Seoul or Tokyo. At night, we get the real stuff. Yi teaches us the inner art, the techniques secretly embedded in the ancient patterns but lost in modern forms. Best of all, Lad..." Nagleson leaned toward Owen and lowered his voice. "He shows us the dirty stuff, the things he learned and used during the war."

Owen thought about that, remembering what his father had told him and the beating he had taken the evening before. The story seemed plausible enough as far as it went, but it begged more questions than it answered. He looked around and saw faces of every race. As the line took them into the pavilion, he heard a babble of languages from all over the world.

He turned back to the big Australian. "Who are all these people?"

"Well now," Nagleson said, scratching his chin. "Not just any old blighter can train here. It's an invitation only kind of thing, and to get invited, someone has to vouch for you. Those of us who know about it… Well, we're kind of a closed network. A lot of us are in similar lines of work, you might say."

Owen was about to ask what kind of work, but thought better of it.

He and Nagleson had almost reached the serving table when a glimpse of someone just leaving the line drew his eyes like iron filings to a magnet. He quickly turned to take in the sight of a tall, shapely woman in her early twenties with corn silk blond hair pulled into a ponytail that swung this way and that as she looked for a place to sit. Finally finding room at a table, she put her tray down and took her seat.

"Aye, that one's a looker, that Sheila is," Nagleson said over Owen's shoulder.

"Who is she?" Owen said, unable to take his eyes off her.

"Name's Anna Norgaard. She's a Danish lass who fights on the European tournament circuit. She comes here every summer to train—at least, that's what she says. A lot of us think she just comes to get her cherries off breaking blokes' noses and knocking out their teeth."

Owen turned in surprise.

"That's right, Mate. She's a bad one, a real chook. If you ever have to spar with her, you'd better forget she's a woman and go full bore. If you don't, you'll likely wake up with a broken jaw."

Owen thought about the beating he had gotten the evening before. But that had been at the hands of Pak, a coarse, mountain Neanderthal. How could this classy looking Danish girl be so bad?

Owen got his breakfast. When he reached the end of the serving line, he turned to find a seat and his eyes fell on the Norgaard woman again.

"You best stay away from her, Lad," the Aussie said, reading Owen's mind. "That one's blue murder and a lady muck to boot."

Owen had no idea what *blue murder* or *lady muck* meant and didn't much care. He saw a vacant spot on the bench across the table from where Anna Norgaard sat. He gave Nagleson a mischievous grin and headed that direction.

"Hello, is this seat taken?" Owen said on reaching the table. The woman looked up, but didn't reply, so he put his tray down and climbed onto the bench. "I'm Owen Powell," he said, putting out his hand.

She regarded him coolly with eyes the color of jade.

When it became evident she was not going to shake hands, Owen recovered with as much dignity as he could manage and turned his attention to his breakfast tray. He picked up a bowl, held it close to his face, and began shoveling the contents into his mouth with his chopsticks, Asian fashion.

Stealing glances over the rim of the bowl, he studied the woman across the table. He noticed then that her large eyes were not green exactly. They were more like turquoise opals, a menagerie of green and blue flecks. She was pretty with heavy bangs and longer side locks framing her face. She was even beautiful, Owen decided, though not in the classic sense. Her features seemed almost too sturdy—her jaw a tad too strong, her cheekbones and nose a bit too angular. But there was something intensely sensual in that powerful face that made his breathing quicken as he explored it.

Anna Norgaard pointedly avoided looking at Owen, so after several minutes of silence, he decided to see if he could get her to talk. Putting down his bowl, he said, "So, how do you like training here? Have you been here long?"

She sipped her tea and stared at him with icy eyes.

"I just arrived yesterday evening," Owen said, undeterred.

Then her eyes widened as if she were seeing him for the first time. "Oh, I know you," she said, lowering her cup, "You're the new boy, the one who lies on the ground and whines. I didn't recognize you sitting upright."

Owen felt as if he had been hit with a hammer. The heat rose in his face, and he was struggling to find something nonchalant to say when someone began jabbing him on the shoulder at the base of his neck. He winced in pain and jerked around to confront the lout. It was Pak Je-man.

"You do not sit here," Pak said, his black eyes unblinking.

Owen stared up in shock. He turned to Anna. She stared back expressionless. Then her sensuous lips curled ever so slightly in a mocking smile. As Owen's eyes returned to Pak's, he glanced around and saw others watching to see what he would do.

"You do not sit here!" Pak said again, louder, more forcefully. His jaw was rigid.

Owen felt the pressure mounting as more eyes turned to him. He hesitated, determined not to submit to Pak's bullying, but he desperately wanted to avoid another beating. *What do I do?* He frantically searched his mind for some way to save face, but he could think of none. His brain was frozen in despair and humiliation and... yes, he suddenly realized, in fear.

Finally, after several agonizing seconds, he turned away from the Korean, his cheeks burning in shame. Staring down at his tray, he got up from the table and said, "I was done anyway."

"See you around, new boy," Anna called out, as he walked away.

CHAPTER FIFTEEN

In all his young life, Owen Powell had experienced neither fear nor failure in any sizeable measure. Growing up a prodigy in the Tokyo diplomatic community, he had learned to thrive in any environment. He was physically and intellectually superior to other kids his age. Whether roving the streets of Shinjuku, or playing his father's faithful squire at embassy receptions, he was a social virtuoso, a chameleon of many subtle hues, a self-styled renaissance youth-come-modern, at ease in every realm he encountered no matter how it was fashioned or what dragons lay within it.

Drifting through his happy youth on an unending wellspring of achievement, Owen had emerged from adolescence with unbridled confidence. He had little experience with failure, less with self-doubt, and was almost completely unacquainted with fear. But he was a young man untested, a radiant blade fresh from the forge, not yet hardened by plunges in the icy waters of reality.

So it is small wonder that the humiliations he suffered those first days at Yi Chung-hae's training camp should have made such a painful assault on his self-esteem. In Owen's mind, he had faced the first real danger in his life, the first great test of his manhood, and had failed. A modern day chevalier only days before, the young renaissance man of Asia now worried that he was a coward.

It was in this dark and oppressive cloud of self-doubt that he embraced the training regime laid out at the mysterious camp hidden high in the Taebaek Mountains. The days were long and arduous—up before dawn for bathing and breakfast, four hours of training in the morning followed by lunch then another four hours of training. Dinner preceded the two-hour special sessions with Yi Sabumnim in the evening.

Owen threw himself into this daunting regimen with such ardor that other students soon wondered whether he was merely obsessive or utterly psychotic. If an instructor demanded the class do fifty punches, kicks, or pushups, he blasted through seventy-five and returned to stance before any of the other students finished. Admonished to strike the forging post and punching bag with spirit, he attacked them with such ferocity that he began destroying equipment until Pak ordered him to ease up. Once ordered to run five miles before breakfast, he ran ten and missed breakfast completely, yet refused to moderate his pace in the four-hour drill that followed and almost collapsed before the midday break.

For Owen, life at the camp was a fanatical effort to drive his body to its physical limits and beyond. He didn't do this because Patrick Nagleson or anyone else told him he should. He didn't do it to impress Pak or Yi or Anna Norgaard. He didn't even do it to prove something to himself or the other students. He did it for penance, pure and simple. He felt compelled to pay for the cowardice he'd shown in the face of Pak's bullying. He was determined to punish himself—for how long, he didn't know. He only knew he had to drive himself until his spirit was cleansed.

It was just as well that Owen was not trying to impress Anna, because she acted as if he did not exist. The woman was utterly maddening. There was no denying she was remarkable—not only was she stunning, she fought like a banshee and all her movements seemed to combine the grace of a prima ballerina with the power of a jackhammer—but she had the infuriating ability to look right through Owen, whether he stood across from her in training or in front of her in line at the pavilion.

Still wounded from the way she had humiliated him his first day in camp, Owen resolved to not give her another opportunity to embarrass him or even the satisfaction of knowing he still found her attractive. So he treated her with the same glacial disdain that she did him, and they fell into a habitual routine of mutual indifference.

Owen might never have come out of his funk if it weren't for the young Korean students at camp and one tiny, awkward kid in particular. Bae was ten years old and small for his age, but he was strong in spirit. He showed up to train whenever there was class; six days a week he struggled through both of the four-hour sessions. But no matter how hard he tried, Bae never managed to get anything right. His balance was poor, his techniques weak. He seemed incapable of retaining any knowledge from one class to the next. The resident adult students would show him the same pattern, time after time, class after class, and each new day he would be unable to get through it without help. One by one, the residents lost patience with him—at first they cajoled, then they yelled, and eventually they avoided working with the boy. Pak just ignored him. Still, Bae kept coming back.

Seeing a kindred spirit in Bae's dedication, Owen started partnering with him whenever he could manage it during class then began working with him one-on-one during lunch breaks. He took the boy through the same form over and over, patiently correcting every error, adjusting every stance, until he got it right. After a couple of weeks, Bae brought a couple of his friends to their private lunchtime sessions, and Owen reluctantly began coaching them as well. Before long their private gathering had grown to a dozen Korean kids between the ages of ten and fifteen.

As Owen got involved with the kids, his attitude brightened. The nature of his training changed, too. He still worked harder than anyone else, but he stopped driving himself in masochistic obsession. To his surprise, he began to feel at ease at camp. What surprised him more, however, was that Anna Norgaard had begun acting differently.

Owen first noticed it one evening when he thought he caught her watching him at dinner from two tables away. Determined not to act like he cared whether she might be looking at him, he tried to avoid turning her direction. But her eyes continued to bore into his peripheral vision, and after a couple of minutes, he couldn't help glancing back. She quickly looked away. Had he imagined her stare? He didn't think so, but his ego was still too tender to stand another bruising, so he pushed the incident out of his mind and focused evermore intently on his *Tangsu*.

Nevertheless, Anna seemed determined to ruin his concentration. Over the next several weeks, she became increasingly open in her attention. She looked at him more frequently whenever their paths crossed in camp and no longer looked away when he turned her direction. He didn't know what to make of this. Was it some kind of trick? Was she trying to lure him into making a fool of himself again? He worried about what she might be up to, but her growing boldness was rekindling the heat he had felt the first time he saw her. Before long, her opalescent gaze was all he could think about, and he found himself lying awake at night, his emotions swinging wildly between hopeful ardor and angry suspicion.

Finally, unable to contain his curiosity any longer, he boldly put his tray down beside hers at dinner one evening and wedged his way into a narrow opening on the bench beside her. Feeling the heat of her body next to his—and immediately wishing he hadn't made such a brash advance—he began eating, his eyes locked on his food in an effort to avoid what he was sure must be an angry glare.

Sure enough, within moments he noticed she had stopped eating and he felt her looking at him. He tried to keep his gaze down, but after a few moments he couldn't resist the magnetic pull of her eyes any longer. He turned and discovered, to his bafflement, that she was smiling. *What kind of spiteful ploy is this?* He braced himself for the insult he was sure would follow.

Already sitting intimately close, she leaned even closer, pressing against him. "I was wondering when you'd work up the courage to come back over," she said softly, her Danish accent caressing his ear. "What does a girl have to do, send a written invitation?"

Owen opened his mouth, but his brain failed to give him any words. "Well, I... I mean..."

"That's okay," she said, rescuing him from his awkwardness, "I don't blame you for avoiding me. I treated you terribly when we first met. I'm sorry, I really am. It's just that most of the men here are such pigs." She straightened and a hard edge came to her voice. "They all have one thing on their minds. They think that when a woman shows up in a camp full of men like this..." She looked down and blushed. "I don't even want to say what they think." Then she met Owen's eyes again. "Anyway, that's why I come on so hard in sparring, to teach the bastards a lesson and show them what will happen if they make the mistake of sneaking into my hooch some night."

She held his eyes with hers. "That's why I was so hard on you, you know. Put yourself in my place—you arrive at camp, and the first thing you do is pick out a woman and go on the make. So what was I to think? I'll tell you what: here's some kid who thinks he's spotted an easy score for his first lay."

Owen flushed, embarrassed to realize how transparent he had been.

"So what changed your mind?" he said after a moment. "I mean, why are you talking to me now? Why the big thaw?"

"What, so now you don't believe me? Maybe you think this is some kind of cruel trick."

"Well, no, but..." He turned an even brighter shade of red.

"It's all right," she said, leaning toward him again, her eyes reassuring. "I don't blame you for being suspicious, and I don't mind telling you why I'm thawing, as you put it. The short answer is simply that I've been watching you, and I like what I see."

Owen's eyes flashed to hers.

"Okay, don't go getting a big head. I'm not talking about your looks or your talent. I'm talking about how you work with the kids. You're so patient. It's sweet. You have quite a following, you know. Do you know what they call you behind your back?"

Owen shrugged, surprised to hear they talked about him at all.

"You're O' Man Pawu. They mean 'Old Man Powell'. It's really cute; in Korea 'old man' is a term of respect. You may be the youngest of the resident students, but you're older than almost all the Korean students and with your skill and all the attention you've showered on them, they've adopted you as their mentor and idol. Old Man Yi may run this camp, but Old Man Pawu is the young hero they all want to emulate."

She paused, gathering her thoughts. "Anyway, seeing what you've done for these kids... Well, I guess I just decided that maybe there's something more to you than arrogance and testosterone."

Owen didn't know what to say. He was humbled and amazed and flattered and aroused all at once. Alternating currents of emotion overwhelmed his ability to fashion an intelligent response. Finally, he said, "So where do we go from here?"

Anna radiated a smile that sent a wave of heat down Owen's spine, and he wondered how he could have ever thought those lips were cruel or mocking.

"Let's take it slow," she said. "We've got plenty of time to get to know each other." She got up from the bench and picked up her tray to leave. "See you in class."

CHAPTER SIXTEEN

For Owen the next several weeks were like a dream. He trained hard and savored both the day sessions, where he worked with his young charges, and the evening classes, where he drank in Sabumnim's wisdom like a Bedouin at the well of an oasis. Anna was right about the Korean kids. They idolized him—he couldn't understand why he hadn't seen it earlier. Inspired by their devotion, he redoubled his efforts to cultivate their talents, and even little Bae improved noticeably. But what Owen savored most in those last weeks in camp was the time he spent with Anna.

They became inseparable. They ate together, spent their personal time together, and even cajoled other students into shifting work details around so they could share those activities as well. During the many hours they spent in each other's company, they shared the stories of their lives, comparing Owen's experiences as the son of a widowed American civil servant in Tokyo—he had long ago learned to leave out the detail that his father was an intelligence officer—to Anna's childhood in a wealthy business family in Copenhagen. Owen soon felt closer to Anna than he had to anyone else in his life. He told her everything about himself. He wanted her to know the essence of him, how he felt about the world and everything in it, and he sensed she was also opening herself to him.

But as close as they had become, they still were not as intimate as Owen would have liked. Their relationship was clearly more than platonic—they touched freely and often. When no one was around, they held hands or walked arm in arm, and they hugged each other tenderly before parting each evening. Occasionally, when everyone else had gone to bed, they crept out to the training field and held one another as they lay under the stars talking. One night Owen kissed her. It was lingering and passionate—at least, it was on his part—but while Anna did not blunt his advance, neither did she open her lips to his eager tongue, and he realized she was gently but persistently resisting his efforts to move their relationship onto more intimate ground.

To Owen's mounting frustration, they had grown comfortably familiar without becoming romantic. Anna had set a boundary on their intimacy. Owen's frustration was more than physical. He was falling in love, and he thought she was too. He didn't understand why she was holding back after drawing so close to him, but he couldn't help wondering if her hesitation was due to his age. He was eighteen; she was in her early twenties. Did she think of him as a child?

Anna's transformation from ice woman to affectionate friend had a peculiar impact on Owen's relationship with the other camp residents. The closer he drew to her, the colder and more distant the others became. Even Patrick Nagleson, who had been Owen's best friend and self-appointed mentor since his arrival at camp, seemed to shun him when he discovered Owen and Anna were spending time together. *They're all jealous,* Owen thought bitterly. But he had to admit his feelings about the matter were mixed. The rejection hurt, but deep down he glowed with pride in having won the affections of the most desirable and most unobtainable woman in camp.

Oddly, Pak Je-man displayed the most dramatic change in behavior as Owen and Anna became friends. He had never been a gentle or compassionate teacher—he was cold and stern and prone to fits of anger—but aside from the humiliations he had inflicted on Owen his first days at camp he had treated Owen no differently than he had anyone else—no better, certainly, but no worse.

Now, the more public Anna and Owen made their growing affection, the more openly hostile Pak became. It began with harassment in class, but soon spilled over into other camp settings. Whenever he came around, Owen knew he was in for a verbal assault. Nothing he did ever seemed to satisfy the Korean, whether it was Owen's technique or something he was trying to teach the local kids. Pak always found fault, always found a way to demean Owen in front of others.

Owen's mental focus and composure had come a long way over the course of the summer, and he generally weathered Pak's insults with an attitude of placid detachment, but when he discovered the Korean had turned his attention to Anna, he could stand it no longer.

Matters came to a head one evening when he went to the pavilion to meet Anna for dinner and found her sitting across a table from Pak. They were engaged in conversation, and neither of them noticed Owen had come. Puzzled, he got in line for food and continued watching them closely. It did not take him long to realize they were arguing about something. Pak's face was contorted in anger, and Anna looked as if she were about to cry.

Suddenly, Anna leaped up and turned to storm out. Then she saw Owen watching her and froze. In the painful seconds that followed, Owen's heart stuttered as he saw several waves of emotion wash over her face. Genuine shock gave way to what looked like shame and finally—God, he hoped he was right—a look he thought might be relief and adoration. Breaking the spell, she marched over and grabbed his arm, pulling him out of line.

"I can't eat, tonight," she said, her voice choked with anguish. "And I can't sit in there with him nearby. Let's go somewhere alone, okay?"

"Yeah, yeah, sure. But what's going on?

She just shook her head and refused to speak as they walked to her hooch. In the day's waning light, Owen could see tears glistening in her eyes. When they arrived, she took him in and sat him beside her on the cot. She turned to face him and took his hands in hers.

"Owen, I didn't want to tell you this, but now that you've seen us, I think I have to so you don't get the wrong impression."

"What's going on?" Owen said again, his voice more urgent now. "Are you and Pak..." He couldn't bring himself to say it.

"No! No!" she cried. "That's exactly what I was afraid you would think!"

"Then what is it?"

She squeezed her eyes shut and shook her head violently, grimacing as if she had something bitter in her mouth, something she desperately wanted to spit out, but could not bring herself to do so.

"He's pressuring me to sleep with him!" she finally blurted. Then it all came out in a rush. "He's been pestering me ever since the day I arrived. Some days he tries to buy me with promises, other days he threatens me. But it's always the same! 'Pillow with me, Anna. Let me come to your bed, Anna. Come to the spring with me, Anna.' He never gives up. I've never let any of it get to me before—I mean, men proposition me all the time—but... but... now it's different."

"What do you mean?" Owen said the blackness of his dread pierced by a pale ray of hope. "Different how?"

"Now he knows he can get to me through you."

"What are you talking about?" Owen said in shock.

"He knows I care about you, so he's threatening to hurt you if I keep turning him down. Oh, Owen, the thought of being with that animal sickens me, but I don't want anything to happen to you. I just don't know what to do." She buried her face in his shoulder, and the tears she had tried so hard to hold back spilled out in hard, wrenching sobs.

Owen wrapped his arms around her and held her tight. "You don't have to do anything," he said, his voice taut.

⊨⊣ ⊢⊨

Owen had put up with Pak's bullying off and on all summer long, first because he was afraid of him, but later because he didn't want to do anything that might jeopardize his standing in the camp. Pak was Yi's senior student and his chief instructor during the day sessions. He managed day-to-day affairs in the little village and reported to Yi on everything that happened. As Nagleson had told Owen his first morning in camp, cross Pak and one was likely to get a beating and be sent home. Owen had long stopped worrying about being beat up, but the last thing he wanted was to be sent home to his father in disgrace—at least, it was the last thing until now.

Now, Owen had higher priorities to consider than his standing in camp. Pak was trying to extort sex from the woman he loved. The very thought of it put Owen in such a state of anxiety that his mind could focus on nothing but ways to inflict pain on the filthy son of a bitch. He was determined to stop this outrage—no, he wanted to do more than simply stop the arrogant, lecherous bastard—he wanted to teach him a lesson he would not soon forget.

The opportunity for Owen to act presented itself almost immediately. That evening, when the resident students convened for the special session, Yi demonstrated a defense and particularly brutal counter against an attacker who lunges with a knife then he told the students to pair off and begin practicing. Quickly skirting the edge of the group, Owen stepped in front of Pak Je-man before the big Korean could choose his own partner. Pak looked surprised, but did not turn him away.

The two men bowed and Owen, as the junior student, took up the wooden practice knife and prepared for the first attack.

"I wish this were a real knife so I could carve you like the pig you are," Owen growled just loud enough for Pak to hear. "You aren't going to get away with what you've been doing to Anna."

For a moment Pak looked confused, but a flash of understanding crossed his face and he met Owen's glare without answering. He signaled for the attack, and Owen lunged out with the wooden knife with all his strength, trying to bury it in the Korean's abdomen. With perfect timing, Pak angled his body and parried the knife to the side then executed the counterattack—a kidney punch followed by a ridge-hand strike to the throat and a reaping throw—forcefully, but with control. Owen was not hurt. He got back to his feet. Pak picked up the knife and prepared to attack.

"I'm going to enjoy pounding your filthy carcass into the dirt," Owen said. "After tonight, sex with Anna or anyone else will be the last thing on your mind."

Pak stared at Owen grimly and hesitated. But after a moment he assumed the ready position and, on Owen's signal, lunged forward in a quick, but controlled, attack.

Owen parried the thrust as expected, but instead of striking Pak's kidney with measured force, he punched the man as if he were hammering a forging post. The Korean's head snapped up and his back arched, his face contorted in pain. Owen seized the opening and drove his ridge-hand up and into Pak's groin with all his strength. Pak crumpled to the ground with a loud groan.

Owen stood over the fallen man and was just about to taunt him when Pak lashed out with a scissors kick, buckling his legs and bringing him down. At once, the Korean slammed a granite back fist down at Owen's head, but found only empty grass as Owen rolled back to his feet. Pak too was up in a lunge and the men collided in a hail of fists and feet. This was not sparring; it was a frantic, ferocious fight.

Patrick Nagleson was working with another student nearby when the fight broke out. "Sabumnim!" he yelled. But Yi had already seen what was going on and was calmly walking their direction. "You've got to stop them before they kill each other!" the Aussie said, his voice betraying not only his concern for the combatants, but also his astonishment that Yi was reacting so casually.

"Let them fight," Yi said in his familiar deadpan manner.

As Yi and the students watched, Owen and Pak proceeded to beat each other until they could fight no more. Both were wild with rage, and neither had the presence of mind to apply tactics or even block many of the incoming blows. Instead they kicked each other's legs and bodies with all the speed and strength they could muster and filled the openings those strikes created with flailing punches to exposed ribs, jaws, and noses. Within a minute, each had knocked the other to the ground several times. Both were bleeding profusely from their noses and mouths, and dark welts were erupting on their chests and faces.

Finally slowing from exhaustion, they stumbled into a clench and danced a peculiar waltz as each expended his remaining ounces of strength trying to wrestle the other down. Then Owen wrapped his leg around Pak's and stomped down hard on the Korean's Achilles tendon. Pak cried out in pain and sank to his knees, but before Owen could back away and claim victory, Pak thrust out his palm heel at eye level, striking Owen in the bladder. Owen doubled over groaning… Then he wet himself.

"I guess you two through now?" Yi said.

Owen stumbled out of Pak's reach, and both of them spent the next couple of minutes doubled over, coughing and spitting blood. Yi said nothing as he waited for them to collect themselves. The other students quietly waited to see what the old man would do. Finally, Pak struggled to his feet, and he and Owen turned to face Sabumnim.

"Go clean up. We deal with this later," was all Yi said. Then he turned and continued the evening session.

Hunched and limping, Owen and Pak headed back to camp, staying well away from each other along the way. Anna covertly watched them over her training partner's shoulder as they hobbled away. She smiled.

CHAPTER SEVENTEEN

I t was after midnight and Owen lay dozing fitfully. He had washed in the spring hours earlier and retreated to his hooch. Hurting everywhere, he had stripped off all his clothes and flopped down on his cot in the hot summer night.

Suddenly, he was awake and alert. Had he heard something? He wasn't sure, but something had prickled his senses. Light from a full moon poured through the single window overlooking his cot. He blinked his eyes into focus.

There was the noise again—someone was in his hooch!

He turned his head just in time to see Anna steal across the room and kneel beside him. He opened his mouth to speak, but she quickly put her finger to his split and swollen lips. Then she bent over and kissed him, slipping her tongue deep into his mouth.

Her pale hair hung loose. She wore a light cotton robe, and as Owen watched in astonishment, she untied the sash and pulled it open. She was naked beneath. Illuminated by the window, her face and hair glowed the color of moonlight, as did the swell of her heavy breasts, with only her eyes, lips, and nipples standing out in deep blue relief.

Without a word, she swung a leg over the cot and gently settled herself, straddling his abdomen, tenting her robe over them. Owen gasped as her wetness touched his stomach. She giggled softly. Tossing her hair over her shoulder away from the window so it wouldn't shadow her face or his, she peered into his pale eyes then, holding his gaze in hers, slowly slid her body down his until she took him into her.

Owen gasped again, louder this time, and his eyes opened wide. For all his bravado with his friends in Shinjuku, he had never had a woman before. Anna was his first.

She gripped him and canted her pelvis in a slow, gentle stroke. "Oh… Oh!" Owen cried out in sudden surprise, and it was over. Immediately feeling embarrassed, he said, "I'm sorry I—"

"Shush, shush, shush," she whispered. "You were wonderful." Then, without another word, she got up, retied her robe, and left.

Owen lay still for a long time unable to comprehend what had happened. She had come and gone so quickly and said so little… The whole experience seemed ethereal. After a while, he began to wonder if it had been a dream. He reached down and felt the wetness then brought his fingers to his nose. Smelling Anna's rich, musky scent, he knew it had been real.

⇌⇋

The next morning Owen rose early and went to breakfast in hope of seeing Anna. He got a tray of food—though he was so nervous he doubted he could hold anything on his stomach—and took a seat where he could watch for her approach.

He didn't know whether to feel relieved or apprehensive when she appeared a few minutes later and headed for his table. He worried about whether she would think he sounded mature as they sorted out how their relationship had changed. But to his astonishment, Anna sat down and began chatting as if nothing had happened. She said nothing about her nocturnal visit and didn't even comment on Owen's swollen lip or the bruises on his face. It was Saturday, the one day of the week on which there were no classes at camp, and she pattered on about wanting to hike up to the nearby village to explore and, perhaps, do some shopping.

Owen listened, but for a moment couldn't figure out what she was talking about. His mind staggered and groped for some outcropping of bedrock on which to anchor itself.

"Nayen, one of the local kids, told me about it," Anna was saying. "It's tucked away in a little valley like this one on the north trail. They have a teahouse. Maybe we could—"

"Hey, wait a minute," Owen said, finally starting to get his bearings. "You're talking about leaving the vale. You know the rules— no resident crosses the ridge to go anywhere without an escort. It's the one thing Sabumnim won't tolerate."

"Hold your voice down," she hissed, leaning across the table. "Sabumnim doesn't need to know. It's Saturday. There won't be anyone out and about. We can slip out to the training field and pick up the trail away from camp where no one will see us. Come on, Owen. We'll only be gone a few hours. We can be back before dinner."

"Well, I don't know," he said. His common sense told him it would be foolish to break more rules so soon after his fight with Pak, but his heart raced at the thought of spending an entire afternoon with Anna.

Then she leaned even closer to him. "We would have some time alone in the woods, you know," she said, staring into his pale eyes.

Owen followed Anna up the north trail and grew increasingly anxious. They had been hiking for forty minutes, and it had not gone well from the start. They had slipped out of camp easily enough—at least, they didn't think anyone had seen them leave—but no sooner had they crossed the north ridge than Owen was startled by a familiar voice shouting behind him.

"O' Man Pawu! O' Man Pawu! Where you go?"

Owen and Anna turned to see Bae standing on the trail about thirty yards back, his eyes wide in alarm. "It's all right, Bae," Owen said. "It'll be all right."

"Don't worry," Anna added. "He's with me. We'll be back in a few hours. Go on home." She turned and continued down the mountainside at a brisk pace.

"Don't go with her! Go back to camp!" Bae sounded almost frantic. "Please, Owen-ssi, please!" he pleaded, addressing him by his first name, something he had never done before.

Owen hesitated, unsure of what to do. He looked at Bae's pleading face then at Anna's hourglass form as it gracefully descended the trail below before disappearing around a bend. He made up his mind quickly. "Go on home, Bae. I'll be back later this afternoon." He turned and scrambled to catch up with Anna.

Now he wasn't sure he had made the right decision. The outing wasn't going at all as he had hoped. About twenty minutes after leaving Bae, Owen spotted a small grassy meadow tucked behind some rocks a short distance off the trail, a perfect spot to steal away for a little personal time with Anna. Stepping up beside her, he slipped his arm around her waist and motioned toward the meadow then he pulled her against him and leaned to cover her mouth with a kiss. But instead of responding as he had expected, she backed her face away from his.

"We'll have plenty of time for that on the way back," she said. "I want to get to the village while it's still early, before anything closes." Then she gave him a maddeningly chaste peck on his frowning lips, pulled out of his arms, and strode off up the trail.

They didn't speak anymore the rest of the hike. Anna marched along in front with Owen following behind, brooding in frustration as he watched her white hiking shorts sway alluringly with each stride of her long, muscular legs.

Then, to Owen's puzzlement, as Anna reached the top of the next rise, she ducked off the trail and crouched behind the ridge, looking over it. She turned and motioned for him to join her, and a moment later he too was kneeling, peering at the village below.

"This is it," she said. "They call it Myongsan-ni. What do you think? See anything that looks like a shop or teahouse?"

Owen scanned the sad collection of dilapidated clapboard shacks that made up the village. It was a depressing sight. Some of the hovels were roofed in tin, others were covered with tarpaper, but clearly none of them had ever seen a paintbrush. With their knotty planks uneven and rotted gray, they looked as dejected as the handful of bedraggled souls who slogged about between them. A badly rutted dirt road meandered through the settlement, more of a cattle track, actually, and still choked with mud from a heavy rain that had come and gone days earlier. Pigs and goats wandered freely through the mire, and even from the ridge above, Owen could smell the stench of rotting garbage. He could see nothing that looked like it might have been a shop, or teahouse, or any other commercial establishment, for that matter. As he took in the gloomy scene, the unease he had felt since leaving camp grew into a sense of foreboding.

"No, there are no shops down there," he said. "There's nothing for us here. Let's head back to camp."

"Wait a minute," Anna said. "You can't tell what's down in the village from up here. There's got to be something for us to do or see. They must have some kind of business. Why else would there be a village? They at least have a teahouse. Nayen said so. I want to go down and check it out."

"No. I think we should go back. There's something not right about this."

"Come on, Owen," she pleaded. She waited a moment then added, "You're not afraid, are you?"

He threw her an angry glare and hoped she could not see the hurt in his eyes.

She stared back. He was just about to cave in when she said, "I'll tell you what: You wait here while I check it out. When I find the teahouse or a shop, I'll step out in the road and wave. Then you can come down and join me." Without waiting for him to answer, she pecked him on the cheek, jumped up, and started down the trail towards the village.

Owen didn't know what to do. He didn't want her to think he was afraid, but he couldn't shake the strange unease he felt about this village. He watched her work her way down the hillside and approach the settlement from behind one of the shacks.

Finally resigned, he was just about to get up and follow her when the side door of the shack she was nearing swung open and Yi Chung-hae stepped out and started walking towards the muddy village road.

Anna quickly leaped behind the shack and looked back at Owen, her eyes sparkling in excitement, her lips rounded into a mischievous *Uh oh!*

They remained frozen like that for a couple of seconds, both of them unsure of what to do next then Owen heard the roar of a heavy truck engine. Anna heard it too, because she peaked around the corner of the shack and watched the olive green, half-ton army truck pull up beside Yi where he now stood at the edge of the muddy road.

As Owen and Anna watched, several soldiers leaped out of the truck and confronted the old man. Anna looked at Owen—the excitement that had brightened her eyes only moments ago was now replaced with a look of fear and confusion—then she turned back to the village scene as raised voices, indistinct but unmistakably angry, reached Owen's ears.

Suddenly, things were happening faster than Owen's mind could follow. A fight broke out, but an instant before that, Owen's eyes gravitated to the markings on the truck's canvas cover—the outline of a red star within blue and red concentric circles—and he thought, *That can't be...*

A man was down! Owen realized Yi Sabumnim was fighting with the soldiers. Another one grabbed at the old man only to career head first into one of the truck's mud-caked wheels.

Certainly, we're not in North Korea. Owen's mind reeled, his eyes drifting back to the red star. *It can't be... It's impossible...*

A shot! Owen's eyes refocused on the fight and saw Yi sink to his knees then tumble over onto his side.

Then Anna leaped out from behind the shack and ran shrieking into the fray. This audacious attack startled the soldiers just long enough for her to take to the air and bowl over the largest one with a flying kick. But the shock effect of her dramatic entrance was only momentary, and as she wheeled to engage the two men on her left, the remaining soldier on her right stepped up and clubbed her, breaking the wooden butt of his rifle on her head.

The sickening crack echoed across the valley, and Owen froze in shock as Anna fell face down in the mud. Unable to move, he watched in horror as the big soldier got to his feet and rejoined his buddies who now gathered around Anna's prone form.

Owen strained to see if she was breathing. He couldn't tell—she laid absolutely still, her face in the mire. Then one of the soldiers squatted and rolled her over. He thrust a hand beneath her muddy shirt and kneaded her breast roughly. The others laughed. They talked a moment longer then two of them hoisted her limp body up by the wrists and ankles and heaved it into the back of the truck.

The sight of Anna's body being tossed like a sack of grain was finally enough to shatter Owen's mental paralysis. "No!" he screamed. He leaped up and started over the ridgeline, but felt something drag him back. For a moment, he struggled mindlessly to get loose then realized someone had a hold of his collar. Wheeling around to see who it was, he glimpsed a face contorted with rage, a face swollen and discolored from a recent beating. It was the face of Pak Je-man.

He saw it only for an instant. Then the fist hit him and everything went black.

CHAPTER EIGHTEEN

Tokyo—Spring, 2001

Owen almost missed his subway stop on the way back to the hotel after leaving Nomura Eizo's high-rise apartment in Asakusa. His mind was in turmoil, both from the flood of memories Nomura had triggered and his exasperation with being unable to get to the bottom of the mysterious research proposal that had brought him back to Japan.

He was angry, too. In fact, the more he thought about it, the madder he got. Who did the old man think he was, anyway, dredging up all those painful memories? And to think, this greasy Yakuza baron claimed to be his father's friend—his father, a war hero, an investigator for the Far East War Crimes Tribunal, a respected officer in the Defense Intelligence Agency! Why, the very idea that his father might have mixed with the likes of Nomura sullied his memory.

Still, Nomura said he had talked to Rhys Powell the last night Owen saw his father alive, and the more Owen thought about it, the more his memory of the man he saw leaving his house that night looked like a younger version of the slight, elderly man he met tonight. He knew that memory has a way of playing tricks on a man, but he couldn't seem to shake that image. He couldn't imagine what kind of relationship his father might have had with this man, but as much as he hated to admit it, in some strange, indefinable way, what Nomura had told him seemed to ring true.

What did Nomura know about his father's death? He wouldn't say, no matter how hard Owen pressed him on the issue, and he had pressed hard. Nor would Nomura divulge what he knew about the current mystery. Who had brought Owen to Japan, and why did the old man think he was in danger? All he would say was, "Now is not the time, Owen-san. I cannot tell you more." It was infuriating!

Owen's memories of his return to Tokyo that summer were vague and dreamlike. No doubt his mind had distanced them to insulate itself from the pain. After being knocked unconscious at Myongsan-ni, he had awakened strapped to a jump seat in a cargo plane headed back to Japan. Stinking of stale booze and covered in vomit, he had no idea how he'd gotten there.

When he got to Yokota Air Base, he was met on the tarmac by the base commander, a Protestant chaplain, and two well-dressed men from the U.S. Embassy. Fluttering about the confused teenager like a flock of birds, they led him into the terminal cafeteria, sat him down, and got him some coffee and a piece of pie that he was too sick to eat. Then, as the other men listened awkwardly, the chaplain told him his father was dead and stumbled through some story about an accident at his house.

There had been a fire. "Your father apparently fell and hit his head. We don't know how it happened or whether the fire started before his fall, but that must be why he didn't get out." He sounded as if he doubted Owen would believe him.

Owen said nothing. Still in shock from witnessing the tragedy in Korea and dehydrated from an apparent alcoholic binge, he was already physically, mentally, and emotionally paralyzed. This new catastrophe seemed to have little impact—at least it didn't hit him hard at first. A day later, at Jim Shelton's house—Shelton, one of the two State Department men who had met him at the plane, had given Owen a temporary place to stay—grief hit him from behind and he suddenly collapsed in tears as Shelton's family looked on in awkward embarrassment. Two days after that, Owen's grief turned to anger when Shelton delivered what he thought would be good news: Word had arrived that he had been granted a full scholarship at Oxford University.

"I'm not going to Oxford," Owen said, his voice brittle. "I've already been accepted at Kansei University here in Tokyo. That's where I want to go."

"But you can't stay in Japan," Shelton said.

"What do you mean I can't stay here? This is my home."

"You don't have a valid visa. You were here on a dependent's visa under the U.S. Status of Forces Agreement. Now that your father is gone, you're no longer a DoD dependent."

"Then I'll get a student visa."

"There isn't time. The Japanese government won't just convert a dependent's visa to a student visa. You'd have to return to the States and apply for a new visa from there. Besides, how would you support yourself while going to school here? They won't let you work on a student visa, you know. Look at it this way, Owen. Oxford is offering you a full ride—room, board, expenses, the whole kit 'n caboodle. Any other American boy would give his left nut to spend four years in England and go to a school like Oxford."

"I'm not any other American boy!" Owen yelled.

Now, nearly twenty years later, walking from the subway station to his hotel, Owen's face flushed with fresh anger as he relived that exchange in his mind. After all he'd been through, they made him leave Tokyo, the only home he had ever known. And Nomura Eizo had churned up those bitter memories again, that son of a bitch!

Strangely, the conversation with Nomura had also triggered other memories, things he hadn't thought about in years. Images of Shelton sitting down with him several times during the days he stayed in the man's house flashed through his mind, and Owen now remembered his host gently prodding him with questions about his dad. The questions had seemed a bit odd even then, as Owen recalled, but given his emotional state at the time, he didn't notice how peculiar they really were. Now, remembering them anew, they seem especially curious.

"Before you left for Korea, did you see anyone unusual watching your house?" the State Department man had asked. Owen said he had not. "Did your father keep anything unusual at home?"

Owen stared off absently, "Unusual like what?"

"Oh, I don't know... maybe something old, some antique kind of thing... maybe an old scroll. Or maybe a short metal tube, something like that."

Owen just stared at him blankly.

Another time Shelton had said, "Hey, do you know if your dad had a safe deposit box somewhere, not just here in Japan, but anywhere? Back in the States, maybe, or in England?"

Thinking about it now, the tenor of Shelton's questions seemed to suggest he suspected his father's death had something to do with something valuable he was hiding. If so, why hadn't Shelton gone to the police? Why would he be the one to question Owen instead of them? *Strange.* He didn't ask the questions all at once. He spread them out over the days Owen stayed with him, asking one here, a couple there, bringing them up in a casual tone and never when anyone else was around. It was only now, these many years later, that Owen connected the questions and remembered them together. *How odd*, he thought.

━━◁+ +▷━━

Owen let himself in the hotel room, stripped off his tweed sport coat, and sank down in the cramped accommodation's single armchair. It was late and he was tired, but he was too troubled to sleep. His mind flashed between images of Nomura now and the man he'd seen leaving his house that night. Images of Shelton's kind but persistent face alternated with Nomura's, and things each man had said kept echoing in his mind. The more he thought about it, the more he struggled to make sense of it all, the more frustrated he became trying to assemble this puzzle, knowing he didn't have all the pieces.

On top of it all, he missed Elaine. He had been gone nearly a week now and had thought about her every day. He wondered if she missed him, if she had tried to call him at home, or find out where he had gone. He wondered if she worried about whether he was all right. Should he call her?

His mind drifted back to the fight they had the day he left, and he felt the anger again. But it was dulled now. Time had cooled his ire, and his longing for her had grown with each passing day. He wondered if it was the same for her. *What time is it in Maryland right now?* he wondered, turning to the phone beside him. Then he saw the flashing light indicating a voicemail was waiting for his retrieval.

Who would be calling him tonight? It was probably the Mijikawa boys wanting him to join their bout of *hashigo*, midstream. *Yeah, that would really top off the evening*, he thought. *Let a bunch of emotional, half drunk company men slobber all over me.* He guessed they would be at least four drinks along by now, and he wasn't about to put up with their antics while he was stone cold sober. He would just leave the message until tomorrow.

Then it occurred to him… Maybe it was Elaine. Maybe she had tracked him down and wanted to talk. He picked up the phone and poked in the numbers to retrieve the message.

The voice that greeted him left him breathless. "Owen, meet me at the Toshogu Shrine in Ueno Park at midnight. Come alone, and make sure you aren't followed." Then a click as the caller hung up.

Owen's hand started shaking. He immediately recognized the voice, but he replayed the message three times, concentrating on every word and intonation. *It can't be. It's impossible!*

CHAPTER NINETEEN

Owen took an indirect route to Ueno Park and just made it to the Toshogu Shrine by midnight. Finding the shrine's iron gate locked for the night, he looked around uneasily, wondering what to do next. The intermittent rain that had harried the city earlier that evening had finally passed, only to be replaced with a damp, chill fog and silence. Owen waited by the gate for several minutes, the dampness slowly saturating his clothes. Ueno Park was deserted and blanketed in darkness.

Growing suspicious about the phone call and increasingly uneasy about his vulnerability there, alone in the silent park shrouded by fog, he decided to head back toward his hotel. Turning back toward the lane he had come up, he faced the long line of massive stone lanterns he had passed that now stood like silent ogres fading into the mist. All was still and silent, but something was wrong. He froze, peering into the fog. Then, among the vague outlines of silent sentries, he thought he could just make out the indistinct silhouette of someone standing motionless in the night. He stared at the blurry figure for several moments. It didn't move. He cautiously walked toward it, and the form solidified and took shape. The face was in shadow, but the silhouette was unmistakable.

"Oh my God," Owen gasped under his breath.

"Owen, is that you?"

Anna's voice. Anna's silhouette.

Owen didn't know what to do. Part of him wanted to rush forward and take her in his arms, but another part of him wanted to hide his face in shame. He had lost countless nights' sleep, endured innumerable nightmares, all because of the guilt he felt for not having come to her defense in Korea. After all these years, he had decided Anna must surely be dead. But now she stood before him, tall and straight, wearing a hooded raincoat belted at the waist.

He approached her slowly, uncertain how she would respond to him and even more unsure of his own emotions. He had loved her once—at least, he had thought so as a boy those many years ago—now his feelings were a tangle of pain and guilt and shock.

"Owen?" she said again as he came near. Her voice sounded uncertain, almost fearful.

"Anna, is it really you?" he finally managed to say.

"Oh, thank God!" she cried. She rushed to him and threw her arms around his neck. "They told me you were dead." She buried her face in the damp tweed of his lapel and began sobbing. "All those years, they said you were dead. They wouldn't let me come to you. They said you were dead."

Owen folded his arms around her and held her close. "Who said I was dead?" he asked, startled and confused. Then the absurdity of the situation seized him. "I thought *you* were dead! What happened? I mean, back in Korea. What happened at that village? Why did those soldiers shoot Yi Sabumnim and take you away? How did you get away from them? Where have you been all this time?"

Slowly, Anna pulled her face out of Owen's coat and gazed into his eyes. Owen was almost afraid to look at her, fearing he might see scars or some other form of disfigurement. But turning his face to hers, he could see none. She was as beautiful as ever, perhaps more so. Her side locks and heavy girlish bangs were gone, but her hair was still the color of corn silk.

"Owen, it was horrible. They locked me up and interrogated me for days. They beat me and… and… Oh Owen, I still can't talk about it. Then our people found out where I was and got me out. I've lived in Copenhagen most of the time since then." She sniffed back a sob.

"When I asked about you, they told me you were dead. I'd have come to you, Owen. I would, really, had I known you were alive." She went on in a rush. "Then, three days ago, my brother, Jürgen, told me he'd heard you were alive and had just gone to Tokyo. I couldn't believe it, but he said it was true, so I told him I had to go to you. Jürgen told me not to. He said it would be too dangerous, but I made him take me to Tokyo. I made him bring me to you!"

"Anna," Owen said in a tone of exasperation. "Who told you I was dead? And who got you out of Korea? Just what do you mean by 'our people'?"

Owen felt her stiffen slightly in surprise. Then she pulled out of his arms and stepped back.

"You still don't know, do you?"

"Know what?"

"Oh Owen, I've got so much to tell you."

Then, suddenly, she turned from side to side, peering into the fog-shrouded blackness as if she had heard something. Owen followed her gaze, holding his breath and listening intently, but he could sense no one else around.

"We can't talk here," she said after a moment. "It's too dangerous for us to risk being discovered together."

"What are you talking about?"

"I'm staying in an apartment in Roppongi. Come there tomorrow night and I'll tell you everything."

"But Anna—"

"Here, I've written down the address for you." She pulled a folded piece of paper from the pocket of her raincoat and shoved it into his hand. "Come after dark, and make sure you aren't followed."

Owen opened his mouth to speak, but she cut him off again.

"Trust me, Owen, you're in great danger. I will be too if certain people discover I've contacted you. I'll tell you all about it tomorrow night."

She started to leave then hesitated. She turned back to him, took hold of his lapels, pulled him to her. She kissed him tenderly. Then she turned and dissolved into the mist.

CHAPTER TWENTY

Owen pressed the button by the door of the apartment at the address Anna had given him. A day had passed since their brief meeting in Ueno Park, and his heart quickened in anticipation of seeing her again. After a moment, the door opened and he faced a tall, powerfully built blond man with hawk-like eyes and a rugged jaw.

"Hello," the man said, putting out his hand and smiling warmly. "You must be Owen. I'm Jürgen Norgaard." He kept his deep voice barely above a whisper, but his grip was firm and sincere. "Please come in," he said with a trace of urgency.

After Owen stepped through the door, Jürgen edged past him and leaned into the hall, cautiously looking one way then the other. Drawing back inside, he closed the door and locked it.

"I can't tell you how glad I am to finally meet you," he said in a more relaxed tone, his Danish accent more evident now that he spoke up. "Anna's told me so much about you." Throwing an arm over Owen's shoulder as if they had known each other for years,

Jürgen guided him towards the living room. "She'll be out in just a moment. You know how women are." He smiled again.

Owen looked around and couldn't help taking in a breath. The apartment was immense by Japanese standards and designed to appear even larger with a cathedral ceiling that peaked high above them and a carpeted floor that sank by levels to a smaller, more intimate area in the center. A large, stone fireplace dominated the far wall, its chimney reaching upwards toward the peak of the ceiling. A fire crackled in it, warming the sunken area.

The room was decorated in a tasteful blend of Asian and modern European styles. Ink drawings and watercolor paintings adorned the walls, and elegant vases graced highly polished side tables. In the sunken area, plush leather furniture was arranged around a low, Japanese-style table.

"This is quite a place," Owen said, knowing it must be worth millions, given the cost of real estate in Tokyo.

"Thank you, but it's not mine," Jürgen said. "It belongs to some distant cousins on my mother's side of the family. They don't spend much time in Tokyo and let me use it whenever business brings me to town."

"Do you come here often?"

"Not as often as—"

Just then Anna entered the room looking radiant.

"Owen, I'm so glad you came," she said.

She hurried over and greeted him in European fashion, taking him by the shoulders and kissing him briefly on each cheek. Then she drew back and looked into his eyes. To Owen's delight, her formality melted away. Sliding her hands from his shoulders to around his waist, she drew close and laid her head on his shoulder. Owen put his arms around her, and they stood that way for several seconds, holding each other without speaking.

"Ah hum," Jürgen said, clearing his throat loudly.

Reluctantly, Anna pulled away.

"I know you kids haven't seen each other for a long time," Jürgen said, "but we have a lot of important things to talk about. I think there will be plenty of time for you to catch up on old times later, yes?" Then turning to Anna, "Perhaps when your big brother isn't standing around feeling awkward." He raised an eyebrow teasingly and Anna blushed.

"Come sit down," Anna said, taking Owen's hand and leading him down to one of the sofas in the sunken living room. Anna sat down beside him, holding his hand in both of hers, and Jürgen took a seat in an armchair across the table from them. Momentarily overtaken by a sense of awkwardness, they chatted about casual topics for several minutes.

The Norgaards were charming and strikingly attractive. Jürgen, dressed in wool slacks and turtleneck sweater, looked the archetypal Viking. He was at least six and a half feet tall, lean, and heavily muscled. Anna, nearly six feet in stature herself, was clearly his sister. They both had the same pale blond hair, sturdy jaws, and aquiline noses, though Jürgen's eyes were a flat green, lacking the blue flecks that gave Anna's their opalescence.

Anna must have been at least forty years old by now, but she could easily have passed for thirty and was undeniably more beautiful than she had been in her early twenties. The sturdy, angular features that had looked too strong on her young girl's face seemed to suit her now. Her hair was stylishly cut, and she was immaculately dressed in wool, cashmere, and elegant jewelry.

She and Jürgen were obviously wealthy and cultured. Strangely, or so it seemed to Owen, they were treating him as if he were a beloved, but long-lost member of their family, though they were veritable strangers.

"Okay, so what's going on?" Owen finally said, his voice betraying his growing impatience. "Both of you said you have a lot of things to tell me. So tell me."

Jürgen and Anna looked at each other and sighed deeply. "Where do we start?" Anna said to Jürgen.

"How about with what happened in Korea?" Owen said. "How did you get out, and what am I doing here in Tokyo?"

"It's probably better to start with the last question," Jürgen said. "That's the one that's most important for you to understand because of the danger involved."

"What danger?"

"Owen," Anna began gently, "you are at the epicenter of an international struggle of epic proportion. It may be hard to believe, but there exists in this world, behind the scenes and concealed from sight, a network of secret organizations that work together to control the more visible institutions of power. Someone in one of those organizations—we don't yet know who—has had you brought here in an effort to manipulate you to their advantage."

"Oh, come on," Owen said. "Certainly, you're not serious. A network of secret organizations running the world behind the scenes?"

"Anna may have overstated the facts when she said we control things," Jürgen said. "We don't run the world, but we do influence a lot of events by working through people we have placed in key positions in governments and other powerful institutions."

"We?" Owen said, raising an eyebrow. "So you and Anna belong to one of these organizations?"

"Yes," Anna said, squeezing his hand more tightly and holding his gaze with hers. "We are Keepers of the Covenant, Owen, members of God's one true church. And though you have never known it, you are one of us. At least, you are in a sense. You hold a special position, a unique station in our society. It's a legacy you inherited from your father."

"What's my father got to do with this?" Owen thought of his disturbing meeting with Jack Fowler and squeezed Anna's hands hard in reflex. She stiffened and grimaced slightly, but didn't pull away.

Seeing her flinch, Owen took a deep breath and forced himself to relax. "Maybe you'd better start from the beginning."

Anna relaxed too, obviously relieved that Owen had loosened his grip. "I'll get us some tea," she said. "If you want it from the beginning, it's going to take a while." She kissed him lightly on the cheek and got up to leave.

Jürgen kept his eyes on Owen as Anna headed for the kitchen. Then he began speaking in a professorial tone. "Owen, history, as you have learned it, particularly the history of Western civilization since the time of Christ, is a sham." He hesitated, waiting for a reaction, but Owen only nodded, signaling he intended to hear him out without interrupting. "To be more precise," Jürgen continued, "it is a history that is, at best, half right. It is a chronicle written, first, by the victors of a power struggle within the early Christian church, and later, by people aware only of surface events without understanding, or even knowing, the machinations behind the scenes that caused those events."

The Dane paused gathering his thoughts then continued. "You have been taught that Christianity began when a lowly carpenter from Nazareth revealed he was the Son of God, the Messiah foretold in Old Testament prophecies, and set out with his flock of twelve disciples to bring salvation to the world through faith and love. Well, the facts tell a different story. Jesus was not a lowly carpenter, and the village of Nazareth didn't even exist before the third century of the Christian era. Actually, the roots of Christianity reach back to a group of ascetics who lived in a community called Qumran, located on the Dead Sea."

"The Essenes," Owen said. Owen had read about the Essenes in his undergraduate studies at Oxford. He had learned they were an obscure sect of Jewish mystics and that they had written the *Dead Sea Scrolls*, but beyond that, little was known about them.

"Right," Jürgen said. "Historians once believed the Essenes were pacifists who had withdrawn from society to live a monastic life of contemplation, but nothing could be further from the truth. They were, instead, a radical messianic movement, a sect dedicated to throwing off the yoke of foreign oppression and reforming Judaism, which had become moribund under a Pharisaic priesthood that was collaborating with the Roman occupation. The Essenes were watching for the Messiah's arrival and cultivating a revolutionary movement to restore the House of David to the throne of Israel."

"It sounds more like you're describing the Zealots," Owen said.

"Very good, Owen," Jürgen said, nodding in appreciation. "I'm impressed by your knowledge of history. Yes, the group you know of as 'Zealots' were dedicated to the same goals. In fact, many Essenes were Zealots, or 'Zadokites'—'Sons of Zadok'— as they called themselves. But the Zadokites were merely the Essenes' military arm. They were a guerilla organization that terrorized the Romans and goaded their own countrymen in an effort to raise an insurrection that they hoped would lead to Jewish independence. The Essenes, on the other hand, were the political and spiritual force behind the Zadokites. They recruited, educated, trained, and blessed members into the holy struggle. You might say the Zadokites were to the Essenes as the Irish Republican Army has been to Sien Fein in the struggle for Irish independence."

"Okay," Owen said, "so how did this radical messianic movement start Christianity?"

"That's easy," Jürgen said. They found the Messiah. John the Essene—history remembers him as 'John the Baptist'—recruited his cousin, a young aristocrat named Jesus bar Joseph, into the movement. Jesus was a direct descendent in the royal line of David, and it didn't take the Essenes long to recognize the signs that the fulfillment of prophesy lay in this young man. He was the rightful king of the Jews and was obviously blessed with great spiritual power."

Jürgen paused again then took a different tack. "Owen, have you ever wondered why the Gospels, at least the ones you know of, are mysteriously silent about Jesus's life over the years between his first visit to the Temple at age twelve and the beginning of his 'ministry', as modern Christians call it, at age thirty? It's because he was in Qumran studying scripture and Essenic doctrine. It was only after years of study and spiritual development did his cousin, John, formally initiate him into the movement with the Essenic rite of baptism."

He hesitated, noting Owen's look of surprise.

"Yes, baptism was an Essenic rite before it was a Christian sacrament, but the Essenes did it only in living water, that is, a moving stream, just as the one true church does it today. After being baptized into the order, Jesus founded the Nazarean Party, a revolutionary movement in Jerusalem. The term 'Nazarean' was later mistranslated to 'Nazarene' and interpreted to mean he had come from Nazareth." He waved a hand dismissively.

"Anyway, building on this political foundation, Jesus began publicly preaching religious reform while secretly assembling an underground network. He did this through a group of twelve disciples that he recruited to be his core revolutionary cell. This first twelve-member council symbolized the twelve tribes of Israel and served directly under the Messiah's leadership. Their plan was to establish similar twelve-member cells in each of those twelve tribes, and each member of those cells would recruit cells of their own, and so on."

This caught Owen's attention. As a former soldier trained in unconventional warfare, he recognized the classic system of compartmented organization, a method guerrillas and terrorists often use to maintain security. Each member would know only the fellow members of his own cell and one person in any cell he founded beneath him. That way, if he were captured, there would be few people he could compromise, even under torture.

"So what happened?" Owen said. "How was the movement disrupted? And how did a revolutionary movement turn into a religion?"

"Well, you already know the answer to the first question, at least, part of it," Jürgen said. "The New Testament Gospels are a flawed historical record, but they do provide some of the essential facts—Jesus's core cell was penetrated. He was betrayed, arrested, and crucified. But that misfortune, disastrous as it was, did not destroy the movement. When Jesus departed the scene, leadership of the House of David fell to his brother James. As for becoming a religion, well, the movement never was secular or purely political. It began as a Jewish reform movement in Qumran, and it continued to be a blend of religion and politics for several decades. You see, despite everything else, Jesus was indeed the Messiah, the Christ. He was the fulfillment of prophesy in the spiritual sense as well as in political terms. During his long years of study and spiritual development, something happened to him that had never happened to any other Jew. He came to know God—he didn't just know about God; he *knew* God. And because he had come to know God, he knew how to guide others to direct knowledge of God. He passed that knowledge on to some, though not all, of his disciples."

"Hey, wait a minute," Owen said, straightening in sudden realization. "You're talking about Gnosticism!"

"Exactly," Jürgen said with a smile. "At least, that is the name the Hellenic world used to describe the true faith."

Owen had learned about Gnosticism in school as well. Named for the Greek word '*gnosis*' or 'knowledge', it was a movement within the early Church that claimed Jesus had taught a secret doctrine to a select group of his disciples who had thereafter preserved that knowledge and passed it secretly to subsequent generations.

Just then Anna returned carrying a tray laden with a teapot, cups, and pastries. She placed the tray on the low table and began filling cups.

"Your Owen is very well read," Jürgen said, smiling.

"Of course he is," she said. "I told you he was extraordinarily intelligent. You don't think he would be 'my Owen' otherwise, do you?" She grinned and winked at Owen, but he was too focused on what Jürgen had said to notice.

"Are you trying to tell me this secret organization that you claim is manipulating world events is some kind of group of Gnostic Christians?" He said.

"Not just 'some kind of group,'" Jürgen said. "It is a network of twelve great houses directly descended from the twelve revolutionary cells Jesus and James established among the tribes of Israel."

"But that's impossible. The early Church may have been Jewish, but it couldn't have been Gnostic. The Gnostics didn't begin to appear until a hundred years or more into the Christian era. They were a heretical movement, one the Church struggled to suppress, and it eventually succeeded. By the mid fifth century, the so called 'Gnostics' were gone."

"Heresy is an ugly word," Jürgen said, his smile fading. "Evil people use it to persecute others and deny their own followers knowledge of God. We are the Church, the true Church. The Pauline church that rose up in Rome is a false movement, a product of fraud and deception."

"Pauline church?"

"Owen," Anna said, hoping to defuse the tension she could sense rising between the men. "I know this is hard for you to accept." She sat down beside him again. "That's because everything you've learned about Christianity is based on a series of New Testament books written or rewritten by Saul of Tarsus and his followers."

"You mean the Apostle Paul," Owen said.

"Yes, that is what the Roman church called him," she said, so that is how he is known today. But, in truth, he was Saul of Tarsus, a Herodian—a cousin and follower of the puppet king Herod Antipas—who persecuted James and his followers."

"But that was before his conversion, before his vision on the road to Damascus."

"Ah, yes, his conversion," Jürgen said, rolling his eyes. "That was a staged affair, Owen. You see, when the Romans and their half-Jewish puppet dynasty failed to suppress the Christian revolutionary movement by overt means, they resorted to subterfuge. They had Saul pretend to receive a miraculous vision of Jesus and stage a conversion to the very sect he was trying to wipe out. It was a brilliant ploy. He changed his name to Paul, returned to Jerusalem, and tried to convince James and the House of David's Council of Twelve that, not only had he become a Christian, but that, because he had seen Jesus in a vision, his authority to interpret Christ's teachings was greater than theirs, greater than the people who had known Jesus personally, greater even than James and other members of Jesus's own family. All the while, he was trying to destroy the movement from within. He was gathering information on its members and reporting directly to the Roman procurator." Jürgen took a cup of tea from the tray.

"Well," he continued, "that put James and the Council in a quandary. They weren't taken in by the likes of Saul, but they were afraid to overtly oppose him. He was a powerful man—he was Herod's cousin and a Roman citizen. So they came up with a ruse of their own. They pretended to accept both his conversion and his authority to preach, only not in Jerusalem. James sent him north to spread the Nazarean movement to the Hellenic Gentiles. He and the Council believed Saul could do little harm if kept away from the cells that were doing the revolutionary work in Palestine."

"Well, okay," Owen said. "But doesn't Paul's behavior in the years that followed prove his conversion was genuine? I mean, look at the record. He traveled all over Asia-Minor preaching Christianity and founding churches."

"Yes he did," Anna said. "But he didn't preach true Christianity. He couldn't have, even had he wanted to, because he never received the true teachings. Instead, he manufactured a doctrine that perverted Jesus's message, creating a mythology fashioned from Mithraism, a pagan cult popular in Tarsus, his home. In Saul's teachings, Jesus was transformed from the revolutionary spiritual leader he truly was into a deified human sacrifice, and Saul taught his followers to celebrate that sacrifice by symbolically eating his flesh and drinking his blood. He taught these things to subvert the true faith and, thereby, defang the Nazarean independence movement it fueled."

"It was another marvelous ploy," Jürgen said. "Whereas the Nazarean Christians in Jerusalem were teaching followers to throw off the yoke of pagan Rome and restore God's chosen kingdom of Israel, Saul claimed Jesus's kingdom was not of this world. According to Saul, Jesus wanted everyone to 'render unto Cesar.' Whereas James and his followers walked in Jesus's footsteps, employing methods of spiritual development he taught the few devotees who were advanced enough to grasp them, Paul taught that simple faith and ritual were the keys to salvation. Anyone could be reborn simply for the asking. It was a brilliant stratagem, one designed to build a counterfeit movement that would quickly eclipse the true faith in size and popularity."

"So, why didn't James try to stop him," Owen asked.

"He did," Jürgen said. "That much is revealed even in the Pauline Testament. Several years after James sent Saul into the Gentile world, stories of his false teachings began to filter back, so James recalled him to Jerusalem. When Saul returned, James confronted him. They had an altercation that turned violent and Saul fled, only to return with a mob of Herodian loyalists who seized James and stoned him to death. That incident, in turn, triggered a spontaneous Nazarean uprising against Saul. They caught him and were about to kill him when the Roman army intervened and took him into custody. Unaware that he was the procurator's spy, the soldiers arrested him for inciting the insurrection. It was at that point that Saul invoked his Roman citizenship and secured his release."

"Owen," Anna said, "you need to understand how Saul's actions set off a chain of events that ultimately destroyed the Kingdom of Israel and drove the true faith into hiding." Her tone was no longer gentle. Her eyes bore into Owen's and her jaws were tight. "The uprising the Herodians caused when they killed James did not end with Saul's departure. The Romans put down the mob that rose up against Saul, so they thought they had put the incident behind them. But word of James's murder and Saul's release spread through the city enraging not only members of the Nazarean underground, but other Jews as well.

"Over the next several years a spirit of resentment festered and grew beyond the reach and strategic control of the Christian revolutionary councils that Jesus and James had planted within the twelve tribes. As the movement grew beyond Nazarean control, citizens became bolder in challenging Roman authority and terrorist attacks grew ever more frequent."

Her voice grew strident. "Finally, the Romans reacted violently. In 70 C.E., the Roman army attacked in force, razing the temple and destroying the city of Jerusalem. Well aware of where the roots of the insurrection lay, they then marched on Qumran and killed every man, woman, and child who lived there. Fortunately, the twelve revolutionary councils that resided with the tribes survived the carnage and fled Palestine. They fanned out, spreading the true faith, first across the Middle East and North Africa and later into Europe and Asia. It was around that time that history began to take notice of the 'Gnostic Christians' as you call them."

"The only problem," Jürgen said, "was that, by then, history was being written by the Pauline church in Rome and its satellite congregations that Saul had founded throughout Gentile Asia-Minor. They depicted us as heretics, people who had deviated from Christ's message of peace and submission. But, actually, they were afraid of us because we knew the true teachings and they did not. They were terrified their followers would find out how little they really knew, how much Saul and the bishops of Rome who came after him had fabricated. Indeed, many of their followers did find out how empty the Pauline doctrines were, and they converted to the true faith, even as they remained in Pauline congregations. But the Paulines preached against us and persecuted anyone who let it be known they had received knowledge of God not doled out by their own pompous clergy."

"Well, this story is all very interesting," Owen said, unable to keep the skepticism out of his voice. "But it doesn't square with the historical record, and I mean secular history, not just the New Testament. If Paul's version of Christianity began as a Herodian scheme to subvert a Jewish revolutionary movement, why did the Romans persecute Christians so aggressively throughout the Church's first three centuries? I'd say that feeding Christians to lions is a pretty harsh way to treat followers of a movement founded by one's own spy."

"Yes it is," Jürgen said, smiling grimly. "No one ever said the Roman emperors were reliable allies. But the blood of those poor dupes who laid down their lives in the name of a mythical Christ was on Saul's hands as much as it was on Caesar's.

"When the explosive growth of the Jewish revolutionary movement revealed that Saul's scheme to undermine it had failed, Rome had no more use for Saul's popular Jesus cult. They ordered him to disband it. But Rome had created a monster in Saul and his followers. Saul had become quite comfortable in his role as revered spiritual leader, and he wasn't about to tell his followers, many of whom lived in miserable poverty, that their blind faith in the myth he had created would not bring them fabulous rewards in heaven. So he continued to preach and Rome turned against him."

Jürgen edged forward in his chair, his eyes blazing. Owen felt an urge to lean away from the big Dane, even though there was a table between them.

"For the next two hundred years," Jürgen said, his voice hard, "Rome persecuted Pauline Christians even as Paulines, themselves, persecuted followers of the true faith. Then, early in the fourth century, things got a lot worse for us when the Roman emperor, Constantine, attempted to reunify his splintering empire under the banner of Pauline Christianity. When that happened, not only did it make the Paulines safe from further persecution, but the Bishop of Rome then had the might of the Roman legions behind him. With Constantine's blessing, he called a conference where he and the other Pauline bishops canonized Paul's writings as Holy Scripture, along with altered versions of several other texts, and vowed to destroy all record of the true faith. From that day forward, they began hunting down everyone who professed knowledge of God."

Jürgen's voice was raised now, and his eyes burned with a ferocity that Owen could feel almost on a physical level. He turned to Anna for a moment of respite, but saw the same fire in her eyes as well.

"The Paulines launched a pogrom throughout Christendom," she said. "They seized every true Christian they could lay their hands on and forced them to recant. Those who would not were put to the sword. They destroyed our scriptures wherever they found them and tried to erase our very existence from history. But they failed! We were driven underground, forced to teach and worship in secret, but we survived!"

"No thanks to Rome!" Jürgen said. "Oh, we tried to live like normal human beings. Again and again over the centuries, branches of the Covenant surfaced and tried to spread the true faith in the open. But did they let us? Did they embrace us with the charity and love they themselves professed? No! They mounted crusades and inquisitions that exterminated God's children by fire and sword. The Valentinians, the Manicheans, the Montanists, the Cathars, just to name a few—all murdered wherever Paulines tracked them down!"

Jürgen suddenly seemed to realize he had been yelling. He stopped and visibly struggled to bring himself under control, staring at the far wall, and the veins in his neck pulsing wildly. Anna too looked flushed, though not as much as her brother. Owen watched them, unsure of whether they meant to continue.

After a couple of moments, Anna spoke more calmly. "That's why we move in secret now and try to control powerful institutions wherever we can. It's for our own protection. We've learned to keep an invisible hand on every sword in order to keep its blade off our own necks."

With that, Anna and Jürgen fell silent. Jürgen seemed to have spent his venom. He sat back in his chair, and both siblings now appeared lost in thought.

"Okay," Owen said after a minute, shaking off his tension with a heavy sigh, "so where do my father and I fit into this?"

"Your family's ties to us, Owen, stretch back to the first century." Jürgen's professorial tone had returned, though his deep voice was gravelly and he sounded tired. "When James was killed, Joseph of Arimathea ascended to lead the House of David."

"You mean the Joseph of Arimathea that gave up his tomb for Christ after the crucifixion?" Owen said.

"The same," Jürgen said, nodding. "He was another member of the House of David, a cousin of Jesus and James. When James died, there were no more direct heirs to the throne of Israel, so the Council of Twelve elected Joseph to lead them. As it was, he inherited a revolutionary movement that was spinning out of control. The night of his rise to leadership, his 'ascension', as we call it, he had an apocalyptic vision that revealed the coming disaster. He foresaw the destruction of Jerusalem and the temple, the twelve great houses driven to the far corners of the earth, and the extended Pauline persecution."

Jürgen edged forward again. "In this vision, God told him he was to take the House of David to a wild and uncivilized island in the distant north. There, he would find a powerful warrior who would embrace Christianity and pledge himself and his descendants to defend the true faith. This warrior would serve as Arbiter between the great houses, an impartial mediator who would maintain contact between them and adjudicate their disputes as they dispersed around the globe. In every generation from then until the end of days, there would be an Arbiter, a direct blood descendant of the first one."

The Dane's green eyes locked on Owen's.

"After the Roman attack in 70 C.E., the prophesy in Joseph's vision began to unfold. When the House of David fled Palestine, Joseph led his followers to Britain. There they landed on the southwest coast and built a church near what is now the village of Glastonbury. And the first warrior they converted there was a powerful Celtic chieftain named Gwilym ap Hywel. He became the first Arbiter, the progenitor of a line of Arbiters that has been unbroken for nearly two thousand years."

Jürgen stopped and looked at Anna. For the first time, Owen thought he detected indecision in the Viking's rugged face. Anna turned to Owen and again took his hand in both of hers.

"Owen," she said softly, "Gwilym ap Hywel was your ancestor. He was the first Arbiter, and scores of others have followed him. Your father was an Arbiter." She hesitated, peering into his pale eyes and squeezing his hand tightly. Then she looked at Jürgen as if unsure whether to continue.

He nodded solemnly.

Turning back, she hesitated a moment longer then said, "Now, Owen, you are the Arbiter."

CHAPTER TWENTY-ONE

Owen didn't know what to say. He tried to imagine his father as a secret arbiter and defender of some obscure branch of Christianity. It was a difficult picture to grasp. He would never have described his father as religious. Not that he was particularly worldly, either. He led an almost monastic life, focusing all his energy on work except for what little he devoted to Owen. So why hadn't he told him about this?

"I don't understand," he finally managed to say. "If my father was a Gnostic Christian, why didn't he raise me as one too?"

"We don't raise children in the faith as Paulines do," Jürgen said. "For us, religion is a matter of personal choice, not one of parental programming. And since our tradition embraces secrecy so strongly, our children often don't learn about the Covenant until they come of age. Since your father was an Arbiter, it's even less surprising that he didn't tell you about it. Not all Arbiters accept the true faith. Most do, of course, and your father did, but it isn't essential."

"How could it not be essential for an Arbiter to embrace the religion he is sworn to defend?"

"The essence of the Arbiter's role is objective mediation," Jürgen said. "It's an honorable service Arbiters have provided through the ages. We don't insist you become a Christian anymore than God insists you accept his wisdom. We only expect you to fulfill your destiny. That is something God will not let you escape, whether you accept the faith or not."

Owen wasn't sure he liked the sound of that. "So this is some kind of diplomatic job?" he said.

"Partly," Jürgen said, "but it's a lot more than that. Over the ages, as the great houses separated and became powerful, they grew increasingly suspicious of each other. They became territorial and competitive, occasionally even combative. Your job is to mediate disputes between them, guiding them to consensus agreements whenever possible. When consensus cannot be reached, you adjudicate the dispute and issue a ruling. If the leaders of any house do not accept your ruling, you impose it on them by force."

"By force?" Owen blurted. "Now, how in the h—" He bit back the curse, remembering he was in the company of people very passionate about religion. "How would I do that?" he began again. "How could I possibly force my will on leaders of an organization I can't even see, an organization you say has people in powerful positions all over the world?"

"It's not as hard as you might think," Jürgen said. "The great houses almost always accept the Arbiter's ruling. After all, the Arbiter's commission is spiritually ordained, so his decision is considered the will of God. In the few cases that one house or another has tried to defy the Arbiter, the other houses have promptly banded with him to bring the rogue leaders in line, providing the necessary intelligence and soldiers to serve under the Arbiter's command until the issue is resolved."

"You've got to be kidding! Are you saying Arbiters have led secret armies and waged secret wars?"

"More like commando raids in most cases. But several Arbiters have led the great houses in military operations to defend the faith from external threats."

Owen pondered these revelations for a moment, staring into a cup of tea that had gone cold in his hands. "So what happened in Korea?" he said, looking up.

"Yi Chung-hae's training camp was a Covenant refuge point," Anna said, "one of several scattered around the globe. We hold these points as neutral ground for Covenant Keepers, places where we gather and cast inter-house disputes aside to take care of business of one kind or another. The purpose of Yi's camp was to train guardians, soldiers of the Covenant who protect the great houses.

"So you're one of these 'guardians'?"

"Well no, not everyone who attended Yi's camp was a guardian. Prominent Covenant Keepers often send their children to camps like this as part of their preparation for life in our society, similar to the way British aristocrats send their kids to boarding schools and some affluent Americans send their kids to military schools."

"Prominent Covenant Keepers?" Owen mused.

Anna hesitated, blushing.

"Our father was a member of the House of Zebulun's Council of Twelve," Jürgen said. "Anna was twenty-three when we sent her to camp. She had been in spiritual training for five years and was close to being ready for baptism into the Covenant. Had she not been taken and violated in the betrayal, she would probably now be married to an influential Covenant Keeper. As it is, no man in our society will ever marry her."

"I am considered unclean," she said quietly.

Owen thought of Myongsan-ni and his cheeks burned with guilt. For a moment he could not bring himself to meet Anna's eyes, but when he did, she looked at him without anger or shame.

"What do you mean by 'the betrayal'?" he asked Jürgen without turning away from her.

"The neutrality of the refuge point was violated," Jürgen said. "We had situated this camp in the remote mountains just inside North Korea because the location was so easy to isolate from people outside our circle—no adventurous tourists or outdoorsmen to worry about. Payoff the local commissars and military commanders and we had the vale and surrounding hills to ourselves. The only problem was, we were vulnerable to traitors within the Covenant. Anyone willing to betray us could inform people above the local cronies that we were there, and that is what happened. Pak Je-man sold Yi and Anna to the North Korean district authorities because he believed they both had gained influence over you, and he resented it."

"Influence over me? Why in the hell would that matter?" Owen said, no longer caring whether he cursed.

"It mattered," Anna said, "because you were the son of the Arbiter, the heir apparent to the legacy. The Arbiter is the single most powerful man in the Covenant. His decisions can literally change the course of history and determine the destinies of the great houses. Knowing that, the leaders of every house are chronically fearful that the Arbiter may be biased in favor of other houses at their expense.

"When you turned eighteen, your father sent you to Yi for training to begin preparing you for your future duties. All of us at camp were notified that you were coming and sternly warned about two things: First, you had not yet been awakened to the Covenant, so we were to say nothing about it around you. Second, we were not to violate refuge point neutrality by fraternizing with you. The Arbiter must maintain his objectivity—he must not become too friendly with members of any particular house.

"That's why Pak became so angry when he saw our relationship developing, his anger festered and boiled until he finally exploded.

That's why he had the refuge point destroyed, had Sabumnim killed, let me be taken and... and..." Her voice wavered then trailed off.

Owen flushed with rage as he thought about Pak Je-man. The Korean was the most despicable man he had ever met. And he was even worse than what Anna described, Owen decided, remembering what she had told him about Pak back at camp. He didn't compromise Yi and Anna just because he believed they had violated neutrality. He did it in a jealous rage born of lust and frustration. He did it because he hated Owen and wanted Anna.

Owen noticed that Anna said nothing about Pak's advances on her and wondered whether she had told her brother about it. He wondered, too, if Jürgen or anyone else knew about what she had done that night in Owen's hooch. He doubted it.

After a minute, Anna found her voice again. It was choked with emotion. "Oh Owen, I was so foolish. It was entirely my fault. I should have stayed away from you like they told me to. I tried, really. You remember how hard I tried to keep you away, don't you? But I just couldn't help letting you get close. I was falling in love."

She leaned against Owen's shoulder and began sobbing openly. Feeling awkward, he put his arm around her. "It's all right," he said, unable to think of anything else to say. "It's all right."

For several moments, the men were silent. Then Jürgen said, "Well, all of that is in the past." His voice was acrid with grief and bitterness. "What is really important, now that you finally know about the Covenant and your legacy, is that we find the scroll."

"Scroll?"

"Yes, the *Apocalypse of Joseph*. Joseph of Arimathea recorded his apocalyptic vision on a scroll. Later, when Gwilym ap Hywel embraced the faith and became the first Arbiter, Joseph presented him the scroll as a symbol of his authority. The *Apocalypse* has since been transcribed many times and translated into multiple languages—it is part of our Holy Scripture—but the original scroll has remained in the hands of every Arbiter from Gwilym onwards, passed from father to son over scores of generations. Its value is incalculable, both as an object of antiquity and as a symbol of power. Should anyone else get hold of the scroll, they could claim your legacy. They could claim the title of Arbiter and alter the course of history."

Owen's eyes opened wide as the pieces started falling into place. *"Did your father keep anything unusual at home?"* he remembered Jim Shelton probing. *"Something very old, some antique kind of thing. Maybe an old scroll? Or maybe a short metal tube, something like that?"*

"There are people who would kill to get this scroll, Owen," Anna said, breaking his reverie. "You've got to find it and make sure it's safe."

"I guess that is why Nomura told me I was in danger," Owen said under his breath.

"What?" Jürgen said loudly. "Has someone else talked to you about the scroll?"

"Well, not exactly. An old Yakuza named Nomura Eizo had me picked up and delivered to his apartment yesterday evening. He didn't say anything about a scroll, but he warned me I was in danger and urged me to go home."

Anna sat up straight, pulling out of Owen's embrace. She and Jürgen looked at each other, their eyes wide in alarm. "Owen, you've got to stay away from that man," she said, her voice suddenly fearful. "He's extremely dangerous. I don't want anything to happen to you."

"Nomura was your father's sworn enemy," Jürgen said. "After the Second World War, your father collected evidence against him for the War Crimes Tribunal and had him imprisoned for unspeakable atrocities in Japanese occupied Manchuria. But they couldn't keep him in jail—Nomura was too rich, too well connected. He managed to get the charges against him dismissed before the case ever went to trial. When he got out, he swore he'd see your father dead and plotted to get him the rest of your dad's life."

Jürgen gripped the arms of his chair. "To make matters worse, Nomura knows about the Covenant. He had eyes and ears all over Japan, still does. He stalked your father like prey and eventually found out about us. If he knows you're back in Japan then he must be the one who had you brought here. He must be after the scroll!"

"But that doesn't make sense," Owen said. "He told me to go home. He practically begged me to leave, said I wouldn't be safe here."

"And did you tell him you'd go?" Jürgen said, his tone cynical.

"Well no, but—"

"Of course not! And he knew you wouldn't. He just said that to gain your trust. Don't you see? The *Apocalypse of Joseph* has been missing ever since your father's death. No one even knows where to look for it. You are the key, Owen, you alone. Only you can find it, and Nomura knows that. So to get it, he has to get close to you."

"I don't know," Owen said. "Nomura's a gangster, a Yakuza *oyabun*, but it didn't seem like he was trying to get anything from me. He just kept urging me to leave Japan and wouldn't tell me why except that he owed it to my father to keep me safe."

"Owen!" Anna cried in exasperation, turning to face him squarely. "For God's sake, put two and two together—Nomura Eizo is the man who had your father killed!"

CHAPTER TWENTY-TWO

Owen spent the better part of Sunday wandering the streets and parks of Tokyo, though he could not have recalled afterward all the places he had been. He wasn't touring the sights. He was walking to think, to try and sort out everything Anna and Jürgen had told him the night before.

Their story was a lot to swallow. A sect of Gnostics had escaped the fourth century Roman purge of the Christian Church and survived secretly into the twenty-first century. Gnostic groups had spread around the globe, penetrating governments and other powerful institutions to safeguard their interests. They had influenced world events, even causing wars and determining their outcomes. The very history of civilization since the time of Christ, at least as Owen had learned it, was in question.

But the most difficult thing to accept was the Norgaards' claim that his father had led a double life. He had secretly been a Gnostic Christian all the years Owen had known him. No, it was even more fantastic than that. He had been some kind of arbiter, an intermediary, judge, and enforcer among the leaders of

Gnostic Christianity. As much as Owen hated to admit it, the picture of Rhys Powell as a Gnostic Arbiter seemed to fit Jack Fowler's theory that he had been involved in some kind of cult with that State Department guy, Michael Dunross. Worse than that, the Norgaards said Owen's father had been murdered, just as Fowler had said.

"One of Nomura's henchmen hit him over the head," Jürgen had said. "They ransacked the house then set fire to it to cover their tracks." When Owen said that scenario was unimaginable, Jürgen had responded, "Do you know why your dad's colleagues called him the "mace"?" Owen only stared. "He got that name during the war, when he was a guerilla leader on Mindanao. Whenever a local peasant collaborated with the Japanese, Rhys Powell would appear in the night and cave in the stoolie's head with a traditional Filipino war club to send a message to the other locals. It became his trademark. After the war, he left the same 'calling card', so to speak, when he enforced Covenant discipline. Nomura knew all that. He set up the murder to look like a revenge killing to Covenant members and an accident to outsiders."

Owen was flabbergasted. Remembering the gentle, soft-spoken man with whom he had grown up, this story simply defied belief. But why would the Norgaards lie to him? What possible reason would they have to make up such a fantastic tale? Such an odd pair—they were essentially strangers who had come out of nowhere, yet they acted is if he were part of their family.

Of course, he had known Anna that summer so many years ago. At least, he thought he had known her. In fact, he had thought he loved her, and last night she said she had fallen in love with him. But now, seeing his memories through adult eyes, he realized what he had felt in Korea was probably no more than a boyhood crush. He wondered how she had really felt about him.

Whatever her true feelings had been in 1982, now, nearly twenty years later, she literally materializes out of the mist and introduces him to this older brother. Together they tell him that history is a sham and his father was not the man Owen thought he knew. On the surface, such claims struck him as absolutely absurd. How could they possibly expect a serious student of history, not to mention a professor of international relations, to believe such a story?

Then a pang of guilt cut through him as an image of Myongsan-ni flashed into his mind. There was no denying that that tragedy had happened. In one respect, he thought, he ought to be thankful. After all those years of thinking he had lost Anna, after all the guilt he had suffered, she was back and didn't seem to hold him responsible for failing to protect her. In fact, she treated him even more warmly now than she had in Korea. It was like he had a second chance with her.

He wasn't sure how he felt about that. He was still powerfully attracted to her. Despite all the years that had passed, his pulse still raced whenever she caught his eye in her opalescent gaze. He had laid awake most of the night thinking about her, and when he finally did fall asleep, images of her naked body straddling him in Korea collided and tangled with visions of her present, more sophisticated persona, spinning out an erotic collage that denied him rest.

Yes, I want this woman, he admitted to himself as memories of those dreams began to arouse him anew, *but... but what about Elaine?*

Above all, despite the guilt it caused him, Owen couldn't help suspecting the Norgaards' motives. In Owen's experience, people who try to get strangers to swallow improbable tales are usually after money. He didn't have any, so what could they be after? Could it be this scroll? Such a thing would be worth a lot, but if that is what they are trying to get then it must exist. And if the scroll exists then at least part of their story must be true. If so, what else?

Once again, Jim Shelton's words echoed in Owen's memory: *Did your father keep anything unusual at home? Maybe an old scroll?* It seemed to fit. Then he remembered Shelton saying something else: *Before you left for Korea, did you see anyone unusual watching your house?* That question had always given Owen a strange feeling. Now, suddenly, it made sense, too. The Norgaards seemed absolutely certain his father's death had not been an accident—he had been murdered. And when they found out that Nomura Eizo knew Owen was back in town, they immediately concluded the old yakuza was behind the plan to bring him here.

Owen's jaw tightened. No, he didn't see anyone unusual watching his house before he left for Korea. But he did see someone unusual coming out of his house after arguing with his dad. It was Nomura!

As if waking from a dream, Owen noticed his surroundings for the first time in hours. The sun had just set. An Edo-period street lantern glowed over his right shoulder, and stars were winking in an amethyst sky. He looked around and realized he was standing on a street corner in Asakusa. He didn't know how he had gotten there, but he was right across the street from Nomura's high-rise apartment.

Seized with anger and determination, he set out across the street. A taxi blared its horn and swerved around him, but he paid it no mind. Slamming through the posh building's double glass doors, he stormed up to the well-dressed goons standing in the lobby.

"Take me up to Nomura!" he demanded in Japanese without bothering with any of the courtesies.

The men looked at each other, startled and unsure of how to respond. "I am sorry, Dr. Powell," one of them finally managed to say, "but Nomura-sama is not expecting you this evening."

Owen looked from face to face, surprised that the man had addressed him by name. He hadn't met any of these particular thugs before. "I don't care whether he is expecting me or not," he said. "I want to see him now!"

He pushed by the men and hammered the elevator button with his fist, although he could see that, like its counterpart in the garage, the lift could not be activated without a key. Looking flummoxed, one of the sentries, apparently the head man, whispered something to the other two then continued trying to reason with Owen. One of the others dialed a cell phone and began talking in quiet, urgent tones, a pained expression knitting his brow. Finally, after several tense minutes during which beads of sweat gathered on the sentries' foreheads in proportion to the volume of Owen's voice, the man on the cell phone nodded and the leader bowed curtly, muttering apologies, and produced a key.

Things went much more smoothly from that point forward. When the elevator opened to the fortieth floor drawing room, Guard Captain Abe Shintaro smiled and bowed then extended his arm motioning Owen to the second elevator, which stood open waiting for him. A few moments later, Owen was in Nomura's penthouse apartment, and the white-coated houseman was leading him down the hallway toward the atrium. They crossed the garden, as before, but instead of taking Owen to the study where he had met Nomura two days earlier, the houseman took him to another door, opened it, and bade him to go inside.

Cautiously, Owen stepped into what turned out to be an elegant dojo, a martial arts training room, matted in rice straw *tatami*. The stark, white walls were lined with racks of *boken* and *bo*, wooden swords and staffs of various lengths and weights. A Shinto *kamiza*, or "spirit seat", graced the far wall. And in the center of the room, Nomura Eizo, dressed in a rich, indigo *hakama* and *keikogi*, was practicing a *jo kata*, a training pattern done with a four-foot hardwood staff.

Nomura's movements were graceful and precise as he the wielded the stick with powerful sweeps and jabs. For a moment, Owen stood transfixed admiring the old man's obvious mastery. Then Owen remembered his anger and decided not to let himself be awed by the man who might have murdered his father.

"I want to talk to you," he called out rudely.

Nomura continued the *kata*, seemingly oblivious to Owen's presence.

"Hey, I said I want to talk!" Owen yelled.

Nomura, who had just raised his *jo* for an overhead strike, stopped mid-stride and looked at Owen. Owen thought he saw the briefest flash of irritation darken the old man's eyes then it was gone. Nomura lowered his staff and bowed.

"It is good to see you again, Owen-san, but as I told you before, your coming here is dangerous for both of us."

"Never mind that. I have to ask you a question."

"All right," Nomura said, sighing as if he had anticipated this moment. "Ask your question."

"Are you responsible for my father's death?"

Nomura looked shocked, as if this were not at all the question he had expected. He looked down at the *tatami* a moment then raised his eyes to meet Owen's baleful glare. "Yes," he said softly. "His blood is on my hands."

Owen was stunned. He had not imagined the man would openly admit that he had murdered his dad, and hearing him do so momentarily paralyzed him with incredulity. Then the impact of what he had heard sank in, and a fury he had never known before filled him like molten steel flowing into a caldron. "Why you murdering bastard!" he screamed, his voice cracking with emotion.

Turning to the rack beside him, he snatched up a *boken*—a large, Japanese white oak training sword, heavy as steel and just as hard—raised it above his head, and charged Nomura. With an earsplitting *kiai* born of hatred and rage, he cut down at the old man, determined to crush his skull like an eggshell.

But Nomura was too quick. Gliding smoothly to *shikaku*, the "dead angle" at which Owen was momentarily defenseless, he angled his *jo* above him and parried the strike harmlessly away. The dojo resounded with the explosive crack of wood on wood then the whoosh of Nomura's staff as it arced around and found the back of Owen's thigh. It could have been a crippling blow, but Nomura stopped it with perfect control, meeting Owen's leg only hard enough let him know the stick was there.

Owen was still mindless with rage. As soon as he recovered the momentum of his deflected sword, he spun and struck at Nomura with a horizontal cut.

With perfect timing, the old man raised his stick under Owen's *boken*, lifted the streaking sword over and past his head then swept it down, thumping it into the *tatami*. In an eye blink, Nomura swept his *jo* up the *boken*, over Owen's arms, and into his throat, stopping the blow, once again, so it did not cause him harm.

But the blaze of Owen's anger would not be so easily quenched. Again and again he struck at Nomura with every cut and thrust he knew, hacking and jabbing with all his strength. Nomura deftly parried each strike and countered with potentially lethal or crippling blows as he continuously stepped around the younger man with the subtle grace born of half a century of persistent training.

Within a minute, Owen's breathing was ragged, and his heavy *boken* had slowed considerably. A minute later, the sword tip was resting on the *tatami* and Owen was bent over, gasping for breath.

"Owen-san," Nomura said calmly, "your technique is respectable, but your temper does not serve you well."

"Well... you haven't seen... the end of it," Owen gasped without looking up. "You may be good... but I'll get you one way or another. You won't get away with killing my father."

"But I didn't kill your father," Nomura said. He saw Owen's sweat-streaked face turn his direction, slightly, and added, "No, I didn't order him killed, either. I told you before, Rhys Powell was my friend."

"But you said you were responsible for his death," Owen said. "His blood is on your hands." Owen slowly straightened, having mostly recovered his breath, but his shoulders still slumped with fatigue.

"Yes, I am responsible," Nomura said, a sad look in his eyes, "but not because I killed him. I am responsible because he was in my territory and I failed to protect him. I carried his *on*—I owed him my life. He was my friend and I failed in my obligation to him. For that, his blood will be on my hands for the rest of my days."

"How could you have been his friend? You were a war criminal and he was an investigator for the War Crimes Tribunal."

"Yes, I was arrested for war crimes, and Rhys-san investigated my case. It was due to his intercession that I was released. He spoke to his superiors on my behalf."

"But I was told you swore a vendetta to get him!"

Nomura stared at him for a few seconds, "Owen-san, who has been talking to you about these things?"

Owen tensed, regretting he had slipped. He had no intention of putting Anna and Jürgen in danger. "That's none of your concern," he said after a moment.

Nomura's face took on a thoughtful expression. "I think it may be time for us to speak frankly, but we need to clean up first. Come."

Without waiting for Owen to answer, Nomura turned and put his *jo* in a rack then walked toward a door at the narrow end of the dojo. Owen hesitated then he racked his own weapon and followed the old man through the door and into a narrow dressing room. There, Nomura opened a hardwood cabinet, pulled out two plastic basins and small stools, and handed one of each to Owen. Then he got out some washcloths and a pair of cotton bathrobes.

Seeing the faucets and floor drains, and smelling the warm, fragrant mist in the air, Owen knew the routine. Without speaking, the men undressed and each went to a faucet, sat on the tiny stool, and began scrubbing down. A couple of minutes later they were done and had slipped on their robes. Then Nomura slid back a *shoji* screen and led him into a chamber made entirely of cedar where a room-sized, four-foot deep pool of steaming water awaited them. Owen breathed in the hot, pungent steam as he slipped off his robe and navigated the steps down into the pool. He eased himself onto a bench, the near-scalding water up to his neck.

In keeping with Japanese custom, neither man had looked directly at the other from the moment they undressed, but Owen allowed himself a sidelong glance as Nomura lowered himself into the steaming water. The gaunt old man, whom Owen had thought frail when they first met, was remarkably sinuous and muscular. What surprised Owen most, however, was the discovery that Nomura had no *irazumi*, none of the full body tattoos for which the Yakuza are famous. But then, not all Yakuza had *irazumi*; those who moved in society's upper strata often avoided getting the conspicuous tattoos.

Nomura took a bench on the opposite side of the pool, spread a washcloth over his liver-spotted head, and closed his eyes. Owen too closed his eyes, and for the next quarter of an hour, both men let the water melt away their tensions in silence.

Then Nomura spoke, startling Owen out of his reverie. "I can understand why you would not want to tell me to whom you have been talking," he said in his precise English, "but I would like you to tell me what you have been told."

Owen remained silent for a minute, considering his options. He didn't want to humor this gangster with any information, but working through the logic of his dilemma, he realized the only way he could test the veracity of the Norgaards' story was to bounce parts of it off Nomura. He decided to gamble.

"I've been told my father was some kind of arbiter for a secret religious group with tentacles all over the world." Owen began cautiously. "I've been told he was murdered and that I have inherited his job in that society."

Nomura stared at him for a long moment. Then he sighed in resignation. "So, it's happened. The Arbiter has been awakened."

"You're saying it's true?" Owen said in astonishment. "You know about this?"

"Yes, it is true. I had hoped you would return home without finding out."

"But why?"

"I told you before, knowing this puts you in danger. I owe it to your father to keep you safe."

"I'm sorry," Owen said in exasperation, "but I just can't see you and my father as friends. I mean, he had to associate with people like you from time to time—it was part of his job—but he didn't get to know those people on a personal level. My dad and a Yakuza, friends?"

"Yakuza?" A puzzled expression furrowed the translucent skin on Nomura's ancient face. "Oh," he said after a moment, a light coming on in his eyes. "The way I had Ataki-san deliver you to me the other night… Oh, I'm sorry, Owen-san. I've given you the wrong impression. I am not Yakuza. I just had you brought here that way because I needed to remain anonymous to anyone who might have been following you. Ataki was only a convenient instrument. He carries my *on* and could not refuse my request for a favor."

Nomura pulled the washcloth off his head, rinsed it in the steaming water, wrung it out, and put it back.

"What brought Rhys-san and me together," he said "was no bond between policeman and criminal. It was much stronger than such an association. We shared religious convictions."

"Oh, you can't be serious!" Owen blurted. "You're not trying to tell me you're a Gnostic Christian."

"Why does that sound so unreasonable to you, Owen-san? Is it because I am Japanese? Surely, whoever told you about the Covenant, told you the great houses spread around the globe."

"Well, yes, and they said it was my father's job to maintain contact with all of them, but I just don't see you as a Christian."

"Then you will need to broaden your idea of what Christians look like." A wry smile momentarily curled Nomura's thin gray lips. "It was, indeed, your father's responsibility to maintain contact between the great houses, a job he inherited from all the Arbiters that preceded him. But actually, the Great Circle—the communion of Illuminati who lead the great houses—had only been restored about seventy years earlier, when your great, great grandfather, Gryphon Powell, toured Asia during the colonial era and tracked down the four missing Eastern houses. We had been 'lost tribes', so to speak, to the Arbiter and the rest of Gnostic Christianity since the seventh century. Gryphon managed to restore the Great Circle, thus fulfilling a prophecy, but it was broken again during the Second World War." He shifted slightly on the bench, sending swirls of heat through the water.

"When Rhys-san became Arbiter after the death of your grandfather, Malcolm, in 1945, he set out to restore the Great Circle once more. To do that, he had to find the surviving members of the house based in Nagasaki before the war. He found me in prison awaiting trial before the War Crimes Tribunal. I was then a member of the Council of Twelve, one of only three who survived the war. Rhys-san, your father, arranged for my release."

"Why would he do that?" Owen said. "I was told you committed atrocities in Manchuria. I can't see my father getting anyone who had done something like that off the hook, even if they were church buddies."

"Atrocities were, indeed, committed in Manchuria," Nomura said softly. "My brother, Ichiro, did that. He got caught up in the

Japanese ultranationalist movement when he was a college student in the 1930s and left the faith for his infatuation with military glory and conquest. He got a commission in the Imperial Army, and toward the end of the war, he ran a prison camp where they did experiments on Chinese prisoners using industrial chemicals our family's *zaibatsu* manufactured."

Nomura paused then continued, his raspy voice quivering. "When the war ended, the Chinese hanged my brother and the War Crimes Tribunal arrested me for supplying the means of his butchery. That was the first I knew of what he had done, but I was overwhelmed with grief and guilt, nonetheless. I was determined to let them hang me, but Rhys-san persuaded me to bear my burden in life."

"So what were you doing in my house the night before I left for Korea?" Owen said, his voice hard. "When I was here two days ago, you told me I had seen you once before, the last night I saw my father alive. You told me to think about it and I'd remember. Well, I have thought about it, and I do remember. You and my father were yelling at each other. If you were such good friends, why were you arguing in our living room?"

"You are right, Owen-san," Nomura said. "We were fighting the night before you left. It was because he was having second thoughts about sending you to Korea. We had been preparing you for years. I had put Rhys-san in contact with the best *budo* masters for your training, and you had done well. But it was time to begin your *bugei* training, your real martial arts education, to prepare you for your future duties as Arbiter. It was time to send you to Yi Chung-hae. But your father had gotten cold feet. You were his only son. He knew it would be very dangerous for you, and neither he nor I could be there to watch over you. He had decided to put it off another year, but I insisted we keep to the plan, and we fought. In the end, I managed to change his mind."

Nomura's black eyes turned to Owen.

"To this day, I don't know if I was right. Look what happened to you in Korea. And had you not gone, Rhys-san might not have been killed. Then again, had you stayed, they might have gotten you too."

"Who might have gotten me too?" Owen demanded. "Who killed my father?"

"If I knew that, Owen-san," Nomura said, his voice suddenly flinty, "believe me, that person would now be dead."

Owen shuddered, though he still sat in near scalding water.

They were quiet for a few moments, each lost in his own thoughts. Then Nomura said, "Come. I have something for you, something from your father."

The old man got up, and Owen followed him out of the pool. They slipped on their bathrobes and went back into the dressing room where Owen was surprised to find his clothes—clean, pressed, and neatly folded—waiting for him atop the hardwood cabinet. A blue, silk, evening *kimono* hung in the corner for Nomura. The men dressed without speaking. Then Nomura led Owen through the dojo and across the atrium into his study. There, he slid aside a silkscreen painting to reveal a wall safe. Seeming unconcerned whether Owen was watching him dial in the combination, he opened the safe and brought out a small, ebony box. Bowing, he handed it to Owen.

"After you left for Korea, your father told me that, should any-thing happen to him, I must give you this after you learned of your identity as Arbiter."

Owen ran his fingers over the top of the box—so small and black and smooth. The lid was hinged, but there was no latch or lock. "What's in it?" he said.

"I don't know," Nomura replied, his face a mask of surprise. "It isn't mine, so I have never opened it."

Owen hesitated then lifted the lid. Inside he found a sealed envelope with something hard and small in it. The following was typed on the outside of the envelope, apparently using a manual typewriter with dirty keys:

BANK LEU (AG), ZURICH,
BOX NUMBER: SM850.

He tore off the end of the envelope and poured its contents into the palm of his hand. "It looks like a key to a safe deposit box," he said, looking up at Nomura.

The old man glanced at Owen's palm then looked up, expressionless.

"Do you know what's in the box?" Owen said.

Nomura shrugged. "I can guess." He hesitated then added, "Whatever is there will be very valuable. If it is what I think it is, many people will want to take it from you. If you bring it here, I can keep it safe for you." Then, seeing suspicion creep into Owen's eyes, he added, "But, of course, that is up to you."

CHAPTER TWENTY-THREE

I t was after midnight when Owen got back to his hotel room. He was exhausted, having not slept most of the night before, but he knew trying to sleep now would be pointless. The turmoil he had felt since talking to the Norgaards had only deepened now that he had confronted Nomura.

This fantastic yarn about his father's involvement with a secret network of Gnostic Christians was beginning to seem almost plausible. He had thought Anna and her brother were insane or, more likely, swindlers trying to pull some kind of scam on him when they first laid out their story, but Nomura Eizo had not only corroborated much of what they said, he had added to it. How could the Norgaards and Nomura both come up with such farfetched tales if they were not true?

The only way that could happen was if they were working together. Maybe this was some kind of elaborate confidence game, and the Norgaards were working with Nomura to fleece him. But that brought him back to the central question: Fleece him of what? Owen was not quite a pauper. He owned a rundown, two-bedroom ranch—well, he held a deed of trust on a thirty-year mortgage—and drove an inexpensive, late-model car that he bought used and kept in fairly good condition. But nothing Owen owned could possibly be worth the time of day to a wealthy Yakuza, or whatever Nomura was, or the heirs to a Danish industrial fortune.

Then there was the fact that their stories did not quite match. More than that, Anna and Jürgen were openly contemptuous of Nomura. They insisted he had had Owen's father killed. Normura, on the other hand, conceded that Rhys Powell had been murdered, but the only guilt to which he admitted was in not having adequately protected his friend. Of course, the Norgaards' apparent hostility towards Normura could be part of the scam, a ploy to throw Owen off the scent and make their story sound more believable. But that still didn't track. Why would they all go to the trouble of weaving such an elaborate plot for so little gain?

And there was Korea and Myongsan-ni.

Owen's thoughts returned to Anna, both as the voluptuous young woman he had yearned for eighteen years earlier and the elegant beauty that had nestled on his shoulder just the evening before. He wanted to believe her. More than almost anything else in the world, he wanted to believe her. But if she and Jürgen were telling the truth, Nomura had to be an extraordinarily calculating murderer, and there was something about the old man's gentle patience that seemed genuine.

Besides, Nomura had passed him the key to a safe deposit box, a key left for him by his father... Or had he? There were no instructions with the key, no note with his father's signature, nothing in the envelope or the ebony wood box in which it had come that proved it was from his dad. Why would his father leave Owen such an enigmatic object with nothing telling him what to do with it? For that matter, why would he leave anything with Nomura, rather than with one of his colleagues at the embassy?

That reminded Owen of Jack Fowler. The CIA man's theory fit both Nomura's and the Norgaards' stories. But then, Fowler was a habitual liar.

For the first time since the summer of 1982, Owen felt helpless and alone. Who should he trust? Who *could* he trust?

On impulse, he looked at his watch and did a quick calculation. It would be a little after 11:00 AM on Sunday in Maryland. He grabbed the phone on the table beside him and had the hotel desk connect him to the international operator. He would tell Elaine the whole story and get her levelheaded assessment. Of course, he wouldn't say too much about Anna—he wouldn't tell Elaine what an alluring woman Anna was, and he certainly would not tell her about their relationship in Korea. But Elaine had a sound, analytical mind. If he just laid out all the available information and posed the questions plaguing him, she could help him work through the mystery and decide what to do next. He was sure of it.

Most of all, he realized as he heard her phone ring, he wanted to hear her voice. He wanted to find out if she had gotten over their spat. Maybe she would tell him she had missed him and wanted him home. Maybe she would say even more. If she did, by God, he'd grab the first plane home, study or no study!

"Hello?" It was a man's voice.

Owen was startled. Had the operator gotten the number wrong? Then he realized the voice sounded vaguely familiar. "Uh, this is Owen Powell," he said, feeling a bit awkward. "To whom am I speaking?"

"Ah, Powell, we were wondering when you'd get around to calling."

Now Owen recognized the voice. "Preston, what in the hell are you doing at Elaine's house?"

"Well, old boy, not that it's any of your business, but I'll tell you since I pretty much have you to thank. I was just moving my stuff in. It seems your sudden disappearance has opened Elaine's eyes to a few things, not the least of which is the availability of other men around her. I think she's been longing for someone for a long time, but with you hanging all over her, she was too stifled to realize it. Well she has, now, and good for her. After all, a woman like Elaine deserves the best, don't you think?"

"Let me speak to Elaine!"

"No, I don't think that would be a good idea. You see, Powell, she's pretty angry that you haven't called. For a while she wanted to talk so she could tell you just where to go—that is, assuming you're not already there." Preston chuckled at his turn of phrase then continued. "I think she wanted some closure, as they say. But now, she just wants to be through with you."

"Let me talk to her, goddammit!"

"I said no, Powell. Don't you get it? She doesn't want to talk. Besides, she can't come to the phone right now, anyway. She's soaking in a tub. I was just about to go in and scrub her back. Jesus, have you seen that woman in soapsuds? Well, I'll tell you—"

"Preston, you son of a bitch! Get Elaine to the phone or I swear I'll—"

"You'll what, Powell? You'll beat me up? That's what people of your ilk do when they're frustrated, right? They resort to violence." Just then, Preston heard the back screen door swing shut. "Well, Powell, old boy, I'd really like to stand here and take a few more of your threats and insults, but Elaine is calling. I've got to go. Don't hurry back." He hung up the phone.

Owen slammed his own phone into its cradle.

Elaine came into the study where Preston was loading software after installing a new modem on her desktop computer. As smart as she was, she was the first to admit what a klutz she was when it came to modern technology. She usually had Owen take care of anything she needed done on her PC, but he had been gone, and she really needed to get her high-speed Internet working so she could get off the slow-drip phone modem that was hindering her efforts to work from home. As a last resort, she had accepted Preston's offer to install the modem for her. The offer had come with strings—Internet setup in return for a dinner date at a fancy restaurant—but she had dickered him down to a casual lunch at a nearby chain diner and insisted he do the computer upgrade first.

Meanwhile, she had spent the morning puttering in the backyard. She didn't care much for gardening, but it was one of the few things that calmed her mind when she was agitated, and she had been agitated for more than a week since Owen disappeared. At least, while she was out planting strawberries, she didn't have to listen to Preston's pretentious babble.

"Randall, did I hear the phone ring a moment ago?"

"Yes, you did," Preston said, sniggering. He kept working at the computer and didn't look her way.

"What?" She watched him and began to grin in anticipation of whatever joke it was that had him so entertained. "So who was it?"

"It was just Powell." He finally turned to face her, eyes glinting like those of a mischievous schoolboy. "I have to admit, I had a bit of fun at his expense."

"That was Owen?" Her voice came out a bit too reedy to sound casual, but Preston didn't seem to notice. She fought to keep her composure. "Why didn't you call me? What did you tell him?"

"I told him you and I were an item," he said, beaming, completely oblivious to the alarm in Elaine's eyes. "I said I was moving in and—"

"You said what?" she yelled. Composure was no longer part of the equation.

The smile ran away from Preston's face as he realized Elaine was angry. "Don't worry, he'll call back. You can tell him I was just kidding, just getting a little payback for—"

"How dare you!" Elaine's voice trembled with rage. "Just who do you think you are, answering my phone and telling someone you're moving in here?"

"Why are you so angry?" Preston said, getting up from the computer. He took a step toward her, but stopped when he saw her expression harden. "Look, I know it was presumptuous of me to tell anyone that you and I are involved, but I couldn't resist the opportunity to play a prank on Powell. It was just a little ribbing between guys. I know you two are just friends—I got him to confirm that for me the night we had dinner at Kazuo's—but I could tell that if he'd had it his way..." His voice trailed off as he saw the fury in Elaine's eyes blaze up, and a glimmer of understanding finally began to take shape in his mind. "Oh my God," he gasped in the tone of a man who realized he had just heard the click of a landmine underfoot. "You... You and Powell?"

Elaine just stared at him, her face livid.

Preston's mind began to race. It was one thing to claim he was involved with Elaine if Owen's own relationship with her was just platonic; it was quite another to taunt the likes of Owen Powell with such a story if he and Elaine were intimate. Preston could not pretend he stood a chance against Powell in a fight, though he had, up until then, done just that. He had told himself that Owen had taken unfair advantage in the restaurant. He had gotten the jump on him, grabbed his arm before he realized what was happening. Preston had told Elaine that story and recited it to himself time and again every day since. He'd even begun to believe it. But the time for self-delusion was past. One day soon Owen Powell would return from whatever mysterious place he had gone, and he was sure to come looking for him.

Preston's breathing became quick and shallow. He began to feel lightheaded. He steadied himself with a hand on the edge of the computer table and was about to sit back down, but looked at Elaine and thought better of it.

"Uh... You are going to straighten this out with Owen, aren't you?" he finally managed to say.

Elaine continued staring at him, the outrage in her eyes giving way to incredulity and then to disgust.

"I mean, you've got to apologize for me, tell him—"

"Get out!"

"But you've got to talk to him. He'll listen—"

"Get out of my house!" Elaine stepped aside and gestured toward the door.

Preston lowered his head and walked out.

CHAPTER TWENTY-FOUR

Owen leaned on the button beside the Norgaards' door. He waited a few seconds then rang the bell again and was just about to start banging when the door opened.

"Owen, what are you doing here?" Jürgen said in a hoarse whisper. "It's nearly two in the morning." The Dane wore an expensive dressing gown over silk pajamas. His bleary eyes did nothing to diminish his patrician bearing. "Come in, come in."

Owen edged past the big man and was heartened to see Anna cautiously leaning around the corner to see who had roused them from their beds at such an ungodly hour. Her corn silk hair was sleep tousled and she wore no makeup. Owen could just see the top of a violet satin housecoat and noticed it brought out the sapphire flecks in her eyes. She was as beautiful as ever. On seeing him, her expression brightened then turned to concern.

"Owen, what is it?" she said, coming out from behind the corner. She hurried to him and took his hands in hers. Owen leaned forward to exchange greeting kisses on the cheeks, but she quickly reached up and guided his face to hers, kissing him on the lips. "What has happened?" she said, cupping his face in her hands.

The kiss was brief, and the way she held his face was almost maternal, but Owen's pulse quickened just the same.

"I confronted Nomura."

"Good Lord!" Jürgen exclaimed.

"You didn't!" Anna said simultaneously.

Both of them looked horrified. Anna reflexively stepped back and held Owen at arms length, looking him up and down as if she were examining him for injuries.

"I needed to hear what he had to say about my father's death," Owen said.

"Owen, we told you to stay away from that man," Anna said. "He's extremely dangerous. You're an important man. We can't afford to lose you." Then her tone softened, "I can't afford to lose you."

"You didn't tell him about us, did you?" Jürgen said, with a hard edge in his voice.

"Of course not! And I also made sure I wasn't followed back here, if that's what you're thinking." He met the Viking's hawk-like eyes and stared back defiantly.

Jürgen glared a moment then sighed. "Well, what is done is done," he said. "And you look none the worse for wear. Come in and tell us what happened. Anna, why don't you put on some tea?"

Jürgen led the way to the sunken living room. The men sat down and for several tense seconds exchanged cool stares, each waiting for the other to begin. "It took a lot of courage to enter the jackal's lair," Jürgen finally offered. "Your father would have been proud of you."

It was a small gesture, but enough to allow Owen to swallow his anger and speak without losing face. "I don't think I'd call it courage," he said. "I struggled all day trying to figure out how my father could have been involved with a man like Nomura. When

I couldn't come up with any explanation that made sense, something inside me just snapped and I couldn't stop myself from confronting him."

"So how did you get in?" Jürgen said. "That building he lives in is like a fortress."

Owen told him about his confrontation with the guards in the lobby. He described how, after bullying his way upstairs, he had been taken to Nomura's private dojo and what had transpired there.

"You attacked him with a wooden sword?" Jürgen exclaimed, "Right in his own house? Why, you're lucky to be alive! That place is crawling with guards. Whatever possessed you to do something so stupid?"

Owen's anger rekindled, but he also thought he saw a glimmer of satisfaction in the Dane's eyes, and that intrigued him enough to continue. "I don't think I was ever in any danger," he said, matching Jürgen's sternness with disdain. "He could have killed me anytime he wanted, but he didn't. For that matter, if he wanted me dead, he could have killed me when I was over there the first time, or had the stooges who picked me up do the job, and no one would have been the wiser."

"The only reason he didn't, then or tonight, was because he needs you. He wants something he can't get without your help—the scroll."

To Owen's relief, Anna broke the tension, arriving with a tray of tea and pastries. Sliding past Jürgen, she kneeled before the low table and put the tray down between the men. The pastries looked decadently heavy, and when the moist aroma of honey and cinnamon caressed Owen's nose, his stomach growled reminding him he hadn't eaten since breakfast almost twenty hours earlier.

He reached for a muffin just as Anna, across the table from him, bent forward to pour the tea, the top of her robe pulling open to reveal the frilly bodice of a gossamer nightgown and the deep, shadowed canyon of her bosom. Owen's eyes fell there and rested a moment. When they reluctantly returned to her face, he saw that she had been watching him. Their eyes met and locked. Anna's face betrayed no expression at first then she slowly raised one eyebrow and smiled.

Jürgen, who sat behind her, oblivious to the subtle heat rising at the table, continued his indictment of Nomura and his nefarious motives. "That man is a serpent, a tempter and deceiver. He will do anything to get the *Apocalypse*. He will tell you he was your father's friend. He will tell you he is your friend. Good God, he would tell you he was your godfather and your father's confessor if he thought that would earn him your trust!"

"He told me he's a Gnostic Christian," Owen said abruptly. With effort, he pulled his eyes from Anna's to watch her brother's reaction.

"That is madness! It's absolutely absurd!"

"You don't believe him," Anna said.

"I don't know what I believe anymore," Owen said with a frankness he immediately regretted.

There was a draught of icy stillness as the Norgaards considered the implications of what he had just said. Anna stiffened momentarily then straightened her robe and rose from the low table, picked up her tea, and curled up in an armchair. Holding the cup to her lips with both hands, she blew on it gently, her large eyes fixed on Owen's. Her lush body was catlike, supple and curvaceous, but powerful. Owen sensed that, even in repose, a current of raw energy pulsed somewhere deep within her. At that moment, the current was flowing toward the negative pole. He almost shuddered as he felt the coolness of her stare.

Jürgen's eyes also bore into Owen's. After a moment he began talking in a low voice, his tone gentle but firm, without harshness, almost as if he were speaking to a child. "Why would there be any question of who to believe, Owen? What has Nomura ever done for you? He says he was your father's friend. Did your father ever introduce him to you or even speak of him? You had a rough time when your father died. Did Nomura take you in? Did he lend a hand in any way?"

Owen chafed under this interrogative lecture, but Jürgen continued without pause. "Now, I can't prove it was Nomura who had you brought back to Japan, though Anna and I are certain it was, but once you got here, how did he treat you? Did he take you into his confidence, tell you about the Covenant and your legacy as Arbiter? No, Anna and I did that. We flew here from Copenhagen the moment we heard you were alive. We came with one purpose and one purpose only, to help you. And now you return our kindness with distrust?"

"I don't mean to sound ungrateful," Owen said. "But this whole affair is so incredible. You and Nomura have both made a lot of fantastic claims. None of it is very believable. You've been very kind to me, and I appreciate that, but there were elements in Nomura's story that, crazy as it sounds, just seemed to ring true."

Anna lowered her cup and shifted irritably in her chair. "Whatever could that man have said to cause you to doubt my word?" she said, never taking her eyes off Owen's. "Have I ever held anything back from you? Have I ever said or done anything to violate your trust?" She hesitated a moment, weighing her words then added, "Have I ever abandoned you in a time of danger?"

Her voice was almost a whisper, but the words cut Owen deeply, and he felt his cheeks flush crimson with guilt. After a moment he said, "I don't know how to explain it. Nomura had a lot of information about my family. He gave me an elaborate account of how my great grandfather found four lost Eastern houses and brought them back into the Great Circle and how my father renewed ties with a Japan-based house after the war. Nomura said he had been a member of that house's Council of Twelve."

"That's utter nonsense!" Jürgen said. "We already told you, he knows about the Covenant. He learned about us over the years he had a vendetta against your father. Don't you see how easy it would be for him to make up a detailed story to convince you he is one of us? After all, he knows a lot more about us than you do at this point. Nomura Eizo a Christian? Absolutely not! He was a war criminal, for Christ's sake!"

"He admitted to being arrested for war crimes, but said it was his brother who committed them. According to Nomura, my father confirmed his innocence and had him released."

"And why would you believe an absurd story like that?" Jürgen said.

"Well, I guess it was less what he said that was so convincing as how he said it."

Listening to his own words, Owen realized how silly they sounded and wished he could take them back. But the Norgaards didn't laugh at him. Instead, Anna uncoiled her lithe form and glided from the chair to the sofa beside him.

"Owen," she said, "now that you've awakened to the legacy, many people will try to deceive you, to twist your perceptions and bend your mind to their will."

She put her cup on the table then moved closer to him and took his hand in both of hers. As her turquoise eyes fixed on his, a flood of positive energy seemed to flow out of her, and Owen felt a wave of heat wash down his body and into his toes, though most of it welled in his loins.

"It is very important for you to be able to distinguish your enemies from your friends," she continued. "You've got to recognize those who want to bring you down, and you've got to put your trust in the people who support you..." She moved her face so close to his that their noses almost touched and added, "... those who love you and want to keep you safe."

Had Jürgen not been across the table watching, Owen would have closed the last two inches between them and kissed her. He knew she would have responded—her eyes and parted lips sent him an unmistakable invitation—but Jürgen was there, damn him, and Owen didn't want to give the haughty Viking the impression he had come banging on their door in the middle of the night to seduce his sister. Nor did he want either of them to think he could be won over to their cause through feminine wiles.

But why had he come? Certainly it was not because anything had happened that persuaded him Anna and Jürgen were trustworthy. Indeed, his encounter with Nomura had made him, if anything, more doubtful of their story. Was that fair? Well, there was Jürgen. Despite the man's open kindness, every time Owen began to feel at ease around him, the Dane's arrogance and fiery temper rumbled to the surface and aroused Owen's disquiet anew.

But Anna... Ah, Anna was a different story. He realized she was right when she insisted she had never done anything to violate his trust, nothing to cause him to doubt her word. She had opened her heart to him in Korea and had flown to his side almost twenty years later when she discovered he was alive and in danger. Remarkably, she had not held him responsible for the tragedy that had ruined her life, made her unclean, unmarriageable to men in her society. She and she alone had remained true to him over the years, whether with him or apart, unlike... unlike Elaine.

Owen suddenly realized what had really brought him to the Norgaards' apartment in the middle of the night. It was not his confrontation with Nomura, as he had told himself earlier. He had come because Elaine had betrayed him. He had come because he wanted to see Anna, because he needed the comfort of her unqualified love and trust, a love and trust he now yearned to return.

With considerable effort, he pulled his gaze from Anna's hypnotic eyes and turned to Jürgen. "I've got something I need to tell you," he said, casting his lot decisively. Jürgen didn't answer, and Owen could sense both of them holding their breath in anticipation. "Nomura gave me something he said was from my father. I think it's a key to a safe deposit box in Switzerland. It said something about Zurich on the envelope it came in."

Jürgen and Anna sat bolt upright in their seats.

"What did he say was in the box?" Jürgen said, his voice crisp with excitement. "How did he say he came by this key?"

"He said my father left the key with him to pass on to me, but didn't tell him what was in the box, if that is really what it is. I don't know—"

"He must have gotten it from your house the night he..." Anna interjected. She hesitated when she saw the shadow cross Owen's face. "The night he had your father killed," she continued more carefully. Then her voice deepened to a throaty whisper as she added, "My God, the *Apocalypse of Joseph* must be in that safe deposit box."

"Maybe," Owen said. "But what I don't understand is, if he's had the key all these years, why hasn't he used it to get the scroll himself."

"That's obvious," Jürgen said. "He can't get into the box without you. Your father doubtless made special arrangements with the bank to ensure that only he or you could access the box. There must be some kind of foolproof procedure for positive identification."

"That must be what this entire charade is about," Anna said, her excitement building. "That's why he had you brought to Japan, why he's been so cagey with you. He needs your cooperation to get the scroll. For that, he needs your trust. He couldn't just appear on your doorstep in Maryland, a stranger claiming to be your father's friend and confidant, hand you a key, and say: 'Hey, let's go to Switzerland and empty your old dad's safe deposit box.' No, he needed you to think you were unraveling a mystery. He needed to slowly and methodically nurture your trust before giving you the key so taking him to the box would seem like your idea."

"But I didn't offer to take him to the box. That never crossed my mind."

"But you are planning to go to Zurich, aren't you?" Anna said.

"Well, yeah, eventually. I thought I'd go there before returning to the States after my research is done here."

"And that will be as good as taking Nomura there!" Anna said. "Don't you see? He has eyes everywhere in Tokyo. He'll know when you've finished your work—this little project he weaved out of whole cloth to lure you here—and he'll know when you leave the country. I bet he'll even know what flight you catch to Switzerland. Then he'll either have you followed from here, or have his henchmen pick up your trail in Zurich. Either way, the day you step out of that bank, you're a dead man and the scroll is on its way to Nomura."

On her last declaration, Anna saw Owen's eyes narrow and his back stiffen. She quickly added, "Darling, I know you're tough. You were a good fighter twenty years ago, and I'm sure you're twice the man now that you were then. But believe me, these people are dangerous. They won't send just one or two men. They'll send a team of professional killers. If they catch you alone, they'll kill you no matter how good you are. Well I'm not going to let that happen!" She let those words hang a moment then added softly, "I lost you once. I am not going to lose you again."

Owen thought about the yakuza thugs Nomura sent to pick him up. He saw from the way they handled themselves that they were trained to fight as a team. Remembering some of the things he had witnessed in military intelligence in Korea and Army special operations in Iraq—hell, some of the things he had done back then—he knew Anna was right. If a team of well-trained professionals wanted you dead, they would get you one way or another, no matter who you were.

"So what do I do?" he said.

"You mean, what do we do?" Anna insisted.

"We preempt!" Jürgen declared. "No doubt Nomura's guessing you will go to Zurich after you're done in Tokyo some number of days or weeks from now. Right now, he thinks you're in your hotel room, asleep. So we get the jump on him. We put you on a plane tonight and you empty out the safe deposit box before he gets his team in place, if we're lucky, before he even discovers you've left Japan."

"I can't just drop everything and fly to Switzerland. I've got a job to do here. I've got obligations."

"Owen," Anna said, her voice insistent, "This is your life we're talking about."

"We can get you to Zurich and back in a matter of days, Jürgen said. "Your research here will hardly miss a beat. Once you get the scroll and put it someplace safe, someplace Nomura doesn't know about, you'll be out of danger,"

"So why don't I just leave the damn thing alone?" Owen said. "It seems to me that I'm only at risk if I go to that bank. I could just toss the key in the river and never go to Zurich, let Nomura watch and wonder for the rest of his life."

"Could you really stay away from that safe deposit box?" Jürgen said. "None of us knows for sure what is in it, but whatever it is, your father left it for you just before he died. It's like a message to you from the grave."

Jürgen was right, Owen realized. He couldn't just leave the box untouched. Sooner or later, he would have to know what his father had left for him. "But flying to Switzerland and back," he muttered to himself. "I can't afford that."

"Don't worry about it," Jürgen said, sliding forward in his chair, his face earnest. "Anna and I will take care of the expenses."

Owen opened his mouth to protest.

"No, we insist," Jürgen said. "I know you're a proud man, Owen. You can repay us later if it's that important to you. What is vital right now, though, is for you to secure the contents of that safe deposit box while you have a window of opportunity to do it safely."

Owen still looked doubtful.

"Leave everything to me," Jürgen said. "Go back to your hotel room and throw a few things in a suitcase. I'll phone the airport and get you on the first flight with connections to Zurich. Then I'll pick you—"

"You'll get both of us on that plane," Anna said. "He's not going anywhere without me to cover his back."

"I don't want you involved in this," Owen protested. "We don't know whether we're really getting the jump on Nomura. He might have anticipated me doing something like this and prepositioned a team in Switzerland. I don't want you putting yourself in danger."

"Where you go, I go, my love," Anna said, her eyes caressing his.

"You know, that might not be such a bad idea," Jürgen said. "You can use an extra set of eyes, and Anna can more than hold her own if things get rough."

Owen considered that. He remembered how Anna had fought in Korea and knew Jürgen wasn't exaggerating. He also could not deny that he wanted her to come along. Despite the gravity of the situation and the danger he might be putting her in, he couldn't repress his excitement in anticipating a trip alone with her.

"Alright," he said. "Let's do it."

CHAPTER TWENTY-FIVE

Elaine Chen knew that Owen was gone. She had overheard students complaining that other professors had been giving his lectures and that teaching assistants would be administering his final exams. She had gone by his house twice that week, driving as slowly as she dared with that busybody neighbor of his always peering around the curtains and scowling. His car was in the carport both evenings. A single light was on—the dim illumination in the living room window suggested it was a hall light, one Owen might have left on for security if he were leaving town. But where would he have gone?

No matter where it was, she had been determined to wait him out. No matter how much it hurt her, no matter how punchy and irritable she would get from lack of sleep, she would not go running to him and become the pliant Dulcinea he wanted her to be.

But all that had changed. That stupid buffoon Randall Preston had ruined everything! Up until his asinine phone antic, she had been confident—well, fairly confident, anyway—that she could handle the likes of Owen Powell.

She had come to consider her little standoff with him to be an exercise in game theory, a branch of strategy in which she had excelled in grad school. It seemed clear to her that their little confrontation had become a two-player, sequential game, one in which the first player to move would place himself or herself—she had been determine it would be him—at a distinct disadvantage, having revealed his vulnerability and provided the opponent an opportunity to make a superior second move.

And Owen had caved. Yes, finally, he had called. She had been on the verge of winning, of getting him back on her terms, until Randall pushed his way into the game and turned the logic upside down. Now she was the vulnerable one, the one who was paying the costs of not moving first, the one who had to move now, immediately, to cut her losses and salvage her relationship with Owen... if there was still a relationship to salvage.

So now she was moving, or trying to, at least. She had begun the moment she threw Randall out of her house. She had grabbed the phone and called Owen's home then his office—no answer at either place—and she had tried both numbers intermittently all Sunday afternoon, evening, and late into the night. She had left several messages on his office voicemail, fuming all the while over his stubborn refusal to carry a cell phone or have an answering machine in his house.

The next morning she called again before driving to the campus to give a morning lecture. After class she returned to her office and checked her voice mail, praying to find a message from him there, though in her heart of hearts she really didn't expect to, then sank in despair when she found her pessimism justified. Finally, with hope nearly lost, she called both of his numbers one last time before setting out across campus to his office in Stradtmann Hall.

Now, on reaching the top of the stone staircase two floors above the lobby, Elaine paused a moment and leaned against the banister, more to gather her nerve than to catch her breath. She peered down Stradtmann's "gauntlet," as the students called it, the hall where professors in the political science department had their offices, and wondered how she might find out where Owen had gone without calling attention to her interest in him. She couldn't ask about him at the administrative desk. Secretaries were the worst gossips on campus. Maybe she would just poke around a bit in his office. Maybe he had left a copy of an itinerary on his desk, or a hotel reservation complete with phone number, or... Well, she didn't know, but she had to find something that would give her a clue to his whereabouts. She just had to.

She took a deep breath to steel her resolve and headed down the narrow, dimly lit hallway. About halfway down, she came to an office with Owen's name posted by the door. The door was closed, but trying the handle, she found it unlocked. She looked up and down the hall to make sure no one was watching her then quickly stepped in and closed the door behind her.

She had never been in Owen's office before, but it was exactly like she had imagined it: obsessively neat. The typical professor would have stacks of books and piles of paper strewn about the office. In her own office, books were stacked on the floor beside her desk and along the walls, and the tops of her filing cabinets were heaped with old academic journals. But not here, "Oh Owen, how can you work in here?" she said to herself. "It's like a sterile operating theater."

She went to the desk and tossed her book bag aside. To her disappointment, there was no hotel reservation or travel itinerary lying around, so she began rummaging through the drawers. She had just moved down to the second drawer when the door swung open, startling her.

"Oh, hello Elaine. We don't see you on this side of the campus very often." It was Owen's boss, Richard Falstaff. He looked surprised to have stumbled upon her in Owen's office, but recovered quickly and did not seem a bit concerned that she was going through his desk. "Is there something I can help you find?"

"Well, uh," she said, her mind racing to come up with a story, "Dr. Powell and I are working on a paper to present at a conference next month and... uh... I thought I'd look over his latest draft, so..."

"Yes, he left town so quickly," Falstaff picked up for her, "he didn't have time to drop anything off with anyone." He stepped over to the desk and began shuffling through the drawer she had already searched, looking for the draft she knew did not exist. "I didn't know you two were collaborating... professionally, I mean. Have you tried his computer? He's certain to have written it there. Did he give you a file name?"

"No, he just gave me a paper copy of the first draft."

"Well, that's our Owen; always trying to keep technology at arm's length. Uses a word processor, but prints paper copies of everything he writes before turning it off because he's certain the first time he doesn't, the computer will eat his files. Won't carry a cell phone, won't send files over email, and doesn't like the Internet. He's about as eccentric as they come—well, among the under-sixty crowd, anyway—but you know that already." He grinned at Elaine as he sat down at Owen's computer and reached for the power button.

She didn't answer. Her initial alarm at being caught in Owen's office was turning to annoyance as she took in Falstaff's tone, his lack of concern on finding her there, his casual references to "our Owen" and how well she knew him. *How much do you know about us?* She thought. *What has Owen told you?*

Falstaff booted up the computer and began skimming the document folders. "What's the working title of the paper?" he asked, hoping for a clue to the file name.

"'Deterrence in the Post-Cold War Era,'" she said. That sounded like the kind of thing Owen would have worked on. At least, she hoped it did.

"Hum," he said after a minute. "I don't see anything that looks like it, and I don't think we want to open all these files, one by one, looking for it. Maybe you can just ask him for the file name the next time he calls you."

Elaine frowned. She felt a fresh flush of irritation at Falstaff's assumption that Owen must be calling her regularly from wherever he was, but was keenly aware that she had found nothing in his office that gave her a clue to his whereabouts, and her little charade about a conference paper was getting her no closer to finding him. She pondered her dilemma a moment, the tension growing. When Falstaff looked up from the computer expectantly, she decided to come clean, to a point, at least.

"That's just it, Richard," her voice sounded small. "Owen hasn't called me since he left. I don't even know where he's gone."

Falstaff swiveled the chair around to face her fully. "You can't be serious."

The utter surprise in his voice all but confirmed Elaine's suspicions—he obviously knew there was more between them than just a professional relationship. With considerable effort, she kept her gaze level and simply said, "I am."

"Well, he's gone to Japan. He got a grant from the Ministry of Economy, Trade, and Industry to study how the Japanese government coordinates competition between private corporations. I can't believe he didn't tell you about it... you of all people."

For the briefest moment, a vein of humiliation opened in her and bled freely. Not only had her private relationship with Owen been exposed, but now Richard Falstaff knew that Owen did not even think enough of her to let her know he was leaving town. Her embarrassment was intense. Then it turned to anger.

"How long has he known he was leaving?" she said, her voice flinty.

"Oh, the grant came suddenly. That's the strange part, well, one of the strange parts, anyway. Right out of nowhere, we get this fax from METI telling us they've approved Owen's research request, but they want him there immediately, the next business day. He had to fly out that night. Funny thing was, Owen didn't even remember applying for the grant."

As Falstaff told Elaine the story, he watched the anger that had hardened her face dissolve into puzzlement then gradually ripen into an expression of alarm. Finally, he stopped mid sentence. "What?" he said.

"You let him go?" she yelled, making him jump.

"Well… uh… yes, of course. We insisted, actually. You see, the grant came with a generous endowment to the university, but the conditions were—"

"When have you heard from him last?"

"Well, he called the day he arrived to tell us where he was staying and give us the phone number, but we haven't heard from him since."

"Give me the number. I want to call him right now."

"Yeah, okay," he said, a little shaken. "I've got it in my office."

He led her out of Owen's office and down the hall to his own. Falstaff went straight to the notepad on his desk where he had taken down the information from Owen's call. "Here it is," he said.

Elaine got the cell phone out of her book bag, dialed the number, and waited a moment. "Hello, I am calling from the United States. Do you speak English?" she said in carefully enunciated words. "Good. I am trying to reach Dr. Owen Powell. He is a guest in your hotel. Please ring his room for me."

Falstaff watched as she waited, his face expectant, trying to reassure her. She refused to meet his eye.

"Thank you," she finally said. "I'll try again later." She clicked off the phone and turned on Falstaff, her eyes hard. "He's not in his room."

"He's probably out to dinner or something."

"It's after midnight there, on a weekday. He would be in his room."

"Elaine," Falstaff said, exasperation creeping into his voice. "Owen's a big boy. He grew up in Tokyo. He's probably visiting friends, catching up on old times."

She ignored him and began dialing her cell phone again. "Hello, Margie? Elaine. I want you to book me on the next available flight to Tokyo."

CHAPTER TWENTY-SIX

"What do you mean there are no rooms to be had in all of Zurich?" Owen said, his temper growing short. It was after 9:00 PM local time and seven hours later in Tokyo, the clock on which Owen's body was running. He hadn't gotten a full night's sleep in days.

"I'm awfully sorry Sir," said a young woman behind the counter at the tourist bureau, "but there's a major technology conference going on this week, and people have come in from all over Europe. Every hotel in town is booked." She tugged at the lapel of her burgundy blazer, her lower lip twitching nervously.

"What about bed and breakfasts?" Anna said.

"I can call around, but I doubt we'll find anything if you insist on separate rooms or even one room with two beds. Bed and breakfasts are people's homes, you know. The rooms tend to be small with one bed. And our chances of finding two rooms in—"

"Call around," Owen said. "Maybe we'll get lucky."

As the clerk picked up the phone and began working her way down the list of local bed and breakfasts, Owen and Anna slumped down on a bench on the other side of the small lobby. They sat a couple of minutes without speaking, sleep threatening to overtake them. Owen was just about to suggest they try to find some coffee when the clerk called out, "I may have something for you, but it's only got one double bed."

Owen sighed in frustration. "I don't think—"

"We'll take it!" Anna said.

It was almost midnight when Owen and Anna got to the bed and breakfast and were taken up to their room. Owen was exhausted and eager to fall into bed. After a minute of awkward discussion about sleeping arrangements and the fact that Anna had brought a nightgown and dressing gown while Owen had not brought so much as pajamas, they agreed that Owen would use the bathroom down the hall first then return to the room and undress while Anna took her turn in the bathroom. They would have to share the bed. Owen would sleep in his underwear. He promised to be a gentleman, and Anna made him swear not to breathe a word about this to Jürgen.

With the critical issues settled, they took their turns in the bathroom and Owen stripped down to his skivvies and climbed into bed, leaving the light on for Anna. He was barely awake a few minutes later when she came in, turned out the light, and slipped into her side of the bed. Owen rolled over, putting his back to her, and was just starting to doze when he felt her slide up against him, spooning his body with hers. Then she put her arm around him and reached for him under the sheet.

Reacting without thought, he snatched her wrist. He heard a sharp intake of breath and felt her stiffen in surprise. He lightened his grip, but did not release her immediately. "I haven't had any real sleep in days," he said. "Let me get some rest, okay?"

She hesitated then let out a long sigh. "Alright," she whispered, drawing back her hand, "Tomorrow."

⊫ ⊨

Anna awoke with the sun warming her face, stretched luxuriously, and rolled over. "It's morning," she purred, reaching for Owen. When her hand found only cool, empty sheets, she rose on one elbow, annoyed, and looked around with bleary eyes.

"Yes, and a beautiful morning it is," Owen said from a chair by the foot of the bed. He was dressed. "I woke early and thought I'd simplify things by showering before getting you up."

"I thought we'd spend the morning in bed," she said, her Danish accent silky. "Afterwards, we could shower and dress together. That would simplify things."

She maintained eye contact for a moment. When Owen didn't respond, she sat up and bunched the pillows against the headboard. In the process, the sheet fell from her shoulders, revealing a gossamer negligee that concealed nothing. Owen looked at her and an image leaped to his mind, an image of skin and hair the color of moonlight, and with it the memory of a cot and a hot summer night in Korea. Anna met his eyes again, saw him looking at her, and smiled the way she had over the low table in the apartment in Tokyo when Jürgen was behind her and couldn't see it.

"We still have time, you know," she said.

"I thought you were in a hurry to get the scroll."

"There's time enough for that. It's been hidden for nearly twenty years. It isn't going anywhere. Besides, what else can we do right now? The bank doesn't open until ten. We have some time to kill, so let's make the best of it."

"What would Jürgen say?"

213

"I don't care," she snapped. "He's my brother, not my father." Then she put the silk back in her voice. "Besides, what he doesn't know can't hurt us."

Owen thought about that. He knew the big Dane was dangerous—he could sense it. Jürgen almost certainly had some amount of training. Owen didn't know how much, but if he had trained in a camp like Yi Chung-hae's, he was a competent fighter to be sure. Of course, none of that would stop Owen if he really wanted Anna—he wasn't afraid of Jürgen or any other man—and he wanted her now. But something wasn't quite right. He couldn't put his finger on just what. Maybe it was just a lingering disquiet from his confrontation with Nomura. Maybe it was something more. It didn't matter. Owen was more soldier than psychologist, and like any good soldier—any soldier, that is, who has seen combat and lived long enough to think about it—he had learned to trust his instincts. Close brushes with death in Korea and Iraq had taught him that when that little voice whispers, *Wait a minute... Something's not right*, it's time to lay low until the fog clears.

"I think we'd better get down to breakfast," he said. "Our hostess is cooking for us. It would be rude to hole up here all morning after she's gone to that trouble." Not wanting to slam the door on future possibilities, he added, "There'll be time for other things later."

Anna watched him for several seconds, expressionless, seeming unsure of how to respond to his rejection. Then she sighed and shrugged her shoulders. "Okay, I've waited nearly twenty years, too," she said. "I can be patient until you're ready."

⟻+ +⟾

At 10:05 Owen and Anna stepped out of a taxi in front of the ornate baroque style building at Bahnhofstrasse 32, and went in through a pair of heavy, plate glass doors with the words "Bank Leu AG" stenciled on them.

"May I see your passport, please?" said Herr Kleistmann, the chief accounts officer a few minutes later. He was a middle-aged man in a charcoal-gray business suit that probably cost as much as Owen's car. His every word and gesture was crisply professional, the personification of German-Swiss efficiency. When Owen handed him the passport, he examined every page then compared the picture to Owen's face for a full fifteen seconds before typing some information on his desktop computer terminal in rapid, clackity keystrokes.

"Yes, I have it," he said after a moment. "The box number you gave me is held jointly under your name and that of a Rhys Powell."

"My father. He died many years ago."

"You will need to provide us an official document certifying his death before we can take his name off the account."

Owen shrugged. "I just need to get into the box today. We can bring things up to date later."

"I assume you have a key."

Owen took it out of his jacket pocket and placed it on the man's desk.

Kleistmann looked at the key suspiciously then said, "There are special security controls on this account."

"What does that mean?"

"It means we will have to take your palm print to verify your identity." Then, seeing Owen's concerned expression, he added, "Don't worry. We do this electronically now. It will take only seconds—if everything matches, that is. Come this way, please."

Owen could not imagine how a Swiss bank could possibly have his palm print on record, but there was no turning back now. He followed the banker to a device with a glass top that reminded him of a copier. Anna, who had sat quietly beside Owen throughout the interview with Kleistmann, trailed behind them.

After typing something into a computer terminal beside the machine, the banker turned to Owen and said, "Kindly place your right hand flat on the glass, please."

When Owen did so, Kleistmann pressed a button on the device's control panel and a bright light flashed beneath the glass. He turned back to the computer terminal, and a few seconds later, several screens of text scrolled across the monitor. To Owen's astonishment, Kleistmann turned to him and said, "Your identity is confirmed, Herr Powell." He smiled for the first time. "If you will follow me, I will take you into the vault and show you to your box."

They started that direction, but Kleistmann stopped abruptly when he saw Anna was following them. "Oh, excuse me, *Fraulein,*" he said, addressing her for the first time. "I am afraid only account holders are permitted in the vault."

Anna turned to Owen, concern darkening her face.

"You are welcome to wait in our guest lounge," the banker said. "I can have some coffee and pastries brought in."

"It's alright," Owen said. "I'll just be a few minutes. I'll bring it right out."

━┿┿━

Kleistmann poked a combination into a keypad beside the chrome-plated, barred gate that secured the room within the vault where the Powell family's safe deposit box resided. The electronic lock snapped and a servomotor rolled the gate aside with near silent precision. They went into a small room. Brushed-steel numbered boxes lined the walls, and a rectangular table stood in the center. There were no chairs.

"Let us see," the man said, running his hand over the wall of boxes. "835, 845... ah, here it is, SM850. Please try your key." He stepped back and watched as Owen inserted and turned the key then pulled the box out a couple of inches. "Very good, Herr Powell," he said, the last quaver of suspicion finally having left his voice. "I will leave you in private now. Feel free to use the table to organize your property. When you are ready to leave, secure your box then press the button by the gate and someone will come and let you out."

He turned and went out, locking the barred gate behind him.

Owen pulled the box out of its wall slot. It was heavy. He could see several large envelopes and some loose papers in it as he put it on the table. His breathing sounded loud in the little room, and he could feel his heart hammering the wall of his chest as he picked up the thick, yellow envelope on top and unwound the tie string.

He pulled out a stack of four-by-six-inch photographs. The top one was a studio portrait of his mother and father. Owen looked at it and smiled, remembering from other pictures he had seen how pretty his mother was. His father, too, was strikingly handsome when the picture was taken—so young, so happy and proud. He beamed in a way Owen could not remember ever seeing in his lifetime. Owen thumbed to the next photo, a baby picture of him. The one after that was of the three of them, his father holding Owen, who looked to be about a year old, his mother sitting beside them, one arm on her husband's shoulder and tickling Owen with the other hand. Owen was giggling. Mom and dad were smiling broadly. There were other pictures, but Owen sighed and shoved them all back into the envelope and turned to the box's other contents.

Shuffling through quickly, he was partly disappointed and partly relieved to find nothing resembling a scroll. He did find another key, a large old looking one this time, and that puzzled him. He laid it aside and was about to open another envelope when the handwriting on one of the loose papers caught his eye. Picking it up, he discovered it was a letter to him from his father.

Dear Owen,

I hope you never have to read this letter. If you do, it will be because I have died before I was able to tell you the truth about our family and prepare you for the grave responsibilities you will have to shoulder. I'm sorry, Son, both for bringing you into such a difficult life, one that will most certainly be fraught with peril, and for not being there to fully prepare you for this burden. The best I can do in these circumstances, is to tell you what I can in writing, from the grave as it were, and transfer to you the properties contained in this safe deposit box and elsewhere.

As you must know by now, you have inherited the mantle of Arbiter for the Keepers of the Covenant, the invisible realm, God's one true church. This burden has resided in our family since the first century. As such, we have adjudicated disputes between the most powerful men and women on Earth. We determine God's will and impose it on his servants. It is a heady responsibility and a terrible one, as it makes us targets of intrigue, coercion, and violence. Yet it is an obligation we cannot escape. Some Arbiters have tried and it has cost them dearly, so do not attempt to thwart God's will. Embrace your destiny, Son, and serve courageously.

In this box, you will find, among other things, the financial means to fulfill your office. This is the Powell family fortune, the wealth we have accumulated over many generations. It is now yours to do with as you choose, but I encourage you to manage it judiciously and live frugally. This is wealth with a purpose, not a license for luxury.

There is one more item I must pass to you—an ancient scroll, The Apocalypse of Joseph. You must present it at your investiture, as it is the source and evidence of your authority. As such, it is too precious to keep in this box. I have hidden it in a place only you will be able to reach. Use the key in this box to retrieve it. Your mother would want you to have it. You will know what to do.

In closing, Owen, I must give you the most important advice I have to offer—be careful who you trust. The wealth in this box alone would be enough to tempt all but the most noble of men and women. But the real source of danger for you is The Apocalypse and the power it represents. After your investiture, hide it in a safe place, a place where no one can guess where it is. Then, for the rest of your life, my Son, be strong, be wary, and always watch your back.

We will meet again in another life.

Your loving father,

Rhys Powell

Owen laid the letter down and sighed. Then he turned back to the box. He opened an envelope and poured its contents out onto the table. They were savings account passbooks from half a dozen Swiss banks, some in Zurich, some in Geneva. He opened one and turned to the balance: fifty-seven million Swiss francs and some change as of the last interest credit recorded in 1982. He wondered what it would be now. He opened a second passbook and found another balance in the tens of millions and the same in a third. In other envelopes he found stock certificates for thousands of shares in major international corporations, as well as government bonds and a variety of other financial instruments. He turned to the loose papers and discovered that most were deeds to property in the United States, Argentina, and several European countries.

After examining these things and rereading his father's letter one more time, he started repacking the safe deposit box. Hesitating a moment, he took the envelope containing his family pictures and slipped it into the inside pocket of his tweed jacket. Then he came to the key. He picked it up and stared at it puzzling. There was something vaguely familiar about this key, something that touched a distant memory that he couldn't quite dredge to the surface. Then it emerged and a series of emotions rolled over him like icy, Arctic swells—the shock of understanding, the horror of anticipation, and finally, the resolve to carry though to the end.

Five minutes later, Owen walked into Bank Leu's guest lounge. Anna sat waiting on a damask sofa, a fine china coffee cup in her hand, her long legs crossed, one bouncing nervously. A large Monet graced the mahogany paneled wall behind her. On a table beside her sat an untouched tray of pastries. Owen's feet moved silently on the plush carpet, but Anna was watching the door and stood up immediately when he came into the room.

"Where is it?" she said, looking him up and down, her brow furrowed.

Owen took her hand and started for the door. "Come on. We're going to England."

CHAPTER TWENTY-SEVEN

"What do you mean Mr. Inoue is unavailable?" Elaine asked the pale woman behind the desk.

"Mr. Inoue is unavailable," repeated Ms. Naguma, as if that answered Elaine's question. She looked up placidly, her hooded eyes betraying no emotion.

"Look, you asked me to wait. Well, I've been waiting for over an hour. I need to see Mr. Inoue on a very important matter. It concerns Dr. Owen Powell."

Naguma didn't answer, didn't blink, didn't so much as twitch. Elaine wondered if the woman could even close her eyes, with her hair pulled back so tightly. She stared back for a few moments, determined to win the contest of wills and kick back the gauntlet this infuriating woman had thrown down between them. It was no good. Naguma was made of stone.

Resisting an urge to stamp her foot, Elaine turned and started back towards the small sofa in the waiting alcove when the glass door to Inoue's outer office swung open and two men came in conversing in quick, hushed Japanese. One was an immaculately dressed man with graying hair and a patrician bearing. The other was a balding man with poor posture and a face that reminded Elaine of a rodent. They hesitated in the middle of the office, finishing their discussion, then Rat Face turned to go. As he walked out, his small eyes discovered Elaine and darted over her body, making her shudder. The elegant man walked past Naguma's desk towards a walnut paneled door. Repulsed by Rat Face's frenetic leer, Elaine jerked her glance away just in time to see Naguma's hand reach beneath her desktop. The electronic lock on the walnut door clicked, and the elegant man passed through without having to break his stride.

Inoue!

On impulse, Elaine sprang for the door, catching it just before it closed, and pushed through it. Naguma, who sat Sphinx-like only an instant before, leaped to her feet with remarkable agility.

"No! No!" she cried. "You cannot go in there!"

She chased Elaine through the door and barked at her heels all the way down the short hallway that led to Inoue's inner sanctum. The two of them burst into Inoue's office just before he reached his desk. He turned to look at them, his face a mask of angry surprise. Naguma began sputtering in rapid Japanese, all the while, bobbing her head in quick, penitent bows.

Inoue put up his palm and said something to Naguma. She stopped talking mid-word and bowed twice more. Elaine took satisfaction in the red patches she saw on the woman's cheeks as she backed out of the room, her head down. When she closed the door, Inoue turned to Elaine. He hesitated, appraising her, then motioned for her to sit down. He took his place behind the stainless steel and glass desk.

"Please tell... who are you and what business here?" he said.

"I am Professor Elaine Chen," she began in a rush. "I work with Dr. Owen Powell at the university. I've come because I—"

"Aaaaaiii!" Inoue said, holding up his hands. He looked down for a moment, frustration clouding his patrician features. Then he looked back at Elaine. *"Gomen nasai. Boku no Eigo ga totemo heta desu."* he said, apologizing for his poor English. *"Nihongo o hanashi-masu ka*—Do you speak Japanese?"

"Skoshi," Elaine said, "A little." She proceeded to explain in broken Japanese that the university was concerned because they had not heard from Owen and could not reach him in his hotel. Nomura stopped her frequently, asking her to repeat phrases several times. He could not seem to follow what she was trying to say, though Elaine was certain she was choosing the correct words and pronouncing them clearly enough, if very slowly.

Finally, in exasperation, Elaine blurted, "Owen Powell! *Doku desu ka*—Where is he?"

Inoue's eyes flashed when Elaine raised her voice, but his face remained calm. "Pawu-san at co-pu-ra-shuns," he said in careful English. "At comu-pan-ies he comu to study."

"How... can... I reach... him?" Elaine said.

Inoue shrugged then offered, "Try hoteo."

With that, he stood up and came around the desk. Elaine understood this to mean the interview was finished—she would get no more time or information from him. He shook her hand, bowing politely, and let her out, following her to the outer office and watching her go out the glass door.

He stood there a moment, his arms crossed, thinking. Then he saw rat-faced Teguchi Kenji, the Ferret, appear at the door. He hesitated there, his face turned toward the elevator, before coming in and scurrying up to Inoue.

"Who was that exquisite creature?" Teguchi said, his eyes darting eagerly.

Inoue continued staring at the door. "That's Powell's Chinese whore," he said, anger tightening his jaw, making the words sound pinched.

"Ah, well, the Arbiter certainly has good taste."

"She is pushy and rude. It's bad enough when Western women act that way. It is doubly insulting coming from a Chinese."

"I could teach her some manners," Teguchi said, his breath quickening. "Give her to me for an hour, and I'll have her whimpering the way a woman should."

Inoue looked at Teguchi and saw a bead of spittle forming at the corner of his mouth. Inoue had heard stories about this man, rumors that he frequented brothels in Shinjuku—well, the few that would still service him, anyway. The whispers spoke of violent fetishes, of humiliation, of prostitutes permanently scarred, and brothel owners paid to keep quiet. Now they say he can only go to houses that cater to his exotic appetites, and the fees are steep.

"Yes, I'll bet you could teach her a thing or two," Inoue said, smiling wryly. "Well, I hear the Arbiter has a new woman, now. Maybe I could talk Brother Saul into giving this one to you."

The Ferret's small eyes widened. "Do you really think you could?" He was nearly panting.

—⋈⋈—

Elaine was tired and her patience was nearly spent. She stood at the end of the front desk of Owen's hotel, talking with the manager, a tall, wiry man wearing round spectacles. His oiled hair was thin and slicked straight back. He sported a kerchief in the breast pocket of his suit that matched his tie.

"Why can't you just give me his room number?" Elaine said.

"Madame," the man said, "I have already explained that to you. For reasons of privacy and security, we do not give out our guests' room numbers. That is our policy."

The man's attitude chafed Elaine to the bone. Who did he think he was, calling her "Madame?" She wasn't married and he most certainly wasn't French.

"Well how do I reach him? This is vitally important. The university where he teaches in the United States sent me to find him. We are very concerned about his safety."

"I assure you that every guest is completely safe and secure in our hotel."

"I'm not suggesting any harm has come to him in the hotel," she said, raising her voice. "But we haven't been able to reach him for days. I need to see him face to face."

"I would be glad to ring his room for you. Then he can come down to the lobby to see you or give you his room number himself... That is, if you are someone he wishes to see."

Elaine resisted an urge to slap him. "I've already called his room several times. No one answers."

"Well then..." the man said, shrugging his shoulders as if that settled the issue. He stared at Elaine a moment longer. When he saw she was momentarily at a loss for words, he bowed curtly. "If you will excuse me, Madame, I have business to attend to." He left her standing at the desk.

Elaine wondered what to do next. She considered staking out the lobby, finding a spot on one of the sofas or armchairs from where she could watch the elevators and front doors. Owen was still registered at the hotel—the switchboard rang a room whenever she called and asked for him—he had to pass through the lobby sooner or later. But that didn't sound like a feasible plan. She was exhausted. If she sat down, she would likely fall asleep, and it wouldn't be long before the hotel staff would be asking her to leave. She bristled at the thought of that snooty manager looking down his nose at her and suggesting "Madame" should find accommodations elsewhere.

Maybe she should just check into the hotel. She had to stay somewhere while she looked for Owen. His hotel made the most sense. She could clean up and get a few hours sleep then come down and—

"Excuse me honorable lady," said a voice behind her in a language she had not heard in several years. It was Cantonese, the native tongue of her birthplace, Hong Kong.

"Yes?"

She turned and saw a young man in an ill-fitted uniform standing at the bellhop's station a few feet away. He was bowing as he spoke, his eyes at her feet in deference.

"Please forgive me for intruding, but I overheard your discussion with the manager. Please accept my apology for his rudeness."

Elaine appraised the young man and decided he was sincere. She guessed him to be one of the thousands of poor, young Chinese who find their way to Japan to work or go to school in an effort to make better lives for themselves. Having heard her talking, he must have recognized her Hong Kong accent and identified her as a compatriot, though one from the upper class.

"You needn't apologize for him," she said. "He is rude but, after all, he is only Japanese."

"Yes, that is true." The young man finally straightened his back, but still kept his head down in respect. "Again, forgive me for intruding, but I also have some information about the man you are trying to reach."

Elaine was immediately alert. "What is it?"

"His room is number 1037—I took his bags up when he checked in—but he is no longer there."

"He's checked out of the hotel?"

"No, he still has the room, and some of his things are still there. One of the tenth-floor housekeepers, Shi Lin, is Chinese and we... well, we talk. But several days ago, Shi Lin and I were both on night duty. I was going up to see her on my last break—it was about 4:00 A.M.—and when the elevator opened on the tenth floor, Mr. Powell got on it to go down. He had a small suitcase in his hand, one of the two I delivered to his room the week before."

"You're saying Mr. Powell's things are still in the hotel, but he left with a suitcase in the middle of the night… well, in the early morning hours?" Elaine said, more to organize the information in her own mind than to question the man's honesty.

"Yes. And there is one other thing I should tell you." The young man bowed again and seemed reluctant to go on. "Please forgive me, honorable lady, but he was not alone."

Elaine's blood turned to ice water. "Go on."

"He was with a *gwai loh* woman. She was holding onto his arm. She was blond and… well, very beautiful."

CHAPTER TWENTY-EIGHT

Owen was surprised to find himself standing in a fog. He didn't know where he was or why he was there. He looked around, trying to get his bearings, trying to find some identifiable landmark, but there was none. The fog was cold and wet on his face, and it had begun to soak through his clothes, but he didn't feel chilled. He was confused.

He stood wondering what to do. Then he felt the onset of an old sense of dread, a foreboding that was troubling, yet strangely comforting if only because it was so familiar. Somehow, it seemed to offer an explanation for why he was there, but he couldn't quite figure out what that explanation was.

I should be afraid of something, but what? A sound... Something about a sound...

He began to walk. Then he heard it and stopped.

It was very faint then gone. He closed his eyes, slowed his breathing, and listened. He could hear the blood rushing in his ears, hear his heart thumping in his chest, but everything outside him was silent, absolutely still.

No, he heard it again, louder this time.

Someone was calling his name... Yes, it was a woman's voice, and she was definitely calling his name. That was different from the way it had been before. But different how? He couldn't remember. He listened intently, trying to figure out who the woman might be, why she would be calling him, from what direction her voice was coming. Then he became alarmed as he realized the voice was Elaine's and she sounded distressed.

"Elaine!" His voice was swallowed up in the impenetrable fog. No echo, no resonance, only dead, wet air.

Elaine called out again, and Owen tried to get a bearing on which direction her calls were coming from. Unlike his voice, hers echoed and seemed to come from everywhere at once. He began walking, hoping to find some landmark, some clue to where he was and where she might be.

She called again, and her voice was louder now. Maybe he had gone the right direction. If so, he was no less anxious, because now she sounded more distraught. She called his name again and again. She became insistent, and the tone and timbre of her voice took on a hopeless quality he had never heard in it before. She wasn't crying in pain or fear or anger. She just moaned in a pitiful, crestfallen way that said she needed him desperately, but held little hope that he would ever come to her.

The despair he heard in her voice cut him like jagged glass, and he felt the first stirrings of panic. He called to her, yelled, screamed until his throat burned, but his words were extinguished in the fog.

Owen walked faster, though there was no distinguishable difference in the terrain, no landmarks to indicate his progress or gauge his speed. He walked on and on, straining his eyes to see through the mist, fighting to remain calm, to keep his rising panic in check.

Then, to his surprise and unspeakable relief, the mist parted and he saw her. In a foggy clearing about fifty feet away, Elaine stood still and alone in her silver-blue, satin bathrobe. The damp chill had compelled her to pull the robe around her tightly, accentuating her graceful curves and hardened nipples. Her face was dark with despair, but Owen called to her, and this time she heard him. She looked up hopefully. Then she saw him and joyful relief filled her almond-shaped, ebony eyes.

"Owen, where have you been?" Her voice echoed all around him. She reached out to him and smiled.

Owen started to walk to her and was about to answer, but a movement in the fog caught his eye and someone stepped out of the mist a few yards behind her. *Anna!* Owen was momentarily puzzled. Anna fixed her eyes on his and smiled. Suddenly, horror gripped him as he watched her move towards Elaine. "No!" he yelled and leaped to protect Elaine. But the fog muffled his voice and his effort to reach her brought him no closer.

Silent as the fog itself, Anna slipped behind Elaine, moving closer and closer until she was almost flush against the smaller woman's slender back. Owen struggled to reach them, but he seemed suspended in space as time moved forward, events grinding toward a cruel, inevitable conclusion.

Elaine, oblivious to the danger behind her, cocked her head in puzzlement. "Come to me Owen. I need you." Her voice echoed in the fog.

"Elaine, come here!" Owen yelled, but no sound left his lips. "Get away from her!" he yelled at Anna, but she only smiled.

As Owen watched in horror, Anna turned to Elaine and raised her hands on either side of the smaller woman's head almost affectionately, as if she were about to stroke her raven hair. Then a wire garrote appeared in her hands, and in one cobra-like movement, she whipped it around Elaine's throat and jerked it tight, yanking Elaine's head back against her, locking it in the notch between her jaw and collarbone. Elaine's mouth and eyes flew open wide, and she clawed at her throat in desperation, gurgling weakly, her knees pumping.

"No!" Owen screamed. "Let her go!" But Anna only grinned, her cheek pressed against the side of Elaine's head.

Both women's eyes fixed on his, one radiating terror, the other delight. As Owen cried helplessly, Elaine's kicking slowed to spasmodic jerks then stopped as the light went out of her eyes. Her hands fell away from her throat and hung limply at her sides. Anna, still smiling and gazing at Owen, let the delicate woman's flaccid body slide partway down the front of her then shoved it away roughly.

Elaine fell facedown in the dirt.

Owen felt as if his gut had been ripped away. All strength seemed to drain out of him. He slowly sank to his knees, his face contorted in anguish. "Why?" he said, looking into Anna's smiling face. "Good God in heaven... Why?"

Anna said nothing. Her eyes, still holding Owen's in their grip, sparkled in satisfaction. Then he heard her thoughts as clearly as if she were speaking: *You caused this. This is your fault!*

"No!" Owen cried out. As he yelled a hissing noise filled his ears and got louder and louder until it became a roar, drowning out the sound of everything else...

He jerked awake and found himself belted into a first-class seat on an airliner, the sound of air and engines filling his senses. He tried to swallow, but his mouth was all sand and cotton. His forehead was clammy. Anna was curled up asleep beside him, hugging his arm, her head nestled on his shoulder. His jolt to wakefulness had joggled her and she stirred, but did not fully wake. She coiled her arms more tightly around his, drawing him deeper into her grasp, and settled back to sleep.

All at once, Owen felt a tide of claustrophobia rise up in him. Fighting an almost overpowering urge to throw Anna off, he closed his eyes, pulled air in through his nose, and concentrated on calming himself.

In a few minutes, the panic subsided.

＝◁┼ ┼▷＝

It was almost midnight when Owen and Anna stepped to the curb outside London Heathrow Airport to wait for the shuttle to the rental car agency. Owen had called ahead from Zurich and reserved a car for them.

"After we get the car," Anna said, slipping an arm around his waist, "we can find a room someplace close and get some rest." When he turned to answer her, she pulled him close and pecked the corner of his mouth.

Owen pulled away from her. "I want to get on the road right away. We need to get to Somerset County well before dawn. It's in the West Country, south of Bristol, and what we need to do can't be done in the daylight. We can't risk anyone seeing us."

"But I'm tired, Owen," she whined. Then, sliding up against him again, she cooed, "Besides, we need to spend some time together. Somerset is less than three hours away. We've got plenty of time."

Just then the shuttle pulled up and the door folded open. Owen turned to get on then turned back, looking around. "Where's your bag?"

"Oh, no! I must have left it in the loo," Anna said, looking alarmed. They both hesitated a moment, trying to decide what to do. Then she said, "I'll go look for it. You go and get the car then pick me up here."

As the shuttle pulled way with Owen aboard, she turned and started running back to the door of the terminal. But as soon as the shuttle was out of sight, she slowed to a walk and dug a cellphone out of her handbag. She dialed a number and gathered her thoughts as she counted the rings.

"Hello," came a deep voice. It was Jürgen.

"It's me."

"Where have you been? Why haven't you called?"

"I'm at London Heathrow."

"England?" Jürgen was incredulous. "What are you doing there? Do you have the scroll?"

"No, Rhys Powell was more clever than we anticipated. He didn't keep it in Zurich. The safe deposit box just had a letter to Owen and another key. Owen's renting a car and we're going to get the scroll tonight."

"And your other task?"

Anna paused. This was the part she had dreaded. "Not yet," she said.

"What?" Jürgen exploded. "But you've been with him for two nights!"

"It's not so easy now. He's not a boy anymore. I'm close, but I can't push too hard and risk arousing his suspicion."

"Anna, you know how important this is. Don't mess up again like you did in Korea."

She felt the blood rush to her face. "Don't start that again! We've been through it a hundred times. I didn't mess up. I had him under control, but that bastard Pak was on to me. I had to move too soon. It was the wrong time of the month. I wasn't fertile. One more week and I would have ovulated, but Pak's meddling forced me to take what I could get, call for the extraction, and hope for the best."

"Well, the best wasn't good enough, was it?"

Anna opened her mouth, but was so angry she couldn't find any words.

"Okay, that's behind us now," Jürgen said, his tone more businesslike than conciliatory. "But before we go any further, I want to make sure you're clear on your three objectives—"

"Yeah, yeah, I know—"

"No, shut up and listen! I don't want you to fuck this up again." Anna drew in a breath to yell, but Jürgen didn't give her an opening. "Your first and most important task is to get the scroll," he said. "We've got to hand that over to Brother Saul to seal the alliance. There's going to be a bloodbath between the houses soon, and Asher is going to come out on top. Saul's leadership is the future—the near future, at least—and when the time comes, we need to be part of his inner circle. But the ultimate destiny of our family depends on your second task. You've got to bear the future Arbiter, so stop fooling around and get pregnant with Powell!"

"I told you, I'm working on it! But if Brother Saul is going to name his own Arbiter once he gets the scroll, what good does my having a baby with Owen do us?"

"Absolutely none at all unless the Arbiter Saul names abdicates in favor of your son, once he comes of age."

"And why would anyone do that?"

Jürgen laughed then waited for her to figure it out.

"You don't mean he's going to name you!"

"It's part of our deal. I get him the scroll and he names me Arbiter. He holds the scroll in escrow to ensure I look after his interests. He thinks he can control me. And he thinks that when I die childless, he or his successor in the House of Asher can simply name another Arbiter, someone even more closely tied to them."

"So Saul knows you're not a whole man." Anna laughed, thoroughly savoring the jab at his ego.

"Yes, little sister, Saul knows I cannot father a child. That's why he's willing to stake his future on my loyalty. But there are a few things he isn't counting on. He won't know about your son—we'll keep that secret. And he won't know that when the boy comes of age, our house and its allies will provoke a confrontation with Asher. Saul will call for mediation, certain I will rule in his favor, but this time the Arbiter will rule against him."

"If you think he'll let you get away with that, you're light in places besides your balls."

"I may be sterile, but I'm not stupid," he sneered. "Of course Saul won't stand for that. He's too proud a man to accept my betrayal. That's what I'm counting on. He'll defy my ruling, and I'll raise a Covenant army that will crush Asher and take back the scroll. Then we will unveil your son as the Powell heir, and I'll abdicate in his favor and wield the Arbiter's mace through him."

"You've got this all figured out."

"I've had nearly twenty years to think about it—ever since you fucked up in Korea and I discovered that son of a bitch Rhys Powell didn't keep the scroll in his house. The first plan came unhinged, but everything's gone more smoothly this time, now that we have Saul pulling strings for us. But for any of this to work, you've got to do your job. The first two objectives are within reach. Let Powell bring you the scroll then lie down and spread your legs—even you can do that." It was his turn to jab. "But are you sure you're good enough to handle your third task?"

"There is no man on this planet I can't kill," Anna said quickly. Then she paused, took a couple of quick breaths, and added, "But don't you think we should wait awhile before I dispose of Owen? I mean, we may need him again. What if I get pregnant, but it turns out to be a girl?"

"You know better than that, Anna. For two thousand years, the anointed line has borne only male children. It's one of God's little miracles, or so they say."

"But what if I miscarry? We need Owen around for insurance. I can control—"

"Don't miscarry! This issue is nonnegotiable. It's part of the deal with Saul. Powell has to be out of the way so he can present his own candidate as Arbiter. So no, little sister, you cannot keep him as a pet. When the rabbit dies, so does Powell!"

With that, Jürgen hung up leaving Anna listening to the dead hiss coming from her cellphone. She clicked it off and tried to stop her hands from shaking.

Kill Owen... Am I really going to have to kill Owen?

CHAPTER TWENTY-NINE

Owen had the highway nearly to himself when he negotiated the roundabout and merged onto route M4 shortly before 1 AM. A three-quarter moon bathed the countryside in blue-gray iridescence and conjured up mist from the boggy moors hugging the highway. Aside from the occasional passing car, only the yellow cones of Owen's own headlights penetrated the ghostly night. Anna slept fitfully in the passenger seat of the rented Jaguar, leaning against the door instead of on Owen's shoulder where she had nestled so frequently over the last several days. She was sulking.

When Owen had returned to the terminal with the car, she had once again urged that they get a good night's sleep and set out in the morning, or even the next evening if he felt they ought to make the trip by night. But he had held firm. The time for waiting was over. He was going to get the scroll now, tonight. When he told her he wouldn't take her straight to a hotel, she first tried silky persuasion then began marshaling a series of arguments. But when he finally explained where they were going and what they would have to do, she had given in without further objection. She just turned her opalescent eyes on him, eyes gone jade in their sudden coolness.

He didn't mind. In fact, her chilly distance was almost refreshing for a change. It was like a cool breeze blowing through his mind, sweeping clean the many conflicted emotions that had made thinking clearly so difficult lately. The quiet of the night alone on the ribbon of highway put him in a contemplative mood, almost like his practice of *zazen*, seated meditation, had so many times in the past.

And Owen had a great deal to think about. He couldn't figure out why his father was sending him on a scavenger hunt for the scroll. If he wanted him to have it, why hadn't he just put it in the safe deposit box in Zurich? He had considered the box secure enough to keep records of the tens of millions of dollars in family assets, so why not the scroll?

Then Owen thought of the key and shuddered. He knew the gate it opened would be the end of the scavenger hunt. There would be no more clues—no letters, no files, no one there to hand him another enigmatic object. The scroll would be there. When Owen stared at the key in Zurich, it had filled him with dread, though, at first, he couldn't remember when or where he had seen it. Then in one icy, horrifying rush, it had come to him.

Owen had seen the key twice before. The first time was when he was ten years old and his father had brought him along on a trip to England. While they were there, Rhys had taken him to lay flowers on his mother's crypt. She was entombed in a mausoleum in an old country cemetery owned by her extended family. Owen remembered the fear that gripped him when his father took him into that house of the dead and explained that her body lay in one of the two granite coffins there.

"One day," Rhys had said, "my earthly shell will lie here beside your mother."

The second time Owen had seen the key was when that day came, the day of his father's funeral. It unlocked the mausoleum's iron gate. Rhys's statement in the letter that his mother would want him to have the key was his way of telling Owen he had hidden the scroll in her sarcophagus. Owen shuddered again and tried to think of something else.

He looked over at Anna, saw the classic lines of her beautiful face in profile, saw the swell of her bosom rise and fall as she slept. She was, perhaps, the most alluring woman he had ever known. He had wanted her desperately that summer in Korea, and she was far more beautiful now. He wanted her still. He longed for her, ached for her all the more knowing he could finally have her. Owen knew Anna would now be his whenever he wanted her. Even as she sulked against the car door, he knew that if he pulled off the road, grabbed her arm and jerked her to him, she would submit eagerly, hungrily. But he was not going to take her.

In the stillness of the misty English night, he finally realized why he had repeatedly avoided intimacy with Anna. It was because he loved Elaine. Despite all the arguing, the hurt pride, and the jealousy over her relationship with Randall Preston, Owen now knew that he loved her and was going to fight to get her back. At this point, he didn't know if their relationship was salvageable. All he knew was that he had to try.

And he would have to explain this to Anna... after they got the scroll.

━◈ ◈━

It was almost dawn when Owen pulled off the country road and killed the engine in front of the high, spiked iron fence that encompassed the old cemetery. The moon had set, and the eastern sky was just beginning to lighten. A heavy mist clung to the ground and pooled in the hollows. Across the road stood an old cottage, a precarious stone structure with a thatched roof, encircled by a waist-high wall. There was no other building in sight.

Owen nudged Anna. She jumped momentarily then was instantly alert.

"We're here," he said, getting out of the car. He went around to the back. *There's a torch in the boot,* he remembered the rental agent telling him. He opened the trunk and found the flashlight, turned it on, and grabbed the tire iron. By then, Anna was beside him. He closed the trunk as quietly as he could, and they set off into the cemetery.

The place was ancient, a miserable assortment of broken gravestones and huge Celtic stone crosses, their inscriptions worn away by centuries of rain and wind, their owners long ago dust and even longer forgotten in graves overrun by brambles. Owen remembered his terror the first time his father had brought him here. He turned to put a comforting arm around Anna's shoulder, but she walked just out of reach, her jaw set, her gait determined.

Toward the back of the cemetery, they went over a rise. An elegant, white marble mausoleum loomed up in the darkness in stark contrast to the crumbling stones around it. Without speaking, they went to the tomb's wrought iron gate. Owen handed Anna the flashlight and tire iron then pulled the big key from his coat pocket, inserted it in the gate latch, and twisted. Nothing happened at first, and he thought the old lock was rusted in place. But he cranked harder, jiggling the key up and down, and the latch finally scraped free. The gate creaked loudly when Owen pulled it. Then it groaned open. He retrieved the flashlight and tire iron and stepped inside. Anna followed closely.

The tomb was dank, smelling of moss and mildew. They heard a rat scratching somewhere on the floor. Owen shined the flashlight around, and his anxiety began to build as he took in the scene that evoked his terror as a child and became the focus of his grief as an orphaned teen. The chamber was a smooth marble cubicle with two granite sarcophagi standing parallel about three feet apart in the center. On the back wall of the mausoleum, at the head of the crypt on the right, was carved the simple epitaph:

Rhys Llewellyn Powell
January 25, 1915 – August 19, 1982
Noble soldier in Christ

The inscription over the other sarcophagus was just as plain and unpretentious:

Olivia Parker Powell
May 21, 1933 – March 30, 1966
Loving wife and mother

Owen stood frozen for a moment, unsure he could follow through with what he had come to do. How could his father have done such a thing? How he could have secreted something in his dead wife's grave. When did he do it, right after the funeral? Or did he come back and open her coffin years later?

Anna pushed past him and went to the head of his mother's crypt. "Come on," she said. "It's this one." She began tugging on the granite lid, but it was either too heavy for her to budge, or it was stuck in place. "Well, are you going to help me?" she flashed Owen an impatient frown.

Forcing himself to move, he stepped between the stone coffins and laid the flashlight on the one that held his father's remains. Then he turned to his mother's crypt and hooked the pry-bar end of the tire iron under the lid and levered downward. A second later, the lid gave way with a hiss and a hollow thunk. He levered some more until it stood slightly ajar over the sarcophagus, leaving an edge under which they could get their fingers. He laid the tire iron on top and they both grabbed the lid and heaved.

It must have weighed hundreds of pounds. For a moment, Owen wondered how they were going to handle it. But Anna surprised him with her strength, and together, hauling and shoving, they managed to wrestle the ponderous stone slab little by little until the length of the sarcophagus was open about a foot and a half.

Taking the flashlight, Owen steeled himself and leaned over the edge. There was no inner coffin. He just caught a glimpse of skeletal legs, desiccated flesh stretched over bones protruding from beneath a green dress, before the air, trapped in the crypt for thirty-five years, rose up and assaulted him and he reeled back in disgust.

"Oh, give me that," Anna said, snatching the flashlight out of his hand.

As Owen recoiled against the sarcophagus behind him, she bent over the open stone coffin and began scrabbling around in its contents. Transfixed in horror, he saw a cloud of dust, dust that was once his mother, rising up in the glow of the flashlight.

"I've got it!" Anna held up a sealed metal cylinder, her face eerily triumphant in the under-glow of the flashlight. "Come on, let's get out of here." She started to squeeze between Owen and the coffin.

"Hey, wait a minute," Owen said, regaining his presence of mind. "We can't just leave everything like this."

Anna stopped abruptly and stared at him. She sighed heavily. Then she laid the flashlight and metal cylinder on his father's sarcophagus and helped him wrestle the granite coffin lid back in place.

They collected their things—Owen carrying the flashlight and tire iron, Anna clutching the cylinder to her breast—and stepped out the door.

Then it happened.

"Freeze!" came a threatening shout. "Don't either of you move."

Owen looked around and saw four county constables, one on each side of the mausoleum's gate, two more in front of them, all about ten feet away. Although the hazy dawn had finally come, casting its dull gray light over the cemetery, the officers still had their flashlights on, and they trained them on Owen and Anna. They all had police batons in their other hands.

Owen saw Anna bend her knees slightly to lower her center of gravity and sensed her preparing to spring. "No," he said. "Relax."

"But we can take these guys," she hissed without moving her lips. She angled her body, widened her stance, and raised her free hand in a fist.

"Stop it!" Owen said. "We aren't going to fight the police." Then to the head constable, "We won't be any trouble. We'll go quietly."

"Drop those things and raise your hands," demanded the policeman.

Owen did as he was told, and the constables moved in to handcuff him. Anna clutched the metal cylinder ever tighter to her breast.

"I'll take that," said one of the policemen. He wrenched it out of her grip.

CHAPTER THIRTY

"How many times do I have to tell you?" Owen said. "I was not looking for jewelry or anything else."

"No, of course not," Detective Sergeant Higgins said, "You and your girlfriend just flew into England in the middle of the night to pay yer' ol' mum a visit. Makes perfect sense. After all, don't we all visit our parents' graves in the wee hours with pry bars in hand?"

The detective was a short, balding man with a pug face and a flat, lumpy nose. He was paunchy, but his jacket was stretched tight at the shoulders. Owen thought he might have been a boxer once, or maybe a wrestler.

"It was a tire iron," he said. "I brought it along in case the gate was rusted shut."

He shifted uncomfortably in the straight-backed wooden chair and decided interrogation cells must be pretty much the same the world over: dirty little rooms with plain, white walls. The furnishings looked familiar, too. Higgins glared at him across a dingy table, its cheap Formica top marred by cigarette burns.

Owen knew the routine—after all, he had been on the other side of tables like this often enough as an Army intelligence officer—so Higgins didn't scare him. But he was tired and hungry, and he wondered what the police were going to make of the stainless steel canister they had taken from Anna at the mausoleum. He worried about how he would manage to get it back, but he kept the worry off his face.

There was a Styrofoam cup on the table. Higgins picked it up and gulped down the dregs of his coffee and made a face. He hadn't offered Owen any. "What's in the metal tube?" he rasped.

"I don't know," Owen said. "Must be something the lady brought along. Why don't you ask her?" He imagined Anna in a separate interrogation room and wondered how she was holding up.

"We did. She isn't talking any more than you are."

"Then why don't you open it and find out?"

"Oh, we will, mate. You can count on that. But we're waiting for the boys and girls from the lab to come in. The way that thing's sealed up, the lads think you might have some kind of biohazard in there. How about it, Powell? You got something dangerous in that tube?"

"I guess we'll find out when—"

The door opened abruptly, and a corpulent, late middle-aged, uniformed officer strode in, followed by a trim blond man in a suit.

"All right, Higgins. We'll take it from here," the officer said from between ruddy jowls.

"Bloody hell," Higgins said, turning on the man. "What the devil are you doing, Chief? And who the hell are you?" he said to the blond man.

The man ignored Higgins and stepped over to Owen. "Dr. Powell, my name is Thomas Jeffries," he said, smiling and putting out his hand. Owen hesitated then took it, and Jeffries shook his hand firmly.

"Jeffries is from MI6," said Chief Constable MacMillan, the beefy uniformed officer. "They're taking jurisdiction on this case. Seems it's a matter of state security."

"State security my arse!" Higgins leaped up from the table. "Since when is grave robbing a matter of state security? And, for that matter, since when can MI6 take jurisdiction on anything inside the UK?"

"Look Higgins," MacMillan said, raising his voice to match the detective's, "I don't like this any more than you do. But I got a call from Scotland Yard. Special Branch thinks this might have something to do with the Glastonbury Massacre. They're sending someone out to take over. He'll be here in a couple of hours. In the meantime, Jeffries here is on the task force, and they want him to handle the questioning."

"But Glastonbury went down in our jurisdiction, and if this has anything to do..."

Jeffries, ignoring the squabbling constables, leaned close to Owen. "Have you had anything to eat this morning?"

"No, I've been shut up in this room since they picked me up two hours ago."

Jeffries turned to the officers. "Get this man some breakfast," he said loudly, "bangers and fresh eggs." The constables stopped arguing mid-sentence and looked at Jeffries, their mouths agape. "You do eat eggs, don't you mate?" Jeffries said to Owen.

"Yeah, but I'm not too keen on bangers," Owen said, looking quizzical.

"Righto," Jeffries winked. "Don't blame ya." He wheeled on the officers who still hadn't found words to express their indignation. "Make that Canadian bacon."

"Now see here," MacMillan finally managed to sputter, his face crimson. "We're not errand boys, you know."

"Then find someone who is and get this man some food. And while you're at it, send in a pot of strong coffee and two mugs." Both constables opened their mouths to protest, but Jeffries didn't give them time. "Gentlemen, I've got work to do here," he said, sitting down across from Owen. "Kindly close the door on your way out."

The policemen stood rigid, looking as if their heads might explode at any second. They stared at Jeffries who stared back, his face relaxed, but his eyes hard as granite. Finally, MacMillan wheeled on Higgins and yelled, "Oh, come on!" They bashed out the door and slammed it behind them.

Jeffries settled back in his chair and grinned at Owen. "What is it you Yanks call blokes like that? 'Keystone Kops'?"

Owen suppressed a smile.

"Sorry you had to put up with a bit of grilling," Jeffries said. "It took time for word to wicker through the proper channels after we intercepted the cemetery caretaker's call to the police reporting your break-in at the mausoleum."

"What is MI6 doing monitoring phone calls inside the UK?" Owen said, raising an eyebrow.

"I didn't say MI6 was doing anything of the kind."

"Who then?"

"Come now, Doctor, you're well past that."

"Gnostics? Covenant Keepers? Here in Britain?"

"Especially here in Britain."

Just then the door opened and a deputy constable brought in a carafe of coffee and two porcelain mugs. Jeffries poured as the man left.

"Now why am I not surprised?" Owen said after the door closed. "It seems I can't swing a dead cat these days without hitting a Gnostic Christian."

Jeffries laughed. "I'll have to write that one down."

"Where are they keeping Anna?" Owen said sharply. "I need to know she's all right."

The Englishman tensed. "Ms. Norgaard is fine. I stopped the interrogation—not that they were getting anywhere with her—and had them move her to a holding cell."

"So what's this all about?" Owen said. "Why would you be intercepting phone calls to England's version of the Mayberry Sheriff's Office? Why would Scotland Yard send you to question me on a petty break-in at a cemetery? What does this have to do with the Glastonbury Massacre?"

Jeffries folded his arms across his chest and smiled. "Why don't you just settle back and have a cup of coffee. It'll calm your nerves. Breakfast will be here soon, and so will someone who is very eager to talk to you."

Owen was mopping egg yolk with the last bite of his English muffin when MacMillan came in saying, "He's right in here, Your Lordship," to someone behind him. Owen looked around to see a well dressed, powerfully built man of about sixty come in behind the chief constable. His curly beard and hair were gray, but his youthful blue eyes sparkled when he saw Owen.

"Owen, my boy, it's so good to see you again," he said, putting out his hand and smiling.

Owen and Jeffries rose from their chairs and Owen reluctantly shook the man's hand. "I'm sorry. Have we met?"

"Yes, several times, but I'm not surprised you don't recall. You were probably too distraught to remember everyone at your father's funeral, and before that, you were just a tyke."

"Powell, this is Lord Robert Huntington, the Earl of Kimberly," MacMillan said. "He owns the property you broke into this morning. He'll be filing charges, I'm sure."

"No, none of that," Kimberly said. "Owen is family. I've come to straighten out this mix-up."

"But... but... Your Lordship," MacMillan said, his jowls trembling. "He broke into the tomb with a pry bar. He—"

"He was visiting his parents' graves," Kimberly said. "And he let himself in with a key. I phoned the caretaker an hour ago. Everything is in order at the mausoleum. He just overreacted he when heard the car and saw someone in the cemetery with a flashlight. It was a reasonable response—calling the police, I mean—but it was all a misunderstanding."

"But Your Lordship—"

"I think we've just about covered it all," Jeffries said, shuffling the chief out the door. "Let's let Lord Kimberly catch up on old times with his cousin from the States." MacMillan was still grousing as Jeffries followed him out, reached back, and closed the door.

"Cousin?" Owen said, sitting down and pouring himself another cup of coffee.

"Your mum was my third cousin, twice removed," Kimberly said, taking the chair that Jeffries and Higgins had used. "It's really good to see you again, my boy."

"Excuse me for not waxing nostalgic with you, Cousin, but just what the hell is going on here?"

"Terse and to the point, just like your father," Kimberly smiled wryly. "Right then, let's get down to business." The smile on Kimberly's face disappeared, and he locked Owen's pale, snow leopard eyes in a stony gaze. "You already know I am a Covenant Keeper. Well, I'm more than that. Within the Covenant I am called Brother Joshua. I am the Illuminatus of David, the enlightened, God-chosen leader of the Covenant's royal house, heir to the sacred legacy of Jesus, James, and Joseph of Arimathea. I preside over the Great Circle."

"Pleased to make your acquaintance, Your Holy Eminence."

"You want to know what the hell is going on?" Kimberly growled. "Well lose the sarcastic, cocksure attitude and listen. You're about to learn something. About six months ago I convened the Circle at the site of the first Christian church in Britain. We gathered to consider a prophecy in our scripture that foretold your awakening and the challenges you would face."

"My awakening?"

"Your awakening to the legacy, to the pivotal role you would play in our society. The prophesy foretold that you would awaken and be forced to make some crucial decisions, and the choices you would make would determine the fate of humankind—continued survival or apocalyptic destruction."

"Apocalyptic destruction? Now that's rich—the fate of humankind on my shoulders. And you believe this prophesy?"

"Absolutely."

"Well how do you know you've interpreted it correctly? As I recall, my last reading of *Revelations* left me more than a little fuzzy on how the end of the world is supposed to go down."

"The *Apocalypse of John*, or "*Revelations*" as you call it, is a semi-synoptic work, part of an incomplete code. God simultaneously revealed half the vision to John and the other half to Joseph of Arimathea. Neither *Apocalypse* can be understood without the other. But when they are examined together—when God's original and unaltered Word is considered in its fullness—the prophecies emerge clearly. And they are infallible. In fact, they are already coming to pass.

"The day we convened to consider the prophecy, the Great Circle was attacked. Our guardians disposed of the attackers quickly, but not before one of the Illuminati fell to an assassin's bullet. We now know the attack was engineered by someone within the Circle, but we don't know who. The great houses are on the verge of war—none of them knows who to trust, who among them is an ally and who is a traitor. The situation is dire. We've infiltrated the earth's most powerful governments, so if house turns against house in open warfare, the outside world will be dragged into the conflict and humankind will devour itself in flame. All of this is foretold, and all of it is coming to pass. After all, you have awakened, and you are being tested. You are the pivotal figure in all of this. The Word is made manifest in you."

Owen fought to maintain his skepticism, his glib attitude, his sarcastic facade, but it was starting to drain away. He felt like he had just taken a punch in the solar plexus.

"So what is this test?" he said, his voice barely above a whisper. "What are these choices I am supposed to make?"

"That, I can't tell you."

Owen exploded.

"Then why the hell are you here?" he yelled lurching across the table. "You Covenant bastards have led me in circles for weeks. 'Go home,' one says. 'You're in mortal danger, but I can't tell you why or what that danger is.' 'Go to Switzerland and get the scroll,' others say. 'No, it's in England.' Just how in the hell am I supposed to know who to believe?"

He leaped up, knocking his chair over, and began pacing around the room. Kimberly folded his arms across his chest and settled back in his chair.

"Two weeks ago, everything in my life was normal. Now I don't know who my father really was, or my mother for that matter. Hell, I don't even know who I am anymore. You tell me the fate of the world rests on my shoulders, but you won't tell me what you expect me to do?" He stopped next to Kimberly, leaned down, and yelled in the aristocrat's face. "Just what the fuck do you people want from me?"

Kimberly didn't flinch. He met Owen's glare with his own, held it a moment, then spoke calmly. "We simply want you to become the great man you've been bred and groomed to be."

That response caught Owen like a short left hook. He stopped yelling and hovered over Kimberly for a few seconds longer then deflated and sank back down in the chair across from him.

"Owen, I can't tell you anything about the challenge you are facing," Kimberly said gently. "I can't tell you what choice you have to make or even what you have to choose between. That would be tampering with the prophecy, meddling in God's plan. All I can do is offer my help in whatever course you decide to follow. And I mean that. I will help in any way I can. You are family."

Kimberly leaned back in his chair and refolded his arms. "So stop whining and buck up," he said firmly. "You are the Arbiter. You are destined for greatness. I know it—I have faith in you. Have faith in yourself. Look deep inside yourself and trust your instincts. You'll know what you need to do."

"You would trust the fate of humankind to faith?"

"Yes," Kimberly said immediately. Then he leaned forward again. "After all, isn't that what this is all about?"

⊷⊱

Every constable looked up when Kimberly and Owen came into the squad room. Owen glanced around then followed Kimberly over to Jeffries and MacMillan who were standing by a counter where a large teapot simmered on a hot plate.

"Dr. Powell has decided he needs to return to Japan as soon as possible," Kimberly told them.

"The chief tells me that, as you're not pressing charges, he's free to go," Jeffries said.

"Where's Anna?" Owen said, looking around again.

"Well, about that," Jeffries said, "it seems she'll have to stay a bit longer to appear before a magistrate."

"In this county, we don't take kindly to suspects resisting arrest," MacMillan said.

"But she didn't resist," Owen said. "We both went quietly."

"Aye, eventually. But the lads say she raised her fist to them. They felt threatened."

"You've got to be shitting me!"

"Now, now, it'll all be ironed out in due time," Jeffries said. "The worst she'll get is a stern lecture and a small fine, but they can't get her on the docket before late afternoon."

"Then I'll just have to wait around," Owen said, his shoulders sagging in frustration. "My credit card's maxed. Anna's been funding this little adventure."

"Well, I think I can see my way clear to lending a cousin a few guineas for a flight to Tokyo," Kimberly said.

"But I can't just leave Anna here in jail."

"She'll be fine, Lad. She'll get no more than a fatherly scolding and a legal slap on the wrist. You've got to get on with what needs to be done. Leave the car for her. She'll only be a few hours behind you. We just need to get you over to Heathrow."

Jeffries looked hard at MacMillan who stared back blankly then flinched as if he suddenly remembered something.

"Oh, uh, I can have one of my deputies drive Dr. Powell to the airport," MacMillan said. He looked around the squad room and bellowed, "Foxworth, I have a job for you."

A stout female uniformed officer with short, red hair and thick glasses got up from her desk and walked their direction. "Come on, let's get your gear into my car," she said.

Owen turned to go.

"Oh, Dr. Powell," Jeffries said. "Aren't you forgetting something?" He reached behind the counter and pulled out the stainless steel cylinder Anna had brought out of the mausoleum. He held it out to Owen. "I think this is yours."

CHAPTER THIRTY-ONE

Owen was practically a zombie when he crossed the lobby of his hotel in Tokyo and jabbed the button for the elevator. He had slept the first part of the twenty-seven-hour, nonstop flight from London, but anxiety had denied him sleep the rest of the trip as he tried to decide what to do when he got back to Japan.

Robert Huntington, Earl of Kimberly—Brother Joshua, that is—had explained that Owen's duty to the Covenant, now that he had the *Apocalypse of Joseph*, was to appear before the Great Circle of Illuminati where he would present the scroll and be officially confirmed as Arbiter. But it could take Joshua weeks to convene the Circle, as it required coordinating the calendars of twelve of the world's most influential men. In the meantime, Owen wanted to find out, once and for all, just what had happened to his father. He wasn't sure how he would do that. He wasn't sure how he would deal with Nomura.

But all he wanted to do right now was clean up and stretch out on a bed for a few hours. Wearily, he watched the numbers above each of the four elevator doors scroll up and down then stepped in front of the one that finally hit "L". The door opened and he stepped forward—and ran straight into Elaine.

"What are you doing here?" he said, staring wide-eyed into her startled face.

She recovered her composure quickly. "Looking for you," she snapped. "But not anymore. I'm on my way to the airport." She pushed past him.

"Hey, wait a minute." She stopped a couple of steps out of the elevator and turned partially, but did not look at him. "How long have you been here?" he said.

"Several days." She looked at her watch. "I have to go. The bellhop already took my bag down. They're calling me a cab."

"Well don't leave now, not after coming all this way. You've waited this long, you can at least give me a few minutes. Come up and talk."

She hesitated and bit her lower lip. Then, still refusing to look at Owen's face, she got back on the elevator. As soon as the door closed, she said, "Where have you been?"

"I've been in Europe—Zurich and England. I'm trying to solve a mystery concerning my father's death."

"Richard said you came here to do research. What could that possibly have to do with your father?"

"I'm not sure. I think the whole research project was a sham just to get me over here. After I got here, I got caught up in this weird thing. I can't explain..."

Just then the elevator door opened on Owen's floor. An elderly couple was waiting to get on. Owen and Elaine stepped out and headed down to his room without speaking. As soon as they got inside, Elaine turned on him.

"Who was the blond woman?"

That caught him off guard. He hesitated then said, "Someone I knew in the past. I ran into her here. She's part of—"

"Were you traveling with her? Did you share hotel rooms?"

"Well, yes, but it wasn't like—"

"Did you sleep with her?" Elaine's face was hard as stone.

Owen felt his anger rising and he opened his mouth to yell, but he saw wetness glistening in the corners of her almond eyes and took a deep breath instead. "There's nothing between us. There was once, a long time ago, but not anymore."

"You didn't answer my question." Her words were clipped, sharp as razors cutting into Owen's tired nerves. He tried to stay calm, but then he thought of Preston and the dam broke.

"Just who in the hell are you to come all the way over here and grill me about who I've been sleeping with? You've got Randall-fucking-Preston living in your house!"

"Yeah, right, Owen. Turn it around and blame me. You know me better than that. You know I wouldn't let any man move in with me. Why do you let Randall jerk you around like that? Are you really so childish and insecure, or are you just using it as an excuse to do whatever the hell you want with an old girlfriend?"

That was the first time he had ever heard Elaine curse, and it startled him. He hesitated. She pushed past him and reached for the door.

"Wait," he said, catching her arm. She stopped but didn't turn around. "There's nothing between that woman and me. There could have been, but I thought of you. I was just traveling with her because she's part of this whole crazy thing I'm caught up in."

Elaine turned. A tear had escaped one eye, and she angrily wiped her cheek with the back of her hand. "Okay, tell me about this crazy thing you keep talking about."

Owen took a breath and sighed. "I... I can't. It's too complicated to explain right now—I don't even know the whole story myself—and if I tell you about it, you might be in danger."

"Right," she said and turned to leave again, but Owen still had hold of her arm.

"Look," he said, "a few weeks ago, one of us said a relationship is about trust. You've got to trust me on this—I haven't done anything wrong."

She turned back and looked at Owen's face. He could see the pain in her eyes. "Yes, a relationship is about trust," she said, her voice deadpan, dejected. "That's why we can't go on. I don't know if I can trust you anymore, and you obviously don't trust me enough to tell me what is really going on." She hesitated a moment then added, "I've got to go."

She reached up, pushed Owen's hand off her arm, and walked out.

Owen watched the door swing shut and tried to decide what to do. He wanted to go after her, but he couldn't think of anything more to say. He stood there uncertain and exhausted. At least she would be safe, away from him, out of all this. He turned and went to the bed, flopped down, and stared at the ceiling. A minute later, he was asleep.

The banging seemed to come from far away. Then it got closer and louder until it sounded like it was in Owen's head. It stopped. Struggling mightily, he forced his eyes open and looked at the bedside clock. He had only been asleep for twenty minutes at most. He lay there confused. Then the banging started again. Someone was at the door.

"Okay, okay!" he yelled, straining to get up. "I'm coming!" He stumbled over and opened the door. It was Jürgen.

"Owen, you look a mess," he said, a smile on his lips.

Owen stepped back awkwardly as Jürgen pushed into the room, letting the door close behind him. "Yeah I'm tired. I just laid down to get some rest." He scratched and ran a hand through his hair then yawned.

"Anna called and told me what happened in England. She's on her way back. Did you get the scroll?" He sounded a bit breathless. His face was aglow.

"Yeah, it's right here." Owen turned to the leather valise he had dropped by the door when he and Elaine first came into the room. He unzipped it and pulled out the stainless steel cylinder.

"Let me see," Jürgen said, grabbing it out of Owen's hand. He immediately hunched over it, turning it over, scrutinizing every side and edge from all angles. "Looks like it's hermetically sealed, maybe to protect it or something."

"Yeah, that's what I thought too. Considering where it was hidden..." Owen let his voice trail off.

"You know, we can't just pry it open or cut it," Jürgen said, looking up. "That might damage the scroll. We need to take it to someone who knows what they're doing, an expert."

"Yeah, but who?" Owen said, thinking more clearly as wakefulness returned. "It's not like we can just drop in on some lab or museum and ask them to open it for us. They'd want to know what it is and what we're doing with it. Word might even get back to Nomura."

"Yeah, you're right." Jürgen scratched his chin. "Hey, wait a minute. I know just the man to help us. He's a metallurgist with a lab over in Yokohama. He runs a little import/export business in antiquities on the side—my family buys from him—so he'd know how to open something like this without damaging whatever's inside, and we can trust him to keep his mouth shut. I've got my car. We can get there just about the time he closes. What do you say?"

Owen yawned again. "Yeah, okay, sure. What have I got to lose?"

CHAPTER THIRTY-TWO

Jürgen parked the Mercedes on the street along a strip of run-down warehouses in a dingy industrial section of Yokohama. The old wooden buildings looked abandoned. Paint peeled from their grimy walls, and years of acidic smog had clouded the windows until they were opaque.

Across the street, a broken down fence marked the edge of the Yokohama railroad switching and freight yard. Rusty signs saying "Danger, Keep Out" in *kanji* hung from the mangled chain-link every twenty meters. Beyond them, strings of empty railroad cars stood rusting on sidings, waiting to be hitched and loaded. A freight train crawled along a mainline somewhere in the middle of the yard.

It was dusk. There were a few other cars parked on the street, but no one was in sight. A distant streetlight was just coming on with a flicker and buzz that suggested it would not light steadily even after the night fully blanketed the area in murky blackness.

Owen didn't like the look of the place.

Sensing his edginess, Jürgen said, "Tanaka's clients are all industrial firms. He doesn't have to impress any retail customers, so he runs the lab in the low rent district to keep his overhead as low as possible. Come on, we want to catch him before he locks up for the night."

Owen grabbed the cylinder from the seat beside him. They got out of the car and crossed a broken sidewalk, weeds pushing up through the cracks, and went up to a graffiti-covered steel door. Jürgen tried the handle. It wasn't locked, so he went in with Owen behind him.

As soon as Owen saw the naked light bulb hanging on a wire from the ceiling fixture and the rotted studs peeking through holes in the dry wall, his sense of foreboding turned to alarm. He drew up short. This was no lab. He was just about to ask Jürgen what was going on when he heard the door close and lock behind him. He spun around and came face-to-face with a powerfully built Asian man with close-cropped hair and wearing a dark suit. A bulge under the jacket told Owen he was armed. The man nodded a perfunctory bow, but kept his hooded eyes on Owen's.

"What is this?" Owen demanded, turning back to Jürgen.

"Easy, Owen. There's no cause for alarm."

Just then, a door in the back of the room opened and half a dozen more men, near clones of the one behind Owen, filed out and took up positions around them, standing relaxed but ready, faces impassive, black eyes hard as onyx.

"What the hell is going on here?" Owen immediately lowered his center of gravity and began scanning, trying to keep as many of the men in his field of vision as possible.

An elderly Asian man came into the room next. "Dr. Owen Powell, at last, we meet. I've been waiting for this moment for a long time. I was a great admirer of your father." He was short and dark with snakelike, epicanthic eyes and a fringe of gray stubble around a baldpate. He wore an expensive looking three-piece suit, white, with a rose-colored tie. His nose was flat. His full lips smiled, but his eyes did not.

"Owen, this is the honorable Zhou Lo-feng," Jürgen said, as if he were introducing a foreign dignitary at a cocktail party. "He is Brother Saul, Illuminatus of the House of Asher."

Zhou did not bow or put out his hand to shake, nor did Owen.

"You can't have it," Owen said, knowing immediately what these men wanted, why he had been led into this trap.

Jürgen sighed loudly. "Owen, be reasonable. Asher is the most powerful house in the Covenant. Brother Saul can keep the scroll safe from Nomura until the Great Circle convenes for your investiture." Then he lowered his voice as if he were conspiring with Owen. "Zhao is a great man, a powerful man, both in the Covenant and in China. He would be a good man to have on your side in the future."

"Give me the scroll, Dr. Powell," Zhou said. He put out his hand.

Owen considered his situation. He faced seven hard-looking men, all armed, though none of them had drawn their weapons. There were eight of them, counting Zhou. Jürgen had obviously set him up, so that made nine. The room was about twenty feet square. If he fought and kept moving, they probably wouldn't draw their guns in that confined area—too much risk of shooting each other. But he was boxed in and badly outnumbered with nothing to get behind, no narrow passage through which he could funnel his attackers to take them on one or two at a time. The door behind him was locked. He didn't know where the other door led.

"Give it to me," Zhou said, his voice more insistent.

"Do it Owen," Jürgen said softly. "You don't have any choice. It'll be all right. I won't let any harm come to you. I know what you mean to Anna… what you've come to mean to both of us. You're like my brother. You can trust me."

Owen looked at Jürgen, probing the big Dane's face. He hesitated then nodded in resignation. Then he did the only thing he could. With two hands, he held out the cylinder to Zhou and stepped towards him bowing slightly. Immediately, two men moved in front of the old man protectively. One of them put his hands out to take the cylinder. Owen laid it on the man's fingers for the briefest instant... then snapped his hips in a tight pivot and swung the cylinder with both hands as hard as he could into the other man's face, following through like Babe Ruth.

For one second, the only sounds in the room were a fleshy slap and a hollow thunk like an aluminum bat slamming a softball. Then, before the man's back even hit the floor, the scene exploded in chaos.

Cries of fury spit the air, and everyone leaped at Owen at once. Drawing the cylinder into himself and pivoting back in one fluid motion, he thrust it out like a short staff into the face of a man grasping for him from behind. This quick jab broke the other attackers' rhythm for a fraction of a second, and Owen leaped upward, swinging the cylinder over his head, shattering the naked light bulb and plunging the room into darkness.

As he came down, he dropped to the floor and dived into a man's knees, rolling through them as the attacker, unable to break his forward momentum, tumbled over him and into another man who charged in from the other direction. Other men collided, and one or two more tripped over their fallen comrades, adding to the confusion. Chinese curses, screamed in rage and frustration, filled the room.

Owen rolled into a dark corner and came up in *hantachi*, a crouch on one knee, facing the open room. It was not quite dark outside. Faint light filtered through the room's two opaque windows, casting his attackers as shadowy silhouettes, faces indistinguishable to him or each other. For a couple of seconds, they groped and flailed, falling into and over one another, as they furiously struggled to find Owen in the tangle. Two figures stood quietly to the side, one short, the other very tall—Zhou and Jürgen.

Zhou yelled something in Chinese then turned for the door behind him.

"No, don't kill him!" Jürgen yelled. "We may need him."

Zhou opened the door and went out with Jürgen on his heels. Light poured in from the hallway. For an instant, all movement stopped as the men looked around the room. Then eyes fixed on Owen and they threw themselves into a ragged attack, three charging hard, two more struggling up from the floor and stumbling over their injured comrades.

Owen sprang up from his crouch with a loud *kiai* and drove a front kick into the lead attacker's chest, splitting his sternum and launching him backwards into a man behind him. Together, they tumbled over the moaning casualties on the floor. Coming down on his feet between the other two hard chargers, Owen used the fraction of a second they took to halt their forward momentum to pivot around and whip the cylinder out in a backhand strike at the man between him and the front door.

The man was just turning to renew his attack and caught the steel tube flat in the face. He cried out and staggered back, hands cupping the blood that sprayed from his smashed nose, and Owen skipped back with him and pile-drove a side thrust kick into the center of his body.

The husky man flew into the door behind him. It was solid steel, but the frame anchoring it was rotted wood. The door tore free and crashed to the sidewalk with the big man on it. Owen ran through the doorway and over the fallen attacker, his foot landing in the very spot it had kicked a second before.

He was out of the snare, but he was far from home free. He heard a torrent of angry Chinese behind him and knew, now that he was in the open, these men would not hesitate to shoot him, no matter what Jürgen had told them. As his foot left the fallen doorman and he hit the sidewalk, Owen chinked to the right just in time. A hail of automatic gunfire erupted from the doorway behind him, peppering Jürgen's Mercedes, riddling the doors and shattering the side windows. He ran two steps down the sidewalk then saw another half dozen Chinese in suits emerge from between the buildings forty meters ahead and swing their machine pistols his direction.

Holy shit! Are they stamping these guys out of a machine, or what?

He chinked left and dived under the back bumper of Jürgen's car just as the new group opened fire in unison with a second burst from the doorway, and the sidewalk rippled in a spatter of chipped concrete.

Owen scurried around to the street side of the car and crouched panting, trying to decide what to do. He knew he would have to move quickly. Nothing would stop the men from just walking around the car and shooting him—they must be moving toward him now. He would have to run for it... or, maybe, leap out at them and hope that the surprise would allow him to get between them again, where they would be less eager to shoot.

But surprise them a second time? Not likely. No place to run, either. His odds weren't good no matter what he did.

Then he heard the deep, hissing rumble of a diesel engine revving up. He looked down the street and saw a big-rig Isuzu truck pulling tandem trailers pass beneath the flickering streetlight, lumbering his direction. It had just wheeled around a corner, and the driver was working the gearbox, coaxing his eight-metric-ton load back up to speed. Owen was in the headlights.

He turned back and peaked over the car door. Two Chinese from the doorway were cautiously approaching the car from the other side. The second group was coming up the sidewalk. Their eyes met Owen's then turned to the truck. They slipped their weapons under their coats and kept walking towards him.

Owen scanned the truck, looking for something to grab onto, but saw only smooth, steel sides, and it was picking up speed.

The truck was nearly on him when the first two Chinese started around the front of the car. Owen looked into the headlights and braced his foot on the back tire of the Mercedes as if it were a sprinter's starting block. Clutching the cylinder tight to his chest, he waited until the last possible second then burst off the block and dashed across the street directly in front of the truck.

An air horn blasted, hurting his ears, but he cleared the far end of the bumper by an inch and, using the big rig as a temporary screen, ran as hard as he could for the chain-link fence. He hit the bowed-over fence with his foot, sprang over it, stumbled momentarily on the other side, but regained his stride quickly and raced for the nearest line of boxcars.

Owen knew the second trailer of the tandem truck had cleared the Chinese about the time he reached the closest boxcar because, once again, the chatter of gunfire erupted from the street behind him. He dove under the boxcar just as a shower of lead began hammering the heavy steel above him. More angry shouts in Chinese echoed from the street, and he heard the chain-link sing with the trample of feet. He rolled out on the other side of the car and found himself between two sidings, boxcars on one, tanker cars on the other.

Still clutching the cylinder, he ran down the lane between the sidings, looking for a place to hide. It was a big train yard and fully dark now. If he could only find a dark crevice to hole up in, he could either wait them out and slip away later, or ambush one of them and take his weapon. He ran along, looking under and between cars.

Then a flashlight beam hit him.

He looked up and saw a group of Chinese at the end of the lane running toward him. Why didn't they shoot? He looked behind him and saw several more coming from that direction. Maybe they didn't want to hit each other in the crossfire. Maybe they didn't want to hit the tankers and risk an explosion. Owen decided it was the latter and cut between two cars.

He scrambled over the hitch, ran down the line of cars, and dived under another tanker. He quickly scanned the yard on that side of the track. It was open terrain for at least a hundred meters—not good. He heard a brief, muffled blast of a train horn, but couldn't spot the train. Then he saw a yellow glow blossom and grow in the middle of the expanse and realized the mainline must come into the yard there from a tunnel. As he watched, a passenger express emerged, raced though the yard, and disappeared on the other side, its red taillight winking in the inky blackness.

He heard footsteps in the gravel behind him.

No time to weigh the odds. He took a deep breath and broke from his cover, sprinting across the open train yard, crossing track after track, stumbling twice but regaining his balance, racing to reach the relative safety of the tunnel. He heard shouts and feet hitting gravel somewhere behind him, but there was no time to look back.

He felt the ground start to slope down beneath his feet and spotted the black maw of the tunnel ahead and to his right just as the machine pistols began barking again. With bullets throwing sparks up from the steel rails and gravel around him, he ran down the track and into the tunnel.

It was narrow—the mainline was a single track. He ran hard, eyes focused on a pale, gray oval ahead, a glimmer of light he knew must be the other end of the tunnel. If he could only reach it before the Chinese got to the entrance of the tunnel behind him, he could get out and disappear into the night. The oval was some distance away, but in the tunnel's absolute blackness, without any frame of reference, he couldn't tell how far.

He hooked the cylinder in the crook of his arm and dashed for the dim, gray light like a halfback sprinting for the goal line. He listened for sounds of the Chinese behind him, but heard nothing over the gentle rumble of a distant train.

Then the tunnel began to light up.

He looked over his shoulder, expecting to see the Chinese shining their flashlights into the opening. What he saw instead was the headlight of a train. A second later, the tunnel roared to life as the engine thundered into the maw.

Spurred on by a fresh bolt of adrenaline, Owen put his head down and gutted out another burst of speed.

He looked back again. Luckily, the train was a freight, and it wasn't going fast, only thirty or forty clicks, but it was coming faster than he could run. The engineer blasted the train's air horn twice then laid on a long, deafening wail.

Panting hard now, Owen looked at the gray light ahead—it was definitely getting closer. He looked back. The train was gaining, but he would reach the end of the tunnel before it caught him. He was going to make it.

Five seconds later, he hit the gray light at the end of the tunnel. His first sensation was the sudden damping of the train's roar as he came out into the open air. His second sensation was the impact of the muscular arm that clotheslined him across the collarbones, just missing his throat.

Owen's feet flew up and his shoulders hit the gravel roadbed. The cylinder went clattering down the track. For half a second he was stunned, but he immediately knew what was happening when the Chinese came down on him and locked his neck and shoulder in a vise-like chokehold. Owen clutched at the man's arm and struggled to get his jaw into the crook of his elbow. He rocked and arched his back violently, trying to break the hold.

The train horn blared again. They were in the middle of the track.

Owen reached up, groping to find his attacker's eyes, but the man buried his face behind Owen's shoulder safely out of reach.

Owen continued to rock and arch, struggling desperately to break the hold before the blood to his brain choked off and his lights went out. As he fought, he saw two more Chinese standing beside the track, their faces pensive and glowing ever brighter in the train's headlight. One picked up the canister and ran up the slope. The other yelled something to Owen's assailant then also turned and ran.

Suddenly, the tension on Owen's neck released, and he realized his attacker was disengaging. The man rolled off him, sprang to his feet, lurching for the side of the track. As he jumped up, Owen lunged for him and snagged the back of his collar. The man's forward momentum helped pull Owen to his feet then it expended like an overstretched spring and the Chinese stumbled back, his panicked face painted in the train's headlight. Owen kicked the man's legs out from under him and pitched him onto the far rail.

The horn blared, and Owen heard the slamming and grinding of metal on metal as the train's airbrakes locked. Turning, he came face-to-face with the train's immense bumper, careening into him, not ten feet away. No time for anything else, he collapsed backward and flattened himself in the roadbed—he heard the Chinese scream for a brief second—just as the engine roared over him.

For several seconds, Owen's world was a roaring darkness punctuated by sparking flashes of light as three tandem diesel engines thundered over him, their brakes straining, their wheels grinding on the rails. He pressed himself as flat as he could, trying to melt into the gravel, his head turned to the side. He squeezed his eyes shut to protect them from the sparks and fragments of gravel stinging his face. Then the guttural roar faded from the crashing noise around him as the engines moved away and a succession of cars passed overhead.

Without turning his head, Owen opened his eyes a sliver and watched the undersides of the cars. In the flickering, sparking light, he saw suspension struts and hydraulic brake lines on each wheel truck that passed over him. Deciding at once, he threw both arms up and grabbed a strut as it flew by. His palms and fingers felt like they had been hit with a baseball bat and he thought his shoulders would be ripped from the sockets, but he held on and his back flew off the gravel roadbed. His legs dragged for a few seconds—the stones bruised his calves and tore at his pants, his socks, his ankles—but he managed to hook them over a brake line and hang beneath the car.

Hanging there felt like an eternity, his back glancing off high spots in the roadbed, the gravel shredding his tweed coat, his shirt, and the flesh beneath, but it took less than thirty seconds and a couple hundred meters for the freight train to grind to a standstill.

With a painful groan, Owen dropped down onto the roadbed. He rolled over and crawled out from under the car then cautiously looked around. He was out of the train yard and appeared to be in a low-end residential area near a railroad crossing. He couldn't see anyone at first, but he heard brakemen yelling fearfully about the two men they had just hit. Then, watching under the car, he saw feet running down the track on the other side of the train.

Owen got up and melted into the darkness.

⟞⟞ ⟝⟝

Elaine looked at her watch then glared at the long line ahead of her at Narita International Airport. Why had she let Owen waste her time back at the hotel? Now she didn't know if she would get to the gate before the last call for her plane.

She dreaded the trip ahead: a long, redeye flight to LA followed by another five-hour flight to Baltimore-Washington International. And that was if she made the plane. Otherwise, she would be hanging around the airport no telling how long for the next flight out.

Her thoughts went back to Owen for the hundredth time. Had she really lost him? She had trouble imagining a future without him, but she could not put her life in the hands of a man she couldn't trust. Why wouldn't he just say what she needed him to say? Maybe he would eventually come around. Maybe he would finish whatever he was doing there and go back to Maryland. Then, maybe, their lives would get back to normal.

Then a chill wind of grief blew over her as reality set in. She had failed. Owen might not make it back to Maryland. Even if he did, their relationship would never be what it had been. Their lives would never be normal again.

She sighed in exasperation and turned her attention back to the long line ahead. Pulling an elastic band from her handbag, she tied her hair back in a tight ponytail then kicked her suitcase another two feet ahead of her in line. At least she had dressed comfortably for the trip in soft shoes, stretch pants, and a sweater. Hopefully, she could get some sleep on the plane… if she made the plane, that is.

"Excuse me Honorable Lady," came a deep voice in Mandarin Chinese. Startled, she turned to see a tall, middle-aged Asian man in a dark suit, bowing respectfully. "Are you Dr. Elaine Chen?"

Elaine's eyes narrowed. "Why do you want to know?"

He rose from his bow and met her cool stare without flinching. "Excuse me, but if you are Dr. Chen, then we have a mutual acquaintance, someone whom we both care a great deal about, and he is in mortal danger."

The man towered over her, and Elaine could see wide, powerful shoulders beneath the suit coat. His graying hair was combed across a balding crown. His brow was heavy, his face was craggy, and his nose looked as if it had been broken more than once.

"I can't imagine that we would have any common acquaintances," Elaine said dryly.

The man accepted the affront with grace, bowing again briefly. "I am sorry, Dr. Chen," he said gently, "but we do, and we must hurry if we are to help him."

Elaine wondered about this curious man. Cantonese was her first language, but she spoke Mandarin fluently, and her ear was keen enough to detect that, though he too was fluent in Mandarin, he was not Chinese.

"Who is this common acquaintance that is in mortal danger?" she said.

"It is Dr. Owen Powell."

Elaine blanched visibly and her eyes grew wide in alarm. "What danger? What are you talking about?"

"There is no time to discuss it here. It may already be too late to save his life. Come, I have a car waiting. I will explain everything on the way."

"What makes you think I'll go anywhere with you? You're a total stranger. I don't even know your name."

"Ah, yes. Please forgive my rudeness, Honorable Lady." He bowed again, and to Elaine's surprise, he blushed. "I am Pak Je-man."

CHAPTER THIRTY-THREE

Owen sat waiting in the dark.

When at last he heard someone fumbling a key into the lock of the apartment door, he slid out of the armchair and crouched in readiness. The door opened, and light from the outer hallway silhouetted Anna's shapely form. She wrestled her heavy suitcase inside then flipped on the entranceway light. She was just bending down to get the suitcase when Owen stood up from his crouch in the sunken living room. The movement caught her eye—she turned in alarm then dropped the suitcase and gasped.

"Owen! Oh my God, you're alive!" She jerked both hands to her mouth reflexively. For a moment she just stared at him, eyes wide in shock and disbelief. Then her face brightened. "Oh, thank heavens! They told me you were dead!"

"Yeah, well, reports of my demise are a bit premature," he said dryly.

Anna rushed towards him, her arms out, but stopped abruptly at the edge of the living room when she realized he was not moving, not responding to her. "What is it? What's wrong?" Then, changing tack, "Oh Owen, you look a mess. Your clothes are filthy and torn to shreds." She took in a sharp breath. "You're bleeding! How badly are you hurt? Let me get the first aid kit." She turned to the hallway that led to the back rooms. "Strip off those rags and I'll clean—"

"I've met your Brother Saul."

She froze mid-step then turned to face him again, but didn't say anything.

"Jürgen set me up. He said we were going to some lab to open the cylinder. Then he turned me over to Saul and his goons." He hesitated then added, "But you know all that, don't you."

Anna still didn't answer for a long moment then said, "I guess I've got some explaining to do."

"Where is Jürgen?"

"I never wanted to hurt you. They made me—"

"Where is Jürgen? Where is the scroll?"

She sighed. "They went to the airport, to Saul's private jet. They would be on their way to Shanghai by now, but there's some kind of maintenance problem with the plane."

"I want the scroll back."

"I know. It's yours and I want you to get it back, but you'll never be able to get it alone. Let me help you."

"Yeah, right, and let you lead me into another trap. How stupid do you think I am?"

"I don't think you're stupid at all." She took a deep breath. "Owen, I don't blame you for not trusting me, but I only wanted the best for you. You've got to believe me. I helped you get the scroll because I want you to be installed as Arbiter. Jürgen was conspiring with Brother Saul behind my back, but even he didn't want them to hurt you. Saul told him he could make him the Arbiter then double-crossed him. Now he's caught up in Saul's web and doesn't know what to do."

She paused, gauging Owen's reaction, then started talking faster. "Listen, I don't care what happens to Jürgen. He used you, used us both, and I hate him for putting you in danger. I just want to help you get the scroll back. You won't be able to get it without my help. Saul has a lot of men, and they're well trained. But I can get past the guards—they know me and think I'm working with them—and I can get you in, too. We can pull it off if we work together." She stopped and waited expectantly.

"Why would they think you're working with them if Jürgen conspired with Saul behind your back?"

"Because Jürgen told them I was," she said, a trace of tension, or perhaps just impatience, raising her voice. "He told Saul we were working together, using you to get the scroll so we could give it to him. He just didn't tell me about it until I phoned him from Heathrow. I was going to warn you when you got back with the car, explain the whole story once we got a room where we could discuss it calmly. But when you came back so determined to get the scroll that night, I decided to put off telling you until afterward. Then we got separated."

Owen studied her face. "I sure as hell would have been more likely to believe you then than now. You could have warned me, but you didn't, so why should I trust you?"

Anna sighed deeply and threw up her arms in exasperation. "Because I love you," she said, her moist eyes searching his.

He didn't respond.

"Oh Owen, I don't blame you for hating me. You think I used you. But you've got to believe me. I would never have done that. And I would have killed them all, even Jürgen, if I ever thought they were going to hurt you." Tears began streaming down her face. "I love you. I've loved you ever since Korea. Can't you see that? I love you."

She started weeping openly, and Owen's anger began to melt. Then she swayed and her knees started to buckle. Owen dashed up out of the sunken living room and gathered her up in his arms.

"It's alright," he whispered. "I believe you. It'll be alright."

She buried her face in his chest and cried. They stood there a minute, he holding her, she nestling in his embrace, then she looked up into his face.

"We can get the scroll back," she said. "Saul's called Beijing for another plane, but it won't get here before daybreak. They're waiting in the private terminal. They've got it sealed off, but I can get us in. We'll hit them hard and fast, get the scroll and get out. We'll have to go into hiding until your investiture, but afterwards, we'll be safe. They won't come after us once you're officially the Arbiter. There won't be any point in it. Then we can be together. I'll marry you and..." She hesitated, watching his eyes, troubled by what she saw there. "That is, if you want me."

Owen looked into her eyes. The openness and vulnerability he saw there cut him deeply. After a moment he said, "I have to be honest with you, Anna. You're a wonderful woman, and you'd be the perfect wife for an Arbiter..."

"But what?"

"But us marrying wouldn't be fair to you." He paused, trying to decide how to say it. Then he plunged ahead. "It wouldn't be fair because I love someone else."

He felt her tense in his arms and pull back. He released her, but held her shoulders gently. She stared at him, her face expressionless, her eyes narrowed, probing him the way she had when he rejected her advances in Zurich and London. Then her body relaxed and her gaze softened.

"All right," she said softly. "I understand. We could never be happy if your heart belonged to another woman." She sighed, stepped close, and rested her forehead against his chest for a moment then raised her face and looked into his eyes. "I'll still help you get the scroll. It's not Saul's or Jürgen's. It's yours. And I'll never press you about us again. But I'll always love you, Owen. I want you to know that." She gazed at him a few seconds longer then said. "Just kiss me one last time, okay?"

Owen smiled and enfolded her in his arms again. She reached up and cupped the back of his neck with her hand, drawing his face down to hers. She parted her lips and reached for his mouth with hers. He closed his eyes. Then she turned her head to the side, jerked down on his neck, and drove her knee into his groin as hard as she could.

Owen gasped and doubled over, his eyes wide in agony and shock. Anna stepped back to set her range then whipped a crescent kick up and across, catching him squarely on the jaw and cheekbone. He spun like a top and sailed back into the sunken living room, crashing on the low table, smashing it to kindling. He lay there dazed and groaning.

Anna calmly walked down the levels of the descending floor. "You stupid son of a bitch!" she hissed.

Owen struggled to clear the fog from his mind. He tried to sit up, but his abdominal muscles contorted from the agony in his groin and he doubled over on his side. Biting back a wave of nausea, he put his palm on the broken table beneath him and pushed, raising himself to a half-sitting position.

Anna walked around behind him.

"Just who do you think you are, rejecting me?"

She viciously kicked him in the kidney. He cried out in pain and his back arched. The force of the blow rolled him off the broken table and onto the carpeted floor, where he lay gasping.

"You could have had it all: power, fame, wealth, and me! I would have done anything for you, Owen. I would have betrayed my family and attacked the most powerful house in the Covenant. I would have stolen the scroll for you, killed for you. I would have married you and bore your children."

She paced around him like a jungle cat toying with wounded prey. He craned his neck to see where she was then rose on his elbow and tried to get up. She quickly stepped in and drove the toe of her shoe into his solar plexus. All the breath whooshed out of him as he fell back on carpet and balled up like a fetus.

"But no, I wasn't good enough for you. Oh, I was good enough to take you half way around the world, good enough to cover your back and help you get the scroll, good enough to share your bed, but not good enough to be your wife."

Owen struggled to breath, and by sheer force of will, managed to overcome enough of the paralysis in his diaphragm to draw a thin wisp of air into his lungs. As his head began to clear, he tried to get a bearing on Anna. He had no way of fighting her while she stood above him, and she wasn't going to let him get up. If he were to survive, he would have to catch her leg and pull her down to his level. But even as he turned to find her, she slipped behind him again, drew back, and kicked him in the kidney with all her strength. He lurched out of his fetal ball and arched his back, rolling across the carpet, writhing in anguish.

"Well, if I'm not good enough for you, you arrogant, pompous bastard, then no one is," she said, following him across the living room. "I'm not going to let another woman have you. You're going to die right here."

Owen lay face up, back arched, unable to move, his muscles contorted in spasm. Anna calmly walked up and raised her foot high, preparing to stomp his exposed throat.

"Get away from him!"

It was another woman's voice. Owen heard it through the crimson cloud of his agony. It sounded familiar. It was… It was Elaine! *Oh, God, no!*

"Well, isn't this a special night," Anna said, her voice taunting. She put her foot down and took a step toward the door. "Not only do I get to kill this faithless bastard, but I can take care of his little Chinese whore, too."

With excruciating effort, Owen rolled over on his side where he could see the door. Anna was just out of his reach. Elaine stood backlit beneath the entranceway light, her raven hair pulled back tight, her stretch pants and formfitting sweater setting off her petite, willowy shape. She stood with her body angled to Anna, feet apart, arms at her sides, head erect, her black eyes hidden in deep shadows from the light above.

"No!" Owen rasped. "Get out, Elaine. Run!"

She ignored him. "Get away from him, I said."

"I'm going to enjoy this," Anna said. She started up the levels out of the sunken living room, slowly, leisurely, like a lion approaching a snared gazelle. "I'm killing Owen because he deserves it. But I'm going to kill you for the sheer pleasure."

To Owen's horror, as Anna reached the apartment's main level, Elaine boldly walked towards her. Anna smiled and closed the gap, her tall, powerful form dwarfing the tiny Chinese woman.

Without warning, Anna fired a roundhouse kick at Elaine's head so fast that Owen's eye couldn't follow it. But just as quickly, Elaine dropped to the floor beneath her and whipped around with a low hook kick that swept the tall blonde's standing leg from under her. Anna's long, powerful legs flew up and she slammed onto the carpet. She took the fall well and immediately sprang up towards Elaine who was still down on one hip, but to Owen's astonishment, Elaine rose with perfect timing and side kicked Anna in the jaw, laying her out flat. Quick as a mongoose on a cobra, Elaine scrambled up Anna's prostrate body until she sat straddling her torso.

Anna was down, but far from beaten. She snapped a flurry of hand strikes and finger stabs at the smaller woman's face, but Elaine's hands moved in a blur, deftly parrying each blow. Then she drew back and nailed Anna between the eyes with the palm of her hand. Anna's head snapped back and hit the floor hard, bouncing off the carpet and right into another blow. As Owen looked on in shock, Anna's head became a blurry cloud of blond hair as Elaine hit her with several more lightning-fast strikes, the heel of her palm smashing the bridge of Anna's nose each time her head bounced up.

Then Elaine stopped and surveyed the damage she had done. Anna's eyes were open and rolling, her pupils dilated. Blood streamed from her nose and one of her ears. Elaine grabbed a handful of blond hair and lifted Anna's head, sliding her other hand beneath and grabbing a wad of hair at the base of her skull. Then she bent down and hissed in the Danish woman's face.

"Look at me." Anna's eyes kept rolling. She didn't respond. "Look at me!" Elaine yelled, shaking the blonde's head roughly.

Anna's eyes slowly settled and focused on Elaine's. Elaine put her nose almost against Anna's and glared directly into her eyes.

"You are never going to touch anything that belongs to me again," she whispered. Then, with a vicious yank, she wrenched Anna's head to the side and Owen heard a loud, crunching pop.

She let go of Anna's head. It fell back to the carpet, bounced once, and rolled to the side facing Owen. Her mouth was open and round as if she were about to call his name. Her once opalescent eyes stared ahead a dull, dead green.

Elaine got up and rushed to Owen.

"How badly are you hurt?" she said gently, taking his arm and putting it over her shoulder. "Come on, we've got to get out of here."

With a strength that surprised him, she helped him to his feet and out of the sunken living room. When they reached the landing, Owen looked down at Anna's body and a flood of conflicting emotions poured over him—grief, anger, remorse, an overwhelming since of waste. He paused there and Elaine's eyes flashed to his face.

"Where did you learn to do that?" he said to cover his emotion.

"There's no time to explain. We've got to go."

They left without looking back.

———

Ten minutes later, they were in a car, weaving their way through the back streets, watching for tails. Elaine drove. Owen sat in the passenger seat, willing his pain to subside, pain from the beating he had just taken and from having been dragged beneath a train earlier in the evening. They hadn't spoken since leaving the Norgaards' apartment. Finally, Owen could contain himself no longer.

"Elaine, how did you do that? I mean, where did you learn to fight?"

Elaine remained quiet, staring at the road ahead, checking her rearview mirror, craning her neck to see down each side street they crossed. After a moment she said, "We both have secrets. There are things about me I can't talk about."

"You can't leave it at that. You're obviously not just a college professor. You've got to tell me how you're mixed up in this."

"Mixed up in what?" She looked at him and raised one eyebrow.

Owen sighed. "Yeah, okay, you deserve more of an explanation than I gave you at the hotel. I didn't tell you then because I didn't want to put you in danger, but I guess that's not an issue anymore. You're in it now whether you like it or not."

Owen gathered his thoughts and continued. "This might sound crazy, but I'm caught up in some kind of struggle between factions in a powerful secret organization."

"Why would I think that was crazy? I'm Chinese. We've had triads for over a hundred years."

"Well, this group is a lot older and more powerful than the triads. I still can't tell you everything, but I've inherited a special function in their world. My father held the post before me, and I think it got him killed. I went to England to get an old scroll that verifies my authority to take his place. Anna Norgaard—that's the woman lying on the floor back there—and her brother pretended to help me, but they were just using me to steal the scroll and turn it over to one of the factions. I went back to their apartment to get it back…" He paused, weighing whether to go on. "Anna offered to betray her brother and help me. She wanted me to marry her, but I told her we would have no future together because I loved you."

Elaine quickly turned to face him, her large eyes wide in surprise. Then they sparkled in a momentary smile, illuminated by the soft glow of the instrument panel. She turned back to the road. "What will you do next?"

"I've got to find a way to get the scroll back."

"I'll help you."

"No! I don't want you involved anymore than you are. I want you to get out of Japan, out of danger." As they talked, Owen struggled to shrug off the remnants of his shredded tweed sport coat. He still hurt all over.

"I'm not going to leave you here alone in the middle of this," Elaine said. "I can help you. Believe me, I've been trained for this kind of thing."

"What are you talking about? What training? Just who are you?"

"I'm the woman who loves you."

Owen froze with his arms still tangled in the jacket. Elaine turned and their eyes met. She smiled sweetly and for a moment he forgot about his pain.

"Now, where are we going?" she said, turning back to the road, all business again.

"To the airport."

"I told you, I'm not leaving—"

"Yeah, okay, I know. But that's where we need to go. There's a private terminal there, somewhere. The people who have the scroll are waiting for a business jet to arrive and take them to Shanghai."

Owen finally managed to get his arms out of the coat and pull the shredded tweed from behind his tender back. He wadded the rag and prepared to toss it into the back seat. Then he felt something stiff inside. He reached in the breast pocket and pulled out a yellow envelope.

"What's that?" Elaine said.

"Some old family pictures I found in my father's safe deposit box in Zurich."

As Elaine turned towards the airport, he took out the pictures and began thumbing through them, straining to make out the images by the occasional faint glow of the streetlights they passed.

"There's a penlight in my handbag," Elaine said.

He got it, shined it on the first photograph, and was immediately captured in the moment. His mother was so beautiful, his father so proud. Baby Owen was happy and innocent. How he wished he could go back to that time. He tried to remember his mother, but couldn't. Maybe it was the stress of everything that had happened that night, but tears began welling in his eyes. He quickly wiped at them with the back of his hand, hoping Elaine hadn't noticed. Why did his mother have to die so young? Why couldn't he have grown up a normal child with two loving parents?

He flipped to the next photograph and stared. It was clearly a wedding scene, his parents'. They were standing side-by-side, elegantly dressed, radiantly happy, and Rhys was slipping a ring on his mother's finger. Several other well dressed people stood in the background. Owen didn't know them, but standing in front of the happy couple was a young, smiling, Robert Huntington, Earl of Kimberly, in a white robe, with his hand raised in ritual piety. He was performing the ceremony.

Then Owen turned to the last photograph and froze. It was an old, black-and-white print. His father, younger here, stood hip deep in what looked like a river with his head bowed, apparently in prayer. Beside him stood a much smaller man, again wearing a white robe and with a hand raised, ceremoniously. He too appeared to be praying. His other hand rested on Rhys's shoulder. Owen blinked to clear his eyes and stared at the short man in disbelief. He was a middle-aged Asian. It was Nomura Eizo. The scene was obviously a baptism.

"*Living water,*" Owen murmured.

"Huh?"

"Turn the car around," Owen said suddenly. "We've got a new plan."

⋙ ⋘

"I still think I should stay and help you," Elaine said. She pulled the car to the curb around the corner from Nomura's apartment building.

"Yeah, I know, but it's better this way. The fewer of these people who know you exist, the safer we'll both be. Anna Norgaard's death is going to send a tremor through their society. My guess is that it won't just be her brother looking for blood when word of it gets around. And if they know about you, they may think they have a lever on me."

"But if they don't know about me then why can't I just go home?"

"Because we can't be sure they don't know about you. You've been hanging around Tokyo for several days asking questions about me. These people have eyes and ears everywhere. No, I want you to go straight to England like I told you. Get a car out of Heathrow and—"

"Okay, I've got it. You've made me recite it twice already."

"Then do it once more."

Elaine rolled her eyes and started reeling off in a petulant mono-tone. "Drive west to County Somerset. Find the estate of Robert Huntington, Earl of Kimberly, outside Bristol. Tell Kimberly you sent me to him with a request for secret asylum until you come to get me."

"Right. I'll be there as soon as I take care of business here." He turned to get out.

"Owen?" She touched his arm and he stopped. Her voice was soft now, her tone fretful. "How long will you be?"

He paused. "I don't know ... days, maybe weeks."

"You said you trust Kimberly because he's family, but can you really trust this Nomura?"

Owen thought about that. "He's the one I should have trusted right from the start."

He leaned over and kissed her hard. Then he abruptly pulled away and got out.

CHAPTER THIRTY-FOUR

"We've got to get a team over to Narita and scour the airport for that private terminal," Owen said, rising up on his elbows. Nomura's houseman shoved him back down on the couch where he lay on his stomach and continued scrubbing dirt and gravel out of the lacerations on his bare back. "Ouch! Jeez, do you have to be so rough?" Owen craned his neck and scowled at the houseman's impassive face. Then he turned back to Nomura, who sat in an armchair a few feet away. "Don't you understand, Nomura-san? We don't have much time. We've got to move now!"

"I understand completely, Owen-san, but we are too late. I know the terminal Brother Saul uses—my people keep it under surveillance. They flew out shortly after 2:00 AM. Apparently, they managed to repair their plane and did not have to wait for the second plane from Shanghai." Nomura's voice was deadpan, dejected.

Owen thought he looked older and frailer than he had noticed before. "Then what are we going to do?" Owen said.

"I am afraid there is little left to do. You lost the *Apocalypse of Joseph*, the evidence of your legacy. Now Brother Saul will petition the House of David to convene the Great Circle. He will present his own candidate to be confirmed as Arbiter."

"But how can he do that? The bloodline runs in my family alone. My father was Arbiter. I am the next in line. The title is mine by birthright."

"This is true, Owen-san, but family trees have many branches. Bloodlines tangle through the centuries, and genealogical records can be forged. No doubt, Saul will claim his candidate is descended from the original Arbiter and charge that your line is fraudulent. The other Illuminati will be skeptical, but Saul is very powerful. Some will support him immediately; the others will eventually follow. With the scroll in his possession, his claim will be credible—possession of the *Apocalypse of Joseph* is the ultimate proof of authority."

"But they stole it from me!" Owen said in exasperation. "Surely they've got to understand that. Brother Joshua knows I had the scroll when I was in England. He knows I got it from my mother's grave. He'll support me, won't he? And you're word has got to mean something. After all, you're a member of the Council of Twelve in the House of..." Owen paused, realizing Nomura had never told him to what house he belonged.

"Levi," Nomura muttered almost to himself. Then speaking up, "I belong to the House of Levi, descendants of Israel's tribe of high priests. But it has been many years since I was on the Council of Twelve."

"Well surely you still have connections. Powerful as you were, you must still be influential even if you are retired."

"I am not retired, Owen-san. I am now Brother Simon, the Illuminatus of Levi."

Owen was stunned. He opened his mouth to speak, but couldn't think of anything to say.

After a moment, Nomura continued. "Yes, I am sure Joshua will argue your case, and the House of Levi will support you too, but in the end, we will either have to accept Saul's candidate or go to war with the other great houses. Possession of the scroll is the ultimate proof of God's will. Even if you had the scroll in England, the fact that someone was able to take if from you is irrefutable evidence that you do not have God's blessing."

"Why are you so damned fatalistic?" Owen said, rising up again. The houseman tried to push him back down, but Owen shoved the man's hand away and swung his legs off the sofa. He sat up and glared at the fragile-looking, wizened old man. "The last time we spoke, you told me you helped my father prepare me for my life as Arbiter. You sought out the best *budo* masters for me, had me sent to Korea for combat training, and kept the key to my father's safe deposit box for nearly twenty years so you could pass it on to me. You said you did all these things because you carried my father's *on*, and after he died, *giri* required you to look after me. Well, if you've invested so much time and effort to help me become Arbiter, why are you giving up so easily? Does my father's *on* mean so little to you?"

The translucent skin on Nomura's skeletal face turned scarlet. "Leave us, Toshi-san," he rasped, without taking his hooded eyes off of Owen.

The houseman looked around, eyes fearful. He got up stiffly, bowed to Nomura and Owen, then went out and closed the door.

"Do not underestimate my commitment to your success, Owen-san," Nomura said, his measured voice like flint on sandpaper. "Your father's *on* and my *giri* to fulfill it are more important to me than life itself. I have not simply found *budo* masters for you or had you sent to Korea—I have watched you and guided your development your entire life. The nanny who taught you to discipline your mind reported directly to me. Your *budo sensei* were my people as well. When your father died, it was I who arranged for you to be educated at Oxford University. While you were there, it was I who arranged for you to study the inner secrets of aikijujutsu. After you graduated, I got you commissioned in the U.S. Army, got you into Ranger School, and then into the Army Intelligence School. Afterwards, I arranged for you to be assigned to Korea, where you could hone your skills and receive training in advanced intelligence tradecraft. After you left the Army, I got you into graduate school at Yale, and I got you your teaching job in Maryland. So do not suggest that I take my *on* to your father lightly."

Owen stared at him in angry incredulity.

"You did all those things for me? Am I supposed to believe I haven't accomplished a damned thing on my own in my entire life? Are you trying to tell me I don't have free will, that I've never made a decision for myself, that I would be nothing if it weren't for you?"

"Of course not, Owen-san. You were born with singular talents, with tremendous potential. But even great potential takes superior education and training to be fully realized. My commitment to your father was to see that you got the best of each."

"But I made my own decisions," Owen shouted. "I've always been my own man."

"Yes, you made your own decisions," Nomura said, his calmness returning in proportion to Owen's rising anger, "but you chose from the opportunities presented you. I simply presented the opportunities and made the best teachers available along the way. Takagawa Masao, the aikijujutsu master who befriended you at Oxford, was a member of the House of Levi. Jack Fowler, the CIA man who trained you in Korea, owed Levi favors for professional assistance we provided him in the past. And there were others. In each case, they trained you in their own specialized field of expertise. Along the way, they gave you ideas, planted seeds in your mind that would ripen and inspire you when the next important opportunity presented itself.

"In that subtle way, I shaped your development, turning you from a brash young prodigy into a combat-tempered soldier with a powerful intellect, savvy in the political world, educated in history and strategy, expert in hand-to-hand combat and unconventional warfare—exactly the kind of man who would be most qualified to arbitrate between the great houses, the man I promised your father I would see you become."

"Well, if you had such an omnipresent hand in guiding my development, what happened in Korea? I would say that was a failed lesson, wouldn't you? I didn't complete my training there and was nearly killed."

"Korea was a costly chapter in your training, Owen-san. Yi Chung-hae was a dear friend of mine and a faithful soldier in Christ. The service he provided the Covenant in training guardians from the twelve houses was invaluable. We all felt his loss immensely. But your experience there was not the failed lesson you think it was. The trials you endured in that mountain camp hardened your body and spirit and played an essential role in making you the man you have become. Your training was essentially complete when you were drawn into—"

There was a knock at the door.

"*Hai, irrashai*," Nomura called out.

Toshi, the houseman, came in and crossed the room to Nomura, glancing at Owen along the way as if he were surprised to see him still conscious. He bent down and whispered something to his master.

"Yes, send him in," Nomura responded. He sat quietly watching Owen's eyes as Toshi went out.

A moment later, the door opened again and a tall, powerfully built middle-aged Asian man with a heavy brow came in. The man had changed considerably since Owen saw him last, but the second he laid eyes on him, he knew who it was and his blood turned to acid. It was Pak Je-man.

Owen leaped off the sofa to attack the Korean. With the agility of a twenty-year-old gymnast, Nomura came out of his chair and intercepted him, bracing both hands against Owen's bare chest. "No, Owen-san! It is alright."

Pak watched Owen and tensed, preparing to defend himself, but he made no move to attack.

"He set us up in Korea!" Owen yelled, glaring at Pak over the old man's head. He pushed forward, but Nomura held him back. "He's the reason Sabumnim was killed. He sold us out to the North Koreans and got Anna—"

"There were no North Koreans!" Nomura said sharply, raising his voice so Owen would hear him over his rage. Owen blinked twice in confusion then, reluctantly, took his eyes off of Pak and looked down at Nomura. "Now sit down, Owen-san. It is time for you learn the truth about what happened in Korea."

Owen looked back at Pak. They glowered at each other a moment longer then Owen stopped pressing forward against Nomura's palms. Pak relaxed slightly. Finally, Owen stepped back to the sofa, keeping his eyes on Pak's. Pak moved to an armchair. Warily, the lifelong enemies sat in unison. Nomura returned to his chair.

"Owen-san," Nomura began again, "you said you thought your training in Korea was a failure, and you questioned why, if I had so much control over your development, that Korea went so awry. Well, I must admit, I could not control circumstances to the extent I would have liked at Yi's camp. It was one thing to provide guiding influences in the outside world; it was quite another to do so at a refuge point, where you were surrounded by members of all the great houses, each wanting to secretly win the affections of a future Arbiter."

Owen remembered what Anna told him about the strict orders everyone at camp was given to not fraternize with him.

"But working through Yi-san—as well as Pak-san—I managed to monitor and guide the forging of your warrior spirit."

"Are you telling me that Pak was your agent?"

"Yes, Pak-san is a member of my house. With Yi-san's full knowledge and approval, I placed him in the camp two years before your arrival to prepare the cover story for his role in your training."

"But this man tormented me. He brutalized me."

"Did you expect your training to be easy? Pak-san's job was to put you under pressure, to bring out the best in you. He was also there to watch over you. His chief responsibility was to protect you from danger and from undue influence from the other houses."

"Well, I'd say he interpreted his mission pretty loosely," Owen said, his anger rising again. He turned to Pak. "Was pressuring Anna Norgaard for sex your way of adding stress to my training?"

"I did no such thing, Dr. Powell," Pak said.

"How about betraying the camp to the North Korean district authorities? Was selling out Sabumnim part of your plan?"

"I already told you, Owen-san," Nomura said, "There were no North Koreans. Yi-san's camp was ten kilometers south of the DMZ. You never set foot in North Korea."

"But I saw them!" Owen yelled. "I saw North Korean soldiers shoot Sabumnim. I saw them beat Anna unconscious and throw her into the back of a truck. They took her and tortured her... raped her!" Turning back to Pak, "I tried to save her but you hit me from behind!" He moved forward in his seat and Pak tensed.

"Owen-san," Nomura said softly. Then more firmly, "Owen-san, look at me." Reluctantly, Owen turned to Nomura. "The attack at the village was a sham. It was staged to fool you. The men you saw were not North Korean soldiers."

"But I saw them shoot Sabumnim!"

"Yes, you did. They killed him because it added credibility to their little drama. But everything else was staged. The woman you knew as Anna Norgaard was acting in a play scripted to ensnare you. Had Pak-san not gotten you out of there, they would have kidnapped you. Then, no doubt, their little play would have moved to a prison scene, one perhaps featuring the Norgaard woman being tortured and raped before your eyes to deepen your feelings of guilt and make you all the more emotionally vulnerable to her. Sooner or later, someone from her house, or whichever house she was working for, would have rescued you both, putting you forever in their debt."

Nomura paused, waiting for a response, but Owen just stared at him, dumbfounded, so he went on.

"Owen-san, you must understand, everything the Norgaards have told you about Korea is a lie. Pak-san was not pressuring Anna for sex. He was simply trying to get her to break off her relationship with you, a relationship that was manipulative and a blatant violation of refuge point neutrality. There was never any capture by North Koreans—no torture, no rape. In fact, Anna and Jürgen Norgaard are not even their real names."

No North Koreans? No rape? Anna and Jürgen not Anna and Jürgen? Pak not his enemy, but his protector? Owen felt a sudden onset of vertigo. The very pillars of his reality were crumbling.

"Dr. Powell," Pak said gently.

Slowly, lethargically, as if in a dream, he turned his puzzled gaze from Nomura to the Korean.

"We did not know it at the time, but the woman who entered the camp as Anna Norgaard, daughter of a wealthy Danish industrialist and prominent member of the House of Zebulun, was actually Russian. Her real name was Roxanna Novikov. She and her brother, Juri, were children of Alexander Petrovich Novikov, a Council of Twelve member of the House of Naphtali, based in what was then Leningrad, but is now St. Petersburg. She had been posing as a Dane on the European competitive karate circuit for several years. It seems she too had prepared an elaborate cover story in anticipation of your appearance at camp."

"But how could she have pulled that off?" Owen said. "Wouldn't someone from the House of Zebulun have caught wind of an imposter posing as one of their own?"

Pak shrugged. "No doubt some of them knew, but money changes hands, favors are exchanged. Not everyone in God's one true church is saintly."

Owen's brow knitted, and his fists clenched in frustration. "Why didn't you tell me about these people? You've been watching me all my life. Why did you let me be trapped this way? Do you have any idea what I've been through, what guilt I've carried since Korea?"

"I am truly sorry, Dr. Powell," Pak said, his tone sincere, "but I did not know these things at camp. Until the incident occurred in which Yi Sabumnim was killed, I thought Anna was simply an impetuous young woman, determined to defy my authority. When she sprang her trap, I realized how wrong I had been, but my first priority was to get you to safety. Later, I dedicated my life to tracking her down, but several great houses closed ranks to keep her hidden. After years of investigation, I discovered her true identity, but the trail was cold. We did not know where she was until she was seen leaving Tokyo with you a little over a week ago."

"But you could have told me about the North Korean sham years ago."

"Would you have believed the man you thought to be your mortal enemy? Would you have even listened to me?"

Owen stared at Pak, unable to answer, then turned to Nomura, "You could have told me about it when we met two weeks ago. You could have warned me about the Norgaards, or whoever they were, then."

"No, Owen-san, I could not. There was much more riding on your actions than your personal destiny alone. Almost two millennia ago, God revealed these events to Joseph of Arimathea. He foretold a time of tribulation in which you would awaken to your role as Arbiter and be tested. You would be tempted and forced to choose between darkness and light, between evil and good, and the fate of mankind would rest on your choice. Keepers of the Covenant were forbidden from tampering with this prophecy. We could do nothing to guide your decisions. When we discovered you had been awakened—that is, when I learned you had been told of the Covenant and your legacy—you were already involved with the Novikovs. I could not interfere. You had to see the darkness in them and reject it."

"But I had to get the scroll, and I thought I needed all the help I could get." Owen's voice was weak, all the vinegar drained away. "How was I supposed to know?"

He raked his fingers through his hair and sighed, suddenly feeling very tired with the effects of sleep deprivation and physical and emotional stress finally catching up with him. Then he realized for the first time since Pak had arrived that he was naked from the waist up. He got up and slipped on the robe Toshi had left for him. As Nomura and Pak sat silently, he crossed the room to the expansive window and looked out over the city. The predawn sky was blossoming peach in the east over Tokyo Bay.

"Shit," he said, almost to himself. "My dad led me across Europe on that silly scavenger hunt—mysterious keys, safe deposit box, breaking into my mother's grave—hell, we even got arrested." He let out a mirthless chuckle. "You'd think he didn't want me to find that damn scroll."

"Owen-san," Nomura said softly, "your father was a man of great forethought. Maybe he knew you would need every possible opportunity to strip off unwanted straphangers—people following you... people with you—so you alone could retrieve the *Apocalypse of Joseph*."

Owen felt the last ounce of denial drain out of him. It was all true. The story Nomura and Pak had given him was the only one that explained everything that had happened to him, not only in the last few weeks, but every bizarre experience he had had in his entire life. It seemed to him that he should feel overwhelmed. Strangely, he did not. He just felt as if he had awakened from a deep sleep to a reality he had known was there all along.

His father had been the Arbiter. Rhys had somehow known he would not live to fully prepare Owen to take over that responsibility, so he had secretly enlisted Nomura Eizo to shoulder the burden. Then he had prepared an elaborate scheme to put the *Apocalypse of Joseph* in Owen's hands alone, so Owen could make the right decisions and take up his role. It all would have worked, except Owen had failed.

"So what do we do now?" Owen said.

"There is very little we can do," Nomura said, his tone of defeat returning. "If only you had not been seduced by the Novikov woman."

"But I was just a boy. How was I to know?"

"I don't mean back at the camp, Owen-san. That was before you awoke—it did not matter then. No, I mean this last time, since you found out about your legacy."

"But she didn't seduce me this time."

Nomura and Pak both looked up suddenly. "Are you serious?" Nomura said.

"Well... yes," Owen said, turning to face them. "I mean... well, she tried, I suppose. We kissed. We kissed a lot, and we shared a bed one night, but we didn't have sex. She wanted to, and I did too. But it never happened. It just didn't feel right."

Nomura and Pak looked at each other. Then they got up and joined Owen at the window. "Are you sure, Dr. Powell?" Pak said. "This is very important."

"Of course I'm sure! That isn't something I would forget."

Pak turned to Nomura. "Do you think Brother Saul knows this?"

"Maybe, maybe not," Nomura said thoughtfully. "Owen and the Novikov woman were separated right after he got the scroll. Saul and her brother departed Tokyo before she returned. Now, she's dead. Maybe she never told them she hadn't fulfilled her mission."

"What does my sex life have to do with any of this?" Owen said.

"Don't you see, Owen-san?" Nomura said. "She was the Whore of Babylon foretold in the prophecy, the great test God put before you. Had you succumbed to her charms, you would have lost God's blessing utterly and irredeemably. But since you did not..."

Owen saw a new light fill Nomura's eyes. The old man who, only a moment ago, had seemed so small and frail, now radiated the vitality Owen saw in the dojo when Nomura bested him with a short staff.

"So what does this mean?" Owen said.

"It means, Owen-san, that you may still have a chance to recover the scroll and claim your legacy as Arbiter, a chance to save mankind from destruction." Then Nomura's face turned grave. "But it will mean putting your life on the line. If you are to redeem yourself in the eyes of God and the Great Circle, you will have to face the absolute test."

"I'll do whatever I have to do," Owen declared.

At that instant, a sliver of the sun's fiery orb breached the eastern horizon over Tokyo Bay, pouring orange light over the city and through the window of the study, illuminating the men's faces. Morning had arrived.

CHAPTER THIRTY-FIVE

"**B**rothers, after all these years, we are finally about to gain control of the Great Circle. The Arbiter has awakened, and he is sympathetic to our interests." Saul looked down the length of the long conference table and graced the room with a rare smile.

"Good! Praise God! That's wonderful!" intoned a clamor of voices, though no one else sat at the table.

Saul was alone in the manor house of his private estate situated on a high bluff overlooking the Yellow Sea. From the windows of his house, Saul could look out over the ocean and watch waves crash on the craggy cliffs of northern China's rocky coast. But he could not see any of that from where he sat today. Saul's conference room had no windows.

It was an elegantly appointed chamber featuring a heavy rosewood table with six leather-upholstered chairs on each side and a larger one where Saul sat at the head. On the wall to his right hung photographs of the last three Asher Illuminati and oil portraits of several before that. The wall to his left was almost completely covered by a map of the world, an immense Mercator projection molded in topographic relief with raised, snowcapped mountains sloping down to green plains and yellow deserts, all surrounded by glassy oceans painted a brilliant sapphire over the continental shelves and a deep cobalt beyond. Red lights twinkled at the world's twelve major capitals—not those of nation-states in the secular world, but the cities where seats of the Covenant's great houses resided.

Above the map, digital clocks displayed the times at those locations over signs listing the cities: New York, Rio de Janeiro, London, Copenhagen, Alexandria, Addis Ababa, St. Petersburg, Damascus, New Delhi, Singapore, Tokyo, and, of course, Shanghai.

There were no other chairs in the room—no gallery in the back, no seats along the wall—and there were no recording devices to capture what was said here. This was Saul's private conference room where he met in secret with his Council of Twelve. But none of those men and women was here today.

On the wall at the opposite end of the room from where Saul sat was a large plasma monitor for closed-circuit television and computer output. The images currently displayed on that screen were divided into quadrants. In each, a white-robed man sat gazing out from his own headquarters somewhere else in the world. These were the men who had answered in chorus. Saul too wore a white robe, and his image was being transmitted to all of the other conferees via the same encrypted satellite links that brought theirs to him. He imagined his image alone filled their screens. After all, did he not lead the Eastern Alliance?

"How did this wonderful event come about?" said a dark skinned man in the upper right quadrant of Saul's monitor. "How did Owen Powell learn of his legacy?"

"Yes, tell us about it," said another man. "And tell us how you managed to bring him around to our cause?" Does he know our five houses are in alliance? Will he really support—"

"Patience, patience, Brothers," Saul said, a broad smile making his snakelike features look even more angular than usual. "I'll give you all the details in due time; but right now what we need to do is prepare for the investiture. The important thing you must know is that Powell is not the Arbiter."

"What?" several said in shocked unison.

"What are you talking about, Brother Saul?" said the dark skinned man. He was Brother Thomas, the Illuminatus of Dan, sitting in his own conference room in New Delhi, India.

"How could Owen Powell not be the Arbiter?" said Brother Timothy, Singapore's Illuminatus of Simeon. "His father was the Arbiter. The legacy has been in the Powell family for centuries."

"The Powell line is fraudulent," Saul said, his eyes growing dark as the smile left his face. "Their distant ancestors were legitimate Arbiters, but in the late eighteenth century, Arbiter Lloyd Powell fathered a son out of wedlock with a Russian woman while in St. Petersburg mediating a dispute between the Houses of Joseph and Naphtali. He kept the affair secret and refused to acknowledge paternity. He later married an English woman, fathered a son by her, and wrongly designated that boy, William Henry Powell, his successor. William Henry then passed the legacy on to his descendants. It has been in the wrong hands for two centuries."

"But how can that be?" said Brother Ibrahim, Illuminatus of Gad, in Damascus. Every Powell Arbiter has had the *Apocalypse of Joseph*. They've all produced it for inspection at their investitures."

"Of course they've had it," Saul said. "Arbiter Lloyd passed it to William Henry, and they've kept it in their line ever since. God did not intervene in this abomination because no one challenged the Powell family's legitimacy. But history has demonstrated how displeased the Lord has been with us for accepting this fraud. Look at what has transpired—wars flaring up all over the world in the nineteenth century then, in the twentieth century, two World Wars and the Holocaust. Our late beloved Brother Ezekiel—God rest his soul—believed God let these things happen because Keepers of the Covenant had interfered in his plan. But God really brought these calamities upon the world to punish us for accepting a fraudulent line of Arbiters."

"Well if Owen Powell is not the legitimate Arbiter then who is?" demanded Brother Ismael, Illuminatus of Issachar, who scowled into the camera from his richly furnished study in Alexandria, Egypt.

"And why didn't this true Arbiter announce himself before now?" added Ibrahim.

"He didn't announce himself because, until recently, he didn't know he was the Arbiter. As Joseph of Arimathea foresaw, we have just emerged from a period in which the Arbiter has slept. Believing the Powell family to be the anointed line, we all thought that prophecy referred to the time between Rhys Powell's death and Owen Powell's awakening to the legacy, but we were wrong. It was a much longer period running from the birth of Lloyd Powell's first son, who was asleep to the truth of his heritage, to the awakening of his present day descendant. That man, a humble, pious pneumatic in the House of Naphtali by the name of Juri Novikov, discovered his heritage by reading letters he found in an old trunk in the attic of his family's ancestral home outside St. Petersburg. The letters were from Lloyd Powell to Novikov's maternal ancestor, Alexis Ivanova Buganin, refusing to publicly acknowledge their son."

"But does he have the scroll?" said Timothy. "How could he if the Powell family has had it for all this time?"

"Yes, he has it now," Saul said, a smile of satisfaction returning to his face. "When he awakened to the truth, he went to Brother Mikhail in St. Petersburg. Mikhail knew what an explosive situation this could be, given the Powell family's incestuous relationship with the House of David, so he asked me to help. I met with

Novikov then together we flew to Tokyo and confronted Powell with his family's treachery. Coward that he is, he surrendered the *Apocalypse* to Novikov without a fight."

"Why would Powell have the scroll with him in Tokyo?" Thomas said, his eyes narrowing in suspicion. "Whether his line is fraudulent, he has not known of the Covenant or his father's role as Arbiter."

"He had it because Brother Simon lured him to Tokyo and exposed the Covenant to him," Saul said, his voice hardening. "Simon and Joshua conspired to awaken their false Arbiter and secretly manipulate him to the advantage of their houses. That is what has brought the Tribulation down upon us."

"That is outrageous!" declared Ismael. "The Houses of David and Levi conspiring against us?"

"Of course!" said Ibrahim, his eyes suddenly ablaze. "It makes perfect sense. The house of kings and the house of priests have supported each other since the days of the ancient tribes. They're still plotting behind our backs!"

A clamor of voices filled the conference room as several of the Illuminati expressed their outrage. Saul settled back in his chair and let them vent for a few moments. Then he reined them in.

"Brothers, put yourselves at ease," he said in the reassuring tone they had come to know and trust. "Yes, the fraud Joshua and Simon have perpetrated against us is an outrageous sacrilege, but we have the situation in hand. I have informed Brother Joshua that their scheme has failed—the true Arbiter has awakened and has the *Apocalypse* in his possession—and I demanded he convene the Great Circle for Novikov's investiture."

"And how did Brother Joshua respond to your accusation?" Thomas said warily.

"How do you think he responded?" Saul snapped. "He insisted the Powell line is legitimate, and he denied any collusion between the House of David and the House of Levi." Saul was growing tired of Thomas's suspicions, but he needed the Indian's support, so he channeled his irritation into the telling of his story.

"Can you believe it?" he continued, "Joshua even claimed Novikov had stolen the scroll from Powell. Leading the Covenant's royal house has given that man incredible gall! But in the end, he gave in. What choice did he have? Novikov has the scroll. God has spoken. Joshua will contact all of you shortly to set a date for the investiture."

"With all due respect, Brother Saul," Timothy said cautiously, hoping to avoid the ire he sensed Thomas had evoked, "but scroll or no scroll, Novikov will have to be accepted by the Great Circle to be invested as Arbiter. We will support him, of course, but there are only five of us."

"Six counting the House of Naphtali," Ibrahim said.

"Can we trust the Russians?" Ismael said. "They've vacillated between East and West for centuries. Since the time of Peter the Great, they have they been unable to decide whether they are Asian or European."

"Surely Brother Mikhail will support one of his own," Ibrahim responded.

"But even with Naphtali, six is only half of the Great Circle," Timothy said. "The others are almost certain to stand behind the House of David."

"Not all of them," Saul said. He put his elbows on the table and leaned towards the monitor, his unnatural grin returning. "I have some more good news, news I've been saving for just such a propitious occasion. I have been negotiating with Brother Zechariah, the new Illuminatus of Benjamin. He does not want to reveal his intentions to the rest of the Great Circle, but he assures me, when the time comes, he will throw his lot in with us and support our candidate for Arbiter."

"I don't believe it!" blurted Thomas, unable to keep the shock out of his voice. "Brother Ezekiel's successor, head of the great house in North America, breaking with the House of David to join the Eastern Alliance?"

"He's not formally joining the Alliance," cautioned Saul. "So he urges us to not do or say anything that might reveal he has pledged us his support. But when key issues come up, he will follow our lead." Saul sat back in his chair and folded his arms across his chest. "So you see, my brothers, when it comes time to confirm Novikov's investiture as Arbiter, there will be seven of us in favor of it."

"Seven is still not enough," Thomas said. "This is not democracy. The Great Circle makes decisions by consensus, not by simple majorities. You will need the support of all of the great houses, including the House of David, to get Novikov confirmed."

"But don't you see, Brother Thomas?" Ibrahim intoned in his rich, Arabic accent. "If we have the support of seven houses, the other five will have to follow. Oh, they will argue and debate. Yes, yes, of course. But in the end, they will relent. Seven houses *and* possession of the *Apocalypse of Joseph*? How can they possibly deny that this Novikov has God's blessing?"

"But what if they do?" Thomas insisted. "What if Joshua stands by his story that Novikov stole the scroll from Powell? What if the Great Circle is broken and we are plunged into war?"

"Then we will prevail!" Saul shouted and slammed his fist on the table. "The Eastern Alliance has several of the largest houses in the Covenant. Why the House of Asher alone can call more than eighteen thousand baptized initiates to the sword!"

Every face on the monitor stared at Saul in stunned silence. That pleased him and he paused to revel in their surprise. Then, with a mocking smile, he went on.

"My Brothers, I am not afraid to reveal my house's strength to you. And I know yours, too. You can be sure of it. Thomas, you have almost sixteen thousand five hundred men and women at your beck and call. Ibrahim and Ismael, each of your houses has more than thirteen thousand members. Timothy, you are the weakest among us, so I will do you the courtesy of not revealing your strength to the others.

"You see my intelligence is very good. I know that the Eastern Alliance, augmented by the House of Naphtali, can field well over eighty thousand men and women at arms. That means the other six houses cannot field more than sixty-four thousand initiates combined, and I'm confident that if war erupts, Brother Zechariah will declare the House of Benjamin neutral, reducing our enemies' strength by another twelve or thirteen thousand souls."

"And how do you know this, Brother?" Thomas persisted. "How can your intelligence possibly be so precise that you know the five Western houses plus the Japanese Levites do not total more than sixty-four thousand members?"

"My intelligence does not have to be that precise, Brother Thomas," Saul said with a knowing smile, "Because God has told us the enemy's strength. Does not the *Apocalypse of John* reveal to us that in the time of Tribulation God's true witnesses will total one hundred forty-four thousand souls? Well, the Tribulation has begun, Brothers, so if we know our strength then we know the enemy's strength as well."

The four faces on the monitor were still as they pondered this simple logic.

After a moment, Brother Thomas spoke again. This time his tone was respectful, almost pleading. "Brother Saul, I urge you to consider what you're saying. Our combined numbers may be greater than those of the other houses. But what does that really mean? One hundred forty-four thousand people spread around the world cannot go to war with one another in secret. This is not the Dark Ages—it is the information age, the age of nation-states. If we go to war, the secular world is sure to be dragged into it, a world with huge armies and terrible weapons. During the Cold War the great houses of the East and West cooperated to constrain the superpowers from rash behavior. How can we do that in the future if the great houses themselves are at war?" Thomas paused to let that thought sink in. Then he continued.

"As you have reminded us, the Tribulation has begun. This is a very dangerous time for God's one true church, dangerous for all of humankind. God is testing us. If we act wisely, he will protect us. But if we fail, we bring about not only our own destruction, but the very end of creation itself."

Thomas's voice grew more assertive as he broadened his petition to address the other Illuminati. "Don't you see the danger, Brothers? We are standing on the doorstep of Armageddon, and already we are referring to our brothers in Tokyo and the West as 'enemies'."

"You are right, Brother Thomas," Saul said, his voice deliberately gentle. "This is a very dangerous time. God is testing us, and if we fail we will be destroyed. The test God has put before us is whether we will reject the false Arbiter and restore the anointed line. The Novikov family is legitimate. The Powells are usurpers. God is watching to see if we carry out his will." Saul paused and sighed.

"And you are right in chastening me for calling the other houses 'enemies'. They are not our enemies. They are our brothers. We can trust them to recognize God's will and make the right decision, a decision that will preserve the Great Circle and save the world from war.

"And with that, my brothers, I bid you all good day. Prepare for Brother Joshua's summons and respond quickly. Go with God, Brothers."

"Go with God, Brother Saul," several of them intoned.

Saul flipped a switch at the instrument panel built into the end of the table where he sat, turning off the plasma monitor. The last thing he saw before the screen went dark was Thomas's stony face staring back at him, seemingly unmoved by his closing remarks.

He sat pondering for a moment, Thomas's expression lingering in his mind's eye. Then a door to his right opened and a tall, muscular, blond man came in and took a chair at the corner of the conference table beside him. For a moment longer, neither of them spoke. Then Saul said, "You saw how it went?"

"Yes, I watched it all on the monitors in the control room," Juri Novikov said. "Looks like they bought it. All of them, that is, except for Brother Thomas. He could be trouble."

"I don't think he will be a problem at the investiture," Saul said, staring at the darkened monitor as if he could still see Thomas there. "He knows the only way to avoid war is to confront the other houses as a united front. But afterward... Yes, afterward. I think the House of Dan will be due a change of leadership in the not too distant future."

Juri smiled. "I have contacts in New Delhi. We could keep Asher's and Naphtali's hands out of it."

Saul turned his hooded eyes on the Russian. "What concerns me more right now is Powell." The smile left Novikov's face abruptly. "You were supposed to kill him, but you didn't. Why?"

"I thought we could use him to our advantage," Juri said, hoping the lines he had rehearsed sounded believable. "Anna thought she could control him, get him to give up his legacy and endorse me as Arbiter. Had she succeeded, none of the other Illuminati would stand in our way."

"But she failed, and now she is dead." Saul's voice was flat, emotionless. He watched Novikov's eyes.

"The bastard murdered her."

Saul noted that Juri sounded angry, but not grief stricken. It was as if Powell had smashed his favorite toy, not killed his sister. "Are you certain she succeeded in seducing him? The post mortem found no signs of sexual intercourse in the hours before her death."

"You had my sister's body autopsied?" Yuri's eyes were wide, his face betraying a sense of violation.

Is there a thread of humanity in you after all? Saul wondered.

He said, "The Tokyo police ordered it. It is standard procedure whenever someone dies under suspicious circumstances. I merely had my contacts get me a copy of the report. The police opened a homicide investigation, but Simon pulled strings and had the death ruled accidental." Saul's lips curled in a thin, rueful smile, but his eyes remained hard, watching Juri's. "Your sister must have been clumsy. It seems she tripped on the steps in your apartment and broke her own neck."

Saul wondered whether Novikov's awkward, eye-shifting pause was the product of discomfort at the mental picture of his sister flayed open on an autopsy table, or whether he was stalling to fabricate a story. After a few seconds, Saul said, "But the question remains: Did she have sex with Powell?"

"I'm sure she did," Juri replied, looking down at the table. "She nearly succeeded in Zurich, but they needed to get to the bank for the scroll. They must have done it before leaving for England, or perhaps on their arrival there."

"But you're not certain? She didn't confirm that the last time you spoke, when she called before flying out of Heathrow?"

"She was rushing for the plane." Juri still did not meet Saul's eyes. "She told me Powell had gotten the scroll and was on his way back to Tokyo. She said we had succeeded, and from the positive tone of her voice, I'm sure she meant in that too."

Saul still stared at Novikov, burning holes in the big man as he fidgeted. "For your sake, you had better be right. I think we can count on Powell showing up at the investiture. If so, you had better hope he has lost God's blessing. It will be your life on the line."

Juri looked up in alarm. "But you said you could control the investiture."

"I am doing everything humanly possible. If Powell shows up, he will not get out alive. But that does not mean you will. I have..." Saul paused as if weighing how much to say. "I've arranged for some... let us call it 'insurance'. But I will only cash in my policy if you fail. It will be up to you to see that Owen Powell is not invested as Arbiter."

Juri finally looked Saul in the eye, his old confidence returning. "Owen Powell will never live to become Arbiter," he said through a bitter smile.

CHAPTER THIRTY-SIX

Russian and Chinese attack helicopters swept over the grassy steppe like giant dragonflies chopping the air with bladed wings. The Mi-28 Havocs and Harbin WZ-9s worked in multiple two-ship formations, methodically scouring the designated area. The stated objective of this drill was to secure a patch of ground at a specified set of geographic coordinates for a high-level diplomatic meeting. Military commanders were responsible for sanitizing the countryside and the air above it over a ten-kilometer radius around the site. Civilian authorities, they had been told, would handle access control on the single dirt road leading to the designated location and security at the site itself. The diplomats and their entourages would be brought in aboard twelve specially marked buses. Any other vehicles attempting to approach the site, regardless of type or marking, were to be destroyed. The choppers had been given free-fire clearance for anyone attempting to penetrate the twenty-kilometer diameter quarantine zone from any direction, whether by ground or air.

The aircrews had been told this was merely an exercise in international military cooperation, but they knew it was more than that—they had been given live ammunition and orders to shoot to kill.

Sanitizing an area of more than three hundred square kilometers would have been a momentous task had it been almost anywhere else in the world, but this part of the Mongolian steppe was virtually empty terrain. The countryside consisted of rolling hills covered with scrub grass barely able to support the few scrawny sheep and angora goats the nomadic herders who lived here raised in their daily struggle to eke out a living. Those people and their flocks were gone now. The Mongolian Army had swept them up a week earlier and trucked them off to a holding camp outside a small town fifty kilometers away. Now the landscape was completely barren, a treeless grassy plain with nowhere for a sniper to hide from the infrared, telescopic sights of the ever-prowling death machines in the sky.

Saul's choice of location was nothing short of brilliant, Joshua had to admit. Having petitioned convocation of the Great Circle, the Illuminatus of Asher had the prerogative of naming the site, and he had used that privilege to his maximum advantage. The Mongolian steppe was isolated and deep in Asher territory. Not only did Saul have absolute control of the terrain here, but the fact that northern China, Mongolia, and the Russian Far East were all under Asherite dominion gave him international passport control of the region as well, allowing him to dictate how many delegates each of the other houses could bring and closely monitor the identities of those representatives.

The setting also gave him the opportunity to flaunt Asher's solidarity with its newfound ally, the House of Naphtali, in the combined military exercise that went on above their heads. Although this handful of Chinese and Russian attack helicopters was but a whisper in terms of worldwide military potential, the suggestion that elements of the world's two largest armies would work together at Saul's bidding sent a chilling message to the other Illuminati, one none of them failed to grasp.

Yes, Saul was clever indeed, Joshua thought. He watched the helicopters sweep back and forth over the grassy hills and wondered how the Western Illuminati and their entourages would escape those deadly guns and rockets if the Great Circle erupted in violence.

"You assured me the helicopters would keep their distance," Joshua said to Saul as the last bus pulled away.

"Don't worry, Brother," Saul said with a satisfied smile. "They will not violate the sanctity of the Circle or disrupt the dignity of our sacraments. They are only making one last sweep to assure our security before moving out to the ten-kilometer perimeter."

Saul signaled one of his guardians with a subtle hand gesture, and the man whispered something into a microphone hidden in the lapel of his coat. Almost immediately, the helicopters gathered into formations and began moving away, three groups of Havocs fanning out to the north, northeast, and northwest, and the WZ-9s spreading toward compass points south of the site.

Joshua watched them disappear behind the hills.

He waited a moment, listening to the rotor chop fade in the distance then turned and called out loudly, "Let us stand before God."

He raised the hood of his brown wool robe and positioned it to conceal all but the lower portion of his bearded face. With an air of gravity, he walked to a stone altar placed there for the convocation. With silent precision, the other 204 men and women at the site moved to their places. The twelve Illuminati took up positions in the traditional manner, with heads of the Eastern and Western houses alternating around a circle formed on Brother Joshua, Illuminatus of David and heir to the sacred, royal legacy of Jesus, James, and Joseph of Arimathea. They stood six feet apart, forming a circle seventy-two feet in circumference, twenty-three feet in diameter.

As the Arbiter's investiture was a historic occasion, each Illuminatus had brought six members of his Council of Twelve to witness the event. Like the Illuminati, these men and women wore hooded robes concealing most of their faces. They stood shoulder to shoulder behind their respective leaders, forming a second circle two hundred sixteen feet in circumference, twenty-three feet out from the first.

And twenty-three feet behind each house's group of councilors stood its guardians, a maximum of ten apiece, per Saul's restrictions. These men usually dressed in business suits, but today most of them wore military fatigues and were heavily armed with an assortment of automatic weapons, high-powered rifles with scopes, and heavy, crew-served machine guns—a limit of one of the latter per house, again, in accordance with Saul's rigid constraints. Together, the guardians formed a protective outer circle where they stood facing out from behind sandbags, scanning the surrounding hills with binoculars and riflescopes. They were determined not to let another sniper take out one of their beloved Illuminati.

Joshua prayed that the contentious drama he knew was about to play out in the Great Circle would not climax with the guardians turning their weapons inward.

One additional figure stood on the Mongolian steppe that day, bringing the total in the formation to two hundred five. Juri Novikov, wearing a white robe, stood immediately in front of the councilors from the House of Naphtali, waiting to be summoned before the Great Circle of Illuminati.

So the stage was set. Within a protective ring of one hundred twenty heavily armed guardians, twelve Illuminati, seventy-two councilors, and one candidate stood stone still in hooded robes. A midsummer lassitude had descended on the Mongolian steppe.

No wind stirred the grass. The only movement to be seen came from the guardians who continued to scan the surrounding hillsides, and even they were nearly stationary and respectfully silent.

"Fellow Keepers of the Covenant," Joshua intoned, opening the ceremony in the traditional manner, "we are gathered today to witness the fulfillment of God's prophecy. The Arbiter has awakened and come forward to take up his sacred post as defender of the faith and executor of God's will.

"As it is written and has been our custom for two thousand years, a candidate for this post must be nominated by a house other than his own. He must be a direct male descendant of Gwilym ap Hywel, the Covenant's first Arbiter, and he must prove he has God's blessing and authority by presenting the *Apocalypse of Joseph*, the sacred scroll of prophecy that Joseph of Arimathea entrusted to Arbiter Gwilym on the day of his investiture. Does any Illuminatus here have a candidate to submit for the Covenant's Great Circle to consider?"

"I have a candidate," Saul announced in a strong, confident voice. "I, Saul, Illuminatus of Asher, submit for the Circle's consideration, Juri Novikov, a son of the House of Naphtali."

With that, Juri walked to the edge of the Great Circle and stood between, but slightly behind, Saul and Brother Mikhail, the Illuminatus of Naphtali.

"This is out of order!" bellowed Brother Matthias in his rich Ethiopian accent. "This man is not of the House of David."

"Nowhere in scripture does it say the Arbiter must always be from the House of David," Saul said. "The *Apocalypse of Joseph* says only that the awakened Arbiter will be a chosen son of a northern House. Is not Naphtali a northern house?"

"But only men of the Powell family are direct descendants of Gwilym ap Hywel," said the Illuminatus from Rio de Janeiro. "Surely you aren't going to claim this Russian is descended from an ancient Briton."

"I claim exactly that, Brother Noah," Saul said. "And is it so unreasonable that a Russian has Celtic Britons in his ancestry? After all, you are Brazilian, are you not? But your ancestors were Portuguese and Spanish, and before that, Israelites from the ancient tribe of Joseph."

"But the Arbiters have always been Powells," Matthias said. "How can the anointed bloodline pass from Rhys Powell, an American of Welsh descent, to this Russian?"

"Anointed blood never flowed in Rhys Powell's veins," Saul said. "The Powell line has been fraudulent for more than two hundred years."

With that, the Circle erupted in a cacophony of angry voices, Matthias and Noah yelling at Saul in outrage—Ibrahim, Ismael, and Timothy trying to shout them down. Brother Mikhail and Copenhagen's Brother Malachi were pleading with all of them to remain calm.

Several of the guardians turned and stared.

Joshua surveyed the emerging dynamics with considerable interest. He noted that Saul was strangely quiet, and he sensed the Asherite was smiling beneath his hood. Brothers Thomas and Zechariah also remained quiet. Unlike Saul, both of them seemed ill at ease.

After following the quarrel a few minutes longer, Joshua slowly raised his hand. The Circle immediately became still, the other Illuminati startled by this gesture, atypical of the Illuminatus from the royal house. "We mustn't let this surprising turn of events sow discord among us," Joshua said. "Brother Saul has submitted a candidate he believes to be anointed by God. We must examine the evidence and judge it on its merits." He paused then called out, "Candidate Novikov, enter the Circle and stand before God."

Juri stepped into the Circle, passing between Saul and Mikhail, and stood before the stone altar, looking across it at Joshua.

Joshua continued. "Brother Mikhail, the candidate is from your house. What do you know of his qualifications?"

"He is an enlightened man, one who knows God and serves him with a pure heart."

Perhaps he is," Joshua said, "but the issue at hand is whether he is descended from Arbiter Gwilym."

"He is," Mikhail said. "I know it is hard to believe. I was skeptical too when he first came to me, but I have seen the evidence and I am convinced." Mikhail then told Joshua and the Great Circle the story Saul had previously related to the Eastern Alliance, how Juri had found letters from Arbiter Lloyd Powell to his maternal ancestor proving the anointed bloodline had passed from the Powell family to the Novikov family in the late nineteenth century.

"I have the letters for your examination," Mikhail said. "And I have Candidate Novikov's genealogical charts showing his descent from—"

"Yes, I'm sure you do," Joshua said. "And I'm sure the documents are very convincing. But what I want to know is do you believe them?"

"I... Well, yes..." Mikhail stammered, surprised that Joshua would ask him such a question. "Yes, I do believe—"

"Is not the real issue whether the candidate has in his possession the *Apocalypse of Joseph?*" Saul said.

"Yes, that is what we need to know," Matthias said impatiently. "The *Apocalypse* is the ultimate proof of authority. Without the scroll, this claimant has no case."

"He can't have it!" Noah declared. "The Powell family holds the scroll. Brother Saul's charge that the Powell Arbiters have been fraudulent for two hundred years is absurd because every one of them has presented the *Apocalypse* at his investiture."

"Candidate Novikov," Joshua said, "do you have the *Apocalypse of Joseph?*"

"I have the scroll." Juri reached into his robe and withdrew a tightly wrapped roll of vellum, about twelve inches long, yellowed with age. He laid it on the stone altar before Joshua.

Several Illuminati gasped.

"Brother Simon, if you would assist me," Joshua said, bending over the scroll.

Simon turned and stepped to the altar. He delicately held the end of the ancient document while Joshua took the roll, and they carefully unfurled the first several feet of it across the altar and examined the text.

"What say you, High Priest?" Joshua said, reciting the ritual words. "Be this the true *Apocalypse of Joseph?*"

Simon hesitated, peering down from beneath his hood. Then he pulled the hood back, revealing his skeletal face, and bent over the altar for a closer look. He gently rubbed the vellum between his fingers, feeling the texture of it. The calfskin was blotchy, and the stitching holding some of the sections together was frayed, but the small, neatly scribed Aramaic symbols were still legible. Simon reached inside his robe and brought out a tiny bottle with an eyedropper in the cap, opened it, and put two small drops of fluid on the scroll, one on the unmarked vellum, another on one of the symbols. After a few moments, he rose and repositioned his hood.

"This be the true *Apocalypse of Joseph*," he announced in his flinty voice.

More gasps from around the Circle.

"But how can that be?" Noah said, his voice shrill with tension, his Latin accent heavier than usual.

"Yes, tell us how this scroll came into your possession, Candidate Novikov," Joshua said, trying to keep his voice level. "I know that Owen Powell had it a month ago. My people saw him retrieve it from his mother's grave."

"When the candidate learned of his true heritage," Saul said, launching into the story he had told the Eastern Alliance, "he first went to Broth—"

"No! I want Mr. Novikov to tell us in his own words," Joshua said.

Juri hesitated. Then he proceeded to explain how, after discovering he was the rightful Arbiter, he and Brother Mikhail had appealed to Saul for help. He and Saul had confronted Owen, retrieving the scroll without a fight. Juri told the story smoothly, his tone defiant.

"I don't believe him," Matthais said. "I want to hear Powell's side of the story."

"Yes, I too would like to hear what Owen Powell has to say about this," said Brother Thomas, the Indian Illuminatus. "If Powell retrieved the scroll then surrendered it to Novikov and Brother Saul, then he now must know of the Covenant's existence. He too has awakened to his heritage. So why would he willingly give up the scroll? Why is he not here to speak for himself?"

"Because he is a coward!" Saul said, trying to contain his fury with Thomas for challenging him in the presence of the Western Illuminati. "When he learned of the Covenant, he didn't want anything to do with it, didn't want the responsibility. He was more than willing to turn the scroll over to its rightful owner so he could return to his quiet life as a college professor."

"Well, I still don't believe it," Matthias said.

"Are you calling me a liar?" Saul said.

The Circle exploded in a tumult of angry shouts.

Almost all of the guardians turned and stared. Several from Asher turned around, weapons in hand, and guardians from some of the other houses followed suit, watching the Asherites carefully.

"Brothers!" Joshua shouted, and the Illuminati fell silent. "We must not let this issue tear us apart. We will either accept this candidate or reject him, but we must do it as a brotherhood, as a unified church. I for one do not believe the candidate is anointed by God, but I want to know where each of you stands on the question of his investiture."

"I stand with the House of David," Simon said immediately.

"As does the House of Reuben," shouted Matthias.

"And Joseph," Noah said.

"The House of Asher stands behind its candidate," Saul said dryly.

"The House of Naphtali stands beside Brother Saul in support of the candidate.

"Issachar supports Candidate Novikov," Ismael declared.

"The House of Gad supports the candidate."

"Simeon stands with Asher for Novikov."

There was a pause then Brother Malachi spoke. "Zebulun opposes Novikov for Arbiter."

Another pause.

"Brother Thomas," Joshua said. "Where does the House of Dan stand on the question of investing Novikov as Arbiter?"

Thomas hesitated a long moment then said, "The House of Dan supports the candidate."

Several Illuminati sighed.

"And Brother Zechariah," Joshua said. "You haven't spoken. How does Benjamin, the great house of New York, feel about this candidate's qualifications?"

There was no answer.

"Brother Zechariah?"

After several moments, Zechariah spoke in a small voice. "Benjamin supports the candidate."

"I'm sorry, Brother. I didn't hear you," Joshua said.

"Benjamin supports Candidate Novikov," Zechariah said loudly, sounding more defensive than defiant.

The Great Circle was quiet for a moment while everyone considered what had just occurred.

Then Saul spoke. "Brother Joshua," he began in a conciliatory tone. "Seven of us support investing Juri Novikov as the Covenant's Arbiter. He has proven his bloodline and presented the *Apocalypse of Joseph* as custom requires. He clearly has God's blessing, and no one has offered any reason why the Great Circle should oppose his candidacy." He paused and sighed as if trying to remain patient. "You said we must not let this issue tear us apart, we must accept him or reject him as one united church. I believe that if you change your position—if the House of David casts its support for the candidate—the four remaining great houses will follow your lead and we will have peace." He paused again as if unsure of how far he should go. "But if you don't—"

"Brother Saul," Joshua said sternly. "I oppose this candidate because I know he is not anointed by God. But you are right. None of us has presented any testimony, much less evidence, that contradicts his story or suggests he is not qualified to be our Arbiter. Therefore, we have no grounds on which to block his investiture unless someone steps forward now."

Then, raising his voice as if addressing every man and woman on the Mongolian steppe, Joshua called out, "So can anyone here tell us why the Covenant's Great Circle of Illuminati should not invest this man, Juri Novikov, as its Arbiter?"

"I can tell you why!" came a voice booming back, seemingly out of nowhere.

"Then step forward!" Joshua shouted. "Identify yourself and present your case!"

A tall, broad-shouldered figure, garbed in a hooded robe that concealed his face, stepped out from where he had been standing among the councilors of the House of David.

Throwing back his hood, he declared, "I am Owen Powell, son of Arbiter Rhys, sole descendant of Gwilym ap Hywel, and I have come to claim my legacy!"

CHAPTER THIRTY-SEVEN

"I object to this breach of protocol!" Saul bellowed. "This man has come here in disguise and disrupted our sacred proceedings. He has entered the country using false credentials and misrepresented himself as a member of the House of David."

Several other Illuminati added their remonstrations to Saul's.

"What do we care how someone crosses the borders of secular states?" Brother Noah shouted back. "And if anyone has call to protest someone posing as a member of the royal house, it is the Illuminatus of David." Then a touch of irony lightened his high-pitched voice. "Tell us Brother Joshua, do you wish to lodge a complaint?"

Several faint snorts of laughter flittered around the Circle.

Joshua ignored the levity. "Dr. Powell stands with the councilors of David at my invitation."

"Then I protest this subterfuge," Saul persisted. "If Dr. Powell wished to address the Great Circle, he could have petitioned for an audience. There was no need for the House of David to smuggle him here under false pretenses."

"Wasn't there?" Joshua said, his voice hardening. "Could Owen Powell have openly petitioned for an audience and gotten to this site safely?"

Saul let the question hang on the still Mongolian air. He found Joshua's insinuation that he would have done something to prevent Powell's appearance at the convocation insulting, but he could hardly deny it was true. He had done everything in his power to keep Powell away from Novikov's investiture, even to the point of sending a death squad to Japan to hunt him down in the weeks before the gathering. But the Asherite killers had come up empty—Brother Simon had apparently granted Powell refuge among the Levites—and now it was clear that the Houses of Levi and David had collaborated to get him here.

Well, so be it, Saul thought. It had been a long shot, anyway. He never really expected to keep Owen Powell away. Now, events would just have to play themselves out.

When it was clear Saul was not going to respond, Joshua called out, "Candidate Powell, come forward and stand before God."

"Now I protest!" yelled Brother Timothy from Singapore. "No house has nominated this man as a candidate."

"Then the House of Levi does," Brother Simon rasped. "Here, let me make it formal—I, Simon, Illuminatus of Levi, submit for the Circle's consideration, Owen Powell, son of Rhys Powell, the last true Arbiter of the Covenant," he said, hanging on the word *true.*

As several of the Illuminati murmured complaints, Owen stepped into the Circle and stood beside Juri before the altar.

"I'm going to kill you, you murdering bastard," Juri said only loud enough for Owen to hear.

"One of us is going to die today," Owen growled back. "You can count on that."

⟛ ⟛

Five hundred meters away on a hillside overlooking the Great Circle, a man in camouflaged clothing and greasepaint pushed open the grassy lid of his spider hole another inch and peered through the scope of his Barret M82A1 .50 caliber sniper rifle. He had been there three days, having hiked in one moonless night after the Mongolian Army swept through the area. He had dug the narrow hole four feet deep, keeping the sod intact to cover the plywood lid he had brought and carefully spreading the dirt into the surrounding grass to dry out in the summer sun. By the time the attack helicopters arrived, he was safely in the hole and under its natural, grassy cover, undetectable from five feet away on the ground, or from the air, even with telescopic, infrared gun sights.

The hole was cramped and stank of sweat and urine and the refuse of three days' rations. He didn't care. He had endured far worse as a member of Delta Force. He had loved that job, loved the adventure, the challenge, the sheer ecstasy of killing. He had thought he would be a career soldier, a "lifer", until the CIA discovered his exceptional talents.

They had gotten him out of the Army and put him to work in places ranging from Latin America to Afghanistan to Burma. That job was great too—lots of travel and adventure, and he still got the opportunity for an occasional kill. But he couldn't say much for the pay, and it didn't take him long to find out how much his special skills could pull down on the open market—only as long as it took for him to discover the Covenant and make contacts among several of the Illuminati.

So now, in addition to working for the CIA, Jack Fowler did contract work for a handful of very powerful, very wealthy clients. In most respects it was the same kind of work he had always done, the kind of work he loved, but now he made a great deal of money for his passion.

Fowler grimaced and pumped his right leg to work out a cramp. When the spasm subsided, he centered the crosshairs of his riflescope on Owen Powell's chest. Confident of the elevation and windage, he swept his aim over to Novikov then back to the American, making sure he could cover each of them adequately.

He had waited patiently for Powell to surface. From what the client had told him, he knew the pompous ass would make an appearance sooner or later. Now he waited for "condition green", the event the client had specified as the precondition for squeezing the trigger. God, how he hoped that event occurred. Adrenaline surged through his veins at the thought of it. This was the best rush he had gotten since popping that blowhard at Glastonbury.

═╬ ╬═

"Candidate Powell," Joshua said when Owen arrived before the altar. "What testimony do you offer that has bearing on Mr. Novikov's candidacy for Arbiter."

"Only that he is a liar and a thief," Owen said, drawing angry grunts from several of the Illuminati. "He and his sister assumed false identities and befriended me so they could steal the *Apocalypse of Joseph* when I recovered it from my father's hiding place. Once I got the scroll, he led me into a trap and took it from me by force. When I went to his Tokyo apartment to get it back, his sister tried to kill me."

"You're a liar and a murderer," Novikov said. Then to Brother Joshua, "Powell came to Roxanna and me several weeks ago, begging us to help him recover the *Apocalypse* after learning about the Covenant from Brother Simon. I refused and cautioned my sister to stay away from him. She promised me she would, but—God rest her soul—she loved the man. She had been in love with him ever since he seduced her at the Korean training refuge nearly twenty years ago. They ran off to Europe behind my back to search for the scroll.

"While they were there, I returned home to St. Petersburg. That was when I discovered my legacy. By the time Brother Mikhail and I contacted Brother Saul, Powell and Roxanna had found the scroll, but had been arrested by the English police. They released Powell immediately, but held Roxanna a day longer. Powell then abandoned her in jail and took the scroll back to Tokyo alone.

"When Brother Saul and I learned Powell was on his way to Tokyo, we flew there and confronted him with the evidence of my heritage. We didn't threaten him. We just explained how dangerous it would be to keep the scroll and attempt to become Arbiter. He whined something about having left that kind of life behind when he got out of the Army and said he didn't want to deal with the stress of it again. He gave me the scroll. He even wished me luck as Arbiter.

"So, Brother Saul and I took the scroll to China for safekeeping. A couple of days later, after being unable to reach Roxanna on the phone, I discovered she had been murdered in our Tokyo apartment. Now I know who did it!"

"The Tokyo police ruled her death accidental," Simon said.

"Yes, and we all know who pulls their strings," Saul said.

"Roxanna's death was no accident," Juri said. Then turning to Owen, "Tell us you didn't kill her, Powell. Go ahead, lie to the Illuminati."

Owen was in a quandary, unwilling to lie, but unable to tell them the truth without revealing Elaine's involvement in the incident. He said nothing.

"See?" Juri said.

"The Great Circle is not concerned about circumstances surrounding the death of Roxanna Novikov," Joshua said. "The matter before us is whether Candidate Powell has testimony or evidence bearing on his or Candidate Novikov's qualifications for Arbiter."

"Yes," Brother Timothy said. "Novikov has presented the *Apocalypse* to prove God has blessed his candidacy. Powell, you say he stole it from you. What evidence have you to support that claim?"

"Only my word," Owen said.

"And the Great Circle has Novikov's word that you are lying," Saul said, "and mine."

"There is a certain amount of circumstantial evidence supporting Candidate Powell's story," Simon said. "Records from Yi Chung-hae's training camp have been recovered, and they confirm that Roxanna Novikov posed as a Danish woman named Anna Norgaard when she trained there with Powell."

Joshua added, "And when she was arrested in England with the candidate a few weeks ago, she was traveling on a Danish passport under that name."

"What of it?" Ismael said. "Traveling under assumed names is common in the Covenant. We've all done it.

Juri added, "Powell may not have known Roxanna's real name when he seduced her in Korea, but we told him who we really were when he approached us in Tokyo."

"I didn't approach anyone from the Covenant when I went to Tokyo," Owen said. "Not Brother Simon, not the Novikovs. Roxanna and this man came to me." Turning to Novikov he said, "You lied to me then, and you're lying to the Great Circle now."

"The question is," Ismael said, "do you have any evidence to support this outrageous story?"

"I have only my word," Owen said.

"Then it would appear that you have no case," Ibrahim said. "Your word is nothing against the sacred word of an Illuminatus. And your claim is baseless compared to that of a candidate with the *Apocalypse*. Possession of the scroll is the ultimate authority."

"Yes, I would tend to agree," Simon said. "As high priest I would have to rule that possession of the *Apocalypse of Joseph* is irrefutable evidence of God's will, regardless of how Candidate Novikov came by the scroll."

"Then it is settled," Saul said with conviction. "Brother Joshua, isn't it time—"

"There is just one minor problem," Simon went on. "According to Brother Saul, God's will was thwarted for more than two hundred years. Did he not charge that the Powell family's claim to the legacy was fraudulent, even though they held the scroll?"

Several sharp intakes of breath could be heard from around the Circle, but no one spoke.

"So if the word of an Illuminatus is sacred," Simon continued, "then history provides us additional evidence supporting Powell's case. Candidate Novikov's possession of the scroll can no longer be regarded as absolute proof that he has God's blessing."

"This is legalistic trickery!" Saul exploded. "Novikov has the scroll, Powell does not. Powell has provided no evidence whatsoever to support his claim. If possession of the scroll is now insufficient evidence then we have no way to determine God's will in this matter."

"There is still a way," Joshua said.

There was a pause.

Then Brother Malachi gasped, "You can't be serious. The Great Circle has not resorted to that for centuries, not since the Dark Ages."

"Nevertheless, the method is still valid," Joshua said, "and it is the ultimate test of God's will."

"The authority of the test is timeless and absolute," Simon said. "But one of the candidates would have to formally request it. Then the other would be free to accept the challenge or relinquish his claim."

"Candidates Novikov and Powell," Joshua said. "Do either of you choose to petition the Great Circle at this time?"

This was the moment Owen had been waiting for, the opportunity for which Nomura Eizo—Brother Simon, that is—had prepared him.

"I petition the Great Circle," Owen said. "I am the true and anointed Arbiter. To prove my claim, I demand my right to trial by mortal combat."

Joshua said, "Candidate Novikov, Candidate Powell has issued a challenge. Do you accept?"

Juri stared at Owen for a full ten seconds. Slowly, his lips curled into a sneer. "Gladly."

"Then so be it!" Joshua said. "Novikov and Powell will fight, and God will reveal his will to us in the outcome of that contest."

Trial by mortal combat was an ancient rite in the Covenant. Frequently used to settle disputes in the first thousand years after the great houses fled the Holy Land, the practice had spread to secular realms around the Covenant seats, inspiring the medieval tournaments of Europe and similar spectacles in other parts of the world. Such secular competitions seldom ended in death, though the contestants wore armor and wielded bladed weapons. Conversely, Covenant trials were fought empty handed, but always continued until one claimant killed the other. It was the only way to determine once and for all whom God favored.

Fowler's pulse accelerated as he watched Novikov and Powell strip off their robes and take up positions about six feet apart in the middle of the Circle. *They're going to do it,* he thought. One was going to kill the other, and if it turned out the way he thought it would, he would have his *condition green.* He saw the head figure spread his outstretched arms, and the others stepped back, expanding the inner circle to a diameter of about thirty feet.

So much the better. Now he had a clearer shot.

Joshua explained the terms. Weapons were prohibited in the Great Circle, even among the Illuminati, so they would fight empty handed. The contest would end in death. "Beg no quarter, for none shall be granted," he said. When he asked if they accepted those terms, they both nodded without taking their eyes off each other. "Then you may begin," Joshua said, "and may God's will be done."

On cue, Owen and Juri began circling each other warily, each peering into the other's eyes, watching for the telltale glimmer of decision that precedes physical commitment.

Suddenly, with a yell that was more a maniacal scream of hatred than a *kiai,* Juri leaped forward and launched into a blur of punches and kicks that caught Owen momentarily flatfooted, driving him back a step. But he recovered quickly and stepped across the big man's line of attack, cutting an oblique angle, and spun back with a vicious *shuto,* a knife-hand strike, at Juri's throat.

Juri was ready and blocked it soundly. But that only exposed his midsection, and Owen whipped a roundhouse kick right under the elbow of the blocking arm. He pounded his instep against the Russian's floating rib with all his strength. Solid as concrete.

Juri didn't so much as flinch. Instead, his hand snapped down and caught Owen's foot, and as Owen tried to recoil the kick, the counter torque turned his body, exposing his back. Juri pivoted and punched him in the kidney. Then, gripping Owen's leg with both hands, he threw his own leg in a looping crescent over it and sat down, driving Owen face first into the ground.

A bolt of pain shot up Owen's back from the punch, but he didn't have time to indulge it. He knew what Juri was about to do. And he would soon be crippled then dead, if he didn't stop him.

Before Owen left Simon's refuge in Tokyo, Pak had briefed him on every bit of intelligence he had managed to gather on the Novikovs. Like Owen, Juri had undergone considerable preparation to become Arbiter. He had graduated with honors from the University of Leningrad and then gone into the Soviet Army. There he had served as an officer in the *Spetznaz*, an elite commando group in Russian special operations, and he had gained considerable combat experience in Afghanistan. That was critical information right now, because Owen knew that *Spetznaz* officers were trained in sambo, a deadly fighting system the Soviet Special Forces developed combining elements of karate, jujutsu, and several wrestling systems indigenous to the Caucasus region of Russia.

Sambo-trained commandos were dangerous enough on their feet, but they were lethal on the ground where they specialized in "grape-vining": locking, and breaking their opponents' legs. Juri had Owen's leg now, and Owen knew that if he didn't do something quick, the Russian would splinter his bones like kindling then kill him at his leisure. Knowing how much Juri hated him, Owen figured he would probably break his other leg too before finishing him off, just for good measure.

⚒

Owen's face hit the turf as Juri took him down. Resisting an urge to try and push himself up, he instead pitched his left arm and shoulder under and twisted his body violently. That threw his right leg against Juri's upper thigh and hooked his left instep behind Juri's ankle, catching the Russian's leg in a scissor action, throwing him to the ground. Rolling onto his back, Owen swung his leg up high then drove it down in an axe kick, his heel aimed at Juri's temple. But Juri saw it coming and parried as he rolled away and sprang to his feet.

By then Owen was up too, and he leaped to the attack, hacking into the big man's knees with another roundhouse kick. That target proved more vulnerable than had Juri's heavily muscled torso, and Owen felt the man's leg buckle under the impact of his foot. He moved quickly to exploit the opening, lunging in with a punch to the exposed side of Juri's face. His knuckles found flesh, but it was a glancing blow—Juri had sensed it coming and spun away.

Unfortunately for Owen, the punch's momentum carried him close to the big Russian. Juri continued his turn and lashed out with a spinning back fist at Owen's temple. Juri's strength and the torque of his twisting body combined to make the blow lethal, a vicious haymaker meant crush Owen's skull, break his neck—hell, Juri would tear his head off if he could. But Owen too had combat-tuned senses, and he instinctively turned away, his body meshing with Juri's like a gear, the instant he felt the Russian start into his spin. Juri's back fist still caught Owen on the side of his face, but it was a glancing blow against a target fading away.

Owen went with the momentum Juri's strike added to his turn, letting it carry him out and away from the danger zone. Then he dove, rolled, and came back to his feet beyond the big man's reach. He turned and raised his guard, ready to continue the fight.

Jack Fowler watched the battle through the scope of his sniper rifle, his excitement mounting with each change of advantage. He watched every attack, defense, and counterattack with the fascination of a professional analyzing the work of two colleagues who had mastered their craft. But he didn't let himself forget why he was there. He swept the scope around the Circle and noted that the guardians seemed just as intrigued as he was. They all had turned around and were watching the fight with rapt attention. He sighed in satisfaction and returned his attention to the fighters. He put the cross hairs on one man then the other. *It won't be long now,* he thought. *These guys can't keep that up forever.*

CHAPTER THIRTY-EIGHT

The fight went on and on. Each man landed solid blows on the other. Both of them now bled freely from the nose and mouth. Owen's right eye was swelling shut, and he was sure he would be pissing blood for days to come—if he lived to see those days, that is. Juri was bruised and battered too, but Owen could tell that he was taking the worst of the battle. He felt himself slowing down, getting tired and losing strength as his body struggled to overcome the mounting injuries and keep going. He realized that if he didn't do something soon, didn't find or create an opening through which to deliver a lethal or crippling blow, Juri would close in and use his superior size and strength to finish him off.

Then it happened. The opening appeared.

It only lasted an instant, a mere fraction of a second, but it was long enough. Owen saw a vagueness pass over Juri's eyes that told him the Russian had momentarily lost his concentration. He seized the opportunity, hurtling in with a one-two punch at Juri's face that forced his guard up and his weight back on the heel of his rear foot. Then he swept the big man's front leg, taking him out of stance. Before Juri could recover, Owen buried a roundhouse kick in his solar plexus. This time he used the ball of his foot, rather than the flatter, more forgiving instep, and the big Russian doubled over, his eyes bulging. Owen immediately followed that with a spinning back kick, nailing Juri between the eyes with his heel.

Juri sailed a good six feet through the air and landed like a sack of grain hitting a barn floor. Owen charged through the kick, chasing Juri's body in flight, and came down on it with all his weight an instant after it hit the ground. Dropping into a quick *kesa gatame*, or "scarf hold", he cinched up on the big man's neck and prepared to shift to *kata gatame*, a variation that would give him the angle and leverage to break it.

Then the unthinkable happened.

As Owen moved to transfer his hold, he raised his center of gravity an inch too high, just high enough for Juri, who was still full of fight, to torque suddenly, rolling Owen across his body. Then, before Owen could counter or disengage, Juri seized him from behind in *hadake jime*, a naked choke.

Immediately, Owen grabbed Juri's arm and tried to wedge his chin into the crook of the elbow to protect his throat. But Juri smelled the kill and was moving fast. He wrapped his legs around Owen's body and grape-vined them around Owen's legs. Then, arching his back, he stretched Owen's spine as if he were a medieval torture rack, pulling Owen's neck deeper into the choke.

Owen arched his own back and started rocking violently, desperately struggling to break the hold. He flailed behind him with his fingers, groping for Juri's eyes. He jabbed back with his elbows, frantically looking for a vulnerable target. Nothing worked. Juri's hold was locked solid, unbreakable.

Owen's field of vision began to narrow as Juri choked off the blood to his brain. He kept rocking and flailing, but he was getting weaker. Fog poured into his brain, stifling his thoughts. Blackness folded in upon him, and all sound stopped, leaving him alone in silent darkness at the center of a shrinking, dying universe. Then, at the very end, he heard Juri whisper something in his ear.

"Powell, before you die, I just want you to know one thing. I am the man who killed your father."

What? What was that? With excruciating effort, Owen pushed a single thought through the viscous fog in his mind. *You killed my father?*

Then, with his last ounce of strength, he drove his chin deeper into the crook of Juri's elbow and summoned his *ki*, his inner spirit, to focus every fiber of his will and force blood through the constricted vessels in his neck. Ten seconds passed without him dying... then ten more. Gradually, the blackness in Owen's world brightened to gray. Then color returned and his brain began to clear. A single thought tolled through his mind like a church bell on a frigid winter Sunday. *Juri killed my father!*

Then rage flooded his body like molten lava and his muscles turned to tempered steal. He began pitching and bucking furiously.

Thinking Owen was all but dead, the sudden burst of violence caught Juri off guard, loosening his grip. He quickly recovered and shifted position, trying to reseat the hold. But for the briefest instant, a sliver of space opened between his body and Owen's.

It was all Owen needed. He reached behind him and drove his hand into that space, digging, clawing, groping. Juri's belly was a granite washboard, but Owen pushed lower and quickly found soft flesh where the big man's legs joined his body. He grabbed, twisted, and ripped with all his might. He felt tissue tearing in his hand beneath Juri's cotton trousers.

Juri howled like a wounded animal. He immediately let go of Owen's neck and disentangled his legs from Owen's lower body. He frantically pushed at Owen's back—Owen obliged him, rolling away and pivoting on his knees to face him—then Juri plunged his hands to his groin and drew himself up in a fetal position.

But only for a second.

Owen dove at the wounded Russian, hitting Juri's chest with both his forearms, knocking him flat on his back. Then, lying chest to chest across the big man, he swung his hand up, forming a *shuto* high above his head and, screaming a desperate *kiai*, chopped it down across Juri's exposed throat.

He did it again. He did it several more times.

Owen wasn't sure how many times he had hit Juri that way, but when he stopped, the Russian was dead.

Jack Fowler watched Owen struggle to his feet and stand swaying with exhaustion, staring down at the dead man. *Condition green!*

His heart raced with excitement. He was virtually panting with exhilaration and realized he would have to calm himself. He needed to focus all his concentration on the task at hand. He closed his eyes and deliberately slowed his breathing. After a few seconds he felt his heart rate throttle back. He opened his eyes and took a deep breath. He let out half of it then steadied the crosshairs on Owen's back one last time.

Fowler's powers of concentration were remarkable when he put his mind to something. He had once submerged himself in a snake-infested swamp in Nicaragua, breathing through a reed and remaining absolutely motionless for three hours, just to get a shot at an elusive Sandinista leader he knew was coming to a secret meeting with a black marketeer nearby. So deep was his concentration today that he didn't sense the lid of the spider hole lift away from his head as he focused on his target. Rock steady, he began squeezing the trigger, bracing for the buck of his sniper rifle.

Then he was confused.

He was looking at the sky... Now a craggy Asian face. *Mean looking,* he almost had time to think. There was a crack. Was that his rifle firing? No. It was his neck.

Pak Je-man let go of Fowler's chin and dropped the body back into the hole. Then he quietly closed the lid and crawled back over the ridgeline, causing barely a ripple in the sparse Mongolian grass.

⟞⟨⟩⟞

All of the Illuminati had pulled off their hoods and were gathering around Owen as he stood over Juri's supine body. Each of them edged in to verify with his own eyes that the Russian was dead, that God's will had been revealed. All of them but Saul, that is. He knew the day held one more dramatic event in store and hung back, drifting instead toward the stone altar. He didn't want to block Fowler's line of fire or, God forbid, stop a bullet that was meant for Powell.

The day had not turned out as he had planned. The man who was to be the Arbiter in his pocket lay dead on the Mongolian steppe. The Eastern Alliance would fall apart now as each Illuminatus groveled to regain favor from the House of David. Saul and the House of Asher would be politically isolated, not quite a pariah— after all, how could he have known any more than Brother Mikhail that Juri Novikov's claim was fraudulent—but the other Illuminati would steer clear of private dealings with the House of Asher for the rest of Saul's life.

At least he and Asher would not have to bear the indignities that a vengeful Arbiter would surely throw their way. Not getting an Arbiter favorably disposed to his house was disappointing;

getting one that bore a grudge would be insufferable. That was why he had arranged for insurance against such an outcome.

But where was it? Fowler should have fired by now.

Saul turned and scanned the hills behind him, wondering why he hadn't heard a gunshot. He looked back at Powell. *Why are you still standing? You're supposed to be dead!*

Brother Zechariah edged away from the men clustered around Novikov's body and looked at Saul. He could sense the Asherite's growing agitation and knew it was time to take his place by the Eastern leader's side. He took a deep breath and let it out slowly. Then he adjusted his breathing to a slow, steady rhythm: five counts in, ten counts hold, fifteen counts out. He cleared his mind of all conscious thought and began working his way around and behind where Saul stood near the altar.

Saul continued staring at Powell. *What is going on? Why don't you fall down?* His temper rising, he looked back at the hills, straining to see some sign of the sniper that was supposed to be there.

"Brothers, let us take our places once again," Joshua called.

One by one, the Illuminati pulled their eyes away from the corpse and started back to their places on the Circle. Saul turned and caught the eye of the Asherite guardian with the communications link to the helicopters and passed him an angry hand signal. Owen started walking towards the altar, passing close to where Saul stood looking around in ever growing agitation.

Mind placid, Zechariah edged up behind Saul's right shoulder and watched Powell approach. He kept his mind free of all conscious thought so no one would sense what he intended to do.

＝⊱ ⊰＝

No! This can't be happening, Saul thought, his emotions swinging from rage to panic and back. *I can't let it happen. I can't let Powell become Arbiter! Anything but that...* He tucked his right hand into the voluminous sleeve of his robe and palmed the dagger he always carried concealed there. He looked around, eyes wild, as if wondering if anyone would notice what he was about to do. He turned back and watched Owen approach. His breathing quickened.

＝⊱ ⊰＝

Zechariah moved up on Saul's right side, keeping his mind empty, staying emotionally invisible to the Asherite's keen senses. He watched Powell's approach and felt Saul's tension rise.

Suddenly, as Owen came abreast of the two Illuminati, Saul lunged at him, a glint of steel flashing from his sleeve as he thrust out at the American's chest. Just as quickly, Zechariah leaped out with him, his arm perfectly synchronized with Saul's, dancers in a graceful but deadly minuet. Then Zechariah's hand pushed Saul's wrist downward, sweeping the knife away from its target. He seized Saul's wrist with both hands and felt the Asherite stiffen, realizing his attack had been parried, but not yet able to comprehend what was happening. Zechariah quickly stomped down on the side of Saul's knee. Saul cried out, and his arm went slack. Then Zechariah twisted the Asherite's wrist and drove the knife in and upward, under Saul's ribcage, directly into his heart.

Saul's face turned to Zechariah's, his eyes full of shock and anger. Then he slowly sank to his knees. Zechariah sank down with him, putting his cheek against Saul's, in a gesture that was almost touching.

"Go with God, Brother!" Zechariah hissed in his ear. Then he shoved the knife deeper and twisted the hilt.

Saul fell face down, dead.

Everyone on the Mongolian steppe froze for an instant, staring in shock at the fallen Illuminatus. Then the councilors of the twelve houses dove for the ground as all the guardians began moving at once. The Asherites carrying rifles swung them around at Brother Zechariah, and the other Chinese drew submachine guns and pistols. The guardians of Benjamin and the other Western houses moved just as quickly, drawing down on the men of Asher. Guardians from the other Eastern houses trained their weapons at the Westerners, but Brother Thomas, who along with the other Illuminati and Owen stood boldly erect, yelled, "No, you fools! It's the Asherites—they are the threat!" and the Indian guardians turned on the Chinese.

Mikhail and Timothy both stared at Thomas in confusion. Their eyes went to Saul's body then back to the Indian. Then they made their decision and began yelling orders frantically. The Russian and Singaporean guardians also turned their weapons on the Asherites. A few moments later, even the Egyptians and Syrians were aiming at the men of Asher.

The Chinese looked around with eyes wide, full of apprehension and outrage. Their Illuminatus lay dead and they wanted blood, but guardians from eleven houses were arrayed against them. Slowly, bitterly, they lowered their weapons.

Then everyone heard the rotor chop of approaching helicopters.

Brother Joshua flashed an imploring look at Brother Mikhail.

The Naphtali Illuminatus nodded then barked something in Russian to one of his guardians. The man pulled out a cell phone and tossed it to Mikhail who dialed and began speaking in urgent Russian.

Six flights of attack helicopters, bristling with guns and rockets, swept over the ridgelines and converged on the Covenant Keepers gathered on the steppe. Three groups of MI-28s came from compass points north of the gathering, their fuselages marked with the tricolor insignia of post-Cold War Russia, and three flights of WZ-9s came from the south, bearing the gold-bordered red star of the People's Republic of China. They came to within a hundred meters of the gathering and hovered, their weapons trained on the people on the ground.

Seeing this, the Asherite guardians smiled grimly and raised their weapons again while those from the other houses crouched behind the sandbags and gunners on the crew-served weapons sighted on the choppers.

Mikhail kept yelling into the phone. Owen didn't know more than a few words of Russian, but he heard the Illuminatus say "Moscow" several times and thought he caught the Russian words for, "Far East Military District Headquarters," a command center on which he had focused a considerable amount of attention as an Army intelligence officer in Korea.

No one moved for what seemed like an eternity.

Then, slowly, the Havocs turned and pointed their weapons at the choppers from China. The Chinese hovered a few seconds longer, apparently considering their options. Then they swept their tail rotors around and flew south. The Russians followed, chasing the WZ-9s towards the Sino-Mongolian border. They disappeared over the hills.

Within moments, the Mongolian steppe was silent.

CHAPTER THIRTY-NINE

"There's one thing I don't understand," Owen said.

"Just one?" responded Nomura.

"Well, several, I suppose, but one in particular has been on my mind since we left Mongolia."

They were back in the study of Nomura's Tokyo apartment. Owen reclined on the leather sofa, his legs crossed. Nomura and Pak sat in armchairs facing him. The mood was much more relaxed than it had been the night Owen came seeking Nomura's help to find Saul's private air terminal and retrieve the scroll, but Owen still did not feel completely comfortable around Pak. It was hard getting used to associating with the man whom he had long thought was his mortal enemy. He wondered if they could ever be friends. He doubted it.

It was late afternoon. Outside the study's expansive windows, steel and glass high rises threw back reflections of an orange sun as the city sweltered beneath a blanket of muggy summer heat. Inside the men sat in coolness and deepening shadows. Toshi had just served the Asians tea and was pouring Owen coffee from a silver carafe.

"What is your question, Owen-san?" Nomura said.

Owen hesitated, looking for a way to frame it without offending the man who had done so much to help him.

"Well," he said, "how could Brother Saul have been so... well, so evil? I mean, he was an Illuminatus, right? A man of God."

He suddenly felt foolish for asking so naïve a question. After all, he was a political scientist, a student of history and power. He of all people knew that men of the cloth were not always pious, nor were they immune to worldly temptation.

But neither man laughed at him.

"We have pondered the same question," Nomura said, staring into his teacup. Then he looked at Owen, seeming to read his mind. "We are not like other religious figures. We follow the true course that Jesus the Nazerean laid out for us two thousand years ago. Ours is not a simple profession of faith, it is an arduous regimen of spiritual training that leads to enlightenment. We become one with God. We know the universal mind.

"That is not to say we don't make mistakes. Of course we do. We are human. Illuminati have made terrible blunders; started wars in the secular world and have even fought each other. But in the past, we always thought we were doing the right thing. We were trying to carry out God's will.

"But this was something different. Brother Saul... No, let us call him by his worldly name, Zhou Lo-feng. He was never our brother, not really. Zhou was one of the most respected Illuminati in the Great Circle. He was deeply revered as a wise and powerful man of God. But he deliberately deceived us. He perpetrated a fraud, smuggled a weapon into the Great Circle, and tried to murder you. We have since learned that he even had an Illuminatus assassinated. He was clearly, as you say, evil. The question of how this could have come about troubles us deeply."

For a moment, no one spoke. Then Owen asked the question that had really been on his mind. "Was Zhou the Antichrist?"

"The Antichrist?" Nomura said raising his eyebrows. He hesitated, considering the question. "No, I don't think so. If he were, we could not have defeated him so easily. No, that trial is yet to come, I fear."

"Then how did he turn out the way he did? Just how does a spiritually enlightened man, one who has become one with God, become evil?"

"Perhaps he was never really enlightened at all," Pak said.

"You mean he was faking it?" Owen said in surprise. "Are you saying a man in the Covenant can pretend enlightenment all his life and rise to lead a great house?"

"No, that is not possible," Nomura said. "At every step of an adherent's training, there are trials, tests that irrefutably reveal to senior pneumatics whether the initiate has glimpsed spiritual truth. These demonstrations cannot be faked."

"Then how did Zhou slip though?"

"The only way that could have happened," Pak said, "was if the training program in the House of Asher is defective, if none of the pneumatics there are truly enlightened."

"That doesn't sound logical," Owen said. "I thought the great houses all preserved the secret teachings of Jesus and passed them down through the generations. If those secrets really lead to true enlightenment, to direct knowledge of God, I can't see how they could have been lost to an entire great house."

"They could not," Nomura said. "That is what is troubling us."

Pak said, "The only way these Asherites could have strayed so badly from the truth is if they never received the inner teachings. And the only way that could have happened is if they are not the real House of Asher."

"Imposters? But how is that possible? They knew everything about the Covenant, its history, its rituals. You've known Zhou as the Illuminatus of Asher for... how long?"

"Since he ascended in 1964," Nomura said. "And before that I knew the previous Asher Illuminatus, Gu Jo-dai, who went by the

Covenant name of Brother Adam. The House of Levi has had close relations with the House of Asher since your great grandfather, Arbiter Gryphon, found them in 1884 and brought them into the Great Circle."

Pak said, "We now believe the group your great grandfather found in northern China, the one he thought was the House of Asher, may be some other Gnostic sect. Perhaps it was a splinter group descended from renegade Asherites that left the legitimate house before receiving the inner teachings of the faith. That would explain how they know our history and rituals."

"And these renegades have posed as the real House of Asher for more than a century?" Owen said. "How could all of them keep up such a pretense for so long?"

"Oh, we are all very good at keeping secrets, Dr. Powell," Pak said.

"Perhaps they don't know they are not legitimate," Nomura added. "Asher was isolated from the rest of the Covenant for more than twelve hundred years. The renegade sect might have split from them centuries ago, set up their own house, and told later devotees that they were the true House of Asher."

"What do Zhou's people have to say about this?" Owen asked.

"Nothing, it seems," Nomura said. "Several houses have attempted to contact the Asher Council of Twelve to offer condolences for Zhou's death and to reopen channels of communication, but they are not responding. It is as if they have disappeared."

"Whatever the case may be," Pak said, "the real House of Asher is still out there somewhere."

"That's if they still exist," Owen said. "For all we know, the renegades murdered their masters and took their place a thousand years ago."

"No, they are out there somewhere," Nomura said. "The scriptures foretold that the Great Circle would be restored. We thought that prophecy had been fulfilled when Arbiter Gryphon tracked down the four missing Eastern houses in the late nineteenth century, but we were mistaken. The real House of Asher had not been found." The old man looked pensive. Staring into his teacup again, he said almost to himself, "They are the lost tribe of Israel. They are out there somewhere. They have to be. The prophecies are never wrong."

Then he turned to Owen, his black eyes flashing. "Owen-san, it will be up to you to find the legitimate House of Asher and restore the Great Circle." His tone was earnest, and he held Owen's eyes in a penetrating stare. "But such a quest will be very dangerous. Before you embark upon it, you will need to complete your training."

"Complete what training?" Owen blurted in surprise. "I've trained and studied all my life. What more do you expect me to learn?"

"Yes, you've come far. You have learned technique and absorbed a great deal of knowledge. You have conditioned your body and your mind. But those things are not enough. You have mastered the physical and mental spheres of existence, but you have neglected your spiritual development. As a result, you are rash and ill-tempered. You have difficulty controlling your emotions. Most seriously, your spiritual insight—your intuition, if you will—is not sufficiently developed to guide you through the trials that lay ahead."

"And just how am I supposed to acquire these vaunted abilities?" Owen snapped. Then he bridled at his own sarcasm, realizing his sudden irritation only seemed to confirm what Nomura was telling him.

Nomura ignored the edge in Owen's voice. "You must embrace the true faith as your father did," he said, his eyes glinting with enthusiasm. "Enter the Covenant as an acolyte and begin the training regimen that will lead to your enlightenment. It is a demanding program—many supplicants devote their lives to it without ever attaining the blessed goal—but with your talents and previous training, I am certain illumination will come to you quickly.

"The first stages are mainly academic. You study Gnostic scriptures and learn the true doctrines of Christianity from a pneumatic mentor. Once you understand and embrace the faith, you are baptized into the Covenant. At that point, you begin your meditations and your mentor will begin to reveal the inner teachings, the things Jesus told only his closest disciples..."

As Nomura bubbled on, Owen's mind wandered back to his training at Yi Chung-hae's camp in Korea. His first days there had been grueling and frustrating, frightening and depressing. He wondered how he had ever gotten through it. *Then he remembered.* It all came back to him in a rush, and a question leaped from his lips before he could bite it back, interrupting Nomura mid sentence.

"Whatever happened to Bae?"

There was a stunned silence. Nomura and Pak stared at him, their expressions blank.

"Bae... Bae, you remember him, don't you?" Owen said to Pak. "The awkward kid at Yi's camp. He must be close to thirty years old now. Whatever happened to him?"

"You mean Pak Bae," Pak said. His face suddenly looked tired, sagging into an expression Owen had never seen in it.

"Pak Bae?" Owen said blankly.

"Pak Bae. He was my brother. He is dead."

Owen felt as if he had been hit with a baseball bat. "Dead?" was all he managed to say.

"When he grew up, he entered service as a guardian of Levi. He was trying to follow in my footsteps." Pak started to say something else, but his words came out sounding strangled and he stopped.

Nomura picked up for him. "In 1990 we got into a minor trade dispute with the House of Simeon. Bae-san was part of a team we sent to Singapore to gather intelligence. Unfortunately, the team was discovered, and a squad of Simeonite guardians liquidated them one by one. Bae-san was the last to be found and killed. Before they got him, however, he managed to get a message to us revealing the identity of the Simeonite squad leader." Nomura paused, watching Owen carefully then said, "I understand it was someone you knew at camp."

Owen stared.

"An Australian named Patrick Nagleson."

Owen flinched, sloshing his coffee. The cup began rattling in the saucer, and he quickly set it on an end table beside the sofa. For a moment he thought he would be ill. Patrick Nagleson, his first and best friend at camp, had killed little Bae? He almost could not believe it. "What did you do?" he finally managed to say.

"I hunted him down and killed him," Pak said. His voice was still choked with emotion, but the muscles in his jaw tensed and his eyes were hard.

"Bae-san was a courageous young man," Nomura said softly. "I grieved his loss as if the Pak family were my own. But that is in the past. What is important now is your future enlightenment. You will need to stay in Japan longer than you originally planned. I can give you lodging here, or you can stay at the hotel…"

Nomura's voice droned on, but Owen wasn't listening. *Nagleson killed little Bae?* He just could not bring himself to grips with it. He pictured the boy's face, impish when teasing, and petulant when he thought Owen was not living up to his potential. Then he remembered Bae trying to stop him from leaving camp with Anna that fateful day. When Owen refused to be dissuaded, he must have run to his big brother, Je-man. In a very real sense, Owen had little Bae to thank for saving him from capture. Tears began welling in his eyes. He tried to push the memories aside, but couldn't.

Owen wondered how many people close to him had died in the name of God and the Covenant. There was his father and

Yi Chung-hae. Then there was Anna and Jürgen—he still had trouble thinking of them as Roxanna and Juri Novikov—and now Patrick Nagleson and little Bae. What about his mother? Was her death really an accident? Would he ever know?

What kind of Christianity is this? Is this what Jesus had in mind when he founded the Covenant in Jerusalem two millennia ago? If these people have really come to know God and are doing his will then just what kind of being is this God?

Nomura was still talking. "I will assign a mentor to oversee your day-to-day training, but I will administer your trials, of course, and direct any—"

"I'm not going to do it," Owen said.

Nomura cocked his head in confusion. "Do what, Owen-san?"

"I am not going to submit to the training."

Stunned silence.

After a moment, Nomura spoke in a voice barely above a whisper. "But you are the Arbiter. You claimed your legacy and accepted the investiture." Nomura's translucent skin had gone geisha white. Pak only stared, eyes wide, mouth open as if he were looking for something to say.

"I've been told that not all Arbiters have embraced the faith. Is that true?"

"Well, yes, but you will need the training, Owen-san. The Tribulation has begun. This is a particularly dangerous time for you, for all of humankind. You will need the spiritual strength and insight of enlightenment to navigate the treacherous waters ahead."

"I'll get by one way or another. Look, I accepted the post as the Covenant's Arbiter, so I'll be available if you need me to mediate disputes, but don't expect me to take action to force rulings on recalcitrant houses. I won't take part in your little internecine wars. And I am not going to become a Gnostic Christian."

348

"What about the Asherites?" Pak said. "They are out there somewhere. It is the Arbiter's responsibility to find them."

Nomura added, "Owen-san, you cannot escape God's will. The prophecy says the Arbiter will restore the Great Circle."

"Well, if prophecy never fails, then I guess an Arbiter will find the lost House of Asher some day," Owen said with a humorless smile. "In the meantime, I have other plans. All my life, someone else has programmed my every decision. I think it's about time I took charge of my own destiny. I finally know what I want to do with my life."

"And what is that?" Nomura said.

"I'm going back to Maryland. I want to teach."

Nomura and Pak stared at him in disbelief. They looked at each other then stared at him a few moments longer, as if expecting him to change his mind. When he did not, Nomura sighed. "As you wish, Owen-san. It is your decision. But there is one other issue we must discuss: the scroll. You must put it in a safe place, one where no one can find it. If you like, I can—"

"I have already made arrangements for that," Owen said sharply.

Nomura stiffened. Then he grunted in resignation. "Very well, Owen-san."

EIPILOGUE

Maryland—late summer, 2001

E laine stood at the counter slicing fruit for breakfast and watching Owen through the kitchen window. He was in the back yard, stripped to the waist, doing his morning *kata*. This particular morning he was concentrating on the powerful, physically demanding patterns from Tomari, Okinawa. His body glistened with sweat, and his muscles rippled as he shifted from one stance to the next.

Your seisan-dachi is a bit too wide, Elaine thought, smiling. *One day, perhaps, I'll show you how to do it right.* Watching him there, her mind drifted back to the evening before, and she grew warm. Then the phone rang on the wall beside her, jarring her out of her reverie.

"Powell residence," she sang.

"Elaine, tell me it isn't true! Tell me the most desirable woman on campus hasn't been snatched off the market." It was Owen's boss, Richard Falstaff.

Elaine giggled. "It's true, Richard. Owen and I were married in England."

"Well congratulations to you both! I can't think of two people more suited for each other. I just wish I could have gone to the wedding."

"Oh, I'm sorry. We did it on impulse, not at all the kind of thing I normally do, but it was beautiful. One of Owen's relatives administered the vows—he's some kind of lay clergyman. He's also a member of the peerage, so we had a handful of lords and ladies from his social circle as impromptu guests. We held the ceremony outside in the ruins of an ancient church, the oldest in Britain, I'm told. It was so quaint and romantic... It was simply a perfect day. I do wish you could have been there."

"It sounds wonderful. Listen, I called to talk to Owen about his sabbatical."

"He's in the back yard. Do you want me to call him in?"

"Not necessary. Just tell him I have the papers ready for him to sign at his convenience. Is it true you're taking a sabbatical this semester, too?"

"Yes, I've got loads of things to do, with moving into Owen's place and getting my house ready to rent out. And since Owen is taking the semester off to finish his book, I thought it would be a good opportunity to spend some time with him."

"Ah yes, the book. I can't tell you how pleased we are that Owen has managed to spin his summer research project into a book and sell it to so prestigious an academic press. And the journal article he has coming out next month—our Owen is really on a roll these days."

Elaine remembered how irritated she was the last time Richard had said, "Our Owen," while talking to her. This time she smiled.

"I don't mind telling you, Elaine," he continued, "the tenure committee meets next month, and word has it that Owen is a done deal."

"Really? That's wonderful, Richard. Can I tell him?"

"Let's wait until it's official, just to be safe, then we can throw him a party. Listen Elaine, I've got to run. Just have Owen stop by my office whenever he gets a free moment this week, okay?"

Elaine said her goodbyes and hung up the kitchen phone. She watched Owen a minute longer then reached for her purse. She took out her cell phone, dialed, then continued watching Owen as she listened to it ring.

"Matsukata Electronics Corporation, America," answered a friendly, high-pitched female voice.

"Line seventeen, please. PIN number 452619."

A moment later another female operator answered with a monotone, "Line seventeen."

"This is Sapphire. I need the red line."

"Are you prepared to authenticate?"

"Go ahead." Elaine turned to the calendar hanging beside the refrigerator.

"Authenticate April tenth," the woman said.

Elaine flipped the page to April and did a quick calculation, subtracting the fourth digit of her identity number from the Julian date. "Nine four," she said with deliberate clarity, providing the coded response that verified her secret identity.

"Okay, you will need to go secure," the operator said.

"Right, standby." Elaine poked in the five-digit code that activated the encryption chip in her cell phone. For a few seconds, she heard a squawking sound like a modem trying to synchronize with its counterpart then the line went quiet. "How do you read me?" she asked.

"You're coming through clearly," the voice answered with only the slightest distortion. "I'll connect you now."

Owen had just finished the last *kata* in his workout. Waiting for her connection, Elaine watched him go to the sliding glass door of the bedroom, open it, and step inside. A moment later she heard

the shower start. Then she heard a couple of clicks on the phone
and a man's voice answered.

"*Moshi, moshi.*"

"*Hai, Yuriko desu. Nomura-sama, kudasai,*" Elaine said.

"*Hai, chotto matte, kudasai,*" the man said.

She waited a moment then heard another click.

"Yuriko-chan, how nice to hear from you," Nomura said warmly in Japanese.

"It is good to hear your voice again too, Father," Elaine said in
fluent Japanese with a Tokyo accent. "I'm calling to let you know
we have returned from England. We arrived safely in Maryland
three days ago."

"Very good. I'm glad everything turned out all right." His tone
was sincere. He paused then turned serious. "The situation was
precarious for a while. Owen-san slipped away from you and got
himself into trouble. It would have been most unfortunate had
he been killed, even worse had the Novikov woman seduced him."

Elaine's cheeks flushed. "Owen's temptation was foretold in
prophecy," she said, keeping her voice level. "He had to face it and
make the choice. As for the danger to him, I took care of that."

"Yes you did, Yuriko-chan. You comported yourself well. I am
proud of you."

"Thank you, Father."

"But I have been told that you and Owen-san are now married."

Elaine drew in her breath. This was the part of her report she
had been dreading. "Yes Father," she said softly.

"That was not part of my instructions to you. Your mission was
to watch over him, not marry him. You must realize how much this
complicates our position."

"Yes, I understand that, but I didn't have any choice." She took
a deep breath and launched into the story she had rehearsed, praying Nomura would believe her. "Owen wanted me to marry him.
I blunted his proposal once before, but I could not put him off any

longer without jeopardizing our relationship and the mission. I did what I had to do."

There was a long silence.

"Very well," Nomura said. "I trust your judgment. You have never failed me, and I know you will do what needs to be done when the time comes."

"Thank you for not losing faith in me, Father." Elaine heard the shower cut off. "I've got to go," she said quickly. She clicked off the cell phone and dropped it in her purse.

Nomura placed the phone back in its cradle and stared at it for a few moments.

"Your daughter is impetuous," said the woman sitting across the desk from him.

"She is young," he said. Then, looking up, he changed the subject. "I understand there was an unfortunate incident at the ministry the other day. You will soon have a new boss."

Ms. Naguma smoothed her tea-green dress and met Nomura's gaze with catlike eyes. Her pale face was expressionless except for the barest hint of a smile. "Yes, very unfortunate," she said. "Deputy Assistant Minister Inoue died at his desk. It was quite a surprise. He seemed perfectly fine when I served him tea not thirty minutes earlier."

"And what was the cause of the deputy assistant minister's death?"

"The coroner's office issued a preliminary ruling of heart attack—shocking for a man so young."

"I trust the toxicology report will not persuade them to change their ruling?"

Naguma's smile broadened a bit. "It was an organic substance. All trace evidence will have dissolved before the post-mortem."

"Very good. And Teguchi-san?"

"Yes, the Ferret is gone too. He met with unfortunate circumstances the day after Inoue-san died. It happened at his favorite brothel in Shinjuku Kabukijo. It seems he was physically abusing one of the girls and she turned psychotic. Killed and mutilated him with scissors then killed herself, I am told."

"That is terrible," Nomura said, genuinely shocked.

"Yes, very messy, but these things happen. She was a drug addict. The barbiturate she took to endure Teguchi's fetishes was apparently cut with an hallucinogen that causes violent hysteria."

"Violent death was God's will for Teguchi," Nomura said, "but how sad for the young woman."

Naguma wrinkled her nose in disgust. "*Eta.* She will be better off in the next life."

"Are any more Asherite agents lurking at the ministry?"

"None of which I am aware. But if any more of them come to our attention, I will deal with them expeditiously."

Yes, I am sure you will, Nomura thought, marveling at her ruthlessness. He wondered about this peculiar woman. What did she ultimately want? What would she do to get it? There would be a vacancy on the Council of Twelve, soon. Tanaka was old and in poor health. Is that what she was after? If so, how might he use her ambition to advance his own agenda? Could he trust anyone so cold and calculating?

"Yuriko-san is jeopardizing the mission," Naguma said sharply. "She was not supposed to marry the Arbiter."

That again. Why are you so preoccupied with Yuriko and Owen? But this time it was Nomura's lips that drew into a thin smile. "Do not concern yourself with that, Naguma-san. Events are unfolding according to my plan."

After breakfast Owen took his coffee into the living room and turned on the TV to get the morning news. His brow furrowed in puzzlement as the old picture tube crackled to life and a cityscape materialized with smoke billowing from the side of a tall skyscraper. Then the camera drew back to reveal a second, identical building with a similar wound, and Owen recognized the twin towers of the World Trade Center in New York City.

Elaine came into the room, a cup of tea in her hand. She glanced at the television then looked back and gasped. Her cup and saucer crashed to the floor, but neither she nor Owen seemed to notice. They stood there transfixed by the horror before them. A commentator's shock-stricken voice talked about airliners having flown into the towers.

"Good God, what are the chances of two airliners hitting the World Trade Center within minutes of each other?" Owen mumbled in confusion.

"My love, nothing in God's universe happens by chance," Elaine said.

Still staring at the television, Owen and Elaine sank down on the sofa, both of them aware that the world would never again be quite the same.

www.ingramcontent.com/pod-product-compliance
Lightning Source LLC
Chambersburg PA
CBHW071213250626
47159CB00001B/300